"Better than *The Mummy's Brain,*" Buzzy said, feeling the effects of the martinis. "Better than *Slave of the Sadist* and *Satan's Daughter!*"

Landis beamed. "That's what I thought. Can you start today?"

Buzzy nodded. "I'm way ahead of you, Woody. I've got the monster stuff all ready to go, and I have some nice ideas for the zombies."

Landis nodded. If Buzzy said it was ready, it was ready. The two men had the highest professional regard for each other. "I'm using the sets from *Satan's Daughter*. What happened was, after RKM spent all that money on those beautiful sets, I wanted to shoot another movie right away before they tore it all down. It seemed like such a waste. So I got Neil to come up with this *Cadaver* script, and the only other scenes we need is in the morgue. Shit, this movie just about shoots itself. We don't have to build a single set!"

"And I came up with the plot line," bragged Neil, his makeup now reapplied with Marine Corps precision.

"Fruity, you're a genius," Buzzy shouted across the empty room.

HORROR SHOW

GREG KIHN

TOR®

A TOM DOHERTY ASSOCIATES BOOK
NEW YORK

HORROR SHOW

Copyright © 1996 by Greg Kihn

Cover art and design by Shelley Eshkar
Photography by Waldo Tejada

A Tor Book
Published by Tom Doherty Associates, Inc.
175 Fifth Avenue
New York, NY 10010

Tor Books on the World Wide Web:
http://www.tor.com

Tor® is a registered trademark of Tom Doherty Associates, Inc.

ISBN: 0-812-55108-7
Library of Congress Card Catalog Number: 96-18278

First edition: October 1996
First mass market edition: October 1997

Printed in the United States of America

0   9   8   7   6   5   4   3   2   1

THIS BOOK IS DEDICATED TO MY WONDERFUL
PARENTS,
STANLEY AND JANE KIHN.

ACKNOWLEDGMENTS

I would like to thank the following people for their invaluable help: Lori Perkins, Peter Rubie, Natalia Aponte, Joel Turtle, Jack Heyrman, Kirk Iventosch, Alexis Kihn, Ryan Kihn, Jay Arafiles, Steve Wright, Danielle Winograd, and Dr. Mark Tidyman. I'd also like to tip my hat to the great musicians, too numerous to mention, I've had the opportunity to play with in my life. God bless 'em all.

HORROR SHOW

PROLOGUE

The kid thought he heard something.

Something was coming up the basement stairs.

Heavy footsteps, ascending slowly, too slowly to be anything good. A squish, along with the creaking of the tired wooden treads. A squish?

The old man mumbled and gripped his chest, but the kid felt his panic rising with each step of the bad thing, patiently making its way up from below.

The fear was a numb blanket that wrapped him so tightly he couldn't move. His arms, his legs, the back of his neck, all tingled to the point of pain. He could hardly breathe.

Even for a kid who usually enjoyed being scared, paid good money for it, it was overwhelming.

The bad thing arrived at the top of the stairs, paused, and turned the doorknob. Time was running out.

"It's locked!" cried the old man.

"Sweet Jesus, it's locked," the kid repeated. His voice sounded strange to him, alien and constricted, as if he were hearing a poor recording of himself played back at the wrong speed.

The kid wanted to run but couldn't move his feet. Instead, he stood facing the door, scared to death of what was trying to break through from the other side. He waited, feet rooted to the cheap linoleum, listening to the wild pounding of his heart, yet, despite his terror, he thought, *I've got to see it.*

"It" pushed against the door. Man and boy heard the frame groan, then bark and snap with the weight of the bad thing pushing it beyond its limit.

The kid's mind raced, frantically searching for explanations. The rules were twisted, he tried to make himself believe, that's all. Hell, he'd always suspected it anyway. That's what a lifetime fascination with having the shit scared out of you did to a guy. It desensitized you to the point where you were ready to believe anything. Even this.

But this was real, not a movie or a novel. Or a dream. It was actually happening—something evil, something *not* natural stalking them.

Let it come, I want to see, he thought, trying to bolster his courage.

But fear is like a drug, and, as with any drug, there are two things to consider: addictions and overdoses. For aficionados of horror, paralyzing fear is delicious. Except . . .

The physical manifestation of that fear stood on the other side of the door! All the crazy dreams that had been causing the kid sleepless nights since adolescence were suddenly real. It was just as he'd always suspected. There *were* monsters.

Even at the movies, when he covered his eyes because he was too afraid to see something that he knew would haunt his dreams for years to come, he always peeked. He had to.

Let me see. I want to see it.

The doorjamb split, the dry wood cracking into a jagged gash. Paint chips and splinters exploded from the point of separation. The molding around the door popped, and the gates of hell opened.

The old man might have been screaming, but the kid couldn't hear it. He was vaguely aware of a roaring ocean in his ears.

This is it, he thought. *This is totally it. Time to run. Time to take off like a jet. Time to—*

He waited just another second.

Got to see what this is all about.

NOW

1

A house is like an old box in an attic, hidden for decades. Then some unsuspecting party comes along and—

—opens it.

Landis Woodley's house was like that. Like a museum full of memories and memorabilia, a place that kept.

It was also a house that didn't want to be found. Clint Stockbern discovered it only after weeks of research and legwork. No easy task.

The damn place had no number. Clint knew the old man had ripped the number down in 1964 to throw off the IRS agents. They found him, of course. They always do.

A faded "No Solicitors" sign hung askew next to a doorbell from which the button had been removed, but that didn't slow Clint down. He'd expected obstacles like that. If the stories were true, Landis Woodley would be a man of few charms. He'd left a list of enemies almost as long as his list of creditors.

He hated the United States Postal Service and refused to empty his mailbox for months on end. The route man had given up with the junk mail. The only stuff he ever got now was official: bills, collection notices, tax liens, legal crap. Never a letter. So it was easy for all of Clint's hand-addressed envelopes to go unopened. They ended up with the rest of the correspondence, in the fireplace.

Landis didn't go out much. He had a feebleminded gardener's son named Emil, who worked for him and lived on the property.

Clint had been combing the Hollywood Hills for days looking for Landis Woodley's home. He worked the area behind Beachwood Canyon, cruising through the ostentatious show-houses built in the 1920s. From concrete European castles to Masonite antebellum Southern mansions, the film industry had brought some rather strange fetishes from the back lots to the construction sights. Most of the places looked like movie sets.

Clint's rusty VW bug labored up and down the winding canyon roads while Clint craned his neck to read the addresses. He was twenty-two years old and almost handsome behind the faded acne scars and styleless glasses. He had a determined, earnest face, and most people liked him. Clint passed unnoticed through the neighborhood, patiently driving the search grid he'd plotted the night before.

He eventually found the house with the help of old newspaper clippings about the wild parties that used to go on there. He learned that actress Vivian Loring, a neighbor of Woodley's, used to complain about the noise. Locating her house was not difficult, and from there he fanned out until he found the Woodley estate. The old man had miraculously kept his address out of the paper for years.

Landis Woodley's house tried to blend into a hill at the end of a tricky cul-de-sac. You couldn't actually see it from the road although you did get a glimpse of tile roof. Clint had to walk down a flight of mossy steps to get to the huge front door.

Constructed of rough gray stucco, the place looked as though it hadn't been painted in decades. The only visible windows were as small and grimy as portholes on a tramp steamer.

Clint knocked for at least fifteen minutes and was about to give up when a mailbox slot–sized view window screeched open, and a pair of bloodshot eyes appeared.

"What do you want?"

"Mr. Woodley?"

"Go away!"

"Mr. Landis Woodley?"

"No Woodley here!"

"I have a proposition for you."

The four-inch-square wrought-iron window closed with the scream of chalk on a chalkboard.

Shut out, Clint stepped back, away from the massive gray edifice that jutted from the withered hillside. He'd expected that, too. The guy was a pro, after all. The king of the recluses. Clint used the opportunity to check out the big building from a different angle.

It rose above him like an amusement park ride, a cracked and forlorn stucco structure largely hidden by untended trees and tangled shrubbery. LA shimmered in the background.

He walked down a narrow, overgrown sidewalk along the side and calibrated the size of the building. It stood three levels high and appeared to be in worse condition when viewed from the side. Dead vines clung to rotting trellises and pointed into the slate-gray sky. The stucco walls were veined with cracks and discolored by a dry, black moss.

The house had been tastelessly refurbished in the early sixties. Sliding doors, wooden decks, a cheesy birdbath, and some terribly inappropriate landscaping had been added, all of it now in a state of advanced decay, and the combination of old and cheap was disorienting.

Clint heard a door open on one of the two decks above him. He heard the old man cough, then hock a brownish loogie over the side. It would have dropped into the near-dead, yellow-brown shrubs that grew out of the hill a hundred feet below the property, but the wind blew it back toward the house, under the deck. Much to Clint's consternation, it sailed in his direction and landed with an unhealthy splat at his feet. He winced.

Clint considered going back to the front door and knocking again, but he knew that would be a waste of time. He crept, cat-like, looking for an alternative entrance.

Some plank steps led up to the first of the two decks. Calculating from the hang time on the loogie, Clint fixed Landis's position to be on the upper deck, at least two stories above.

He put a foot on the first step and tested his weight on the wood. It creaked and bent in protest at his 150-pound body.

"Who's that?" a phlegmy voice called.

Clint froze.

"Who the fuck's down there?"

He considered trying to sneak off, but knew his chances of getting inside would not improve with that strategy. Better to confront the problem directly.

He was still choosing his words when the old man shouted, "Stop right there! I'm warning you, whoever you are, I've got a gun, and I'll blow your goddamn head off if you take one more step!"

"It's me, Mr. Woodley, Clint Stockbern. I was just at the front door."

"What the hell do you want?"

"I want to talk to you, that's all."

There was a pause, then Clint heard another extended bout of coughing.

The cough trailed into his words. "No talk, go home."

Clint worked his way to the edge of the steps, hooked his arm on the railing, and swung out over the hill. Looking up, he could see the unshaven, dour visage of Landis Woodley.

"Sir? If I could just have a few minutes of your time. I work for *Monster Magazine,* and I'd like to interview you."

The answer came back disappointingly fast. "I don't do interviews."

"I understand that, sir. The press hasn't exactly been kind to you over the years. I can relate to your attitude."

Landis cleared his throat. Clint got the distinct feeling he was loading up for another loogie. "Speak English, punk!"

"I have a check for five hundred dollars here in my pocket. That's what my publication is willing to offer you for a three-hour interview."

Silence.

He must be considering the offer, thought Clint. *I'm home free.*

"You're not a cop?"

"No, sir."

"IRS? Process server?"

"No, sir."

More coughing. Clint saw a blue plume of dense cigar smoke billow and rise above him. A match fluttered in the wind.

Clint waited. He was prepared to wait all day. He'd been pursuing this story for too long to give up now. At least, now, his offer was on the table.

"Not enough," came the brusque reply.

What? Where was this old shit coming from? Five hundred dollars was damn good money, nearly twice the going rate for this type of thing.

"All right, six hundred, that's as high as I can go. I'll put in the extra hundred from my own money."

Clint hated to use his own meager resources, but a story was a story, and he'd already invested too much time in this one.

"My editor, Ms. Bachman, wants this story, sir, and I'm prepared to—"

"Wait a second. Roberta Bachman?"

"Yes, sir."

"Roberta Louise Bachman from Melrose Avenue?"

"Yes, sir."

"Well, I'll be damned."

"You know her?" Clint smiled, squinting up at the old man, trying to be pleasant.

"Yeah, I knew her many years ago, 1957 or '58. She sent you over here to interview me?"

Clint was perplexed. Why hadn't she mentioned that when she approved the story? "Yes, sir," he replied. "Then you'll do the interview?" he added hopefully.

"I didn't say that," Woodley snapped.

"I wish you'd reconsider. There are lots of your fans out there who would love to hear what you have to say."

The old man snorted. "Right. What are you smokin', kid? Nobody gives a fuck about me. I haven't made a film in over thirty years."

"Nevertheless, there are people who remember."

The old man spit again, this time in another direction, away from Clint. "Just how the hell do you expect to interview people by sneaking around their houses? You're a prowler, for Christ sake. You coulda got your head blown off! I should call the cops."

"Sir, with all due respect, I've sent several letters outlining my proposal."

The old man coughed again; more smoke billowed. Clint's neck began to hurt. He'd been staring straight up at Woodley, getting an unpleasant, distorted view of the jowly, downturned mouth and oversize nose. From where Clint stood, Woodley appeared to be all nasal hairs and eyebrows.

It was not a position from which he liked to negotiate. However, a level playing field was not a Landis Woodley characteristic. Clint got the distinct feeling that he'd been manipulated since he'd knocked on the front door.

He craned his neck back up and saw a glass of amber fluid in the old man's hand. Drinking? Before noon? Yeah, that fit the profile.

Woodley hadn't responded to Clint's comment about the letters. He seemed to be looking off into the sulfurous distance, deep in thought.

"She'd be about, what, fifty-five, sixty years old now?"

"Huh?"

"Still pretty? Still a redhead?"

Clint realized that Woodley was talking about his boss. That surprised him. He'd never thought of her as anything but an unyielding authority figure. With the vast age difference between them, he'd never been objective enough to wonder if she'd ever been considered attractive.

"Yeah, still red."

"She's your boss?"

"Uh-huh."

"You poor son of a bitch. I'll bet she's tough as nails."

"You got that right."

Landis Woodley, unconcerned about the passage of time, let some more of it pass. Clint noticed that the old man didn't seem to care about "flow" and "dialogue" when he spoke. He probably liked those big chunks of silence in his conversations, Clint realized. It put people off.

While he waited for Woodley to speak, Clint wondered if the old man had had the hots for Bachman back in the fifties. It presented one hell of a mental picture, and he stifled a laugh.

"Cash," the old man said.

"Excuse me?"

"It's got to be cash."

"I have a check from my magazine," Clint stammered.

"No checks, cash." Woodley was as blunt as an old sword. He had a marvelous voice, and he used it to great advantage. Clint, with his community college degree in journalism and two years on the job, was no match.

He thought about it. The old man gave him all the time he needed.

"Yeah, I can do cash, if you insist, but I'd rather not."

Shit, Clint thought. *I'll have to go down to the ATM for my hundred, back to the office, then over to the publication's bank to cash their check.* He glanced at his watch. *With traffic it's a couple of hours. Damn. Half the day wasted, then I have to drive all the way back here.*

Woodley spit again. "Well, I'd rather not waste my time talkin' to you."

Clint watched the gob sail past him. "Okay, I'll get the cash."

"Go get it now. I'll be here."

"But—"

"Take it or leave it."

"I'll take it."

The old man went back inside. Clint heard the door close.

"Thanks a lot, you old turd."

Clint Stockbern had grown up with monsters and parlayed his knowledge of all things creepy into a job writing for his favorite publication, *Monster Magazine*.

As a youth, he'd built plastic models of the Wolf Man, Frankenstein, and Dracula. The walls of his room were adorned with lurid movie posters and lobby cards, the stranger the better. Creatures carrying half-clad women were his specialty.

A robot holding a woman in a skintight space suit, a werewolf carrying a blond bombshell back into the swamp, a look of utter depravity on his face—these were the things Clint cherished. The inference was always the same. These monsters were going to *do it* with the women.

Those horrible claws were going to caress her breasts, those fangs were going to . . . It didn't matter. He loved the come-on, the promise of mystery. The movies were never as good as the posters, of course. Usually the scene depicted never occurred in the film. His imagination always created a better story than the one up on the screen, anyway.

In the end he was usually disappointed.

He graduated from posters to other, more advanced items of memorabilia. At a shop in Burbank he bought props, old scripts, and pictures of his favorites.

He studied journalism in junior college and took his share of film courses. His beloved creatures were never far behind. When he applied to *Monster Magazine,* he had no idea that he'd be hired just six weeks later, and sent out on one great assignment after another. He'd done profiles on all his favorite filmmakers: Tod Browning, Ray Harryhausen, William Castle, Roger Corman, and more.

The enthusiasm of writers like Clint kept the magazine afloat.

The Landis Woodley story was Clint's idea. Roberta gave him her blessing and sent him on his way. She never said anything about having actually known the old man.

Later that day Clint stood at the front door of Woodley's house. This time his response came much quicker. Once again the view window opened, once again the bloodshot eyes.

"Yeah?" the old man growled.

He's not making this easy, Clint thought. *He can't have forgotten already, it's only been a few hours.*

"It's me, sir, Clint Stockbern."

"What do you want?"

"I've got the money."

"Let me see it."

Clint held up the packet of cash to the view plate. "Six hundred dollars."

The view plate slammed shut, the locks began to turn, and a half minute later the big door groaned open. Clint got the feeling that the old arch-topped entry hated to be used. It shrieked and moaned with an almost-human quality.

Landis stood in the doorway, a smaller man than Clint had expected, but every bit as feisty and unpleasant.

"Give it." Clint passed him the packet. Woodley shoved it in a pocket without comment. Clint watched and waited, his reporter's senses taking in everything.

Woodley clutched a spit-soaked cigar and a cheap ballpoint pen, giving each equal physical attention. *What is he writing,* Clint wondered. *A new screenplay?* The afternoon came alive with possibilities.

The old man wore a maroon fifties-style, racetrack flash sport shirt and a pair of wrinkled gray pants. Everything he wore was shiny and threadbare, just like most of the upholstered furniture in the house.

The frown never left his aged, television face. Lines, almost too many for one lifetime, crisscrossed that landscape in angry vectors. He'd combed what little hair he had left from the sides of his head across the top, giving it a thin, greasy blanket of yellowish-white thatch. It seemed an ill-advised hairstyle for Landis, one that only made him appear even more cheap and depraved. His eyes were deep-set in his pale face, ruthlessly scanning for carrion, two red wet spots in a gaunt mask.

He stepped aside and drew his arm across his chest, "Come in, kid," he mumbled.

Clint followed him into another world. As Woodley shuffled a few paces ahead of Clint, the young man could see that Woodley was wearing battered bedroom slippers instead of shoes.

Once inside, the first thing Clint noticed was the smell.

An oppressive atmosphere of mustiness and decay permeated the high-ceilinged rooms. Air had been denied circulation here for a long time. Clint had been in old people's houses before, and they all had that peculiar, closed-in odor. His grandmother's house smelled like that, except that hers had the subtle bouquet of mothballs in addition to the dusty stillness. Here, in Woodley's horror hotel, the mothballs had been replaced by the sour scent of cheap cigars and rotgut whiskey. And something else, too, something unclean and animal, a fetid, corporeal stench. Clint guessed the place hadn't been cleaned in years.

The interior of Woodley's house resembled a Gothic rummage sale furnished primarily from film sets: oversize wooden chairs, a standing suit of armor, a Styrofoam coat of arms, some faded plastic plants. Like the movies he'd made, the mansion was a low-budget, fright night turkey, the second feature at a drive-in in some dismal town where there was nothing better to do on Saturday night.

It reminded Clint of the old man's cinematic visions, and his own earliest memories.

He had learned something about himself watching that twisted crap, something that would stay with him for the rest of his life. He discovered that he loved to be scared.

"Isn't that the Iron Lady from *I Married a Vampire?*" Clint asked. Fake blood, now the color of dried chocolate, flowed down the side of it in gaudy patterns.

"Yeah, I used it in *Attack of the Haunted Saucer*, too," Landis said through phlegm-clogged vocal cords. Clint could hear the old man wheeze. He sounded like he had emphysema. "Buzzy Haller built it. We loved it so much we tried to use it in every damn picture. The thing photographed great. It's made of plywood and polyurethane foam."

"*Attack of the Haunted Saucer* is one of my all-time favorites," Clint said.

"Yeah," Landis coughed. "A real piece of work. Did you read what *The New Yorker* said? They called it the worst movie of all time, can you imagine that?"

"Yeah, I've heard it called that, but I don't see it that way. I recently saw it at a festival of fifties horror films, and the audience loved it."

Landis rummaged through some papers and ignored him. He picked up a clipping and read, "Woodley's trashy production is a depressing, hopelessly conducted farce. The acting, sets, plot, camera work, and laughable special effects all bear his indelible stamp of ugly cheapness. He makes Ed Wood look like Kurosawa. A big fat piece of crap!" He looked up at Clint and scowled. "Worst movie of all time? Fuck them. What do they know?"

Clint was about to answer when Woodley continued.

"What these guys don't realize is that *Attack of the Haunted Saucer* was a quickie. I don't argue that, but I defy anybody to make a feature-length movie for five thousand dollars in three days and have it show a profit. Even in 1956, which was a great year for low budgets, that was a record."

Landis's rage kept like bottled steam. Clint knew it was a ponderous cross for the retired filmmaker to bear, and he decided to keep the interview light . . . until the end.

They sat facing each other on an ancient sofa that belched and farted when Clint eased his slim frame into it. The old man collapsed into a battered, vinyl Universal-Lounger. A half-full bottle of generic whiskey dominated the tiny end table next to him. Woodley made no attempt to hide the fact that he enjoyed drinking the world's cheapest booze in the middle of the afternoon.

"Want some?" he wheezed.

Clint shook his head.

"I guess you want to hear about *Saucer,* the so-called worst movie of all time," Landis blurted out to Clint's surprise.

"Yeah, among other things. How do you feel about that?" Clint asked, getting his notebook out and depressing the "RECORD" button on his cassette machine.

"Well, you gotta understand, making movies was different in those days."

A flutter of wings and a high-pitched shriek interrupted Woodley and drove Clint from his chair in a burst of panic.

Something sailed over his head.

Woodley laughed, his throaty guffaw thick and mean.

"If you're a red-blooded horror fan, you won't mind my bats. There's only a couple of them left, and they aren't rabid."

Clint noticed his hand shaking. He sat back down, his eyes scanning the rafters overhead.

"Scared the shit out of you, didn't it?" Woodley said.

"Yes, sir, it did."

"Good. Scaring people has been my main gig for over fifty years . . . and I still get a kick out of it."

"You were saying that making movies was different in those days," Clint prompted.

"Right. Well, all I can tell you is that we had to improvise all the time. We had to think on our feet. I'd like to see Spielberg or Lucas try to pull off some of the stuff we did. Forget it! Anybody can make a movie for fifty million dollars. Hell, it's as simple as making a few phone calls. In those days, we were forced to really get creative. We put our balls on the line every time. These guys today don't have a clue."

Clint nodded. *Good start, now let's get the old fart to open up.*

"What was your favorite film to work on?"

Woodley took a sip of the whiskey. It had been fermenting in the glass, looking like a curious mixture of motor oil and urine. Clint noticed a slick on top. The old man's frown straightened slightly, then cracked. What passed for a smile on Landis Woodley's face appeared as joyless as a dog baring its teeth.

"Favorite film? Let's see . . . probably *Blood Ghouls of Malibu*. We got to work on the beach all day on that one, plus the late Jonathon Luboff was such a joy to work with. He was the consummate pro, always knew what to do. We never had to waste any time with him. Not like that idiot Tad Kingston."

"Kingston gave you problems?"

Landis snorted unhealthily. "He was a royal pain in the ass. Of course, the kids loved him, so we had to use him. He did most of his acting with his hair."

Clint laughed. The old man had made a joke. It was the last thing he'd expected.

"Did Buzzy Haller have anything to do with that hair?"

"No. That's about the only thing he didn't have a hand in. The man was a real genius. He worked on every one of my productions, and believe me, if he couldn't do it, it couldn't be done. We were pretty close . . . used to play poker every week. He lived over at the Roosevelt Arms, a basement apartment. The Roosevelt's a shit-hole, you know."

Clint nodded. Buzzy Haller became a true legend around Hollywood and his special effects work ranked right up there with the best of them in the early days. It was Buzzy's misfortune to fall in with the B-movie people, and he never had a decent budget to work with.

Also, Haller had a drinking problem. Judging from the look of Landis Woodley, it must have been the one true bond that held their friendship together. It seemed the height of irony that, in this town of successful drunks and dreamers, alcohol and imagination kept Buzzy Haller from working—until he killed himself.

Clint decided not to broach the subject of Buzzy's suicide.

"Tell me about Luboff."

"Jonathon was a master. He knew what to do when the cameras were rolling, I'll tell you that. Unfortunately, the man had a major drug problem. He was addicted to heroin for twenty years.

It was starting to affect his work toward the end." Landis paused to relight his cigar.

"You helped Luboff, didn't you?"

"Yeah, I dragged him to the hospital a couple of times so he could kick. The guy was a real mess. You'd think that being a veteran actor with hundreds of films to his credit, the damn Screen Actors Guild would have covered his medical expenses, but they couldn't have cared less.

"It was a real battle, but eventually we got them to cave in and foot a small part of the bill. You know, I was probably the only guy in Hollywood who gave two shits for Jonathon Luboff in the later years of his life."

Clint nodded. "Some of his early work, like *Curse of Nosferatu* and *Doctor Death,* is Hall of Fame stuff."

"They loved his accent. That Eastern European double-talk was the most imitated shit in town for a while. He was big box office, too, at one time. The man was an institution. Of course, at the end he was broke and strung out. Kinda sad, you know what I mean?

"When Luboff was in the hospital we put together a benefit at some theater downtown. We showed a few of his films . . . and *nobody came.* Not one fuckin' person! Can you believe it? We didn't sell a single ticket. That's the way this town takes care of its own. But I will say this, the man was a class act, a sweetheart. Everybody in the crew loved him."

The old man seemed to be softening; his voice became less hostile. Talking about Luboff had opened a door.

"Those scum-suckin' pigs who ran the major studios forced us all out of business." The old man's voice cracked. "They drove that poor bastard Luboff to drugs, and Buzzy to drink. In Haller's case, they said it was suicide . . . and there was a note. I saw it. It was in his own handwriting."

"But his body was never found."

Landis coughed again, spraying the air in front of him with an unhealthy blizzard of sepia-toned particles.

Clint leaned back.

"Right, no body. To tell you the truth I'm not sure I believe it even now. I guess it is possible that he went and threw himself off a cliff or into the ocean or something like that. But I wouldn't be surprised to see old Buzz walk in here right now." .

Clint checked his notes. "He was a good friend, wasn't he?"

"None better. And he was a real artist, too. When it came to clay and latex he could do anything. He made the monster suit for *Blood Ghouls* for a hundred dollars. The damn thing was so unwieldy that nobody could wear it, so Buzzy ended up playing the monster himself. He had to keep it on all day. We were shooting around the clock. Anybody else would have passed out. Not Buzzy. He built a flexible straw into the headpiece and sipped his vodka tonics for hours. If you watch the finished cut, you'll see the monster starting to weave a little. That's Buzz."

Clint smiled. He had seen the finished product, and he knew exactly what Landis was talking about.

"That was one of my favorite monsters. It really seemed to breathe and have expression."

"That was the thing about Buzzy—he could make a monster human. If there's nothing human in a monster, it won't scare you much. The trick is, you gotta make the audience see some of themselves in it. That's when you scare the piss out of them. Buzzy knew that. That's why he went the extra mile under all that latex."

The old man leaned forward, his breath like kerosene. The more he leaned in, the farther Clint leaned back.

"Tell me the story about *Attack of the Haunted Saucer.*"

"You mean Buzzy's effects?"

"Yeah, that's a classic, and I'm sure our readers would love to hear the truth."

Woodley sat back in his chair and took another sip of whiskey. Clint relaxed.

"We'd come to the end of the line on *Saucers.* The budget was gone. We were flat out broke, and I literally had only a few feet of film left. That wouldn't have been so bad, but we still didn't have an ending. We were screwed. I didn't know what I was gonna do. We had these spaceships that had to be destroyed to save the earth and some footage of Tad Kingston telling Deborah DeLux not to worry, and that was it! No more money for actors, cameramen, not even a cup of coffee. So Buzzy glued some paper plates together, soaked 'em in gas from outa my Buick, and set 'em on fire. He threw 'em at the camera and I rolled the last of our film. It wasn't great cinematography, but it gave us an ending. People paid to see that movie, too."

Clint found himself enjoying the interview. This was just the kind of stuff he'd wanted. The readers would eat it up. The booze had loosened the old man's tongue sufficiently. The time had come for Clint's big scoop, and he felt the tension rise as he wondered how he would get into it.

"Ahh," Clint stammered, "just last week I was reminded of another film you guys worked on."

"Which one?"

Clint took a breath. "Well, I was researching another story, and I happened to be reading about the LA County Morgue . . ."

Landis squinted. "Yeah?"

"And it reminded me of a rumor that's been floating around Hollywood for years."

The old man's face froze. His eyes bored into Clint's face like a pair of blue steel drills.

"Yeah? What about it?"

Clint began to sweat. It surprised him how scared he felt just talking about it.

"Well, I was wondering if there was any truth to that rumor."

Clint imagined Landis Woodley's goodwill drying up like a desert stream. His voice took on an icy edge.

"What rumor is that?"

Clint cleared his throat.

"The rumor that you used real corpses in *Cadaver?*"

Silence.

Clint thought he'd blown it. The rumor happened to be one of those old Hollywood chestnuts repeated by every film student since 1957. Like the famous Tijuana donkey story and the Spanish fly myth, it was neither fact nor fiction. It had become legend.

"I guess it's time I told the truth about this and got it off my chest," Woodley sighed. "I'm sick of all this bullshit. People have been whispering behind my back for years, and it's been haunting me. That rumor, that story, is what put me out of the feature films business."

He stared at Clint, and the young man looked back at him, unblinking. Clint could imagine the old man reading his mind.

If he wanted to blame that rumor on why he was drummed out of the movie business, fine. Clint wasn't about to mention the fifty other reasons, starting with the fact that his films stopped making money.

Clint knew from discussions with Roberta Bachman that the rumor had actually improved business for a short while. There had been talk that the old man himself had started it. Whether it was true or not, it had kept interest in the film sharp over the years, giving it a whole new cult audience as time went by.

The old man cleared his throat and rocked back, warming to the task. "You have to remember the way we made movies back then, like I said, it was different. There were no rules. We took chances. The budgets were minuscule, time was tight, the business was bizarre. I don't know, looking back, it all seems so . . . so grotesque."

Clint checked his tape recorder.

Landis cleared his throat. "It was Buzzy's idea. He figured out how to get those drawers open."

2

"We were shooting at the morgue and we had to be out by 5:00 A.M. They let us work the graveyard shift, no pun intended. In those days you could do a location like that without too much crap, and of course we were in and out before anybody had a chance to complain. The LA County Morgue was a great place to shoot. It had been used in a bunch of cop shows, but never a horror movie. We were the first. I had gotten permission to shoot late-night as long as we were out by dawn, when the bodies started coming in from the night before. LA was bad even then. The morgue was a busy place."

Landis Woodley stopped, tried to puff on his unlit cigar, and raised an eyebrow.

"You ever been to the morgue?"

Clint nodded.

"Inside?"

"Well, no, never inside," Clint replied.

"It's a scary place. Smells like a sausage factory in there. They keep it pretty cool, too. I guess that goes without saying. Everything you touch is sort of, I don't know, clammy . . . Working down there all night was giving all of us the creeps.

"There was only one guy there, a custodian, and he liked wine. We were basically on our own.

"Anyway, we were getting twenty shots a night, a breakneck schedule. RKM was breathing down our backs like a pack of goddamn hyenas. They were outgrossing us over at National, making millions on the *Unearthly Terror* series. There was a war going on between the two film companies. They kept trying to outdo each other in the horror department. We found out that they were using pig's blood and cow brains in *Terror,* trying to be the scariest, the bloodiest. Well, one thing led to another . . ."

Clint heard the bats flutter behind him and fought a natural inclination to duck. He lost.

He dived to his side on the couch, keeping his head well below the horizon line of the back of the overstuffed monstrosity that protected him. Shivering with revulsion, he imagined their ugly little black bat-feet dancing through his hair, scratching his scalp as they frantically tried to escape.

"Those bats bother you, don't they?"

Woodley coughed again, violently. He doubled over and gasped for breath in between the spasms. Despite the tremors in his hands, he managed to take another sip of whiskey, calming his convulsing frame.

"I love 'em," Woodley said at last, sliding back into the Naugahyde backrest of his adjustable Universal-Lounger. "They're fourth generation, you know. They've been scaring chumps like you for years."

Clint blinked. What could he say? He righted himself and took a peek over his shoulder. The bats had settled.

He compulsively checked his tape recorder yet again.

"Yeah, they bother me. Bats give me the creeps. I didn't expect it, you know?" Clint said.

Woodley nodded. He knew.

"Would you like to move outside and finish the interview out on the deck?" Clint asked, knowing what the answer would be.

Woodley shook his head defiantly, then plowed ahead with his story as if the question had never been asked.

"We were under the gun, over budget, the usual situation. My special effects budget was about a hundred bucks. You can't make a good monster for that price, at least one that will scare people. Shit. I had two zombies in full makeup, Buzzy Haller and some other guy, some beatnik. I'd used them in every shot and I was concerned that the audience would recognize the same two faces. I needed something different. We were shooting a scene where one of the cadavers rises up from the slab and strangles Tad Kingston, who was playing his usual dim-wit teenager role.

"I couldn't have Buzzy do it, cause he'd been in the last shot. The other guy was no good either. I'd overexposed the both of them. There was supposed to be a whole army of zombies, and I was trying to make two seem like fifty.

"So Buzzy gets this wild idea to use some of the real cadavers. They keep 'em in this big refrigerated vault with drawers that slide out."

Clint shivered, visualizing. "Jesus . . ." he muttered.

Woodley smiled. "Yeah. So Buzzy figures out how to get the drawers open. They had every kind of corpse you could imagine. Some of them were pretty horrible, I'll tell ya.

"We checked about five of them, until we found this one guy who was really ripe. I think he was an itinerant, a bum. God knows what he died from. He'd been dead for a while, that was obvious. I even remember the drawer number, I don't know why. Sometimes you remember little details like that years later. It was drawer 66, like in 'get your kicks on Route 66.'

"So Buzzy hauls him out, gets behind him, and . . . ah, you sure you want to hear this?"

"Yes. Absolutely. Please go on."

"He works him like a marionette."

"Holy shit," Clint whispered. He resisted the urge to check the cassette machine again.

"This guy stank. I don't know how Buzzy did it. He was a trouper, or one sick puppy. Probably a little of both. He had to work like hell to get the guy to bend. Rigor mortis, you know. It was positively ghastly, if I do say so myself."

Landis smiled again. Thin, dry lips parted, revealing stained teeth. Pale, receding gums flashed. It was the smile of a very old and sick predator.

"I could light my cigar, you know. The smoke keeps 'em away."

"What?" Clint asked.

"The bats."

"The bats?"

"Yeah, they can't stand the smoke, it makes 'em keep their distance. Should I light up?"

Clint nodded.

Landis chuckled, another first. "Works every time," he smirked, his lungs rattling, "So, where was I? Oh yeah. Kingston balked. I can't say that I blame him. He threatened to walk out on the whole production, said he had 'standards.' Ha!, that's a laugh. I wound up offering him more money."

"How much?"

"Chump change," the old man said with obvious disgust. "That turkey would do anything for money. Believe me, I know."

"He did it?"

"Damn right he did it. In one take. Kingston should have gotten the Academy Award for that, except that he wasn't acting. He was scared shitless. The guy looked great on film—the dead guy, not Kingston. He wound up being the star of the picture. We used him in at least twenty shots, and he never complained."

Landis paused, waiting for a laugh, then continued. "We even used a few of his dead buddies. Easiest bunch I ever worked with. Real pros. They worked cheap, too."

Clint's jaw dropped. Never in his wildest dreams did he think he would get all this. But there it was, immortalized on tape. Did the old man tell the truth? Could this be just another one of his scare tactics?

"Are you serious?" Clint asked.

"As a heart attack," Woodley replied. He edged forward on his seat.

"I go in for a close-up. Chet Bronski is the cameraman, a prince, and he's pulling in just as Buzzy thumbs one of the eyes open. I'll tell ya, we all shuddered to see what was gonna happen. The camera zooms in and . . ." He paused. ". . . and it's full of worms."

Landis flopped back in his lounger again. He raised his glass to his lips, then stopped, leveling his gaze into Clint's face.

"That shot made the movie," he said, then swallowed the last of the whiskey.

"Worms?" Clint whispered.

"Yeah, squirming like amoebas. They started coming out, right on cue, and I held that close-up for at least sixty seconds. Onscreen, it seemed like a half an hour. People in the theaters shrank down in their seats and gasped. Christ, what a moment! I was at the Royal Theater in Anaheim for the premier. In those days you always opened out of town, and people started screaming. Some lady barfed. It was my crowning achievement on film. I scared the shit out of 'em."

He put the glass down and tapped his knee.

"That's my business, scaring people.

"That poor son of a bitch was a movie star after he was dead. Can you believe that?"

Clint shook his head.

"I guess you could say people were dying to get in my flicks," the old man rasped, more coughing laughter spraying from his mouth.

Landis Woodley's eyes glimmered. Pig's eyes, Clint thought. Cruel and tiny, they were perpetually squinting out at an unforgiving world.

"*Cadaver* went on to become my highest-grossing movie ever," the sandpaper voice continued. "It played the drive-ins for years. I still see it on late-night TV.

"I should have gone on to bigger and better things, but that shyster Sol Kravitz talked me into those idiotic rock movies. Nothing but trouble. Music stinks. It's death at the box office. These kids, these teenagers, they don't spend money. They steal. I lost so much of my own money on *Big Rock Beat*, I almost went out of business.

"I learned my lesson—there's nothing like scaring people. They never get sick of it."

"That's the truth."

"You know the sound of a gunshot?" the old man asked. Clint nodded. "Everybody overdubs a big boom," Woodley pointed out. "It's a standard sound effect, every library has dozens of 'em. What I did in *Snuff Addict* was, in the scene where the guy kills the chick, I let the actual sound of the gun, a crack, stay in.

That evil little crack is nasty. That sound scares people more than those cannons you hear in all the movies now. Listen to a real gun, it sounds like 'pop!' and it's ominous. Sometimes, when you want to scare someone, less is more. The real fear is up here,"—he tapped his head—"inside your brain."

Clint nodded. "What do you think scares people the most?"

Landis considered the question, then said, "Many people fear the dark, you know, and movie theaters are dark. I don't know. They're afraid of dying, of being alone, but isn't that what happens to you when you pay your way in and sit there staring at the wall? Your own life is suspended, forgotten temporarily. You huddle in the dark, alone, waiting to be seduced by what's up there on the screen."

He tried to light his cigar, but it was too wet and short to function. He gave up and put it down with a sigh, as if his whole life was like that now, a used-up cheap cigar. "People are scared of what they don't understand," he continued. "I scare people because no one has ever understood me."

Snuff Addict was a very disturbing film. Clint had seen it, of course. Woodley made it during the 1961–65 era, a very dark time for him. He'd been reduced to making skin flicks, peepshow loops, and worse. Landis had, once again, preyed on people's worst perversions, and his sick movies went for the jugular even then. He sought out the strange, the bizarre, the most depraved fetishes for his subject matter. It ultimately proved too much for even the porn houses.

Clint wondered if *Snuff Addict* contained a real murder. Now that he knew the truth about Woodley, nothing was out of the question.

In the early seventies, when the sex film industry was somewhat legitimized, the world left Landis Woodley in the cold once again.

After *Cadaver,* and the ill-advised *Big Rock Beat,* he only made one more legitimate feature, the rarely seen *Cold Flesh Eaters,* a waste of celluloid in every critic's book.

The rapidly diminishing quality of his work eventually eroded what little credibility he had, and in a few short years Landis's name meant box office death. You could only fool people so many times, then they got wise.

Sitting across from the old man, Clint felt himself becoming strangely detached. He felt as if he'd stepped outside the scene, watching himself doing the interview.

He knew everything about Landis Woodley that had been made public. His infamous career, his brief success, his spectacular failures, his scandals, and his well-documented perversions.

Tip of the iceberg, Clint thought.

"Those bats are only active at night. That's why I keep it so dark in here," Woodley said, changing gears again. Clint nodded. The old man seemed as much a creature of the dark as the bats.

"They eat everything."

The old man's conversation had a peculiar kind of logic to it once Clint began to recognize the pattern. There could be only one topic, whether he talked about the bats, the film industry, Buzzy Haller, the IRS, or dead bodies. The topic was fear. Landis Woodley appeared obsessed with it.

Fear. Clint was the addict, and Woodley the dealer.

"Nobody ever found out, of course, and we all took an oath of silence. The shoot was wrapped up in three days, and that was it. The censors were all over that picture, though, as if they knew something, which they didn't. I had to cut some stuff, but we still outbloodied National. RKM was happy, and we brought home a winner.

"*Cadaver* was your apex?"

Woodley nodded. Outside the windows the sun was setting. He'd noticed the lengthening shadows and the diminishing light before Clint and was reveling in it. In the dark he came alive.

Woodley leaned forward. "It's a hell of a world, isn't it? When the pinnacle of a man's life's work is a low-budget horror movie full of real corpses."

He looked at Clint as if he expected a response. Clint remained silent.

"You want to see some footage?"

Clint cocked his head. Did he hear that right? Did the old man want to show him some film?

"I got some outtakes, some footage the censors made me take out. They said it was too gory, not suitable for public viewing.

Those wimps, they used to run this town. Shit, you couldn't even say the word 'sex' until 1967. I got some great stuff, Buzzy and the corpses at the morgue, some mutilation stuff . . ."

Mutilation stuff? Clint almost said something, then caught himself. What had they been doing down in the abattoir? Carving people up?

"Sure, I'd love to," he heard himself say. "Can I bring a photographer?"

The thought of watching those grainy old black-and-white films, full of real corpses, alone in this house with the old man made him uneasy.

"No, no photographers, just you."

Clint looked a shade doubtful and the old man picked up on it. "I've got stills, posters, half-sheets, lobby cards, scripts, everything, your article would really kick some butt. Maybe you could make some *real* money. You want to make money, don't you, kid?"

Clint nodded.

"Good, thought so," Woodley rasped. "You've got a hell of a start. Come back tomorrow night, nine o'clock. I'll show you some shit that'll make your hair stand up."

Landis busied himself pouring another shot of booze.

A strange noise knifed up from below. Clint was about to turn off his tape recorder and end the interview when the sound froze him. It sounded like a moan, a painful, horrible, half-human moan.

"What the hell was that?" Clint asked.

Woodley's face blanched. The sound had clearly alarmed him as well.

He spilled a portion of his drink on the already-stained rug at his feet. His head turned to one side, like a dog listening to a violin. The moan came up again, low and pitiable, from beneath their feet. It was the most unpleasant and disconcerting sound that Clint Stockbern had ever heard.

"What is that?" he asked again.

Clint stood up, suddenly acutely aware that it was no longer light outside.

Landis looked up at him. He was still seated, still in denial.

"You heard it, too?"

Clint nodded.

"Christ, I thought I was the only one," Landis growled. "I thought it was in my mind."

Clint surveyed the room. The bats were still. Only the sound of the moaning disturbed the quiet. It came again, the low frequency of it raising Clint's blood pressure another few notches.

Landis rose slowly from his chair. His hands trembled even as they grasped the arms. His fingernails, Clint noticed, were too long. Their color was an unhealthy yellow.

Woodley looked to the hallway, his mind far away.

"It's coming from beneath us," Clint whispered.

"Yeah," Landis croaked.

"What's down there?"

"The projection room. There shouldn't be anyone down there; I keep it locked up. That's where I store all the films."

Landis said the words Clint didn't want to hear. "Let's go down and take a look."

Clint turned back to the old man. "I . . . I don't think so—"

"What are you, scared?" Landis leered. Clint considered turning around and walking out, but he didn't want to destroy the relationship he'd spent all day nurturing. Suddenly it occurred to him that this could be another one of the old man's tricks, a test to see how much Clint could take.

"Well—" Clint felt like saying yes, and letting it go at that, but the fear excited him to new heights. Something inside would force him down there, he knew, something would make him face more fear. "Okay," he said.

They descended the steps carefully. Clint stayed close behind Woodley, his eyes darting from corner to corner. The stairs were narrow and creaked like stage props, the light stingy and unreliable. Clint's hands tingled.

"Watch out. My pet owls are in here," Woodley droned. Almost on cue, wings beat through the air in front of them. Unlike the bats, these wings were large and dry, moving across the ceiling in long, feathery flaps. Clint ducked.

"Christ, they're big!" Clint gasped as one sailed past his head.

"Ketupa owls. I get 'em from Central Africa."

They reached the bottom of the steps and entered a long

room with a door at the far end. Light came from a bare bulb hanging from the ceiling. It cast sharp shadows, well-defined and ugly, on the discolored walls. It smelled like a basement.

Clint stepped on something that crunched under his foot. "What the hell? Aren't these—"

"Bones. They eat mice whole, and spit up the hair and bones afterward."

Clint winced and tried to avoid stepping on the little bundles of horror. Landis, ever the keen observer said, "Are you all right? You look a little pale."

Clint wiped his face with his hand and nodded. "Yeah, I'm fine. Do you have rats?"

"Nah, the owls get 'em."

They crossed the room and opened the door. Landis led the way into a large, windowless, rectangular room. A movie screen occupied the far end, with several rows of theater seats arranged in front of it at a discreet distance. A huge old commercial projector, the kind used in movie theaters in the fifties, sat on a table behind the rows of seats. It was a gray metal monstrosity, all reels and gears, and it dominated the back of the room like an evil robot.

"I watch my old movies down here," the old man said. "I've got original prints of all of them, first-class stuff. The seats and projector are from the old Avalon Theater in Westwood. Beautiful, huh?"

"Yeah, nice," Clint replied. The thought of the old man down here alone at night, watching those horrible old movies with real corpses in them while the projector flickered behind him, was too much. The room fascinated Clint. It heightened his fear, providing a rich growth medium of mystery. He could imagine the wet cigar and the whiskey, the bloodshot eyes staring up at the images of Buzzy Haller and Tad Kingston as they manipulated the legions of the dead. He shook his head to clear away the demons.

"Great seats, great theaters, and some damn good movies," Landis muttered, "It was another era."

Clint nodded.

"These seats are from the balcony. I wonder how many kids—"

The moan came again, cutting the old man off like a clap of thunder. It was loud in here, unnaturally loud, and in it Clint could hear the unmistakable sound of pain. Hideous and gutteral, it rose from the floor like a wounded spirit.

It hung in the air, slowly fading away, as if it were recorded in an echo chamber. Clint held his breath.

"Holy shit," he whispered. "It's coming from the floor. It sounds like someone's dying down there. Is there a . . . a subbasement?"

Landis shook his head. "A crawl space. Just a dirt floor crawl space."

Clint didn't want to see the crawl space; he didn't even want to know it existed. What if the old man wanted to investigate further?

Woodley pulled back a filthy Persian rug to reveal a trapdoor in the floor.

"That's the way down," Woodley said. "You want to look?"

Clint shook his head. "Maybe some other time."

"No taste for the creepy-crawlies, eh, kid? I don't blame you. I've never looked down there myself. It's probably the wind. Maybe it broke through down there somewhere and it's swirling around under the house."

Clint knew it wasn't the wind. That kind of thinking usually got guys killed in horror movies. The wind doesn't make your heart stop beating or bring acid to your mouth. The wind isn't in pain. He cleared his throat and asked, "Have you ever heard that sound before?"

The old man nodded. "Yeah, a long time ago."

THEN

HOLLYWOOD, 1957

Buzzy Haller put down his unfinished burger at Barny's Bar and turned his seat to watch some juvenile delinquent play a game of pinball. It was hot and bright outside, but in here it was the exact opposite.

Buzzy was dressed in the casual style of most twenty-five-year-old guys in Hollywood: a sport shirt, open at the neck, khaki slacks, and a dark blazer. His blond flattop crew cut needed trimming, and a closer look at his shoes revealed heels worn from too much walking.

The door opened and Landis Woodley walked in. Light spilled through the breach like liquid fire, blinding everybody at the bar. Another figure materialized from the dazzling silver background, Neil Bugmier.

"Oh shit," Haller muttered. "Here comes Princess Laughing Water." He took a swig of beer. Woodley sat on one side of Haller while Bugmier sat on the other.

"Hello, Buzz," Bugmier said softly. "Aren't you glad to see me?"

"Fuck no," Buzzy said flatly.

Bugmier adjusted his skirt and began to peel away his white gloves. Woodley ordered three beers. Once the gloves were off, Neil flexed his fingers.

"A little hot for gloves, ain't it?" Haller said.

"Well," Bugmier replied, "I just don't feel fully dressed without them."

The beers arrived. Two guys farther down the bar stared at Bugmier with mouths agape. Buzzy hated that. Neil raised the frosted mug to his mouth and took several man-size swallows of the beer. His Adam's apple bobbed up and down with the rhythm of his chugging. He drained half the glass in one pass and replaced the mug on the bar. It carried the vivid red lipstick traces of his constantly pouting cinema lips.

He'd smudged his lipstick, and the stubble of his beard was beginning to poke through the Max Factor foundation and heavy powder. For a man who dressed as a woman, Neil Bugmier had an extremely heavy beard; his five o'clock shadow began to make its appearance around noon.

It was hard being a transvestite in full drag in 1957, even in Hollywood, a place Buzzy Haller considered "the last great fruitcake capital of the world." Neil noticed the two men staring at him and waved.

"Christ, don't do that," Buzzy whispered. "It's bad enough I gotta be seen in public with you, but I gotta drink here, you dig? These guys are probably gonna run into me later and start talkin', you know what I mean?"

Neil winked. "You're such a baby, Buzz. So they talk, who cares? What do you have to be afraid of?"

Buzzy frowned. "My reputation, that's what. Believe it or not, I still get a lot of chicks around this town. Ask Woody."

Woodley wrapped his hand around the mug of beer and smiled. "Don't get me involved in your little lovers' spat, fellahs. I got bigger fish to fry."

"Shove it, Woody," Buzzy barked, loud enough for the two guys farther down the bar to hear. "Lovers' spat, my ass!"

Neil laughed, a high lunatic titter that bordered on parody. "Exactly!"

"Shut up, you nutski," Haller roared. "The world's going

straight to hell in a handbasket. It's gettin' so a guy can't even have a friendly drink anymore."

Landis Woodley smoothed his oily black hair with a hand. He tended to use too much Wildroot Cream Oil and the excess lubricated his palm. He wore a silver-gray, short-sleeve sport shirt with a rolling dice motif. The vertical black stripe over the pocket and the hideaway buttons were the height of fashion, but no matter what he wore, he always looked like a bookie. Buzzy called it racetrack flash.

At twenty-six years old, Landis Woodley was whippet thin and energetic. He wore a mustache, thin and sinister, because he thought that "the chicks dug it." His eyes were beady, constantly moving, shaded by an awning of bushy eyebrows. They were the kind of eyebrows that would, in coming years, grow wild in every direction. Right now they were still reasonably obedient.

The three men sipped their beers and watched highlights of the World Series on the indistinct black-and-white television screen behind the bar. "I hear the Dodgers are moving out here next year, and the Giants are going to San Francisco," Landis said. He liked to use his hands when he talked.

"So? Who gives a shit?" Bugmier cooed. "It won't help make this town any hipper. I swear, you'd think it was the Midwest around here the way they carry on over my clothes."

"You're a fruitcake, Bugmier," Buzzy said.

"Get off my back," Neil replied. "I was in the marines, you know. I landed on the beach at Iwo Jima."

"Yeah? What were you wearing?"

"Under my battle fatigues? Hmm, let me think, black bra and panties, if my memory serves. I had my nylons in my pack."

"You're crazy!"

The bartender, who had been wiping glasses with a white towel and listening to the conversation, laughed. "You kill me, Neil, you really do."

"He may be crazy, but he works cheap," Landis Woodley chimed in. "Why don't you show Buzz the script rewrite, Neil?"

The man dressed as a woman reached into his oversize handbag and withdrew a sheaf of typewritten papers. He put them on the table and smiled. "Best thing I ever did," he said proudly.

Buzzy Haller belched loudly, scooped up the papers, and began to read.

"You're not going to read it here, are you?" Neil asked.

"Of course I am," Buzzy said. "And then I'm going to have a preproduction meeting with myself and decide on a shooting schedule, then design and build the monster within the next forty-eight hours."

"Tonight's the party," Landis said slyly.

"You got the place all fixed up like last time?" the bartender asked.

"Better. Ed, you won't believe it," Landis answered. "Buzzy's got the tree house rigged, the grounds, everything."

"Got something big planned?"

Landis smiled. "I can tell you, right now, that this will be the greatest stunt in the history of Hollywood."

Ed the bartender was impressed. "You guys . . . You're unbelievable, you know that? Nobody does a party like you do."

"It's that hoodoo that you do," Buzzy joked, nodding at Landis.

"You're goin', right?" Neil asked.

"Wouldn't miss it for the world," Ed replied.

Buzzy clapped his hands together. "Man, I can't wait. I invited that cute little publicity girl from RKM, Roberta Bachman."

Landis snorted. "Why waste your time? You'll never get in her pants."

"Wanna bet?"

"I'll bet," said Neil happily. "But we'll need a witness!"

"You guys are dreaming. She's as cold as a blue Sno-Kone. Believe me, I've tried," Landis, the voice of reason, offered. "Are you coming as a man or a woman tonight, Neil?"

"I haven't decided. Some chicks dig that cross-dressing scene. But then again, it scares a lot of potential talent away."

"I can't imagine why," said Buzz, rolling his eyes at Ed. "How about another round?"

Landis nodded. "Speaking of scaring people, tonight should be the greatest. I've got some real beauties lined up. The torture chamber, bats, coffins, and my best prop yet, the guillotine . . ."

"Better than last time?" asked the bartender as he delivered the frosted mugs to the thirsty patrons.

Landis nodded. "This one's the ultimate, Eddie baby. I'm gonna roll some film, too. Luboff's coming, Lana Wills, that Saturday night horror lady from Channel Two, what's her name?"

"Devila," Neil interjected.

"Wow, Devila's coming? I watch her all the time. Man, this is gonna be great. I can't wait," the bartender replied. "Best Halloween party on the planet."

"Did you check out the morgue?" Landis asked Buzzy.

"Uh-huh. It's perfect, really wonderful." Buzzy's eyes sparkled with excitement. "I don't know why we never thought of it before. you should see this place! I swear, it looks like a million-dollar set! I talked to the guy there, and it's no problem. Seems that cop shows shoot there all the time, just never *inside the abattoir.* He said he'd be glad to help, that he *wanted* us to shoot there. Of course, I had to offer him a part, but I figure that can't hurt, right? We can have it from midnight to five for three nights."

Landis chuckled. "What people won't do for a chance to be in a movie. It's frightening. Well, I can use him as one of the doctors, and we can shoot him early the first night. That way he'll be out of our hair after the first hour."

Neil Bugmier pushed the script at Buzzy. "Read," he said.

Buzzy ordered an extra-dry martini, which he referred to as an "ice-cold see-through" and another beer, and sat back, the script in his hands. He knew what to look for and could read a script in less time than most people could read a menu. He began to plow through it, raising an eyebrow now and then. Eddie the bartender cleared away the remains of his lunch.

After twenty minutes, two more "ice-cold see-throughs" and another beer, Buzzy looked up and smiled. "This is pretty good, you know?"

Landis put his hand on Buzzy's shoulder and said, "That's what I've been tellin' ya. Fruitcake here does good work."

Neil smiled.

At first Neil's elaborate costumery had put Buzzy off. Buzzy's homophobic impulses flared at the sight of a man in a dress. Neil patiently explained to him that he was not a homosexual, just a cross-dresser. He loved women as much as Buzzy did, he insisted. He just liked to wear their clothes. It took many months, but eventually Buzzy got to the point where he could work with Neil.

Landis was the man who brought them together. He "discovered" all sorts of interesting and odd people. Hollywood—not only the film capital of the world, but the weirdo capital of the world.

Buzzy knew Landis Woodley loved unusual people. He seemed to surround himself with them, which further alienated him from the old guard of the movie business. Hollywood was trying to clean up its image. Independent filmmakers like Landis Woodley, mavericks and rebels, were always treated the same. First, the big studios tried to drive them out of business, then, if that didn't work, they bought them out.

Landis had had a few modest successes, and he really knew how to stretch a budget; guys like that were always in demand in Tinsel Town. In fact, most director/producers wouldn't even attempt a film on the kinds of budgets Landis routinely worked with.

The Woodley modus operandi went like this: he'd start shooting a film, usually on a miniscule, unrealistic budget, then run out of money in mid-production. At that point, he'd gotten the investors in too deep and he would beg, borrow, or steal to complete the project. He'd oversold a picture more than once. As a consequence, he had very few repeat investors. Landis Woodley was not a money person. For that, he had Sol Kravitz. Sol was the kind of guy who could go out and make investment money materialize out of thin air. He'd been successful in the fledgling peep-show business and various other shady permutations of the film industry. It wasn't really actually the movie game, but it did involve the concept of "film."

Sol loved Landis, and he viewed the younger man as a potential superstar.

Landis came to depend on Sol for the raw material that ran his two-bit B-movie empire—cash. Buzzy knew who signed the checks.

Sol had raised the funds to start *Cadaver,* and Landis was off and running. The drive-ins were hot, and Landis had a deal with RKM to distribute the movie. Even after the lackluster performance of *Attack of the Haunted Saucer,* he'd managed to talk RKM into rolling the dice one more time.

As he sat in the cool, dark confines of Barny's Bar on this

muggy Thursday afternoon in the heart of Hollywood, Buzzy thought about Landis's annual Halloween party, a tradition in the hills above Beachwood Avenue.

The party was a debauch, pure and simple; Landis and his friends were perverts. Liquor and reefers were everywhere. Many an aspiring starlet had been led down the devil's path by that combination, liberally applied by the charming Landis Woodley, with the assurance that "nothing bad would happen" and that the young lady would be considered for the lead role in his next epic.

If that didn't work, "Doctor" Buzzy Haller could always be called upon for more exotic intoxicants. More importantly, the party gave Buzzy and Landis a chance to try outrageous stunts on unsuspecting people. Their goal was to shock and frighten. Of course, they filmed everything. Party scenes from last year showed up in *Haunted Saucer.* Buzzy was sure that this year's performance would be the best ever.

Neil got up to go to the rest room, and that was always interesting.

Today he chose the men's room and avoided any unpleasantness. The bar was empty at this point. The other patrons had departed, and Neil, ever the diplomat, had decided to forgo his usual "powder room" scene and just urinate quickly.

When he returned, Buzzy was finishing up the last few pages of dialogue.

"Better than *The Mummy's Brain,*" Buzzy said, feeling the effects of the martinis. "Better than *Slave of the Sadist* and *Satan's Daughter!*"

Landis beamed. "That's what I thought. Can you start today?"

Buzzy nodded. "I'm way ahead of you, Woody. I've got the monster stuff all ready to go, and I have some nice ideas for the zombies."

Landis nodded. If Buzzy said it was ready, it was ready. The two men had the highest professional regard for each other. "I'm using the sets from *Satan's Daughter.* What happened was, after RKM spent all that money on those beautiful sets, I wanted to shoot another movie right away before they tore it all down. It seemed like such a waste. So I got Neil to come up with this *Ca-*

daver script, and the only other scene we need is in the morgue. Shit, this movie just about shoots itself. We don't have to build a single set!"

"And I came up with the plot line," bragged Neil, his makeup now reapplied with Marine Corps precision.

"Fruity, you're a genius," Buzzy shouted across the empty room.

Roberta Bachman got ready to go out. Her roommate, Janice Devin, an aspiring actress, stood behind her as she looked in the mirror. Both were in their early twenties and attractive.

"Are you sure you want to go?" Janice asked.

"Sure I'm sure. What's the big deal? Besides, I heard that a lot of big stars are going to be there."

Janice put a hand on Roberta's shoulder, causing Roberta to stop applying her cosmetics and look up at her.

"Just be careful, okay?"

Roberta went back to her eye shadow. "I'll be careful. Why are you so sure something's going to happen?"

"Because I've heard all about Landis Woodley. He's a sick man who makes sick movies."

Roberta laughed. Her delicate titters were as fresh and clear as stream water. She was just out of college and eager to get ahead. Her three-week-old first job, as a publicist for RKM Motion Picture Company, excited her. Everything seemed new and different now that she was out on her own. Although she'd lived in Hollywood all her life, this was her first taste of freedom.

Raised off Melrose Avenue in a tiny house with her mother and Auntie Clarice, she'd often dreamed of what it would be like to have her own apartment. Now, not only did she live by her own rules, she worked for one of the hottest new motion picture companies in town. Life for her had never been better.

"Anyway, Buzzy Haller is a very nice man," she said convincingly.

Janice turned away. She went over to the window and looked out. "It gets dark so early these days. I hate winter."

"It's not winter yet, just Halloween," Roberta said.

"Don't you think your costume is a little risqué?"

Janice took a cigarette from the ornate brass case on the table and lit it with a lighter that looked like a gun. She blew the smoke out dramatically, pausing to replace the lighter, then turned back to Roberta. Her image, much smaller now in the mirror from across the room, stared back at her best friend with thinly disguised disgust.

"I'm going as a cigarette girl, what's wrong with that?"

Janice frowned. "It's just that it's so . . . so sexy. I mean, there's more of you showing than costume."

"Oh, for God's sake, Jan, this is the 1950s! People are much more modern now. Believe me, there will be sexier costumes than this one, I'm sure. This is Hollywood. Don't you want to come with me?"

"Forget it. Besides, I wasn't invited."

Roberta went back to her face, glancing at the clock on her vanity and making a mental note that she only had fifty minutes left before Buzzy showed up at her door. Janice kept the pressure on, pacing the room, appearing and disappearing in the mirror as she moved in and out of the field of vision.

"I heard that Buzzy Haller smokes reefers," she said.

"Come on, Jan," came the reply. "That's just a stupid rumor. They say that about half the men in Hollywood these days."

"God knows he drinks enough," she continued.

"No more than anybody else I know," Roberta countered.

"Are you crazy?" Janice snapped, "That man sucks up martinis like ginger ale!"

"Aren't you overreacting to what Mary said?"

Janice took another deep drag off the unfiltered Chesterfield, leaving a crimson lipstick ring, and crossed the room. "Mary should know, she works at the commissary. She said he drinks every day, flirts with all the girls, and gambles."

Roberta stopped doing her eyes again and turned to face Janice. The smoke from her cigarette curled seductively around her head, looking suddenly like a crown of thorns.

"Will you calm down? God, it's like you're my mother or something. If anything happens, *anything,* I'll grab a cab back home in a flash," Roberta explained evenly.

"Well—" Janice stubbed out her cigarette and exhaled sharply in her best Bette Davis impersonation.

"Come on, Jan. It's okay. Buzzy Haller is a very nice man.

He's taking me to a party where there will be lots of other people. What could possibly happen?" Roberta finished off her sentence with a sobering look, designed to assuage her friend's fears.

"A lot," Janice replied, unconvinced.

"Like what?"

"He could get fresh with you, lure you into one of the bedrooms, get you drunk, and slip you his pepperoni."

"His *what*?" They burst into a torrent of giggles.

Tad Kingston had no talent, at least that's what everybody said behind his back. To his face they were more diplomatic. "Lots of potential," the agents would say, or, "the right looks." Never, "He's a great actor." And it was the truth. Thadeus Willinger, AKA Tad Kingston, couldn't act his way out of a paper bag, but he did not aspire to be a great actor. What Tad Kingston wanted was to be a movie star.

In Hollywood, that was a much more realistic goal.

Tad did have the looks. He'd toyed with being a rock 'n' roll singer, but his inability to carry a tune turned off the record companies. So, Tad embarked on a career as a matinee idol. He found an agent who liked his face, had some pictures printed, and waited by the phone. It never rang.

He ran into Landis Woodley at a party, and the brash filmmaker took him under his wing. He wound up with the lead teenager part in *Hot Rod Monster, Blood Ghouls of Malibu,* and *Attack of the Haunted Saucer.*

The kids loved him. Overlooking his massive shortcomings as an actor, they focused on his hair. He had what Landis Woodley referred to as "star quality hair."

It was blond, longish for its day, swept back, and greasy. It flared with intricate patterns back from his forehead. His pompadour cascaded in front like a frozen waterfall, then swept back severely on the sides and ended up in a classic "DA." He spent hours working it with a comb. If he'd spent as much time learning his lines, he might have gotten more work.

His credits with Woodley probably helped him lose more jobs than gain them around Hollywood.

Tad was wolfing down a ham sandwich his mother had made him when the phone rang.

The telephone in the hallway of his mother's house was black and heavy. It sat on a tiny table next to the most uncomfortable chair his mother owned. That was by design, of course. Tad knew her reasoning: that he would spend less time talking on the telephone, and thereby reduce the amount of her monthly phone bill. Coupled with the postage-stamp-size table, it was as severe an environment as she could muster for conversation.

None of it mattered to Tad. He didn't give two shits for comfort, and he talked as long as he liked, whenever he liked, regardless.

She kept the ringer at its loudest setting and it reverberated off the flowered wallpaper with eardrum-rattling intensity.

Tad picked up the weighty receiver. "Hello? Tad Kingston speaking."

Landis Woodley sounded pissed off. "Hey, Kingston, I heard you're not bringing Lana Wills to the party tonight, and I thought I'd call you and find out for myself."

"Mr. Woodley—I . . ."

"I know you wouldn't screw me like that, would you? I went out of my way to line this up for you. Lana Wills is hot now."

Tad stammered. He decided to be forthright and just tell the truth, an ill-advised strategy when dealing with Landis Woodley.

His voice quivered slightly as he said, "Ah, Mr. Woodley, actually I was going to take Becky Sears."

Landis snapped back without dropping a beat, "Becky Sears? Are you crazy? She's just a script girl, a nobody. Lana Wills is a star!"

Tad sat in the uncomfortable chair and put his elbow on the tiny tabletop. He could sense his mother upstairs listening. The old lady really loved to eavesdrop. It was the only way she ever got any information on her son.

"But I like Becky Sears," Tad whined.

"Tough shit. You're taking Lana Wills and that's that. I'm sending a limo over to pick you up, and you better be ready."

Tad could hear his mother wheezing on the landing above him; the cramped house and narrow staircase carried sounds like a hollow tube. "Jeez, Mr. Woodley, what am I gonna tell Becky?"

Landis laughed. "I don't care. Hell, tell her the truth; that you have no say in this, that you're a piece of shit, and that I made you do it."

"But she's such a sweet girl, it's gonna break her heart."

Landis sighed. "Kid, you're hopeless, you know that? Have you *seen* Lana Wills? She's built like a brick shithouse. Jesus, Tad, every other guy in America wants a piece of that. The boys over at RKM insist that she go with you. She's in *Son Of Tarzan,* and they want her name out there for everybody to see."

"I just can't tell Becky . . . it's gonna break her heart. She'll cry."

Landis sighed again, this time deeper and with more resignation than usual. "Okay, I'll tell her. What's her number?"

"Would you? Jeez, that would be great! Mr. Woodley, you know I'd do anything for you."

"Cut the crap, kid. I'll do your dirty work, but don't think you can get away with this shit forever.

"Here's the deal. I can only afford one limo, so it's gonna be for both of my stars. Get this, you're double-dating with Luboff. The grand master of horror and the young apprentice, going off to the party of the year together. He's taking some bimbo from Paramount, and you're with Wills. I'm gonna send a photographer over to get some shots of you getting ready, you know, combing your hair, stuff like that. 'Star gets ready for fright night bash!' Brilliant, huh?"

Tad blanched. The thought of sharing a vehicle with the dirty old man made him queasy. "Luboff? Aw man, do I have to? Shit, the old man's always getting loaded and putting his hand on my knee. Plus he smokes those disgusting cheap cigars."

Landis cut in. "I bought him some good ones for the party. Can't have the star smoking garbage in public."

Tad stopped. He knew he had no choice. "All right." He sighed. "What time is the limo coming?"

"Eight. Be ready. I'll tell Luboff to keep his hand out of your lap."

"You'll call Becky?"

"Sure."

Tad heard the phone click. Landis never said good-bye—he just ended a conversation like he was picking up a phonograph needle. Tad had grown used to it. He owed Landis Woodley his professional life and didn't complain about the hundreds of antisocial, crude, and humiliating things he did all the time.

Would Landis call Becky? Tad hoped so. He really liked Becky, but was too spineless to call her himself. He eased the receiver back into its cradle and stood up. His mother called from upstairs, "Thadeus? Are you going out somewhere?"

Tad shouted up the stairs, a darkness creeping into the voice that he saved exclusively for her. "Yes, Mother."

Landis Woodley smiled wickedly. All seemed in readiness. Tonight's party was going to be his best yet. He would *really* give these people something to remember. The king of low-budget horror was going to deliver the goods.

He looked down at his list of calls. The numbers blurred. He ran his finger down the list and stopped at only the most important names. *Damn,* he thought, *I need a secretary for all this shit. It's too much work.*

He had already forgotten about calling Becky Sears. Tad Kingston and his pimply adolescent problems didn't rate very high on his list. The kid would just have to learn to take care of his own butt.

Buzzy Haller entered the room and gave him the thumbs-up sign.

"Ready to go, boss," he said.

"Beautiful," Woodley said through his teeth.

"How about a drink before we change?"

They drifted into the living room, where a full wet bar waited for customers. Landis automatically prepared two vodka martinis, very dry, no olives. He handed one to Buzzy.

"I gotta tell ya, Woody," Buzzy said honestly, "there's nothing like an icy see-through."

Landis held his glass up and said, "Here's to old H.P. Lovecraft."

"Who?"

Landis smiled. "Just a guy."

Buzzy took a sip and made a smacking sound with his lips. "Ahh, perfect. You always get just the right ratio of vodka to vermouth."

They drank as Buzzy scanned the guest list. He tapped the

paper and said, "We're gonna scare the livin' shit out of these people tonight."

Landis nodded. "You think we'll get into trouble? I mean, this is some pretty heavy stuff."

Buzzy raised his glass and winked. "Aw, who cares? It's worth it to shake these assholes up a little."

4

Albert Beaumond was haunted. He didn't know how, but he did know why. As the world's leading Satanist and leader of the First Satanic Church of America, he'd been doing research on the nature of the devil in different cultures when something unexpected happened. He overturned one rock too many.

He stood on the sidewalk in front of the fledgling Los Angeles International Airport and squinted into the hazy sunshine.

Albert was a tall, distinguished man in his late forties, always well dressed, with a European flair. He wore a neatly trimmed goatee and kept his silver-streaked brown hair combed straight back. He cut a handsome, striking figure.

His daughter was late. She was always late. For a college student at UCLA she didn't seem to have much of a mind for punctuality. Didn't they require her to go to her classes on time?

He smiled when he thought about the way her mother had been when they first met in San Francisco twenty-two years ago. Albert studied anthropology with a minor in botany at the University of California in Berkeley. Thora's mother was a botany student as well. Now *that* woman had been a stickler about being on time. She chided him endlessly about being late on their first date. He learned his lesson and was seldom late after that. When she died ten years later, he was late for the funeral.

Thora took after Albert.

Over the years he'd adjusted to the point where he expected it, even planned for it.

Except today it was a nuisance. His plane had arrived a few minutes early, he'd cleared customs in record time, and now he was anxious to get home.

In his suitcase were artifacts that could change the way western civilization thought about God forever. He shifted it from one hand to another, not wanting to put it down even for a second for fear that something might happen to it.

He need not have worried. The battered brown leather bag looked sufficiently scruffy not to attract the least attention from the usual airport thieves. Even if it were stolen, the artifacts he prized above all else were nothing anyone would know the value of—anyone but a trained anthropologist, that is.

To Albert, it was a miracle. The two twenty-inch silver alloy pieces, hand-polished and odd in appearance, had amazing powers. They were tucked away in his bag, wrapped in towels and tied with a piece of rawhide. The customs inspector didn't even bother opening them. He just waved Albert through the turnstile with a yawn and a look of bored indifference.

Albert fished a cigarette out of his breast pocket and lit it with a flick from his monogrammed Zippo lighter. It always worked on the first try. He trusted that lighter like he trusted nothing else in this godless world.

Godless? Well, maybe not, thought Albert. Now that he'd seen it with his own eyes, he couldn't say for sure what omnipotent beings ruled our festering universe. He knew about one for sure. The devil was real.

Every culture has a religion, and every religion has a devil, or so it seemed to Albert when he began his scholarly quest to catalog and investigate every reference.

It turned into an enormous job that kept him busy for years, but Albert had a mission. He wanted to establish the face of Satan around the world. He wanted to compare and understand what characteristics stayed the same from culture to culture.

Maybe, among those statistics a pattern would emerge, a common thread of belief in the Prince of Darkness that Albert could use to conjure him up.

So far his best efforts seemed to fall on deaf ears. Like the monk who prayed for years in vain and never saw the slightest sign that his lifetime of prayers had been answered, or even heard by an indifferent God, Albert had been trying to raise the devil without success. He reasoned that a universal approach might work. After all, there was really no such thing as good and evil, just man's interpretation of it.

A scientific approach was called for.

It was the modern way, and in 1957, modern was the name of the game.

People everywhere were searching for new ways to do things. Albert saw himself as a pioneer. He was, after all, the first person to establish the only openly Satanic church in America, a bold move in any era.

In his research, he'd found no fewer than 1,665 references to Satan, spanning hundreds of cultures.

There were many similarities, too. Belief in Hell, eternal damnation, demons, demonic possession, sin, and evil incarnate seemed to be universal concepts.

For Albert Beaumond, it was vindication. He felt a breakthrough was just around the corner. His ultimate goal, of course, was to conjure the Prince of Darkness, to be the first in modern times to commune with him. His search went on for years.

"Do what thou wilt shall be the extent of the law," he said, muttering his favorite Aleister Crowley quotation.

In South America, in the high country of Peru, on the misty plains beyond Machu Picchu, he found something truly staggering, truly magical. There, cut off from the outside world, lived a tribe of Indians who worshipped a demon they could summon whenever they wanted through the use of an ingenious device.

His liaison to the local scientific community, a smarmy little man named Carlos from the Anthropology Department at the University of Lima, had mentioned it to him in his hotel room in Ecuador. He had arrived there en route to Peru to study some quaint local human sacrificial customs among the native population. The Ecuadorians were less than enthusiastic when he approached them to photograph their rituals.

He then prepared to travel to Peru and explore the mountainous regions there. In addition to his anthropological pursuits, Albert planned to study the native flora, taking specimens of the numerous unknown and uncatalogued species along the way. Albert's encyclopedic knowledge of flowering plants, especially the narcotic and hallucinogenic varieties, had proved valuable. In the past, he'd sold the rights to several of his discoveries to pharmacological companies, offsetting the cost of his expeditions.

Albert's hotel room sweltered in the oppressive tropical heat. Humidity so intense that it made the wallpaper peel debilitated him. He was reduced to sitting on the rattan chair beneath the ceiling fan and drinking whatever chilled beverages he could procure. Today it was beer, tepid and barely cooler than room temperature. He offered one to Carlos, who greedily accepted and paced the room as he drank.

The ceiling fan turned agonizingly slowly, stirring only the faintest breeze, imperceptible but for the slight cooling of the sweat on his brow.

"It is a Stone Age tribe, Dr. Beaumond," Carlos said hopefully. Albert had passed himself off as a doctor of anthropology from USC, referring to himself as "Doctor" Beaumond. No one asked to see any verification, and so far no one had bothered to check his background.

Albert Beaumond certainly looked like a professor. His goatee, close-cropped to fetishistic proportions, gave him an intellectual, and slightly evil, persona. The overall effect was convincing. And then there was Albert's natural intelligence and upper-class background. Carlos had no reason to doubt his authenticity.

Albert had loosened his tie and removed his lightweight summer jacket. His white suit was wrinkled and moist, soiled here and there by the general dirtiness of the country.

White, though reflective of heat, was an impractical color for clothes here. His shirt stuck to his back, defined in geographic detail by the sweat-stained suspenders that hung from his shoulders. As he leaned forward, the pattern of rattan was branded lightly on his back. Albert had been uncomfortable every minute he'd been here. How could these people live like this?

Carlos didn't seem to mind the heat. He swigged down the warm beer and talked excitedly. Albert could smell Carlos's body scent; it lathered the air with an odor of oniony sweat. He wondered why these people didn't use colognes.

The air barely stirred. Albert mopped at his brow with a dirty white handkerchief. He watched the research assistant pace.

For his part, Albert thought Carlos boorish and common. The little man seemed only interested in the payment that Albert had mentioned for reliable information that might add to his research.

"A tribe so ancient that no one knows how long they have been there. The ruins near their village date back to pre-Inca times."

Albert seemed mildly interested until he learned of their methodology, then he was intrigued. He would spend much money and many days searching for the tribe to see with his own eyes if Carlos had reported the truth.

This tribe believed that all things, all emotions, and all spirits were born of vibrations. They worshiped the vibrations and had kept a detailed account of every spirit they had conjured over the centuries and what vibration contacted it.

It was the combination of vibrations that did the trick.

They did it through the use of long metallic vibrating devices that resembled tuning forks.

As the fork was struck and resonated, then combined with another vacillation wave coming from a second fork, it summoned forth an entity that was sympathetic to that frequency. Different combinations produced different results. Certain frequencies oscillated between themselves, canceling each other out. Their discord made new vibrations, and those rang with unknown dissonance. The effect built on itself.

Two certain forks, Albert was told, two mysterious antiquities from the dawn of man, had the miraculous power that, once struck, together, made contact with . . . the other side.

The other side of what? Albert wondered.

Carlos said it was a demon who came forth in the form of a serpent. A Snake God.

To Albert, of course, that entity represented something else entirely. The face of Satan. It appeared in their drawings as a serpent, complete with horns, forked tongue, and a tail. Familiar turf for Albert.

"Will this information be worth money to you?" asked Carlos. "I have gone to great expense to contact a man who can help us, a medicine man. He can help us locate the tuning forks."

Albert fanned himself with his notebook. Carlos grinned like a successful thief. To Albert, the entire experience of being in the room with Carlos had become unpleasant, but now, with this new information, Albert was revived.

"Yes, Carlos. I think it could be worth something."

Carlos caught his breath. "How much?" he asked.

"We'll see, we'll see," said Albert.

"I think," said Carlos, "that I can persuade this man to do business with us. For a price."

Albert immediately set forth on an expedition to the high plateaus to find the sacred tuning forks and unlock their secrets. Carlos arranged for a translator/guide to accompany them.

For weeks they climbed and searched, enduring hardships of every description to reach the hidden village.

Albert gathered plant specimens as he went, amazed at the dizzying number of varieties. He discovered a giant flower that greatly resembled the *Papaver somniferum*, or opium poppy. The seedpods had grown to twice their normal size. Albert named the new discovery *Papaver somniferum gigantus Beaumond*, and collected as many pods as he could fit in his specimen bag.

This discovery alone could pay for the expedition, he thought.

When at last Albert discovered the backward, isolated Stone Age tribe, he went about trying to obtain the tuning forks.

Like most twentieth-century men, Albert grossly underestimated the power of the spirit world and blindly called forth the power of evil as if he were placing a long-distance phone call.

That's when his problems really started.

It began the first night he was in the tribal village. The high priest, whom he had made an instant effort to patronize, invited him to watch as he used the summoning devices to conjure up the Snake God.

The tuning forks were not kept hidden. In fact, they were kept in a hut in the center of the village, in the open, where everyone in the village could see them. No one, not even the enemies of the tribe, dared touch them except the high priest. Fear could be one hell of a deterrent, Albert decided.

The living conditions within the village were deplorable, yet the hut that housed the tuning forks stayed clean and well maintained.

The sacred objects seemed to be the center of village life.

Albert got his first look at the tuning forks as the sun faded over the ridge behind the village. It illuminated the square in front of the hut with golden twilight.

The high priest removed the forks from their leather pouches and held them over his head for all to genuflect.

The people of the village became very excited at their unveiling, and, although Albert could not know what they were saying, he sensed their fear and reverence.

The people bowed down with their foreheads to the ground. They chanted and prayed, whispering like leaves in the wind.

Albert stepped forward and examined the two objects with the appraising eyes of a scientist.

The sun exploded off the polished metal surfaces with the intensity and brilliance of fire. They were, without a doubt, the most curious antiquities he had ever seen. They resembled two tuning forks, the type used by musicians. One was slightly larger than the other, the bigger of the two being about two feet in length. The other appeared to be a scaled-down version of the first, about fifteen inches in length.

Both forks were of the same design, a matched set of two U-shaped silver bars, roughly one inch in diameter, bent in the middle. The two prongs ran parallel, separated by an inch of space. At the top of the elbow there was a perforation through which a leather strap had been threaded. The tuning fork was thus hung so that it might vibrate freely.

At the four ends were unusual designs that caught Albert's attention. There, sculpted intricately by hands of talent, were four snake heads, accurate in every detail. The heads all seemed to be the same. They were all baring fangs.

These tuning forks appeared to be constructed in a manner inconsistent with the level of skill of the locals. Albert felt sure that they were the work of some older, more advanced culture.

The surface of the silver had been meticulously polished. It wasn't perfect, as a machined modern piece would have been, but it looked damn close. The tolerances were obviously hand-wrought.

The striker was an animal's cloven hoof.

After the sun had set, the priest selected a man from the village, and, against the victim's will, he was dragged forward and tied to a stake set firmly in the ground. This, only after much protesting and lamenting, was met with cautious resignation by the rest of the villagers.

The unfortunate man's fate appeared sealed, and no amount of argument would change it.

A ring of wood and dried shrubbery was placed around both the man and Albert's party and lit with a torch of burning pitch. All those involved in or witnessing the ceremony were within the circle of flame.

In the center stood the tied figure. The flickering light of the fire played across the man's terrified face. He screamed and pleaded in an unintelligible tongue, his limbs straining valiantly against the rough fiber of the rope to the point where it cut into his skin and blood began to ooze.

The priest stepped forward and marked the victim's forehead with ashes.

Albert's native translator began to shake and seemed mortally afraid of what was about to transpire. He became reluctant to translate the words of the high priest, reluctant to be a party to the damnation of this poor creature's soul.

The victim howled and fought the bonds that restrained him.

Albert had to shout at his translator to continue. Within the ring of fire, the priest, his assistant, the translator, and Albert stood facing the center. The bound man continued to struggle.

The high priest said a few words, chanted what Albert believed to be the name of the demon, then struck the larger metal fork with the cloven hoof striker.

It made an unbelievable sound, a low vibration that seemed to rattle Albert's very soul. The ominous tone filled the night.

The insects stopped singing. The sound grew until the vibration became painful to hear.

The priest then struck the second fork, and its vibration joined the first, oscillating in and out of the sympathetic harmonics of the two wildly dissonant notes. The combination began to have a strange effect on Albert. Intoxicating and hypnotic, it insinuated its way through his eardrums and into his brain, canceling out all else.

With an effect like rolling thunder, Albert felt his internal organs vibrate. He felt as if he were standing next to railroad tracks while a train rumbled past.

He blinked, trying to hold back a steady flow of tears that began involuntarily to stream down his face. Looking around, he could see that every man in the circle was crying.

The tuning forks hummed with a sustained tone that defied the laws of physics.

His eyes were drawn to a shimmering cloud, hovering a few feet above the tied man's head.

The head of a huge, glistening, horned snake materialized, coming into focus before Albert's incredulous eyes. It wavered for a moment, then snapped onto the body of the bound man with a terrible finality, wrapping its wet coils around the hapless native and crushing him like a piece of meat. The coils flexed, then tightened. Albert listened for the sound of bones snapping, but the only snapping he heard was the crackle of the fire as it sputtered around them.

A terrible metamorphosis then took place.

The sinuous body of the snake began to blend into the body of the man, melding into his shape and taking on the characteristics of a human form. The blue-green scales melted into arms, legs, a torso. The form of a human emerged from the coils of the reptile as if being sculpted from living tissue by a master artisan.

Albert wiped his weeping eyes as the snake-man was born before him, the skin reptilian, iridescent, but with a form suggesting humanity. It was a grotesque melding of the two entities that Albert now beheld, half–snake demon, half–man. The body of a human, the head of a snake. It twisted and pivoted on its slender neck, watching the people and the fire.

A forked tongue flickered the air around it; the lidless eyes seemed to rotate as it studied the scene.

What Albert watched was impossible.

The snake head looked at Albert. Its whiplike tongue danced in his direction. Albert stood transfixed as, one by one, the ropes snapped and the changeling stepped away from the tree.

The priest remained rooted to the ground, but the others present, including Albert and the translator, faded back, away from the center and closer to the wall of fire. The flame barrier held them, just as the coils of the serpent had held the sacrifice. They were trapped. The snake creature stepped nearer, its tongue darting in and out, and Albert could smell a fetid, unpleasant odor coming from it.

The priest cried out something, and the translator, shocked from his terror by the urgency in the priest's voice, interpreted and shouted at Albert.

"Stay within the circle of flames!"

Albert's back was now hot, the hair on the back of his head began to singe as he pressed closer to the fire. He wanted to run, to jump through the wall of flame and take his chances, but he did not.

He realized the terrible beauty of what he saw, the heart-stopping monstrosity of it. Without a doubt, without an ounce of uncertainty, he knew he was looking at the face of Satan.

When, after almost an hour, the serpent dematerialized and the fires burned down, the tribesmen lowered the dazed victim from the stake. He began to weep, and after a short time became hysterical. They dragged him before the priest, who at first comforted the man, then unceremoniously put him to death. "To prevent the demon's return into the same body," he explained to Albert through the interpreter.

"Does the host body have to be human?" Albert asked, concerned for the victims. "Could it be an animal?"

The priest nodded as the question was translated. "Yes, it can be any living thing, but only man can bring the full power of the demon."

That night, as Albert lay in his sleeping bag, his mind raced.

The incredible event he'd witnessed had left him shaken but also exhilarated.

He schemed to get his hands on the tuning forks. He thought about offering to buy them, but quickly rejected the idea. The concept of money meant nothing to these people. He considered various scenarios to trick the priest and the villagers, but dismissed each one.

All the while the tuning forks tempted him, unguarded in the center of the village.

He came to the conclusion that he would have to steal them.

Albert abhorred violence, and he rejected any thought of using force to take them. He had a rifle, but that would not be effective against the entire village if they turned on him.

He decided that the best approach would be to purloin the tuning forks under cover of night and make his escape. The only problem was the natives, who, better suited to the jungle than he, would quickly overtake him in a chase.

So Albert devised a plan.

He noticed that the villagers all drew their water from a single well.

Albert prepared a narcotic extract of *Papaver somniferum gigantus Beaumond* and surreptitiously poisoned the well.

Over the course of the next twenty-four hours, he successfully drugged the entire village. When the natives were all asleep, he put the tuning forks in his pack and left the plateau.

Knowing that the villagers would sleep for days, he nevertheless hastened his retreat through the jungle.

Albert opened his eyes as the blaring of an automobile horn awakened him from his daytime nightmare.

He looked up to see an attractive teenage girl driving a green-and-white Pontiac Star Chief convertible. She had the top down, and her blond ponytail bobbed in the breeze.

His daughter had arrived.

He smiled and waved when she called his name.

"Oh Daddy, would you please hurry up! I'm late!"

"That doesn't surprise me," he said as he slung his bag into the backseat.

"Welcome home," she chirped.

"It's good to be home, Thora," he replied.

"A woman's been calling for you."

Albert looked bemused. "A woman?"

"Yeah, she said it's really important that you call her as soon as you get in."

The car pulled away, cutting into the traffic like a speedboat. Albert leaned over and kissed his daughter on the cheek before the inertial force pinned him back into the vinyl seat.

"Does she have a name?" he wanted to know, genuinely curious.

"Yeah, get this," she said as the Pontiac careened into a turn. "It's that late night horror show host on Channel Two, the one who looks like a sexy ghoul!"

"Devila?"

"Uh-huh. Isn't that exciting? She's a big star!"

Albert knew about Devila. He'd seen her many times on television, hosting a plethora of dreadful movies while she vamped for the cameras. He liked her look—pale skin and clingy black dress, with a witchy silver streak in her long, straight, midnight hair. But he had never met the woman.

She was very big with the beatniks and the teenagers in Los Angeles. Albert Beaumond wondered what the connection could be.

A horn blasted as his daughter swerved in front of another car.

"Why would she call me?"

Thora weaved in and out of traffic with the brazen skill of a New York City taxi driver. Albert hung on for dear life, having forgotten how aggressive his daughter could be behind the wheel. "She wants to take you to a Halloween party."

Albert laughed. "That's absurd."

"Oh Daddy, you are the most handsome, available bachelor in town, you know," she gushed.

"I rather doubt that," he replied, flattered by her assessment. "But, seriously, why me?"

"Well," said Thora proudly, a flash of smile splitting her face, "she said that you're the scariest, sexiest man in Los Angeles, and that she's the scariest, sexiest woman. She said everybody's afraid of you, and that you'd be the perfect date for this party she's going to tonight."

5

Darkness fell around the Landis Woodley fun house like a lead curtain, further sealing it off from the world of sanity and reason.

Even though the clock showed eight o'clock on Halloween night, no trick-or-treaters came to the door. Not that Landis cared. If any costumed children ever did find the uninviting gray stucco building, down from the road and visible only from certain angles, he would have ignored them. Landis hated to answer the door.

He had once thought of having a doorbell made that played back a tape recording of a dog barking and an angry voice shouting, "Go away! We don't want you here!"

He had Buzzy Haller go so far as to actually tape the warning, but he never got around to doing the wiring. Buzzy was much too important to Landis to waste his time working on small projects like that. Buzzy made the productions run. He was the monster maker, and, as Landis insisted, without a monster, you don't have a movie.

Landis stood upstairs in his bedroom, putting the finishing

touches on his undertaker's black tux, when he heard the front door slam.

"Buzz?" he shouted.

"Yeah!" came the reply.

"Come on up!"

He heard the thumps of Buzzy Haller coming up the stairs, two at a time.

"You'll never guess who's comin' to the party, man!" he gushed as he entered the room.

Landis straightened his bow tie and cussed at his clumsiness. He ignored Buzzy, who continued talking.

"Neal Cassidy! He's the cat who's the hero of the Jack Kerouac book, *On the Road*, you know, the one that just came out?"

Landis finished with his tie and turned stiffly to face Buzzy.

Buzzy whistled. "Nice monkey suit."

"Thanks," came the terse reply.

Landis looked at Buzzy, saw the scruffy blue jeans, cutoff gray sweatshirt, and fake goatee. "Don't tell me, the beat generation!"

"That's right, Woody. That's my costume this year. I'm a beatnik!"

Landis winced.

"Complete with reefers!" Buzzy concluded, and pulled out an envelope with half a dozen rolled joints in it. He flashed it open and showed Landis.

"You're incredible, Buzz. Where'd you get them?" Landis asked after taking a good look.

"Some cats I know from San Francisco just blew into town. That's where I met Cassidy. The man's a legend! *On the Road* is the Bible of the beats, man, and it's all about him!"

Landis was not visibly impressed. "What's with the term 'beatnik'? Everything's got a 'nik' at the end of it since that damn Sputnik went up three weeks ago. Christ, it's on the front page every day. It's even affected the way you talk."

Buzzy laughed and removed one of the reefers from his envelope and lit it. He took a huge drag on it and held it in. As he exhaled, and a cloud of intoxicating blue smoke filled the room, he said, "Sputnik, nutnik, beatnik, neatnik, who cares?" In his hippest tone, he said, "The beats are all about beatitude, man.

It's not about the beat, as in bongo drums, it's about beatitude, you know, being cool."

Landis accepted the reefer from Buzzy and inhaled himself a dream. He rolled his eyes in a parody of Buzzy and said, "Crazy, man, crazy."

Buzzy laughed, "You got it, Daddy-O! That's the reef, Chief."

Roberta Bachman checked herself one last time and hurried to the window. She had heard a car door slam and thought it might be Buzzy Haller, come to take her to the party. It wasn't. It was Janice's friend, Gladys.

"Hi, Gladys!" Janice said as she jerked open the door.

"Hi, Jan! I got the popcorn!"

They hugged and spilled into the house, full of girlish good feelings and smiles. Roberta sat back down on the couch, smiled in Gladys's direction, and went back to the book she was reading.

Gladys plunked herself down on the couch next to Roberta and whistled.

"Wow! That's some sexy outfit! My mother wouldn't let me out of the house with something like that on." Her eyes widened in admiration. "And I don't know if I'd have the guts or the body for it anyway."

Roberta adjusted her costume, slightly self-conscious now that Gladys had become the second person in ten minutes to make a comment.

"Well . . . my mother would have a heart attack, too, but she's not here, is she?"

"You guys are so lucky to have your own place! God, I would just die!"

Janice came in clutching her *TV Guide.*

"Popcorn's on!"

"What's on television tonight?"

"Need you ask?"

Janice and Gladys were both diehard TV fans. They watched everything and knew all the actors and actresses on every show.

Hollywood had taken it on the chin when TV became the number one form of entertainment in America almost overnight, but the two girls didn't care. They loved TV as much as the movies. LA had simply shifted gears and was fast becoming the TV production capital of the world.

To aspiring actresses like Janice and Gladys, it only meant more opportunities.

And the guys were sooooooo cute.

"Let's see, 'Wagon Train', 'The Millionaire', 'Ozzie and Harriet'."

"I just love that Ricky Nelson. He is *so* handsome!"

Gladys jumped up. "Oh, didn't I tell you?! I got an audition for that new show, 'Wyatt Earp'!"

"Oh my God! Hugh O'Brien!"

Roberta frowned. Her friends were idiots. "You two are completely cracked, you know that? I mean, is that all you think about? These TV shows are as dumb as comic books."

"What's wrong with comic books?" Janice asked.

Roberta sighed. No hope. "Comic books are for children, just like those TV shows you like to watch."

"Oh, and I suppose Buzzy Haller, who works for the one and only Landis Woodley, a real Ingmar Bergman type, I might add, is a sensitive intellectual!" Janice replied.

"Well . . . all I'm saying is that TV is mostly fluff, and films are a little more stimulating. At least, they have the potential to be. There are some great movies out there, it's an art form. TV's just throwaway stuff, free entertainment."

Janice huffed. "Listen to you. Now you're putting down TV just because you're working for a film company, that's great. Take a look at yourself, Roberta. Tonight you're going to a Halloween party at a guy's house who makes movies like *Attack of the Haunted Saucer*, with another guy who makes rubber monsters, dressed as a sexy cigarette girl. And you've got the nerve to put down TV shows because they're too lowbrow for you? What's wrong here?"

Roberta considered her answer as the doorbell rang.

"There's Buzzy now," she said gratefully.

"Einstein has arrived," Janice mocked.

"Oh, leave her alone," said Gladys. "Let her have some fun. You're just jealous."

Janice inhaled sharply, another one of her many overly dramatic stage moves, and made a derisive sucking sound she once saw Bette Davis make. She might have spoken again, getting in the last word, when Roberta opened the door and there stood a tall, ruggedly handsome man with a blond crew cut and a fake goatee. His sweatshirt was torn and his jeans were faded. On his feet were sandals covering black socks.

Roberta gasped.

"Cool, baby, like wow! Nice costume!" he said. His eyes scanned her body. The cigarette-girl outfit revealed a tad more than Roberta felt comfortable with, and she was now unsure about her choice. This afternoon it had seemed so sophisticated, so exciting, so daring. Now it seemed like too much, or too little, as the case may be.

Roberta, stunned momentarily by his unabashed stare, looked down at her costume and blushed. She was embarrassed in two ways, once for herself and once for him. For a second there, she thought that Buzzy was actually dressed that way, then she realized, the beatnik getup was his costume.

Janice and Gladys stared from behind her, mouths agape. *It's a costume*, she thought, *thank God, it's only a costume*. She would have died of embarrassment in front of her friends if this were the real Buzzy Haller.

"Like my costume?" Buzzy asked.

"A beatnik?" Roberta asked.

"That's right, Daddy-O."

"Cool," said Janice, deadpan.

A sharp, acid look from Roberta cut Janice's tongue, and she refrained from further comment.

Roberta introduced Buzzy to her friends. He seemed nice enough. His hands were clean, and his teeth were white.

"It's interesting," said Roberta. "But why a beatnik?"

"Why? You won't believe this, but Neal Cassidy is coming to the party."

The three girls looked at each other blankly.

"I'm sorry. Neal Cassidy?"

"Yeah! From Frisco!"

More blank stares.

"Jack Kerouac? The book *On the Road*? Neal Cassidy is the character Dean Moriarty."

Janice rolled her eyes, Gladys looked confused, and Roberta

smiled. "Oh," she said, "I've heard of that! It's a popular book right now, isn't it?"

Buzzy tugged at his sweatshirt. " 'Popular' is not a word I would use. Are you into Zen? You see, this whole thing *just is*. *Why it is* doesn't really matter, does it?"

"What are you talkin' about?" Gladys asked.

"I'm afraid I don't understand either," replied Roberta, stealing a glance at her friends to see if they were making faces yet. Buzzy was a bit peculiar.

"Neal's gonna be at the party," Buzzy finished. "He's a beat generation hero."

Roberta smiled again, this time sweetly and with real amusement. "Really? Just what does this Neal Cassidy do that makes him a beat generation hero?"

"He drives around the country in old cars," came the unpretentious reply.

Janice ran back to the kitchen, smelling burning popcorn, laughing like a maniac. Gladys was too interested in this strange man to laugh at him yet. Roberta got her coat.

"So," Buzzy said as he led her out the door, "the reason I'm dressed as a beatnik is that the king of the beats is coming. It's in honor of him."

"I see," Roberta said, and closed the door behind her.

Albert Beaumond unpacked his artifacts first, before thinking of anything else. He placed them carefully in a cabinet behind the altar in his worship area. The familiar images of Satan that adorned the walls of his "church" were comforting, but now that he had seen the true face of the antigod, all other representations were little more than quaint.

He would change all that soon. He would show the world the real Prince of Darkness in all his glory.

The cameras would roll, the skeptics would be forever silenced, the pilgrims would be converted, and his name, the name of Albert Beaumond, would live forever.

He had no doubt he would become the most famous man in the world.

And oh, the trouble he would make among the Christians!

While their God hid and confused his legions, Albert's would appear on the television, proving his existence every Friday night.

The priests would come to see for themselves, and Albert would laugh as their terror mounted. To the world's great religions, this would be their worst nightmare.

Proof of the devil's existence but not of God's.

Albert could visualize the new hordes of followers he would attract and command. The new power he would gain might destroy weaker men. Not Albert. Not the high priest of the world's biggest religion, the one that proves itself on demand.

The only religion in the universe that could actually reach out and grab you.

Thora stayed upstairs, listening to her collection of 45 RPM records, which she kept in a special case. She had over eighty different sides, mostly by all the new rock and roll artists that were exploding on the scene. Her favorite was that sullen, pouty "Hillbilly Cat" Elvis Presley.

Albert couldn't tell the difference between Ricky Nelson and Fats Domino, but he loved the spirit of rebellion in youth, and this new music captured that spirit like fireflies in a jar.

Little Richard boomed down the stairs. "The Girl Can't Help It" was as loud and raucous a record as Albert had ever heard. He smiled as he thought of his daughter jitterbugging around her room.

Apart from the Satanic worship, life in the Beaumond house seemed as normal as the Nelsons'. The phone rang, and Albert answered it in his office in the den.

"Hello?"

A woman's voice, dark and husky, suggestive of gin and cigarettes, came down the telephone.

"Albert Beaumond? This is Devila. Did your daughter tell you I called?"

"Why, yes."

"I saw you on TV last month, talking about your Satanic Church, and I thought you were absolutely marvelous."

She pronounced the word "marvelous" as if it were "mahvelous," and Albert smiled without thinking.

"Thank you," he said modestly.

"You're a very handsome man, Mr. Beaumond."

"Thanks . . . again."

"I hope this is not too forward of me. May I get right to the point?" Her voice sounded quite deep for a woman.

"Yes, of course."

"Well, I understand that you're single, and I was wondering if you'd accompany me to a party in Hollywood tonight. There will be lots of publicity, and I think you might actually enjoy yourself."

Albert sat down behind his desk. A ram's skull mounted on the wall in front of him glared down as if to say, "Don't mock me." The twisted horns and vacant eyeholes had a haunted, disorienting effect on him. Sometimes he would stare at it for hours.

"But why me, Miss Devila?"

"Because it's good publicity. You scare people, Mr. Beaumond. So do I, although you do it on a much more serious level than I do. The photographers will be there, and any picture of me with you would be sure to get in all the papers. Not to mention Jonathon Luboff—"

Albert leaned back. "Luboff? The great Luboff? He'll be there?"

"Oh, yes, and many more. Most of the people in the horror movie business will be there. It's Landis Woodley's house. His Halloween parties are famous."

"Landis Woodley? He makes some pretty bad movies, doesn't he?" Albert's own voice sounded boorish compared to hers.

"The worst. I should know; I show them all the time," she said. Albert wondered if she were wearing her Devila costume as she spoke to him. In a flash of cognition he realized that she would definitely be wearing it that night to the party. The thought made him itchy.

"What time would we have to arrive?" he asked slyly, barely suppressing his delight.

"No particular time," she replied. "We're celebrities—we can go whenever we want. I've hired a hearse and driver for the evening."

"Perfect," Albert crooned. "Absolutely perfect."

Jonathon Luboff injected the heroin into his left leg rather than fool around with the collapsed veins in his scarred arm. Being right-handed, he'd abused the left half of his seventy-year-old body so horribly, every fix had become a nightmare for the trembling old actor.

He checked the dose twice; he didn't want to get sick or nod out before the party. His career was already in ruins. More bad publicity, especially among the Hollywood insiders, would finish what pitiful little he had left in the way of work.

Luboff waited a few heartbeats before pulling the syringe out. It was a good, clean hit. His leg warmed and he felt the sweet numbness climb into his aged torso. A few moments later his brain reacted, and he experienced the familiar dreamy lightness that he'd spent the better part of his twilight years chasing.

He had considered suicide again today, but he procrastinated, hoping against hope that one of the big studios would call. The truth was he contemplated suicide nearly every day now, until he'd had his fix. Then it faded from his conscious mind like the ice melting in his morning glass of Scotch.

He had a monkey on his back that would have killed a younger man, but Jonathon Luboff was tough as nails. He'd already lived the equivalent of three lives in the space of one.

From the heights of stardom to the depths of despair, his roller-coaster karma never slowed down.

He looked in the mirror.

The face that looked back at him was as frightening as any monster or madman he'd ever played in the cinema. It was the eyes.

Now sunken and carrying a wrinkled mass of flesh around them, they still gleamed with an intensity that made most people shrink from his stare. Luboff's eyes penetrated.

His eyes were diabolical, mad, passionate, and searching. They sent complicated, mixed messages of pain to those who chose to look into them. The windows to a troubled and unhappy soul, they glared back at him from the mirror. Even with the pupils constricted to mere pinpoints, they still expressed enough raw anguish for a thousand lifetimes.

Once, they had looked out from the movie screen at millions of paying customers. From his classic 1930s films, which made him a matinee idol, to the cheap, shoddy Landis Woodley productions of the 1950s, those eyes compelled generations of moviegoers.

As a young, darkly handsome leading man, women fought over him. He'd been married five times, bought and sold numerous Hollywood mansions, starred in over a hundred pictures, and was known the world over. Now, in a low-rent apartment in West Hollywood, he waited for the smack to deaden the pain of living so he could once again pull off the illusion of life.

Luboff staggered backward, bounced off the wall, then collapsed heavily in a metal-and-plastic kitchen chair. How the chair had made it from the kitchen to his bedroom, he didn't know. It had appeared there last week, migrating across the filthy expanse of the living room floor to where it now supported his emaciated frame.

His breath came shallow; the room spun.

He knew he had to get up and get ready to attend the party, but his limbs refused to cooperate. Luboff, the consummate actor, knew how to force his body to do things it didn't want to do. He'd been doing it for years. Desire was the key, desire and pacing.

He was still dressed in his bathrobe, a garment he wore constantly unless he had to go out. His black tuxedo with tails hung by the door, still encased in plastic from the dry cleaners. Landis had taken care of that chore for him. He had also purchased a box of decent cigars so that the star of his latest movie wouldn't appear too destitute. Luboff's taste in tobacco ran to the cheap, unpleasant-smelling varieties he bought at the drugstore.

Luboff felt the rush of the narcotic sweep through his system, wiping away the failures and the humiliations that had accumulated since his last fix.

The great Luboff sighed.

He lurched from his chair and bumped into the dresser. His shoulder collided with a framed movie poster proclaiming, "Luboff at his most frightening! The story of a curse that wouldn't die! Experience the horror of THE MUMMY'S BRAIN!" It rattled against the wall but didn't fall. Jonathon steadied himself. This was Luboff at his most frightening right now, far more disturbing than anything he'd portrayed in that or any other film.

His hands were clumsy and huge as he opened the cigars and attempted to light one. Everything seemed small and delicate, and he felt as if he were wearing gloves. He fumbled with the cigars, managing to unwrap one and put it in his mouth. Lighting it was another story. The matches fought him, frustrating him to the point of mental exhaustion. At last he struck a match and brought one of the fine cigars to life, puffing it frantically. His hollow cheeks worked in and out like a bellows as he fought to keep the ember glowing.

Luboff's eyes burned like distant warning signals.

He swayed and leaned, his shrunken, quivering body as unsteady as his mental state.

As the plumes of bluish smoke filled the air, he felt warm and weightless. The skeleton of a smile crossed his lips.

He stayed, leaning across the dresser, cigar in hand, for almost thirty minutes. His legs had locked into position, and, instead of falling, as he often did after a fix, he remained upright, his mind wandering.

He vaguely remembered Landis Woodley telling him he'd arranged for a starlet to accompany the actor to the party.

Could it have been a dream? Luboff's mind swam. His sex drive had shriveled away years ago, and now the only vicarious thrill Luboff got from beautiful women was in the status of their proximity.

His hands shook all the time now, so he could no more caress a shoulder or a breast than he could perform brain surgery.

For the great Jonathon Luboff, the grave beckoned.

Eventually he donned his tuxedo, slipped a worn vampire's cape over his shoulders, and straightened his back. A comb slicked his graying hair back, and a little theatrical makeup added color to his pale visage. He looked in the mirror and compared this latest reflection to the one he had beheld earlier.

It was improved. Not greatly, but some.

The heroin had left him dazed, and he stayed in that dreamland between worlds even after the doorbell rang, signaling the arrival of his car and driver.

He walked slowly to the car, in character, high as a kite.

Landis Woodley's house was lit up like a nightclub. Cars lined the street in front on both sides. Neighbors complained bitterly to the police, but nothing came of it. This, after all, was Hollywood on Halloween, a town and a holiday made for each other. People in costumes paraded past the gawkers. There were dozens of Draculas and Frankensteins, handfuls of mummies, and a small army of sexy witches.

The guest list included over a hundred names, many from the horror film business. The stars were Jonathon Luboff and Devila.

Landis stood by the front door and welcomed people by filming their arrival on 16 mm film. When Devila and Albert Beaumond drove up in their hearse, the flashbulbs popped.

Once inside, Devila played the room like the pro that she was, posing and vamping for the cameras. Most people didn't know or recognize Albert. Devila herself knew that the delayed reaction to that would be worth its weight in gold. Wait until the world put two and two together! The Satanist and the horror show girl!

Luboff's entrance came off a bit less splashy but every ounce as electric. The limo wheeled up to the house and ejected the fragile actor and his young cohort. Their arranged "dates" trailed behind. People rushed to greet them and get a closer glimpse at how bad Luboff looked. He drove them off with his eyes. One level stare, and they were repelled back into the faceless crowd.

Landis and Jonathon embraced, cigars puffing, and exchanged pleasantries. Woodley was pleased to see that the old man had controlled his dose to manageable proportions. Tad Kingston stood by impassively. His hair, of course, was perfect.

Landis had hired photographers to photograph the celebrities, knowing that some of the pictures would run in various newspapers and magazines and thereby promote his movies. In this way he could not only control the dissemination of information, but he would own the photos. Landis Woodley loved publicity.

Plus, he had a few surprises planned.

Buzzy Haller and Roberta Bachman entered arm in arm and went straight to the bar, where Buzzy began the night-long project of trying to get her drunk.

She thwarted his efforts by sipping a controlled amount of champagne, pacing herself and making Buzzy crazy. Roberta knew how to take care.

When Neal Cassidy arrived, the upstairs bedroom became the reefer room and guests came and went all night. Bongo music drifted into the hall along with the sweet scent of burning pot. Poetry was being recited, people were expressing themselves. Neal was a magnet for the beats. He spent hours pontificating about Kerouac's real mission, the message of Zen. Everyone listened with the rapt attention of tea-heads.

Luboff himself spent at least an hour in there, inhaling marijuana and making small talk. His date, the actress Lillian Mansville, abandoned the old junkie five minutes after they arrived. The cigar smoke made her sick, she complained. Before she dumped him for a male fashion model from Santa Monica, though, she made sure that they had their pictures taken by every available photographer in the place.

Neil Bugmier, wearing a baby blue chiffon prom dress and white pumps, attracted as much attention as the celebrities. He laughed and danced, enjoying the limelight. Halloween meant a lot to him; it was a chance to show the world his most inventive side with total legitimacy.

He circulated freely, leaving a trail of astonished looks and rolled eyes. As per his instructions, he talked about the new script to anyone who would listen.

In the center of the house, next to the great spiral staircase where the ceiling stood as high as the structure would allow, was a twenty-foot-high guillotine. It dominated the wild landscape of the party like a huge antique curiosity. The blade, perched high above the crowd, gleamed mirrorlike and appeared razor-sharp.

In conversation, Landis explained to anyone who would listen that it was real, an original French Revolution model. He claimed that he'd purchased it from a broker in Paris for a movie he would eventually make about Marie Antoinette, *Headless Beauty.*

People looked up at the blade with ghoulish fascination. Landis explained that this particular guillotine had been in service for many years and had the blood of hundreds of victims soaked into it. This instrument of death, he declared, must be respected and feared. "It's probably haunted."

Partygoers stared up at it all night, wondering what happened when that heavy blade was loosed. They could almost see it in action, the headless bodies jerking spastically while the heads thumped into a bloody wicker basket.

In general, folks gave it a wide berth as they passed—but they couldn't help but look. When the shivers ceased crawling up their backs, they edged closer, eyeing the blade poised above them, a graphic reminder of Landis's monstrous imagination.

Buzzy introduced Roberta to Landis, and he promised to star her in his next movie if she would "go for a walk" with him around the grounds. She declined, but he persisted. At some point during the evening, he paid Buzzy one hundred dollars for the right to steal his date.

Her cigarette girl costume was drawing the wrong kind of attention, and she now felt uncomfortable. She draped her jacket over her shoulders to dampen the effect.

Roberta's modesty made an impression on Landis, and his desire for her increased in direct proportion to her rejection of him.

"Come on, you've got to see the tree house," he insisted. He pointed out the window to an elaborate building perched in an old oak tree.

"That's the fourth time you've asked me," Roberta replied, becoming annoyed.

"It's a special place; you've got to see it."

"You're not going to leave me alone until I go out there and see your stupid tree house, are you?"

Landis smiled. "Nope."

"All right, I guess I have to, but the only way I'm going out there is if my friend Laura goes."

"Laura Grootna? The costume designer's assistant? Sure, the more the merrier, I always say."

"And Buzzy."

"Why Buzzy?"

"Because he's my date."

They climbed the ladder and entered through a trapdoor in the floor. Buzzy made the girls go first so he could sneak a peek up their dresses as they ascended.

There were three windows in the tree house, all shuttered. Landis insisted on opening all three, the last one affording a beautiful panoramic view of the city.

The two girls watched as he unlatched the shutters and folded them back.

Framed in the window, backlit by the lights of the city below, was a body hanging by the neck. It pivoted slowly in the slight breeze. The face was discolored, the lips blue, and the tongue lolled grotesquely out of the mouth like a huge purple slug. As the body swung into view, Landis shone a flashlight in its face. Laura screamed.

"My God, it's Fred, the key grip!" Landis shouted.

Roberta felt the champagne rise in her throat and knew she was going to be sick. She looked down at the trapdoor and the ladder below with trepidation. Her eyes went back to the dead man, his face now fully in view as Landis's flashlight illuminated the terrible grimace there.

Then, Roberta's legs turned to rubber as she saw something that scared her beyond reason.

The dead man's eyes snapped open, the purple tongue curled

back, and an ugly smile split his unearthly lips. The mouth opened, and a voice from the grave crackled, "Hey, baby. How about a little kiss?"

Roberta screamed again and bolted for the trapdoor. She was through it and down the ladder in a matter of seconds, Landis right behind. Buzzy stayed above in the tree house, laughing maniacally.

Roberta bent over in the bushes and vomited. Landis stood behind, quiet and concerned.

He waited respectfully while she emptied her stomach, then offered her a handkerchief as she straightened up.

Their eyes met, hers wild and fearful, his strangely excited.

"What was it?" she coughed.

"A joke . . . I think."

"What?"

"A sick joke, that's all."

Roberta looked at Landis with undisguised disgust. He winced. She held her gaze for several seconds, then turned abruptly on her heel and began to walk briskly away.

"Hey, wait a minute!" Landis shouted.

"Don't talk to me!" Roberta said with icy conviction.

"It wasn't my idea! It was Buzzy's!"

"You knew?" Her angry eyes surprised him. It wasn't the reaction he'd anticipated.

"Yeah, I guess I did."

"You're an asshole, Landis Woodley!" she shouted, and began to walk away again.

"Are you leaving?"

She answered by walking faster, up the incline toward the street.

"Laura's still up there!" Landis said quickly. "What about her?"

Roberta stopped and turned to face him. "Oh! What's he got planned for her? More fun and games? You guys are really sick!"

Roberta heard Laura's voice calling.

"See? She's all right."

"No thanks to you."

Laura ran after Roberta, her face still wet with tears. They embraced, Roberta staring daggers at Landis over Laura's shoulder. Then the two women turned and marched up the hill.

"Wait! Where are you going?"

"We're going home!"

Landis hurried after them. "I'll drive!"

"Stay away from me, I'm warning you!" she said, her voice cracking with emotion.

"How are you gonna get home?"

"That's no concern of yours."

Landis watched her go. From back in the tree house another scream rose. Buzzy was having some more fun with another guest.

Inside the house, Albert Beaumond was explaining the aspects of Satan in South American Indian cultures to Sol Kravitz when Landis and Buzzy reentered the house.

Fred, the hanged man, swilled champagne and jammed pretzels in his mouth, the rope still trailing from his neck. "I'll hang myself every half hour, you'll love it," he boasted.

Devila danced with Luboff while the cameras clicked away.

Then, at midnight, all the lights went out.

"Don't panic, folks!" Landis called out. "It's probably the fuse box. We'll have it fixed in no time!"

As soon as Buzzy and Landis disappeared into the cellar to make repairs, a nervous pall settled over the crowd. The old house became terribly uncomfortable in the dark. The guests huddled together, speaking in whispers. The mood went from celebration to consternation in a few short moments.

Almost as soon as the two men disappeared, strange things began to happen, and the guests began to grow increasingly uneasy.

First, in the great fireplace, which had been cold all evening, a fire sprang up spontaneously. A gasp went through the crowd, followed by nervous laughter.

"Good trick," cried one of the special effects people.

Then some torches along the wall of the stairwell, which most people assumed were fakes, ignited with a surprising "whump." A few women gasped. The leaping fires threw unsettling shadows across the room. At the center of it all, the guillotine stood tall. The fires burned in pagan ritual all around it.

"Bravo!" one of the cameramen shouted. "Landis Woodley, a master!"

People gathered in the light of the torches, drawn to the guillotine.

The rest of the guests shifted uneasily on their feet, looking up at the blade.

The edge gleamed ominously high above the floor, lit by the dancing flames of the torches. The staircase, now swathed in sinister half-tones, reclined like an evil creature, curled around the beheading machine. The wrought-iron filigree became a demonic face in the shadows.

Buzzy Haller emerged from a door behind the guillotine and waved to everyone.

"Almost fixed," he chirped, his cheerful banter in stark contrast to the mood of the guests. "It's just a matter of a fuse, it shouldn't be too long. In the meantime, have you been admiring this beautiful piece?"

He ran his hands along the rough wood beams of the guillotine. Buzzy was drunk, but he wasn't slurring his words yet. In the early stages of intoxication he was invariably entertaining and engaging.

"It's a genuine antique. Mr. Woodley paid a small fortune for it. It will be the centerpiece for our next film, *Headless Beauty.* Shares are still available, by the way." Someone in the back of the room giggled. "Seriously, this is the real thing, folks, comes complete with curse."

"Why didn't he just have one made?" a woman's voice shouted from the back of the dark room. There was a smattering of nervous laughter.

"Ahh," Buzzy replied, "a good question. Perhaps Landis himself should answer that."

At that moment Landis entered through the same door Buzzy had: a small Gothic, round-topped aperture located halfway up the stairs on a landing behind the guillotine. It was almost like a secret passageway.

"My technicians are working on the lights. They should be back on in a few minutes. Were you curious about this?" He put his hand on the guillotine, directly in the path of the blade, where the head would have been locked into place.

"Be careful!" a woman shouted.

Landis smiled. "No need to worry. The blade, although razor-sharp, is locked in place with four thick bolts. There's no chance of it falling."

"Someone wanted to know why you didn't just have one made?" Buzzy reported.

"I can answer that question with another question. Would you want to own a copy of a great painting when you could have the real thing? You see, I had a rare opportunity to purchase this historic piece in Paris last year." Landis paused, and looked around the shadowed room, slowing his pace for maximum dramatic effect. He spoke as if reading from a script. "The price was right, a bargain actually. It seems the previous owners wanted to dump it quickly, they thought it was haunted."

"Haunted? Surely you don't believe that?" a man's voice challenged.

Landis's smile never wavered. The entire line of questioning amused him, and he instinctively began to milk it for all it was worth.

"Who knows what the spirit world is capable of?" another man answered. He stepped forward out of the throng of people and looked up at the gleaming blade. His eyes sparkled.

It was Albert Beaumond. He was dressed in his all-black, Satanic priest's outfit, a silver pentagram pendant hung from a chain on his neck. He waved his hand dramatically at the looming specter of the guillotine. "This machine is for beheading. The removal of one's head from one's body leaves the soul . . . shall we say, confused? Those poor creatures who were its victims left this world rather quickly and against their will. Their spirits may indeed linger here, attached to this device forever."

Landis nodded. "Our esteemed guest has hit the nail directly on the head. The question is: how could it not be cursed? If this blade could speak . . ." His voice trailed off, and his eyes rose to the razor edge. "Imagine the things it could tell.

"In my opinion, the curse makes it even more valuable, more of a collector's item. If I could be so lucky as to capture a real ghost on film, well, we could all retire.

"Let me demonstrate for you how it works."

He approached the machine casually, touching it now as if it were nothing more than a hat rack. "Ghosts or no ghosts, it's a hell of a thing, isn't it?"

Albert answered in the affirmative.

"Named after Dr. J.I. Guillotin, a physician who thought it would provide a more humane method of execution, the guillotine is a formidable piece of equipment. The blade is weighted and extremely sharp, it runs along this track and severs the head cleanly into this basket." Landis pointed to the appropriate features. "They say that the severed head lives on for a few moments after it has been removed from the body, and that it is actually *aware* that it's falling into the basket. During the revolution, there were always a few heads in the basket. A gruesome harvest, eh?"

"Were the heads buried separately from the bodies?" Albert asked. "That might have had an influence on the hauntings."

"I couldn't tell you," Landis replied. "Want to see how it worked?"

Without waiting for an answer, Landis walked around behind the machine and placed his head in the yoke. The guests gasped.

"Be careful," Albert warned. "If this machine really is haunted . . . well, just be careful."

"Nothing can hap—"

Before Landis could finish, the blade came down, slicing his head off with no more effort than a paring knife moving through a carrot.

When people looked up and saw the blade beginning its descent, they screamed. The whole thing seemed to happen in slow motion. Landis's headless body jerked away from the yoke, a gout of blood issuing from his neck. It stood before the crowd— the screaming never stopped—then reached into the basket and retrieved its head.

Albert Beaumond was speechless. He stood stunned while the headless body of Landis Woodley held the trophy high and shook it. Then it turned and staggered through the door. A trail of blood marked his path.

Screaming and shouting filled the room.

A moment later the lights flickered on. Buzzy Haller watched as several women fainted, men dropped their drinks, and more than one person became sick.

The lights revealed their astonished, frightened faces blinking at one another in the harsh glow of the electric bulbs.

Too stunned to move, they stood around rubbing their eyes and wondering what they had just witnessed.

Albert Beaumond was the first one to laugh.

7

"Did you see the expression on Luboff's face?"

Devila laughed hysterically. They were in the hearse being driven home, sharing a bottle of brandy. When the enormity of Landis Woodley's pranks revealed themselves, a new level of respect among the horror community sprang up. The guy may have been a maker of B-movies, but as far as parties went, he was A-class all the way.

To pull off a prank like that required planning, expertise, and true devotion. He would go to any lengths to scare people.

And he had succeeded.

Devila loved it. She'd seen the guillotine trick before—it was a standard—but never before had she seen it done with such believable subterfuge, such elaborate groundwork. Landis Woodley was obviously cut from different timber than the rest of the men in this town. *He's got guts, vision,* she thought.

Albert Beaumond thought so, too.

The brandy had lubricated him to the point where he'd actually been able to put some moves on Devila. She was attractive beneath her ghoulish makeup. Albert found her tacky, vampirish countenance a turn-on. Her pale skin and slinky black dress were alluring to him in a way that Devila would have been alarmed to understand.

Then he began to tell her about South America.

He explained it all to her in a casual way, as if he did this sort of thing every day.

She received it in the same spirit.

"I find that a little hard to believe, Albert."

"Yes, it's fantastic, I know. But every word is true."

She leaned forward and batted her eyes, letting her impressive cleavage perform its magic. "How about a little demonstration?"

"Of course," he answered immediately, anxious to impress her and take her interest in him to a new level.

The driver parked the hearse in the driveway of Albert's modest, two-story San Fernando Valley bungalow. Thora was still awake when they entered, watching TV with her friend: a sullen, quiet, overweight girl. Thora jumped up and ran toward them. The friend stayed on the couch, watching them with petulant shyness.

"Wow! Devila! I just LOOOOOVE your show!" Thora gushed. Suddenly her father wasn't so boring and predictable.

"Thank you," she replied in a normal voice. Thora hadn't expected that. She half expected Devila to use her television voice and say, "Dahling, I vant to drink your blood!"

"Thora," Albert said sternly, "I think it's time you and your friend went upstairs. It's way past your bedtime."

"Oh Daddy," she replied, "I'm in college now. I'm grown-up. Besides, Carla's parents let her stay up as late as she wants."

Her friend, the quiet Carla, looked away quickly.

Albert laughed. "Maybe so, young lady, but in certain cultures, children who disobey their fathers are beaten until they're well into their thirties."

Thora sighed. "We're beyond that, I think. This is 1957. Our society is much more enlightened than that."

"Don't be so sure," Albert said firmly, then, turning to Devila, "Thora is a first-year anthropology student at UCLA."

Devila looked at her approvingly. "How wonderful. You must be so proud."

"I am, sometimes," Albert replied, looking into the living room where Carla feigned interest in the television show.

"Does that mean I can stay up?" Thora asked her father hopefully.

"No," he answered. The finality of his voice was convincing, and Thora knew she had been defeated. She could see that Devila and her father wanted to be alone.

She signaled to Carla, and the two of them walked dejectedly toward the stairs. "Good night," she called out as they disappeared around the first landing.

"Good night," they echoed.

"Teenagers," Albert sighed. "They're the same in every culture. Would you care for some brandy before I show you my church?"

"Church?" Devila asked.

"Of course. Freedom of worship is guaranteed under the Constitution."

He led her to the dining room and poured her a generous glass of brandy. She drank it without a hitch, and he filled her glass again. They drank in silence, each wondering about the other.

The quiet of the house was accentuated by a ticking clock in the next room. It was past two. Albert was beginning to feel the effects of all the booze. The room spun slowly, Devila's smile captivated him, and he desperately wanted to impress her.

After an appropriate amount of time, he put down his glass and took hers gently from her hand. He put her glass next to his on the table and licked the sweet residue from his lips. Then he turned, took her into his arms, and kissed her passionately.

"Come with me," he whispered.

Albert led Devila through the house, into the "church." It used to be a family room before he'd modified it into a soundproof, light-proof fortress. The heavy oaken doors closed behind them with a meaty click.

Inside, it was quiet and dark. Subdued light illuminated just enough for her to see the alien landscape inside the room. As normal as the rest of the house was, this room was peculiar.

Devila looked around in amazement, her eyes drawn to the

ram's skull on the wall. A red-painted pentagram covered the floor. The altar at the rear of the room was covered with black cloth, the same black cloth that sealed the windows. Curious items hung from hooks along the walls: whips, hoods, black robes, knives, and torches.

Devila's senses tingled.

The occultism she toyed with in her shallow, public life was nothing more than a game compared to this. She knew that. She also knew that Albert was as real and serious about his belief as any Catholic priest could be about his.

God in heaven, the devil in hell, these were concepts that everyone agreed upon. Albert Beaumond sought to prove the one by proving the other.

He dimmed the lights and lit a bank of colored candles. Their faces began to glow. Devila's black eye shadow and pale makeup stood out dramatically in the half-light. Shadows danced on the wall behind her, casting strange messages.

She batted her eyes, letting the elongated lashes dip and flutter seductively.

Her yearning for him increased. Albert gazed at her as if she were naked, sending bolts of excitement through her chest. The chemical reaction between the two of them seemed to detonate as soon as he lit the candles. The uneven light heightened their desire.

The chamber closed in around them.

Something brushed against her leg and she jumped. A large black cat jumped onto the altar.

"Oh, that's Mephistopheles. He's a big nuisance, but harmless."

From a secret hiding place behind the altar, he retrieved the tuning forks. It was little more than a converted liquor cabinet with a wooden door set in the wall. He held them out to her, and she wanted to take him right then and there.

He smiled. The forks glinted and glowed, pulsing with invisible power; he gave them to her, and she took them hesitantly.

"They don't look like any big deal," she said. "These can open the gates to hell?" Her voice, husky and low, filled the mysterious chamber like smoke.

"Yes," he whispered, "they can."

Devila handed them back to Albert, who took them reverently. He walked across the room to the front of the altar and hung them on a wooden hook in such a way that they would be able to resonate freely. Devila's eyes sparkled with anticipation. *What would this man show her? Was he serious about opening the gates of hell, and if so, shouldn't she be afraid?*

Somehow she felt safe, as if Albert's dominating presence would protect her no matter what happened. Besides, *he* was not afraid. He acted as if he knew exactly what he was doing. He made sure the tuning forks were hanging in precisely the way he wanted, then he turned to her and spoke. His face was electric.

"This is not magic, black or otherwise. It is not any sort of occult hocus-pocus. It is the actual manifestation of a demon, a demon man has called many names—the devil, Lucifer, Mephistopheles, Belial, Beelzebub, Asmodeus, Apollyon, and of course, Satan. Since time immemorial, men have called to him, to conjure him to do their bidding, to gain his power. But now, I, Albert Beaumond, have discovered the ancient secret. The absolute truth!"

Devila swallowed, her heart pounding. The low-cut black dress she wore rose and fell with her breathing. She looked from his eyes to the tuning forks, then back again. Taking a striker made from the leg of a hoofed animal, he paused, and let the crushing strangeness wash his feverish brow.

He spoke again, his voice hypnotic. It compelled her, and she became further aroused. The very evil of the room itself, of Albert's claims, of the tuning forks, brought her pitch higher. She felt a dampness come over her, her ears tingled, she felt lightheaded.

"I want to show you something incredible, something that no modern, civilized human being besides myself has ever seen. Something so fantastic that you will not believe your eyes. Something that will make you understand that the universe is *nothing* like you thought it was."

He waited for her response. All she could muster was a hoarse, "Okay."

"But first," he continued, "you must swear that what you are about to see will never be repeated to anyone, at any time, for any reason."

Devila smiled wolfishly, beads of moisture glistening on her upper lip, just above the smear of her wine-dark lipstick. "For any reason?"

Albert nodded. "Yes, darling, there are those who would pay you for your eyewitness account, and I will not stand for that. So, if you plan to go to the newspapers with this, I'll refuse the demonstration and take you home."

She looked at him as though he were crazy.

"Jesus, you're serious, aren't you?"

Now it was Albert's turn to smile. He looked at her in a superior way and gave a quick nod of the head.

"All right, show me!"

The aftermath of Landis Woodley's party was a horror show. Most people had left by 5:00 A.M., and the cleanup had begun. It was a scene of utter desolation in the living room. Empty bottles, cigarette butts, confetti, vomit, discarded bits of costume, broken glass, and someone's pants were all scattered about the floor. The rug had been destroyed, one artistic guest had drawn pictures on the walls, and in the kitchen a candle had burned down and started a small fire that burned the back door.

All in all, a success, thought Landis. Damage was within acceptable limits and the cops had not showed up.

The corps elite gathered downstairs in the screening room for some after-hours libations. Neil Bugmier and Deborah DeLux made a pot of coffee and Landis sipped his cup thoughtfully, still savoring the guillotine illusion. The fake neck was uncomfortable to wear, and he'd only had to use the detachable head for a few seconds, but it was worth it. Tomorrow it would be the talk of Hollywood.

The Great Romano, a washed-up magician and carnival sleight of hand artist, stood up and raised his glass of champagne. He wore his usual costume of threadbare white tie and tails, the same one he'd been wearing since vaudeville.

Other people, sporting a plethora of beverages from coffee to bourbon to soda water, followed suit. Romano's bombastic, irritating voice rose to a crescendo as he waved his arm around the room.

"Dear friends," he started, "I implore you. A toast!"

The glasses, mugs, and bottles went up. Of the eight people in the room, all of them participated.

"A toast! Are you with me?"

Everyone considered Phil "The Great" Romano to be full of hot air except Landis, who seemed to have a soft spot for the old carny. He was old-time showbiz, a living piece of vaudeville.

"I am usually known for my predictions, prognostications, and prophecies, and as you know, my success rate is 87 percent . . ."

"Eighty-seven percent wrong!" shouted a drunk Buzzy Haller. Everybody laughed except Romano.

"Eighty-seven percent right!" corrected the silver-haired huckster.

"Why don't you guess his weight?" someone joked. There was more laughter.

Romano cleared his throat. "As I was saying, tonight I make my boldest prognostication! Based on a thorough astrological investigation, and in conjunction with the reading I got from my always-reliable Tarot cards, I predict success for Landis Woodley's next picture!"

There was polite applause. Landis smiled.

Romano continued, "To the man who lost his head tonight, I give you Landis Woodley!" He raised his glass high. "A toast!"

"Hear, hear!" they all shouted.

Landis stood and tipped his coffee mug. "Thank you! And here's to all of you who make it possible!"

Buzzy Haller stumbled to his feet. His speech, slurred by the alcohol, was almost incomprehensible. He was a bad drunk, given to violent antisocial behavior at his worst. Landis knew that tonight, for some reason, Buzzy was out of control.

"Jess a minit! Jess a goddamn minit!" He lurched from side to side, reeling into Neil Bugmier, who caught and steadied him.

"Take it easy, Buzz," Neil said gently.

"Get your fuggin' hands offa me, you faggot!" Buzzy shouted.

"Buzzy—" Landis began to say.

"Shaddup! Alla you, shaddup! Lissen to me, you buncha fuggin' losers! I got sumpin' to say."

The room quieted. Buzzy swayed from left to right, front to back, his eyes crossed and his mouth drooling. Landis considered stopping Buzzy, but decided to just let his friend do whatever he was going to do, and then pack him off to bed, by force, if necessary.

"Thish ain't the movie business, thish is the bullshit business! We ain't making movies. Nobody could make movies on the budgets we got! It's bullshit!, you hear me? Bullshit!" the last word he screamed at the top of his lungs.

"I'm sick of it! The fuggin' scripts thish fruitcake writes are crap! The acting is crap! The direction is crap! The distribution is crap! The reviews are crap! It's all crap! It's a big, fat fuggin' piece of crap!"

No one said a word. The faces all looked away. Buzzy continued, bellowing at the walls, throwing his head back and howling like a mad dog.

"Remember the flyin' saushers ending in *Haunted Sausher*? I threw a fuggin' paper plate at the camera, fer Christ sake! A burning paper plate! Izzat filmmakin'? Huh? The poor muthafuggers in the seats paid to see that! Can you believe that shit? They paid to see a couple of burning paper plates! Shit, they coulda done it themselves at home!"

Landis stood. He leveled his gaze at Buzzy. Buzzy stopped talking and leered at his best friend.

"They didn't pay to see burning paper plates, Buzz. They paid to see a lot more than that. They paid to see the illusion of flying saucers being destroyed by the heat rays of a hopeful, dying planet. They paid to see Tad Kingston shoot down the aliens, whether they were paper plates or twenty-thousand-dollar special effects. They paid to see the *magic*. They want to believe, Buzzy, they want to dream. And that's what we sell 'em . . . we sell 'em nightmares. We sell 'em illusions. And you ought to be pretty damn proud of what we do, 'cause only a few people in the whole world can do it."

Buzzy looked at Landis with one eye closed. Neil caught him as he slumped backward and laid him on the rug, careful not to bang his head.

Hoyt Lovejoy stepped forward. A swashbuckling actor from the early days of talkies, Hoyt was a proud, vain, macho leading man gone slightly to seed. He'd appeared in two Woodley productions. He looked at Buzzy, passed-out wasted on the floor, and sneered, "Who says my acting is crap? Get up, you little shit. Get up or I'll crack your fuckin' cranium!"

Buzzy opened one eye and said, "Chuck you, Farley."

Hoyt reached down and hefted Buzzy up by the front of his shirt. Hoyt held Buzzy in a standing position for a moment, cocked his fist, and punched Buzzy in the face. Buzzy flew back into Neil Bugmier's arms like a rag doll.

Hoyt leaned over him and shouted, "Had enough? Ya little turd! Don't you ever call me a crappy actor again, ya hear?"

Buzzy was out cold this time.

Landis Woodley carried Buzzy Haller upstairs and laid him out on the couch. He needed Neil's help to do it. In a few moments, Buzzy was noisily sleeping it off. Landis returned to the basement screening room, with Neil a step behind him.

"How can you put up with that guy?" Neil asked.

"Buzzy's all right. He just has this massive Hollywood paranoia, you know? He thinks the whole world's out to get him."

Neil grunted. "Well, it is. As long as he keeps acting like that."

Landis paused on the basement stairs and said, "I know that Buzzy's a little nuts, but damn it, the guy's my friend. He's loyal, and he's brilliant. You know that ending for *Saucer* he mentioned? The one with the paper plates?"

"Yeah?"

"Well, that was pure Buzzy. I don't know why he's so ashamed of it. All he did was work with what he had, which was zip. The fuckin' guy makes something out of nothing, and he's actin' like it's the end of the world."

Neil looked sad. "Paper plates and gasoline?"

"Yeah, and the gas came from *my* car, so actually, all he had was the plates. So, he created an ending, saved the movie, and saved my ass. The investors were going to pull out the next morning, and I'd have been ruined. I guess I owe him, you know? If he has a problem, then I'll try to help. It's only fair."

"But he's hates that scene," Neil said. "You heard what he said."

"He didn't mean it. That scene typifies what we do—we make something out of nothing. Art from paper plates, from garbage. Look, nobody's proud of that ending, but, shit, we pulled it off. There's something to be said for that."

Neil shook his head. "You're too sentimental. The guy's an asshole."

They descended the stairs.

On the way down they ran into Jonathon Luboff sitting on the bottom step, slumped over. He, too, appeared to be in bad shape.

"Oh shit, what next?" Neil asked nobody. "It's a goddamn sanitarium around here!"

At some point during the evening, Luboff had scored and shot some more smack. Now he was stretched out on the stairs, nodding out and drooling.

"Jonathon?" Landis asked, "Are you all right?"

Jonathon looked up, his pupils pinned.

"Jonathon?"

He stared into Landis's face, his haunted eyes boring worm holes. Landis felt a chill. No one on earth could be a bigger Jonathon Luboff fan than he, and he was thrilled to have the opportunity to work with the veteran film great. Yet, Landis knew that this was the end of the road for Luboff.

Once, Landis had succeeded in getting Luboff checked into a drug rehabilitation clinic. They kept him there for over two months, while the old man fought a legion of tenacious and powerful personal demons.

Landis did what he could. But Luboff did the suffering.

Sometimes it seemed like the old fucker didn't want to be saved.

In Landis's petition to the Screen Actors Guild for financial and medical assistance for the aging actor, he'd pointed out that Luboff had once been a major star, a proven box office winner who generated millions of dollars. They acknowledged that when they turned him down.

Hollywood traditionally turned its back on has-beens, casting them out like old shoes. Like shoes, faded stars washed up somewhere, no longer worth the money it cost to repair them.

Luboff had been all that and more—a classic crash and burn story with a bitter twist.

Tad Kingston, with leading lady Deborah DeLux in tow, found Landis and Neil standing over Luboff.

"How're we gonna get him home?" Tad asked.

"He can stay here," Landis replied. "Christ, I'm running a halfway house for these loaders. I got Buzzy on the couch and Luboff on the stairs."

"I wonder where he got the junk?" Deborah asked.

"Good question. If I knew, I'd kill the guy. Shit, can't they see what it's doing to him? He's a mess. I thought tonight we could drum up a little publicity for him, you know, jazz up the next movie, but he spent most of the time upstairs getting whacked." Landis sighed. He tilted up the old actor's chin with a hand so that Luboff's faraway eyes were looking up. "What am I going to do with you, Jonathon?"

The glazed windows to Jonathon's soul looked past Landis, off into the distance. Landis let the head drop.

"I hope he can keep it together for the next picture," Neil said.

Deborah put her hand on Landis's shoulder and whispered in his ear. "Come on, there's nothing you can do. We'll carry him up later. Let's have some coffee."

They entered a basement room that passed for a den, and talk soon turned to the next movie. Everyone was anxious to hear the plans. "Come on, Mr. Woodley, tell us about the new one," Tad asked.

Tad and Deborah were particularly excited because this time they would receive star billing along with Luboff and Hoyt Lovejoy.

They had paid their dues, and in Landis Woodley's world when you worked hard and played team ball, you got rewarded. You got to keep playing. Money was slim, but Landis kept you working. That was the important thing.

Everyone in the room made some sort of living off Woodley Productions.

"You really want to hear about it?" Landis smiled.

"We all do," Deborah answered.

The others nodded. Outside, the sun was coming up, but down in the basement of Landis Woodley's house, midnight hung eternal.

His voice, racked by a night of too much booze and too many cigarettes, unwrapped the story of *Cadaver.*

"It's a beauty. Neil here came up with a pretty decent script. You know, I've always wanted to shoot in the LA County Morgue. It's cheap, and it looks great on film. I had Buzz go down and check it out today, and it's all set. The challenge was building a script around the morgue. That's why Neil was such an important part."

Neil stood up and took a bow. "It was really nothing," he crowed.

"Of course, it was my idea," finished Landis. Neil shut up immediately.

Landis took a sip of coffee and shook a Pall Mall out of a maroon soft-pack. He lit it with a wooden match and exhaled slowly.

The smoke hung in the air like a motionless hurricane. He coughed and said, "I wanted to use a set over at RKM. They had just finished with *Vampire's Kiss,* and they had this gorgeous set—a lab, a castle, interiors up the kazoo."

Neil giggled. "Interiors up the kazoo," struck him as funny. With Landis, everything was, "up the kazoo."

"It must have cost a fortune," Landis continued. "It was absolutely incredible. Well, you know me with finished sets. I just naturally started working on an idea.

"To me, it was like saving two-thirds of the production cost. I mean, the set *is* the movie . . . pretty much. I couldn't let it go to waste. I heard they were gonna do a Spanish production on it a few weeks later.

"All I needed was a script, so I called Neil and told him my idea. Then, for some reason which I'll never understand, RKM pulled the set out from under me, said I couldn't use it. *They tore it down."*

Hoyt looked confused. "They tore it down? What kind of an asshole thing is that to do?"

Landis shrugged.

Hoyt cracked open a beer and whistled. "No wonder they're losing money. That was like a free movie, and they wasted it."

"They didn't want *me* to have it," Landis replied. "There are people over there who hate me, and they'd rather eat the set than let me use it. It's because of the kinds of movies I make. They think it's beneath them."

"Beneath them?" Hoyt asked incredulously. "That's a joke."

"Until the money comes in," Landis finished.

Hoyt belched quietly, his voice smooth and resonant, befitting a leading man. "Have you seen the shit they're putting out this fall? Christ, *Brazen Teenage Hussy* and *Carnival Girls* ain't exactly *Gone with the Wind,* if you know what I mean."

Landis smiled. "Don't blame them. They're just doing what the stockholders tell them to do."

"Making trash?"

Landis nodded.

"Well, hell, we can make better trash than that," Hoyt said.

"It's true," Landis replied. "I don't deny it. But someday . . ."

"Someday they'll kiss your ass!" Neil exclaimed.

"Damn right," Landis said. "Someday, they'll let me do what I really want. Give me a nice big budget, some decent distribution, a professional set, and I'll show those fuckers what I can do!"

Neil clapped. "Bravo!"

Landis raised his hands. "When that day comes I'm gonna stick it right back to 'em, where the sun don't shine. Our job is to survive in the meantime. We're all just paying our dues here. Eventually we'll get the shot.

"I'm gonna earn respect at the only place they recognize, the box office. I'll make the greedy fuckers notice me. You see, working down here, at the bottom of the food chain, is a wonderful opportunity. I can really get creative and show some smarts.

"That's what this town is built on, people who make it up the ladder the hard way. I don't mind. When they make it harder for me, it just makes me tougher. So . . . fuck RKM! I'm making the movie anyway, on my own. That's when I got the idea to use the morgue."

"What about the interiors?" Deborah asked.

"My house," Landis said slowly. "I'll use my house."

* * *

When Albert Beaumond kissed Devila, she tasted like brandy and cigarettes, sweet and bitter.

She accepted his advance without hesitation. She opened her lips and let his tongue explore.

Albert was consumed with the urge to excite her. After all, they were the most diabolical couple in Hollywood. He considered the anticipated publicity. Dating Devila would be the best move he'd ever made and being linked publicly with her would be instant media credibility.

His church would soon be on the map. After he filmed and demonstrated the conjuring of Satan, he'd be front-page news. With her by his side, he was sure to get more than his share of press.

They were deliciously glamorous.

She broke off the kiss and pushed him away, stirring his feelings more than she knew. He looked into her eyes, knowing what she would ask for before she opened her wine-colored lips.

"Show me," she whispered. "Show me now."

"Sure." He smiled. "No problem at all. Here, help me light these candles. I need enough to make a circle."

They lit the candles together, placing them in holders a few inches apart to form a large circle, filling the room. In the center were the altar, the tuning forks, the sleeping cat, and Albert.

He used his belt to tie the complacent cat to a hook embedded in the altar. He'd designed the slab to accommodate the ritual sacrifice of small animals.

He then marked the cat's head with ashes.

Without preamble, he struck the tuning forks so that the hard, cloven hoof made contact with the tubular shanks. First one, letting it ring for a moment, then the other.

They resonated together strangely, vibrating the inside of Devila's head as if she was standing inside a huge church bell. The two tones oscillated, ringing wildly. Albert watched the air around him. The candles flickered and the forks began to blur. Devila stood dead still.

The cat jumped at the sound and began to struggle against the bonds.

The air in front of the tuning forks began to waver like heat rays radiating off a desert highway. The shimmering waves distorted the light passing through them. At the center of that distortion, a shape began to take form.

Albert let the forks resonate, resisting the urge to strike them a second time. The shape became more distinct.

It looked like a serpent, or rather, an apparition of a serpent, huge, with powerful-looking ghostly coils and a massive head. As they watched, the figure became more distinct.

Roberta Bachman drank coffee. She sat in her Hollywood kitchen, the sun streaming through gauze curtains, and read the papers. Sputnik orbited overhead and the world was no longer safe for democracy. The reds were everywhere. Same old shit.

She got up from the peach-colored Formica tabletop and walked over to the percolator to pour another cup.

Through her windows, LA looked bright and new, the smog had yet to settle across the basin, and traffic was still manageable.

She knew all that would change soon. She switched on the radio.

The disc jockey talked fast and bubbly, typical of the genre. He hawked his products and touted the radio station. He was one of the good guys in the white hats, and he said so every few minutes.

Roberta let the coffee swirl in her cup, a rich brown/black liquid with aromatic steam coming off the top. She spooned in some Half & Half and stirred absently while she listened.

"And it looks like rain is on the way!" chirped the radioman. "Eighty percent chance of showers this weekend! So take your umbrellas, kids! Didja ever notice that when you take your umbrellas it never rains, and when you don't take 'em, it pours? Well, on Saturday, I want all the good-guy listeners to take their umbrellas with them everywhere they go. We'll chase those old rain clouds away, right gang?"

"Right," Roberta said in a sarcastic monotone.

"And now, here's Ozzie and Harriet's famous son, the *irrepressible* Ricky Nelson!"

"I'm Walkin' " came on the radio, and Roberta hummed along. She knew the Fats Domino version, unlike most other white listeners, and was mildly amused by Ricky's performance. Still, it had a nice groove, and it beat the hell out of Pat Boone.

The phone rang.

Roberta looked at the wall clock. Seven-thirty. Who would call at that time? Janice was still asleep, and being the day after Halloween, neither one of them was going to work even though it was only Friday.

She turned the radio down and picked up the receiver.

"Hello?"

"Roberta Bachman?"

"Yes, who is it?"

The voice on the other end of the line was familiar, but she couldn't quite place it. She sat back down, her coffee in front of her.

"This is Landis Woodley," the voice said.

Roberta's muscles stiffened at the sound of that name.

Her voice took on a frigid flatness. "Yes?"

There was a slight pause, then, "I'm calling to apologize for last night . . ."

"Apologize? Listen, buster, that was a sick joke you pulled on us! You've got a lot of nerve calling me up this morning. I never want to hear from you again!"

"I'm sorry," he said quickly. "We didn't mean any harm, and I think Buzzy got carried away."

"That's right, put the blame on him. You guys are all the same."

Landis laughed. "What? Hey listen, lady, I just called to say I was sorry, don't lump me in with Buzzy or anybody else. It's just that . . . I saw your face, and I know how upset you were, and I just wanted to see if you were okay."

Roberta took a sip of coffee and snorted. "Hmmph! And where is your asshole friend this morning? How come you're calling and not him?"

Landis let his voice drop smoothly, "Because I like you, and I didn't want to see you get hurt. Sometimes Buzzy gets a little overzealous. Last night he was drinking a bit much, and I was a little worried that he might—"

"Might what? Try to rape me? Well, let me tell you, he never got a chance . . . and he never will. I think both of you are animals. You can tell Mr. Haller, when he wakes up, that I never want to see his ugly face again."

Landis let a moment slip away, then said, "What about me?"

Roberta was confused. "What about you?"

"Well, would you ever see *my* ugly face again?"

Roberta stopped. She hadn't expected Landis to say anything remotely like that. "I . . . I don't know what you mean."

"I mean, if I asked you out, like for dinner, would you go?"

Roberta was flattered and at the same time disgusted. "No. Probably not," she said.

"Why not?"

Roberta's voice toughened. "I don't know you. And what little I do know about you, I don't like. You and Buzzy are like two peas in a pod. I don't think I'd ever want to go out with either one of you."

Landis sighed.

"Is that a no?"

"Yes, that's a no. You're unbelievable, you know that?"

She hung up before he could answer.

Devila gasped at the image of a huge snake Albert had conjured before her eyes.

It wavered and thickened, then became more solid. There could be no doubt about it. What she was seeing was incredible, impossible. It frightened her.

She took a step backward. The image began to move, its coils flexing and undulating. It hovered in the air above the cat, but its evil black eyes were fixed on Albert. Devila became aware that Albert was not moving. He seemed paralyzed. The snake floated toward him, relaxing its massive torso as it went.

Devila screamed.

The serpent slid around Albert.

Devila backed up farther, knocking over several of the candles.

Albert disappeared beneath the ghostly coils of the Serpent Demon. It wrapped around him until only the head of Albert Beaumond showed. Then, with a snap and a shifting of realities, Albert's head was gone. In its place, the head of the snake.

Devila screamed again.

The scales around the thing's mouth parted, and an evil grin seemed to grow. Its malicious eyes flashed at her, raping her. She stood transfixed as the two inhuman slits seemed to look right through her, into her soul, devouring it. She shuddered and shrank back.

The scaly nonlips opened and a black, whiplike tongue darted out. Devila screamed again. The tongue shot out so quickly, so unexpectedly, that the burst of adrenaline she felt nearly shocked her into unconsciousness.

It touched her face, the moist, black tentacles of the forked tip caressing her pale skin. As lovers do.

She needed to scream but didn't want to open her mouth, lest the probing, quivering feeler find its way inside her. Instead she made a piteous, high-pitched moaning sound.

The black tongue darted in and out of the serpent's mouth sharply, as fast as lightning, emerging a split second later wet with stinking saliva.

It played with Devila, toying with her inability to scream and run. The tongue ran over her, leaving a snail's trail of iridescent slime wherever it touched.

A few moments later she was lathered from head to toe, her hair slick with the foul-smelling spit. She kept her mouth clamped shut tightly. The tears and reptile saliva burned her eyes. Fear exploded in her heart.

At last the demon tongue withdrew and the Snake God pivoted its head to survey the room. Devila stayed absolutely still, afraid to move yet shivering with revulsion.

Albert, or what used to be Albert, dropped to his knees and began to crawl to the wall of candles. It stopped and extended a finger.

The flame licked the tip, burning the flesh.

The Snake God withdrew the finger, now black and smoking, and looked at it quizzically.

Its eyes fell back on Devila, then something popped.

She found herself looking at Albert Beaumond again.

It happened in the blink of an eye. The Snake Demon disappeared. The flames on the tips of the candles fluttered, as if the air had been disturbed, but Devila felt no breeze.

Albert's eyes were glazed. He shuddered and felt his face with the palms of his hands. He looked at Devila, confusion in his features, and began to cry.

"Jesus Christ, what a hangover!"

Landis looked at Buzzy with thinly veiled disgust. They sat drinking coffee on the deck overlooking Beachwood Canyon. From behind a pair of dark glasses, Buzzy groaned again. "The sun is killing me!"

Landis snapped open the newspaper and ignored his friend's suffering. "You're a fuckin' vampire," he said.

"Ohhh, I think I must have pushed the old panic button a little too hard last night. My eyes hurt."

"You deserve to suffer. You know, it serves you right. You were an asshole last night. Hoyt Lovejoy punched you out, don't you remember?"

Buzzy's hand came up to his face, felt the swelling under his eye and around his nose, then returned to the coffee mug. The sunglasses could not hide the damage. "Is that how I got this?"

"I'm afraid so."

Buzzy smiled, as if suddenly remembering something funny. "That guillotine trick was a knockout, huh?"

Landis nodded, his eyes scanning the paper. He said nothing.

He was searching the *LA Times* for any mention of his Halloween party. So far, to his dismay, he'd found none. Ignoring Buzzy was easy to do. He could hear the man's labored breathing behind the wall of newsprint. Landis's mood continued to sour.

"It hurts to smile," Buzzy said softly.

"Don't strain yourself," Landis replied, his tone dark.

"Why are you so pissed off?"

Landis put down his paper and leveled a gaze at Buzzy. "You really want to know? Okay, I'll tell you. I'm pissed off at you because—"

He stopped, wondered if he was wasting his time, then continued, slower, determined to make a point while Buzzy was still in pain. "—because of what you did to Roberta Bachman."

"Roberta Bachman?"

"Yeah, your date, don't you remember?"

Buzzy pushed the sunglasses farther up his swollen nose, took a sip of black coffee, and grimaced.

"She left screaming."

"Exactly. So, what's your point?"

Landis shook his head. "The point is, I don't want you alienating people like that. That girl is a sweet young thing. You didn't have to scare the shit out of her so bad. Now she's going to go all around Hollywood and tell everybody what a bunch of assholes we are. Negative publicity we don't need, even if it's word of mouth."

Buzzy squinted, mouth agape. "So?"

Landis continued, "Yeah, that's what she's probably doing today. Listen to me, I love to scare people. That's my job, and I love shaking them up like we did last night, but I don't want people like her to run away crying. It creates ill will, and the only reason we're throwing these parties is to drum up some industry talk. We're in the horror movie business, remember?"

Buzzy tilted his head, made a face, then leaned forward. His eyes locked with Landis's. "Hey, wait a minute. Have you got the hots for Roberta Bachman?"

Landis stood up. "You're fucked up, you know that? I can't tell you anything!"

"Do you have the hots for Roberta Bachman?" Buzzy repeated, slowly. "You never cared what people said before. In fact, you never gave a fuck about anybody. Now you're tryin' to tell me that you care what this little chick at RKM thinks? Don't try to shit me, man. I know you."

Landis looked off into the city. Palm trees waved down on Franklin Avenue. Cars crawled along the major traffic routes. A few forlorn birds pirouetted in the sky.

"You do, don't you?" Buzzy said.

Landis didn't answer.

"Look," Buzzy said, "I don't care if you take her out. After last night she'll never talk to me again anyway, so you're welcome to her. It's just that you and me are brothers, man, and I want to know. I want the truth, that's all."

Landis moved to the railing and lit a cigarette. He looked back at Buzzy's beaten face and smiled wickedly. Youth was still a part of him, and even though his hair had started to thin, he still had the heart of a little boy. There sparkled a mischievous energy in his smile.

"I think she's kind of cute," he said.

"I knew it! So, the truth is out! You could have any girl in Hollywood, but you want this mousy little publicity girl from RKM. That makes zero sense, man."

Landis's smile faded. "Well, you took her out."

"Yeah, but you tried to talk me out of it," Buzzy said defensively. "You said I'd never get in her pants."

"I was right."

"Hey, I personally don't care if you take her out or not, okay? I just want you to level with me. Do you or do you not have the hots for Roberta Bachman? No trick answers, yes or no."

"Yes."

The sliding door slid open and Neil Bugmier stepped onto the deck carrying a thick sheaf of papers. He wore a halter top and shorts, a pair of tan pumps, and a pair of cat's-eye sunglasses that made him look like something from a Milton Berle comedy skit. His makeup appeared garish in the bright sun; the effect was surrealistic.

Landis and Buzzy looked up and almost laughed. No matter how used to Neil's wardrobe preferences they became, they still had to stop themselves from making comments now and then. Neil sensed this and became indignant.

The fresh fingernail polish glinted as he handed over the papers to Landis.

"Here they are, all the latest changes."

Buzzy rubbed his forehead. "Could you get me some aspirin?" he asked Neil.

"I'm not your maid," Neil snapped, obviously as unhappy with Buzzy as Landis was today.

"No, but you dress like her."

"Fuck you!" shouted Neil, and lunged for Buzzy. For his size, Neil was an amazingly strong person. He'd always been athletic and kept himself in good shape, unlike the perpetually whacked-out Buzzy, who was about as inclined to exercise as he was to volunteer for an IRS audit. Neil pulled him out of his chair and pinned him against the railing.

Landis tried to pry Neil's hands loose, but the incensed transvestite would not give an inch. He pushed Buzzy's head back until it was hanging over the cliff, his upper body bent over the wooden rail. The red fingernails squeezed into his neck.

"Hey!" Buzzy yelled. "Hey! Let me go!"

"I've put up with your shit too long!" screamed Neil. "I'm gonna teach you a lesson you'll never forget!"

Landis wedged an arm between and tried to separate them, but Neil pushed him away. He released his right hand from its death grip on Buzzy's Adam's apple and slapped him hard across the face, aggravating the injuries he'd already suffered. The sunglasses were jarred off his head and spun out into the canyon, helicoptering down into the brush below. Beneath the shades, Buzzy's eyes were red and squinting, one of them already discolored in a classic shiner. He tried to turn away from the sun, but Neil held him tight. Buzzy yelped in pain.

"Say you're sorry," demanded Neil.

Buzzy looked at him with grim determination not to give in. Neil, not really waiting for an answer, slapped him again. This blow caused Buzzy to bark in pain.

Landis considered trying to intervene again but knew that it was useless. Neil was truly enraged and beyond Landis's control. He wondered if the tough little tranny was going to heave Buzzy over the side and put him out of his misery once and for all.

"Say it!"

Buzzy coughed, making choking sounds. His eyes rolled back up into his head.

"Say it, asshole!" Neil demanded.

"I'm sorry," Buzzy said softly.

Neil released him and he slid back onto the terrace. Buzzy was embarrassed and his face throbbed. He looked over the edge to see if he could locate his sunglasses. They were nowhere to be seen.

Neil glanced at Landis and said, "I'm ready to start whenever you are."

Landis nodded. "Okay, let's work in the kitchen."

Leaving Buzzy to his own hell on the terrace, Landis and Neil slipped back inside and sat down at the big kitchen table, where Neil had set up his typewriter. Landis preferred to work in the kitchen rather than in an office. He could think with more clarity and had access to the coffeepot. The informal arrangement made for better decisions.

"Let me see page sixty-one," Landis asked.

He read in silence, then looked up and said, "Could we read this together? I'll be Luboff and you be Tad Kingston. Take it from the top of page sixty."

The script was cool and crisp in his hand. Landis scanned the pages like a shark.

CADAVER
Script by Landis Woodley and Neil Bugmier
Scene 41.
INT. NIGHT. LA COUNTY MORGUE
JOHNNY CONFRONTS DR. EZEKIAL

JOHNNY
I don't understand. These corpses are fresh. They haven't been prepared.

DOCTOR
That's just the way I want them, Johnny. You see, I have a special need for them, different from the medical college.

JOHNNY
Doctor, I don't think I can do this.

DOCTOR
Sure you can, Johnny. You want to be a medical doctor
someday, don't you?

JOHNNY
Well, yes, I do.

DOCTOR
Your mother would be very disappointed if you dropped out
now, wouldn't she Johnny?

JOHNNY
Yes, Dr. Ezekial.

DOCTOR
Bring me that cadaver over there, and remove the sheet. I want
to examine its organs to see if they're suitable for my purposes.

**JOHNNY GOES OVER TO THE CORPSE, PULLS BACK
THE SHEET, AND GASPS. IT IS THE BODY OF HIS
BEST FRIEND, NICK GARBO. JOHNNY DROPS THE
SHEET BACK ONTO THE CADAVER.**

DOCTOR
What is it, Johnny? Somebody you know?

JOHNNY
Doctor! It's Nick! He's dead!

DOCTOR
Of course he's dead, Johnny. That's how you get in here. But
don't worry, we'll give him a nice clean dissection.

JOHNNY
No! You can't! It's insane!

DOCTOR
Insane? You call me insane? That's what they said back in Vienna when I told them I could transplant live organs from one
body to another. They said I was mad. Mad! But who's to say
what madness is? Certainly not the doctors! They condemn
me, but they have no right! It is I who should condemn them! I
am not insane! I have never been insane!

BEHIND JOHNNY, COVERED WITH A SHEET ON
THE SLAB, THE BODY BEGINS TO RISE UP. THE
SHEET FALLS AWAY TO REVEAL THE HIDEOUS
DEAD FACE OF NICK. IT SITS UP, SWINGS ITS LEGS
OVER THE SIDE, AND STANDS. JOHNNY AND THE
DOCTOR TURN AROUND AND SEE IT SHUFFLING
TOWARD THEM.

JOHNNY
It can't be!

DOCTOR
Get back! Get back I say!

THE CORPSE LURCHES FORWARD. JOHNNY STUM-
BLES TRYING TO ESCAPE.

DOCTOR
Something has caused it to reanimate! If I could just—

JOHNNY SCREAMS. THE CORPSE REACHES OUT
AND STRANGLES JOHNNY WHILE THE DOCTOR
LOOKS ON, FASCINATED BY THE REANIMATED CA-
DAVER. THE CADAVER KILLS JOHNNY AND TURNS
TO THE DOCTOR.

"Okay, hold it right there, Neil. This is where I want it
changed," said Landis, breaking character.

"Changed?" Neil asked.

"Yeah, I can't kill Tad Kingston this early in the movie, it's
gonna hurt the door."

Neil ran his hands through his hair. "It's halfway through at
this point. I think you're free to kill him off if you want."

Landis smiled. "No, I want him to live. Look, Neil, there's
two reasons for it. One is I'm paying that chump Kingston
enough money where he should be in every fuckin' scene, and
two is if he dies halfway through, the teenagers will be turned off.
Believe it or not, Tad draws the kids into the theaters. If the
word gets out that he dies halfway through, the door goes down."

Neil stared at the page in his hands. "You can't be serious. I
wrote this scene exactly the way you asked me to. Kingston dies,

the sheriff gets suspicious and comes after the doctor. It's a crucial plot point. How else is the sheriff gonna start investigating the doctor?" Exasperation colored his voice. On certain words he sounded almost whiny. Landis let him finish and waved his hand in the air, as if shooing away a fly.

"Nope, that's not gonna work. We'll have to change it."

"But—"

"No buts. Change it!"

Neil looked dejected, as if he'd been chastised by the teacher in front of the whole class. Landis caught his look and said, "Let me explain something to you, Neil. You never kill the hero, and in this movie, Tad's the hero. It turns people off. Now, if you heard me say that, it must have been a misunderstanding, because I never, ever kill the hero. It gives people hope, it makes them feel good about themselves, at least for the first seventy minutes."

Neil laughed. "This is a movie about cadavers! Dead bodies! It's not *Rebel Without A Cause*, and that's Tad Kingston up there on the screen, not James Dean. Nobody's gonna give a shit if he dies!"

Landis looked at Neil, his eyebrow cocked. "Not true to a teenager. You judge an actor by his hair, and I know for a fact that Tad's hair is better than James Dean's. I've surveyed it!" Landis paused, then frowned. "Why are you arguing with me? That's not like you, Neil!"

"This script has got my name on it too, you know."

Landis raised his voice, "Hey! I don't give a fuck if it's Ernest Hemingway's name. This is *my* movie, and what I say goes!"

Neil became quiet. His head bowed slightly and he let the page drop from his fingers. Landis put his hand on Neil's shoulder and said, "What's the problem, Neil?"

Neil looked at Landis. "I don't know," he mumbled. "It's Buzzy and Luboff. They're so . . . so screwed up, and they're trying to take us down with them. It makes me mad, I guess. I want this movie to make it. Then I see those two doing their best to fuck everything up, and it makes me mad that you just let it happen."

Landis leaned back and scratched his head. He had a precious expression on his face, one that Neil had never seen before. Bemused, a little beatific around the edges.

"Cool it, Neil. I know what I'm doing. This movie is going to be just fine. As far as the goon squad goes"—he hooked his thumb back in the direction of the sliding doors—"let me deal with them, and you just worry about the rewrites."

Neil shook his head. "I don't know—"

"You're a damn good writer, Neil! But, nobody will hire you 'cause you dress like a woman. But I did, didn't I? The way you dress don't mean shit to me. You're fast and you're affordable—notice I didn't say 'cheap'—and I value your work.

"You could clean up in this town, but you're a goddamn fruit-cake! Was that a conscious decision?" He paused, not expecting an answer, then forged ahead, "You could get a crew cut, wear a gray suit, kiss butt, and wind up working for Walt Disney if you wanted.

"I'm the only one who hires you the way you are, fishnet stockings and all." He grinned; Neil did too. "Now, Buzzy is the same way, except he's an asshole, and Luboff's a junkie. What can I do about it? Each one contributes what they can, in their own way. I try to give them all a chance. Can you dig that?"

Neil nodded, "Yeah, I can dig it."

"Okay, then, let's get to work. I have a million changes I want to make in this script, starting with Tad not getting killed."

Behind them, the sound of the sliding door opening caught their attention. Buzzy reentered the house.

Neil turned around just in time to see Buzzy walk into the kitchen. He tensed, preparing himself for another fight. Buzzy walked toward him, a hangdog expression still dripping off his face.

Neil started to speak, "If you're here to—"

Buzzy cut him off. "I'm here to apologize, man."

Nobody spoke for a moment. Buzzy stood there, his hair askew. The black eye looked painful.

Buzzy's voice rumbled. The vocal cords, burned by booze and cigarettes, were rough, texturing the words as he spoke. "I'm sorry, it was the booze talkin'. I've been a jerk . . ."

Landis laughed. "You can say that again."

Buzzy shot him a look, and in that moment Landis could see the terrible pain in the man's eyes. Buzzy coughed and looked away.

"Don't agree so fast, okay? Christ, it's hard enough without having you guys up my butt. I just want to apologize to both of you. It's been pretty rough around here for me lately, and I shouldn't take it out on you."

Neil and Landis looked at each other.

"Besides, for a guy dressed as a girl, you pack quite a punch," Buzzy finished.

Neil smiled and put his hand out. Buzzy shook it tightly, and the two men hugged.

"Sit down, Buzz," Landis said, "I want you to hear this, too. I'm making some major changes in the script."

Buzzy pulled up a chair and sat down.

"I've been doing some thinking about this," Landis continued. "This movie is a parable of my life, of all our lives, when you think about it." He looked at the other two. "You follow me?"

Neil shook his head, so did Buzzy. "Explain."

"Well, it's like this," Landis began.

10

The room felt cold, even though the candles created tiny dots of heat. Albert Beaumond lay on the hardwood floor holding his head.

"Are you all right, Albert?" Devila knelt over him and asked.

Albert shook his head. A trickle of blood oozed from the side of his mouth. He coughed, spraying pink. "What? What happened?"

Devila helped Albert into a sitting position. "You were . . . I'm not sure how to say it, you were possessed. That thing you summoned covered you, its head became your head, its body became your body."

His eyes were glazed, unfocused. "What's that smell?" Albert sniffed the air.

"Snake spit, I think. Jesus, I can't put it into words . . . it was horrible. The most horrible thing I've ever seen."

Albert's head rolled. Devila touched his brow and found it burning. "You saw it?"

"Saw it? Jesus, yes. It hovered in the air for a minute, I can't describe it, it was horrible. Then it came down over you and . . .

and it *became* you. Albert, I'm scared. That thing was evil. You shouldn't be fooling around with something like that. I could sense the power of it. God, it was like a bad dream." She looked into his glassy, frightened eyes and put her hand on his shoulder. "Never again, okay? Never again."

Albert coughed again, shook his head, took a few deep breaths, and said, "It took over my body."

Devila nodded vigorously. "It licked me with its disgusting, slimy tongue. I thought it was going to kill me. Were you aware of anything?"

"I didn't feel a thing, physically, except a shock when it came in and went out. Mentally, though, I feel like I've been raped. I sensed it taking over my body, it shared its mind with me. I could feel it in there like a goddamn parasite. Jesus, it was unbelievable. I wasn't in control of *me* anymore—*it* was. I was powerless inside my own body."

He looked at her again and his face clouded over. The wrinkles on his brow were as deep and crooked as cracks in a sidewalk. "I shared my brain with it," he said with a shudder, "and I could read its thoughts for a split second before it stopped me. I got the feeling that it didn't want me to see inside there.

"Once it knew I was able to read its consciousness, it closed that part of my brain off like a light switch. But in that one split second, Jesus Christ, it revealed a lot to me."

Devila smoothed his hair, brushing it off his face, mothering him. "Like what?"

Albert struggled to one knee and felt his head. The rubbery feeling and dizziness that had overwhelmed him earlier had begun to subside. He could almost stand.

"Help me up," he said in a whispery, shaken voice.

Devila supported his arm as he worked his way to his feet and stood unsteadily. His mind still reeled at the invasion. Everything hurt; every muscle in his body had been tensed when that thing was in charge. Adrenaline had been pumping at an unbelievable rate.

But, as spent as his body was, it was the mental strain that hurt the most. Albert could not stop thinking, reliving that awful moment when his mind and the consciousness of the demon were joined.

He shivered involuntarily.

During that moment of possession, when the thing entered him and gave him its brief glimpse of hell, Albert knew he had made a grave mistake. In the inky blackness that overwhelmed Albert, the background against which the thing emerged, he could sense that the demon knew exactly where it was. It knew that it was no longer deep in the jungle among ignorant, savage people. It knew that it had materialized in a modern city, teeming with sophisticated beings, electric with possibilities. It knew it finally had a host it could use to its advantage. And it was happy. It was ecstatic.

Albert could also feel the malice in its cold heart. He could sense it measuring him and gauging the new world into which it had been, with Albert's help, admitted.

He could feel the pressing darkness, the timeless void from which it came, and knew in a heartbeat that it was ancient beyond man's understanding. It had been pent-up, controlled, and frustrated for too long. Now, excited at the prospect of freedom, of seeking destiny and power in this bold new century, it rejoiced.

Albert saw the evil of its desires and knew that misery and submission awaited him and his daughter as long as they were forced to serve this cruel master.

For mankind, worse.

What Albert had glimpsed, ever so briefly, was hell.

Not the understandable, classical hell of Dante—no, this was a new hell, built on true suffering and real destruction. It was the end of nature, the rise of death and chaos, the submission of man as a race.

In Albert, it had learned everything about our culture. It had seen man's inhumanity to man, man's own damnation, weakness, and greed. In that instantaneous linking of their minds, it sucked every bit of knowledge in Albert's memory.

So it knew exactly how to exploit all these things. The Serpent Demon had been unchanged for thousands of years. It waited and watched, as patient as the stars. While man, for all his technology and ideology, was the same slimy rock crawler he had always been. Thousands of years were just a blink. The species never changed.

That pleased the demon.

Albert knew that, because of him, the end was near. The fate of humanity had just slipped through his fingers. In that moment, the last few tenuous strands of Albert's sanity snapped.

At Landis Woodley's mansion, the light slanted through the kitchen as the sun's angle shifted. It cut interesting shafts through the smoke from Buzzy's cigarette.

"The movie's got to have a point," protested Neil. He'd been hunched over the typewriter with his arms folded over the roller, his head down. Now he raised it, the indentations of the keys on his forehead.

"No, it doesn't. It doesn't have to have anything," Landis snapped back. "Think about it. The point is—it has no point."

Neil rubbed his face. Today he was dressed in a simple black dress. "Aw shit, Landis. Speak English."

"Our only job is to shock the moviegoer. That's it, just shock his ass. My philosophy of shock is that it's got to be unexpected, okay? It doesn't necessarily have to have a rhyme or reason; it just happens. The more unexpected it is, the higher they jump." He leaned back, smiled, and pointed his finger at the ceiling, holding it up as if to say "number one." It gathered the attentions of Buzzy and Neil effectively, and they stared at him, listening hard. "Shock is the total reversal of polarity in a situation," he said.

Buzzy shook his head. "Christ, you're gettin' kind of deep for me, Woody. What's all this shit about 'reversal of polarity'?"

Neil swept the hair back from his face, revealing the drying, chalky layer of thick makeup that he constantly applied to hide his whiskers. As a writer, he knew what Landis was driving at, but he was genuinely surprised at the man's artistic approach to this particular project. Landis intended for *Cadaver* to be his masterpiece. Usually it was wham-bam, thank you, ma'am.

Neil always kept a paperback dictionary in his pocketbook for situations just like this. Whipping it out, he quickly flipped to the esses and found the appropriate definition for "shock." "The dictionary says: 'to strike with surprise, terror, horror, or disgust.' "

Landis slapped the table, causing the coffee to jump and splatter.

"That's us! We're shockers!"

Buzzy yawned. "So what's that got to do with us?" he asked.

"Everything," Landis replied, "Every goddamn thing! That's exactly the way I feel about horror movies."

"Huh?" Buzzy squinted through his black eye.

"What's the reason for the cadavers coming to life? Is it evil scientific experiments? Black magic? Voodoo? Atomic radiation? No! There is no explanation! That's the beauty of it! It just happens. Who cares why? The important thing is that the cadavers start moving, there is no explanation. When they start killing people, it really doesn't matter how it got started, does it? No! It's happening. That's all you need to know. It's better not to explain. Let the people draw their own conclusions. All I'm concerned with is the action, not the explanation. The truth is, there is no answer to the mystery of why the cadavers come to life . . . because life has no answers."

Buzzy rolled his eyes.

Neil clapped his hands together and shouted, "My God, the man's an existentialist!"

"Right," Landis barked. "A horror existentialist!"

Landis beamed at them, and the entire kitchen radiated his infectious enthusiasm. For each of them, there was nothing better than making horror movies.

"Neil," Landis said, "I want you to get started right away on the rewrite. Make any necessary adjustments in the plot to support our new . . . our new attitude. Make it work, baby. Make it fuckin' sing!"

"What about an ending?" Neil asked.

Landis smiled. Leaning back in his chair, he said, "Don't need one. There is no ending. The cadavers win. No explanation, no nothing. They win, period."

"Bleak. Fatalistic," Neil droned. "Horror show noir."

"Uh-huh," Landis concluded. "Just like life. The only ones who win are dead."

The First Satanic Church was dark, its doors locked.

Elsewhere in the house, Albert and Devila sat on a couch drinking more brandy. The sun was up now, casting its full spectrum of light upon the magic of night, killing it effectively for another twelve hours.

The brandy warmed their throats and tranquilized their racing hearts.

Albert wondered how he could undo the horror he had unleashed. He hated himself for performing the ceremony without proper preparation. Drunk, horny, and boastful, he'd let himself be seduced by the idea that he could control it.

The demon didn't take the cat. Why would it when it could have me? How many more times can I do that before the damn thing breaks free?

Then he remembered why the village priest killed the host after the ceremony: *to prevent its return to the same body.*

Certainly, he did not want to act as the host again. That had been the most painful and terrifying experience of his life.

He had been naive and foolish to conjure the serpent. Again he cursed his brandy-swollen male ego and its sophomoric attempt to impress Devila. It was just the kind of ignorant mistake he hated in others, a misguided, boastful bit of idiocy that could have cost him everything.

God, he hated himself.

Far from being some kind of theological doctrine, some intellectual argument, this foul demon was the very soul of evil. It meant to destroy or subjugate not only Albert and his daughter, but the rest of the world as well.

Albert's plan had been foolhardy and based on nothing but greed. Now, the force of evil would use Albert to return from a prison, millennia-old.

Albert knew what the demon wanted. After all, it had been inside him.

A question nagged Albert. Was this demon really Satan? Or was the universe full of such creatures? Once the door between the two worlds opened, what else would come slithering through?

Albert had been worshiping Lucifer all his adult life. But he had never equated it with just pure evil. In fact, to Albert, the argument was that there was really no such thing as good and evil.

Do what thou wilt shall be the extent of the law.

There was only life and death. It was what it was.

The Prince of Darkness exists, he thought. *It's here in this very house and it means to destroy me, and the people I love.*

Devila watched Albert.
He was as pale as a sheet, shaking and wild-eyed. He didn't look like a man who had just pulled off the hoax of the year. Then maybe it was all real. Her mind raced.

My God, she thought, *if demons exist, and mankind can summon them . . . what the hell else is out there?* Albert had the power in those tuning forks.
Devila found herself scanning the room constantly, afraid that the thing might come back.

The forks are still in the other room, the church, he called it. God, that's frightening. That place is about as far from a church as you could get.
Yet, it was a place of worship. Albert Beaumond worshipped the wrong things, she decided. He was one sick puppy.

Her eyes went back to the mirror again, locking on her face.
And you're a sick puppy for even being here with him. This man's religion is evil.

Devila's was a much more practical theology. She worshiped money.

She knew that if she could get her hands on those tuning forks, even for just an hour, she would be richer than her wildest dreams. And famous.

She wanted to ask Albert, but he spoke first.

"I've got to destroy those forks," he said in a trembling voice.

11

Devila's Spanish-style, white stucco apartment building was in the slums of Beverly Hills. The same three-block section of four-to-six-unit buildings would have been an upper-middle-class paradise in any other neighborhood, but in Beverly Hills it was the low-rent district. It occupied a small, ten-block strip of land just below Wilshire Boulevard, still technically Beverly Hills, but in name only. People there enjoyed the prestigious postmark, but none of the status of the exclusive neighborhood where the movie stars lived.

Devila liked her one-bedroom apartment. It was cozy, "cute" in a California way. There were colorful Mexican tiles in the kitchen and bathroom and a nice picture window that looked out onto the quiet street. A palm tree grew in the front yard. She had her own parking place.

Tonight she couldn't sleep. The shock of what she had experienced at Albert's house had begun to wear off, replaced now by a numbness, a disbelief, that made her relive it over and over again in her mind.

The tongue of the serpent touched her a thousand times in

her dreams, haunting her relentlessly until she was forced to believe.

But Devila was a practical woman. She had fought her way up
the ladder of success in one of the toughest, most competitive
markets in the world. What she had seen shook her faith to the
core.

Like most people in LA, she had come from someplace else.
Raised a Baptist, she had enough fire and brimstone in her to
fear both death *and* life. She acted in high school plays, won
a couple of beauty contests, and bought her bus ticket to
Hollywood with money she made waiting tables in a skimpy
outfit.

She spent the next few years getting the runaround from
agents, producers, and other, less interesting hustlers. She grew
up fast, got tougher every day, and eventually decided that
whatever she wound up doing in Hollywood, she would have to
make the position herself. She began to live life on her own
terms.

She lay in her bed, staring at a movie poster for *Daughter of
Dracula,* and remembered how she got the idea for her character.
She heard that the job of "Creature Features" host had opened
at a local TV station.

She made a costume that showed off her figure, dyed her
brown hair black, and auditioned. Two weeks later, the young
program director, who couldn't take his eyes off her cleavage,
called to give her the job.

I am the mistress of my own destiny, she thought.

But how far could she take the "Devila" character? It had
gone just about as far as it could in the local TV market. It was
time to branch out. She was sick of showing the same stupid
grade-Z movies every week, pandering to a bunch of adoles-
cents and beatniks, and having to act the role of bimbo. It was
time to move ahead.

Into the movies.

*Fuck this crummy job. Fuck this lame TV station, fuck the ignorant fans.
I want more. So I'll I have to go out and* make *more.*

As she lay gazing at the *Daughter of Dracula* poster, Devila knew
what her next step would be.

* * *

Albert Beaumond sweated. The moist sheets stuck to his body like molting skin. His nightmares scorched the inside of his head, making him wish he were anything but asleep.

He was in the dark, but it was a darkness he could feel and smell. A musty odor seemed to curl off him, making his head swim and his eyes water. He writhed in the sticky void, slithering back and forth across the uneven floor of his lair. He was not alone.

With him were hundreds of other, lesser entities. They squirmed against him, pushing their snouts into his flesh, burrowing, searching. For what? The sensation was appalling. The things, whatever they were, clung to him desperately.

Then, a layer of understanding was peeled back and he knew the terrible truth.

He was their mother.

They were his hatchlings.

Then another layer drew back and Albert screamed.

They were snakes.

Albert screamed again, but could not hear himself. He could feel his throat constrict, sense the air being pushed past his vocal cords and—

He had no vocal cords.

More layers peeled back. Albert was a snake himself. He writhed and curled, flexing his serpent body in a hopeless attempt to escape. The skin around his head split. It separated and cracked away from his eyes, revealing a fresh, wet, new layer beneath.

The new layer felt the cold. The old layer stretched taut, pulling beyond its limits, peeling away. The feeling was indescribable.

Albert shuddered. He bucked and convulsed, disgusted with the sensation. The old skin repulsed him, a coat of dead flesh, as crawling and rotten as roadkill. He struggled anew, frantic to remove the itchy cocoon that enveloped him. The new skin, as soon as it was exposed, felt radiant and alive. It breathed through open, robust pores, filling his body with energy.

Albert twisted and turned. He flexed and rubbed against the hatchlings. The old skin peeled back, halfway now. The hatchlings squirmed more violently, and he could feel great rips of skin come off.

They began to feast on the dead skin, nibbling at it with their hungry mouths. Their forked tongues licked and tickled against the dead shell, pulling at it. Then they began to tear it away more quickly.

They were anxious. They knew that the doorway to Albert's world was open.

When he realized what he was and what he was doing, he screamed again. Only this time he could hear it. He could hear it growing like a deafening siren, bouncing off the walls and echoing through the night.

Then a hand touched him. He jumped.

His eyes jerked open, and he looked into Thora's face with wide, terrified eyes.

"Daddy! Daddy, wake up!"

He kept screaming until the last shards of nightmare melted from his consciousness.

He was aware of the wetness of the sheets, how they clung to him, how he'd pulled them back but in so doing only tangled himself farther.

Thora unwrapped him gently, watching in horror as her father's body quivered spasmodically beneath her fingers. The terror he felt was so intense that it had raised welts across his back and shoulders.

The panic in his eyes when she switched on the lights caused her to step back. That panic burned into her memory.

Landis Woodley's office was in the kitchen. At one time he had a proper office on Sunset Strip, but soon found out that most of his business got done in the bar. The cost of maintaining an office was bleeding him dry; the receptionist, the furniture, the framed movie posters, it was all a colossal waste of time.

Trying to play with the big boys was not working. When you played in their ballpark, you had to be able to swing with the checkbook in a way that made Landis nervous. He started cutting costs after the first month. The receptionist went first, then the fancy furniture, and in less than a year he was down to one phone, a card table, and some folding chairs. The next logical step was to work out of his house. The commute was only twenty feet, and the price was right.

Now he actually enjoyed working at home, and he was absolutely convinced that he got more things done.

Landis made a mental note to have someone clean up the place. Cartons of Chinese food and empty pizza boxes littered the counter. Dirty dishes filled the sink.

The phone rang, next to the coffeepot. He moved some cups and a newspaper out of the way and picked it up.

"Hello?"

"Mr. Woodley? This is Devila," a throaty female voice said.

Landis smiled. Devila was one of his favorite people. "Devila, darling, how did you like the party?"

"It was wonderful. You did an unbelievable job. People are still talking about the guillotine bit."

"Thanks. Nice to hear that. So, what's on your mind?"

"Well, I don't know how to say this, but . . . I've got something I want to discuss with you. A movie project."

"I'm always up for a film project," he said, "except that, right now, I'm going into production on *Cadaver* in a few days, and I'm afraid I'll be busy for a while."

Devila's voice softened. "Could we get together this afternoon?"

"I'm pretty busy," Landis said truthfully.

"It'll only take a few minutes," she cooed. "This is something big. Huge. I can't talk about it over the phone. All I can tell you is, this is the most incredible thing you've ever seen. If you can get it on film, you'll be a legend."

Landis pondered the offer. "Hmm. It sounds interesting. You can't tell me anything more?"

"Not over the phone."

"I see. Well, Devila, I really would love to work with you, but I'm swamped right now."

"Mr. Woodley?" Devila said.

"Call me Landis."

"Okay, Landis. This is really big. I've seen something truly incredible, something that defies logic—a supernatural entity. It's real, and it's scary as hell. I've seen it with my own eyes. Are you interested?"

Landis coughed. "Well . . . I can't really get into anything right now."

"How about if I make it worth your while? I can be very persuasive." Devila's voice had changed, it was softer, sexier.

That's all Landis needed to hear. He smiled at the phone and said, "Okay, how about we meet at Barny's at, say, two?"

Devila's voice toughened slightly. "I'll be there, but please come alone," she said. Her vocal range was amazing, and Landis had always wanted to use her in a movie. She was a natural and already famous, at least in LA.

"Barny's, alone," he repeated.

"Good. I'm looking forward to this," she said. "See you there."

Barny's was dark, as usual. Devila was not in her costume, but she still drew stares from the handful of men at the bar. Without the witchy makeup, Devila was a very attractive woman.

She found Landis at a booth in the back.

"I've never seen you out of character," Landis said with a smile. "You look great."

Devila returned his smile with one of her own. She sat across from him and ordered a glass of white wine. They made flirtatious small talk until her wine arrived, then she got down to business.

"I've seen something," she cryptically repeated her earlier claim.

Landis looked into her eyes and waited for her to complete the thought. When she didn't, he asked the obvious question. "Okay, I'll bite. What did you see?"

Devila leaned forward. Landis could smell the sweet wine on her breath. It mingled with the French perfume she favored, applied liberally.

"This has to remain between us, not to leave this table," she said.

Landis inhaled her scent. "Are you swearing me to secrecy?"

Devila nodded. "No bullshit, now. I'm serious. What I am about to tell you must never leave this table. Agreed?"

"Agreed," Landis answered, his curiosity aroused.

Devila's voice dropped. "I've seen something amazing, something that scared the shit out of me. The thing was—*it was real*. At least, as far as I know, it was real. I checked. It would have been a bitch to fake."

Landis sipped his beer. "So, what did you see?"

"I can't tell you any details," she said. "So don't ask. But, to make a long story short, I've managed to get my hands on something truly supernatural."

Landis chuckled and shook his head.

Devila looked surprised. "I thought you were into the occult."

Landis shook his head. "Just because I make horror movies doesn't mean I'm into every cockamamie, hocus-pocus load of shit people try to sell me. I'm a realist. I'm into money."

"Good, then we understand each other," she said.

Landis narrowed his eyes, letting his voice fall an octave. "Let me get something straight right now. You don't believe in this shit, do you?"

"You mean the supernatural?" she asked, wineglass in hand.

Landis smiled as his head bobbed slowly up and down. "Yeah, right, the supernatural, the occult, whatever you want to call it."

"What do you take me for, an idiot? I don't believe in anything, but just hear me out. It makes what I have to tell you all the more incredible."

Landis signaled for another round of drinks. Devila began her story. "I saw a real demon," she finally said. "It materialized out of thin air."

Landis smiled. "What have you been smoking?"

Devila's face changed. Her mouth bent downward at the corners, and she pushed away from the table. "Don't mock me. I don't have to take this shit."

"Okay, okay, relax. It's just that, well, it's hard to believe, you know?"

"I know it is. I know you must think I'm crazy, but I swear it's true."

"You say you actually saw this thing? And you want me to film it?"

She nodded.

"What's it look like?"

Devila looked around the room. She leaned forward and whispered, "It looks like a giant snake."

"A giant snake?" he whispered back.

"A serpent. A demon serpent."

Landis looked into her eyes, searching for signs that she was lying or crazy, and found none. Devila lit a cigarette in a long silver holder and blew smoke across the table.

She believes what she's saying, he thought. *She believes it one hundred percent.*

Landis decided to be diplomatic and humor her for the time

being. "You know, I've always said that if anyone brought me a genuine ghost, a haunted house, a flying saucer, whatever, and I could film it and verify it, that film would be worth a million dollars. Now you tell me that you can produce this phenomenon for my cameras?"

Devila nodded. "Guaranteed."

"What do you want out of it?" Landis asked.

"I want you to make a movie about it, starring me," she said firmly.

Landis's face remained immobile; he had a great poker face when he wanted to use it. "I see," he said. "Documentary or drama?"

"I don't care," she answered. "As long as I'm the star, and I get a share of the profits. A big share."

"How much?"

"Sixty-forty split. I get the sixty, you get the forty."

Landis laughed. "I don't make deals like that. If I did, I would have gone out of business a long time ago."

Devila was not laughing. Her eyes bore down on him like bad weather. "Take it or leave it," she said coolly.

He wondered if she was serious. *It's too far out*, he thought. *A demon? Nah. I'd be a sucker to believe that.*

"I think I'll leave it," he said.

"Suit yourself. I'll go to National with it, I'm sure somebody there will listen." She started to rise and swilled down the last of her wine. "Thanks for seeing me. Too bad we couldn't do business."

She stepped away from the table. The men at the bar watched to see what she would do. As she took her first few paces toward the door, Landis stood and went after her. The men craned their necks to follow the action.

Landis grabbed her arm. "Hold it," he said. "Let's talk about this a minute."

Devila gave him a look of utter determination, saying, in a glance, that she was not to be trifled with. She let him gently lead her back to the table.

"Do you realize that I don't even know your real name?" he asked in a friendly voice, one as nonthreatening as he could muster.

"I know that," she replied. "No one knows my real name. I don't give it out."

"If you want to do business with me, I'll have to know. It shows trust, good faith," he said.

Devila snapped a smile at him, just a short, unfriendly baring of teeth, but it made him relax.

"Trust? I don't trust anybody," she said.

"You're gonna have to trust me," he said, his voice thick and sweet.

"Why?"

"Because . . . because I think you might have something here. I don't know why, but I don't think you're lying about this. It's completely insane, but that's what I like about it. It might be worth a chance, anyway."

Now it was Devila's turn to be smug. She looked over at the bar. The men who had been staring at her all looked away quickly.

She looked back at Landis. "My name is Julie."

"Julie what?"

"Julie Greenly," she replied.

"Come on, Julie Greenly, let's go over to my office and talk about this some more."

Thora Beaumond cared for her father, wiping his fevered brow and spoon-feeding him chicken broth. She'd called Dr. Segwick, but he'd not been able to find anything physically wrong with Albert.

Dr. Segwick suggested she consult a psychiatrist. He suggested that whatever was wrong with her father was born of mental problems. Many of the people who had contact with the Beaumond family held the opinion that Albert Beaumond was quite insane and had been since the death of his beloved wife.

Albert had turned to the occult in his grief, they opined. In a vain attempt to reach out to her from the grave, Albert had dabbled in many of the darker, esoteric arts. His Catholic upbringing laid the groundwork for his beliefs, giving him delusions of heaven and hell, Satan and other diabolical beguilements.

Dr. Segwick believed Albert mad.

Apart from sedating Albert and prescribing rest, there was little else he could do.

"Your father is a very disturbed man," he told Thora in the hall. "He needs help that I can't give him, professional help."

"Is my father insane?" she asked.

"He's suffering from some form of mental collapse. I don't know enough about such matters to give you an opinion. That question is best answered by a trained analyst."

He reached into his pocket and withdrew a card, which he handed to Thora. "This is a colleague of mine, Dr. Winnet. He's a top man in his field. If anyone can help, he can. Call him, Thora. Call him first thing tomorrow."

She looked at the card and then at Segwick's aged, responsible face. Her unblinking eyes registered, but failed to reflect, all the numbing information she'd had to absorb.

"Yes, I'll call . . ."

Dr. Segwick left. His heavy footsteps receded from the house, across the wooden porch and beyond. Thora was left staring out through the screen at him. She wondered what to do.

Thora stayed up with her father, wiping the sweat from his face, assuring him that there was no demon in the room with them, and trying to calm him down.

It was the longest night of her life. When the moon rose outside his window, her father howled.

12

The morgue was a wonderful place. Buzzy and Landis loved it from the first moment they walked in.

"Isn't this cool!" Buzzy whispered to Landis as the coroner lead them through the rooms.

"It's perfect, absolutely perfect," Landis whispered back. "I love it. Look at those metal tables, and the walls. Jesus, look at the white tile walls. It's like a fuckin' slaughterhouse. I couldn't have designed a better set."

At last Dr. Meune paused and turned to face them. He had a sly smile on his face that Landis found difficult to read. "Would you like to see some of our customers?"

Buzzy and Landis exchanged looks. "Customers? Yeah," Landis answered. "Why not?"

"You have a strong stomach?" the doctor asked.

"I guess so," Landis replied.

"How about you, Mr. Haller?"

"I can handle it," he said without hesitation.

"Okay, follow me."

Dr. Meune, the aging coroner for LA County, led them into

the abattoir. It was cold, and the smell was extraordinary, a weird combination of death and Lysol. He walked up to one of the drawers that were built into the wall, pressed a release on the handle, and slid it open.

The stench was horrible, like bad meat, and Landis fought his gag reflex. The faint scent of the deodorizing agent, which Landis now noticed was coming from the air vents, did little to off-set the pungent smell of the corpse. Their hot breath in the chilly room made fog clouds that hung for a moment before dissipating. In that moment Landis was reminded that the tiny clouds were a sign of life, and that no such mist issued from the customers here.

The stainless steel drawer slid out noiselessly; it was well-made and terribly efficient. Landis noticed the intense look on Buzzy's face. His keen interest in the business of dead bodies was beyond what he needed to research the movie. That thought gave Landis pause. A chill shivered through him.

The body bag was dark brown and zippered. The coroner gave them a last glance and pulled it down. The whine of the zipper cut the frigid air like a dentist's drill. "Here's one of our recent patients."

"Patients," Landis said. *That's funny*, he thought.

"As you can see, this man was the victim of a rather nasty automobile accident. I haven't examined him yet, but I suspect that he died from that massive head trauma."

He pointed to the side of the man's skull. It was caved in, as if somebody had smashed him with a baseball bat. Just above the left eye there was an indentation the size of a grapefruit. White bone peeked through the mass of blood and gray matter. His eyes were open. Landis saw that they looked dry and flat. A slight dry film had formed over them, and they stared up at the ceiling blankly.

Nobody said anything. They just stared at the corpse for a few minutes, then the coroner zipped the bag back up and slid it into the wall.

"You know, I did some acting back in high school," the coroner said. The fact that they were in the presence of death many times over did nothing to lessen this man's dedication to the theatrical arts. The possibility of being in a movie had so titillated him that he spoke of nothing else from that point on.

"I could see that, from the self-assured manner in which you carried yourself," said Landis in a parody of thespian diplomacy.

Buzzy raised an eyebrow. He was interested to see how Landis would handle the coroner's dreams of stardom.

"I would like to hear you read, if you don't mind," Landis said, feigning interest.

"Of course, of course," came the reply.

Landis walked out of the room, leaving Buzzy and the coroner alone. The doctor looked at Buzzy and smiled uncomfortably. "This place is neat," Buzzy said. "I really liked that dead body you showed us."

The coroner nodded, glanced at the door through which Landis had disappeared, and coughed. Realizing that Landis would not return immediately, he decided to engage in conversation with Buzzy. "What do you do?" he asked.

"I make monsters." Buzzy grinned.

The coroner attempted another smile, this one even weaker than the last. "Oh, I see."

"For the movies," Buzzy added. "I do the special effects."

"Oh!" the coroner exclaimed, finally understanding.

"You didn't think I made real monsters, did you?"

"Of course not," he replied nervously. "Where did Mr. Woodley go?"

Buzzy shrugged. "He goes wherever he wants."

The room was still.

"Could I see another body?" Buzzy asked, his eyes twinkling like fireflies.

The coroner gave Buzzy a look of consternation; part irritation, part curiosity. Showing them the first body had been a scare tactic, designed to impress the filmmakers. It was something that the coroner did with visitors, a little reminder that they were in his world, the world of corpses. Now, the monster maker wanted to see more. It was not normal.

"There's a girl, she just came in this morning. Nice lookin', too."

Buzzy began to nod vigorously.

"Well, since you're with the movie and all, I suppose it wouldn't hurt. It ain't like she's gonna complain."

They both laughed nervously. The cold air bristled with electricity, Buzzy obviously as excited as Dr. Meune. The coroner looked around and said, "She's in twenty-two. Come on, I'll let you have a little peek."

They walked toward the locker, ten strides from where they were, and Meune put his hand on the handle.

"I should tell you. Sometimes, we get some interesting cases. Young girls, murder victims usually, their bodies are in real good shape. We get a lot of prostitutes here."

He twisted the handle and jerked the drawer open.

"This one's in excellent condition, no outward signs of trauma."

He let the drawer slide almost into Buzzy's groin. In a peculiar motion he flipped the sheet down, revealing her naked body.

"No bag?" Buzzy asked.

The coroner looked up. "She's fresh, just came in. We don't bag 'em till they're ripe."

Buzzy whistled. "Jeez, she's, like, I don't know, like dead."

"Yes," the doctor sighed. "So young and beautiful, too. Cause of death? I'll find out soon. I can tell you from experience, they can't hide from me. I see it all, inside and out." He paused and looked into Buzzy's eyes. "If you know what I mean."

Buzzy swallowed, his throat dry. "Yeah," he whispered. "I can only imagine. It must be pretty intense."

"It is," Meune agreed. "This one's, I don't know, kind of nice, actually."

"Yeah, she's real nice," Buzzy replied. "Better than that other guy we saw. Shit, if I had my choice of which one I had to work on . . . well, no contest."

Meune smiled. "That's why I love being the boss."

They turned back to the girl, her pale skin nearly the same color as the sheet. "Nice figure, too," Meune whispered. "Too bad she's dead."

Buzzy's hand reached out toward the girl's naked torso, hovering inches above her chest. "May I?" he asked. Meune nodded, admiring the man's nerve. He understood the compulsion.

Buzzy lightly touched her breast; the cold, dead skin excited him.

The doctor was about to comment when Landis reentered the room carrying a script. He handed it to a surprised Dr. Meune.

"Here, read this for me," he said loudly, slightly out of breath. "It's the role of the coroner; I thought you might be perfect for it."

The coroner smiled. He scanned the pages while Landis and Buzzy lit cigarettes.

Fifteen minutes later they had Dr. Meune out in the parking lot fighting off imaginary zombies. Landis pronounced him a great actor and promised him the role of the coroner in *Cadaver* after five minutes of "emoting" under the hot California sun.

People really would do anything for a chance to act in a movie, even a Landis Woodley production.

Landis and Buzzy drove away laughing, convinced that the location alone was going to make *Cadaver* a hit. Landis was having a cast meeting at his house, and it was his experience that Jonathon Luboff should be picked up several hours before and watched like a hawk to avoid any unpleasant drug situations. That job was Landis's alone—he trusted no one.

He drove to Luboff's apartment, successfully surprising the old man before he'd had a chance to have his afternoon fix.

Albert Beaumond's mental condition continued to deteriorate, manifesting itself with worsening hallucinations. He woke up screaming hourly, giving Thora nightmares of her own.

The demon talked to Albert in his dreams.

"I'm coming," it said. "I am coming to destroy your world."

"But why?" Albert pleaded. "I have worshiped you. I have glorified your name, Lucifer."

The snake hissed. The forked tongue flickered. "Because I can, you puny, idiotic fool."

Albert watched the reptile head twist and rotate unnaturally on its human body. The shocking metamorphosis of man to serpent jarred Albert's fragile senses every time he focused on it. The only adjective that could possibly describe it was "unGodly."

The snake-headed abomination pointed at him. "Man is done," it spit. "To destroy him is to destroy the work of God, which gives me great pleasure. I will use *you*, little man. I have waited for you all these centuries. Now, at last, you have released me to my destiny."

"God exists?" Albert asked.

The snake head pivoted, its terrible, lidless eyes moving coldly in the oversize sockets. It took in the room constantly, always aware of change or movement. "You are more of a fool than I thought," it said.

Albert strained at the confines of his dreams like a man tied to a rack. Good and evil were abstract ideas that man had created to explain his own compulsions. *Weren't they?*

Wasn't that the whole point?

Do what thou wilt shall be the extent of the law.

Was the black widow spider evil for devouring her mate? Albert's whole world had been based on the answer to that question's being "no."

"Evil is everywhere," said the snake. "Nature is full of evil."

Thora entered the room. Even though Albert was deep in his drug-induced sleep, he was aware of her. So was the demon. It let a series of thoughts, too horrible for Albert to comprehend fully, pass into his mind.

Albert shuddered, revulsion leaving a taste of bile in his mouth. He realized that since his possession, he was linked psychically with the demonic entity. The door between the two worlds somehow passed through him.

He realized, with cold certainty, that the demon wanted Thora's young female body. It was only a matter of time before it possessed her as it did him.

The afternoon was fading into evening. Thora, about to leave for her night class, checked on her father, who seemed to be sleeping quietly.

She slipped back out of the room and descended the stairs. The house was still. A clock ticked in the hall, creating a melancholy ambience. The door to her father's studio was locked; she couldn't seriously bring herself to call it a church.

She knew he was the head of an esoteric cult that practiced odd and primitive rituals, but what he did wasn't *evil*. His Satanic practices were merely an attempt to gain insight into non-Christian theologies.

Thora was in the act of opening the front door when she was startled by a figure standing on her porch.

"Oh! You scared me!" she said.

"I came to see if your father was all right," said Devila.

Devila was not dressed in her costume. She wore a simple dark skirt and blouse. Even without her makeup, Devila's distinctive face was easily recognizable by the college student.

Thora looked down, her posture changed, and from the shift in her body language, it was clear that Albert Beaumond was far from all right.

"He's . . . sleeping," Thora said, faltering.

"Oh, I thought maybe I'd visit him."

"Well, I'm about to go to school, but I'm sure he'd love to see you when he wakes up. Would you like to come in and wait?"

Devila smiled, appearing embarrassed at Thora's childlike trust in a woman she barely knew. "I don't know . . ."

Thora took her arm and gently pulled her through the door. "Don't be silly. Please, come in. I think you might be able to cheer him up or something. I'm really worried about him, I mean, really, really worried. I've never seen him like this. The doctor says he's having a nervous breakdown, but that can't be true, can it? My father is one of the strongest men in the world."

Devila glanced up the stairs in the direction of Albert's room. "I don't know," she stammered again.

"He's a brilliant man. Nothing ever bothers him. This just doesn't make any sense."

Thora's tiny voice quivered as she went about her act of trying to convince herself that nothing was wrong. "You know what I think?"

Devila shook her head.

"I think he got something down there in South America. I think he contracted some virus or other, and it's affecting his brain."

"That's possible," Devila replied.

"Won't you stay and wait for him to wake up? I hate to leave him alone, and I know he'd like to see you. It would mean a lot. Please?"

"I don't know; it's not right to be here when you're not and he's sleeping."

Thora held up her books. "Look, it's getting late, and I have to go. Please stay. There's stuff to eat and drink in the refrigerator. I'll be back in three hours. Dad's up in his room. Why don't you go on up?"

Devila smiled. "If you insist, but I feel weird."

"Don't. Stay a while, please. I know he would want that."

Thora checked her watch and sighed. "I gotta go." She walked out the door before Devila could respond.

Devila stood in the living room, her heart beating rapidly, listening to the house. She looked at the arch-topped, Medieval-style door to Albert's "church," standing like a heavy wooden barricade between this world and the next.

As if in a dream, she was across the room and had her hand on the wrought-iron lever before she realized what she was doing. Whatever force was driving her tried to unlatch it.

Of course, it had to be locked, she thought. The tuning forks were probably still in there. Standing at the threshold for another few, time-distorted moments, she thought about the man upstairs. What had happened to him? Was he truly insane now? It was easy for her to believe that, having seen Albert's possession by the snake demon. An experience like that would be more than enough to drive any man permanently mad.

Certainly Albert was suffering.

Devila hadn't actually planned on physically taking the tuning forks with her today. She'd wanted to just check out the situation. But now that the opportunity presented itself, it seemed like destiny. Even though she was terrified by the forks and didn't even want to touch them, she knew the value of the cursed things. Greed motivated her.

She looked around the room and wondered where the key to the door was. *Probably right here,* she thought. Her eyes scanned the ornate molding around the door. Above was a small shelf, ideal for hiding the key, and she ran her hand across it until it stopped at a small protrusion. She pulled it down and looked at it. It was an old-style key, long and cylindrical.

She weighed it in her sweaty hand, asking herself one last time if she had the stomach for what she planned, then she fitted the key in the large hole and turned it.

The click was loud and disconcerting.

The door was heavy but swung cleanly. She entered the room

cautiously. It was colder than it should have been, noticeably cooler than the rest of the house.

She switched on the lights.

The place seethed with the memory of the demon, and she prayed silently as she approached the altar.

Something jumped across her path and startled her. She cried out. The huge black cat, Mephistopheles, hopped onto the altar and hissed.

She tried to shoo it away, but the cat stood its ground.

"I don't have time for this," she said.

The cat hissed again. Devila looked around at the ritual objects strewn about the room. She picked up a wooden staff and waved it. "Get the fuck off that altar, or I'll knock you off, you stupid cat."

The cat jumped away, back into the shadows.

"That's a good kitty."

Her hands were tight and stiff as she pulled away the tapestry that concealed the hiding place.

It was a small compartment, hardly bigger than a bread box, built into the wall, without a locking door handle. Without thinking, she opened it and felt inside. The forks were there, wrapped in a towel, lying on their sides like pieces of pipe.

She lifted them out carefully, closed the small door, and, holding them away from her body, carried them out of the room.

Her skin crawled and her heart pounded. The dryness in her mouth was affecting her breathing. She wheezed and tried to swallow, but only about half a lungful of musty air passed her constricted throat. She walked directly to the front door, then remembered that she had to reclose the door and return the lock to its original position. She turned back reluctantly.

The forks were heavier than she'd imagined, substantial and hard beneath the white cotton towel. Even through the layers of cloth she could feel the power of evil in them as they shifted in her grip. They were so heavy that she had to resort to cradling them against her body like a baby. The thought of them touching her in that maternal way made her nauseous. They radiated an almost imperceptible tingle, as if they were vibrating among themselves. It made uncomfortable the flesh of her arms, like a low-level electrical shock.

She walked as quickly as she could, closed the door, replaced the key, and—

—a moan from above made her jump. It rose to a shriek and shocked a double shot of adrenaline through her veins. It pumped through her like amphetamine, instantly and without warning.

She froze as the second shriek cut the air from the direction of the stairs. All the hair on her body bristled, and she felt a numbness in her legs. The adrenaline was now a metallic taste in her mouth.

It's Albert, she thought. *It's poor Albert up there losing his mind. And me with the tuning forks. Jesus Christ, what am I doing?*

It was the pain in Albert's voice that made her change her mind about running. It sounded so pathetic, so tortured.

She hesitantly approached the steps and listened for signs of consciousness from his room.

Taking a few steps up, she realized there was another sound coming from up there, a ragged, tortured breathing that was audible even above the pounding of her heart.

Leave. Get out now. Run. Don't look back.

No. Devila still had an ounce of humanity left inside her; that, and a jigger of curiosity.

It sounded as if he was dying in there. She couldn't leave him just yet.

I'll just peek in and call an ambulance, she thought, *then get the hell out. It's the least I can do for him, poor soul. He needs some kind of help.*

She mounted the stairs and walked carefully to his door, the tuning forks still in her arms.

As her line of vision swept into room, she saw the outline of his legs, still and tightly defined against the white cotton sheets. Her eyes traveled up his torso and saw that he appeared to be sitting up.

She considered putting the forks down but decided against it until she could ascertain whether he was asleep or not. It was hard enough picking those awful things up once. She might not be able to force her hands to do it a second time. If she needed to, she could always put them against the wall by the door, out of sight.

Holding them back, away from him, she slid into the room sideways, her face first.

"Albert?" she said softly. "Albert, are you awake?"

Farther into the room, now, and very tense, she came. She saw an arm move. Was he awake?

"Albert?" Her voice came up in volume slightly. "Albert? Are you awake, dear?"

She stepped around the corner of the door and looked directly at him.

Her scream rang out through the empty house like the sound of breaking glass. Albert's head was gone. In its place was the snake's sinuous gray neck, tapered head, and blunt snout, from which the ropish tongue flicked.

The demon's flat eyes followed her movement ominously. She stepped back, her mouth open, the sounds of shock coming from her throat. Her legs tangled up in themselves, and she stumbled backward.

The neck snapped and the jaws opened. It happened so fast that Devila didn't have time to react. A baseball-sized globule shot from the snake's mouth and whizzed by Devila's head.

It landed with a splat on the wall behind her.

What?

There was a fleck of wetness on the back of her hand.

It's spitting at me. It's spitting, and it would have hit me if I hadn't stumbled just then.

The thing was deadly accurate . . . a spitting viper.

She fell into the hall and scrambled to her feet. Her hand was beginning to throb, and the thought occurred to her that the spittle was acid. A few seconds later it was burning like hell.

She wiped it frantically on her shirt, but the tingling only worsened. She ran down the stairs, paying close attention to her feet so she wouldn't fall, and found the kitchen sink. The cold water helped a little, but she began to feel a numbness around the fiery spot on her hand. Then she couldn't feel the water. Ironically, she still cradled the tuning forks like a baby in her arms even though her hand was throbbing.

Tears erupted from her eyes and streamed down her face. She began to tremble. *Was it the fear or the poison?*

God help me, she thought, *the thing spit at me, and it's poison. If I hadn't stumbled, I'd be dead. Get out of the house now,* she told herself. *Get out and don't look back.*

13

The rehearsals were excellent. Jonathon Luboff crawled out of his shell and delivered his usual professional character study. His eyes broadcast pain that was almost unbearable to watch. Landis knew that it was those eyes that would sell the role he was playing; so dark and strangely compelling.

Tad Kingston gave Neil's inspired script a one-dimensional reading. He looked good in his makeup, hit all his marks, and kept his hair from upstaging him—a serviceable performance by Tad's standards.

The interior shots, now being done at Landis's house, were easy to block, and Buzzy worked as they went along. He'd enlisted the aid of two of his beatnik friends to play cadavers, promising them both a screen credit and a few reefers. They agreed readily. It was a kick to dress up and scare people, they told him. "Tell me something I don't already know," he had said in reply.

The day flew by. Landis directed the action, and everything seemed orderly and dignified. No wild party today. When Landis worked, he was a man possessed. There was too much work to do for anyone to be falling behind the pace. Landis planned on completing twenty to thirty shots a day, an unheard-of pace, even among the B-movie miracle men. It allowed for precious few second takes, so Landis liked to have his actors well rehearsed and prepared to jump into any scene at any time.

Landis let most mistakes go; he was too cheap to repair the damage. Why fix something that most people would miss anyway? Luboff's accent washed everything he said in a general European mishmash that most American teenagers just took as additional shtick. Horror movies didn't have to make sense—they just had to scare you.

Jonathon Luboff was beyond caring. The demons inside him were all too real, the pain in his soul far deeper than mere acting. Jonathon shrugged it all off. He was emoting with his essence, portraying pure pain that transcended the role he played.

His own life was a horror show; what was role-playing to others was truth to him. He was the reflection of his own misery.

When it came time to deliver, Luboff was flawless. Under the watchful eye of Landis, he kept his drug use controlled and memorized his lines. A lifetime of experience carried him through difficult times that would have destroyed lesser men. Jonathon Luboff was made of steel in some regards. Landis marveled at his tenacity to keep working, to keep surviving personal travails, and bend but never break under the massive weight of his sorrow.

Landis always hired the same cameraman. Chet Bronski was another Woodley special, blackballed from the rest of the film-making community by his left-wing politics—he was a zealous socialist in an era where that sort of thing could ruin your career. Brought before the House Un-American Activities Committee, he told them all to go straight to hell. Consequently, he stopped being hired by every production unit in a Hollywood driven to extremes by paranoia. Landis Woodley liked Chet Bronski and hired him to shoot all his films, although lately he'd talked him into working under an assumed name, Chet Lens.

Chet mapped out the camera angles and made notes on the lighting for each scene. Landis was over his shoulder every inch of the way, shouting and directing the movement of people and props.

He smiled when, near the end of the afternoon, he realized that *Cadaver* was ready to shoot.

What remained of Albert Beaumond stood on the stairs, looking down at the open door. Devila had been here, he knew. Even though possessed at the time, he still retained the image of her through the serpent's eyes.

He saw her screaming and watched her flee.

He had no knowledge other than that. His legs were weak, and his head throbbed. He could barely focus his eyes. Every time the serpent possessed him, it seemed to tense every muscle in his body to the point of snapping.

Albert wept. He knew that the possession had taken place *without* the tuning forks this time. That meant that the demon had complete access to reach into him, and, even more terrifying than that, it could come forward at any time. Albert's mind resisted the only thought, the only plan that made sense.

He had to save Thora from this fate.

He had to save the world.

He staggered down the steps and across the living room.

The tuning forks must be destroyed.

When he found that they were missing he became confused and even more afraid. Had the demon taken them? Had he, Albert, already hidden them and couldn't remember? Had Thora gotten rid of them?

He ruled out the Thora possibility, realizing that she had no knowledge of them or their terrible power.

Then he remembered—

—Devila!

She could have taken them! She knew their power, and she knew where they were. The thought screamed through his brain like a rocket. No! Not Devila! Albert pulled at his hair and paced the room frantically.

He had to warn her.

But the weight of derangement hung heavy across Albert's shoulders. He knew it was only a matter of time before the demon returned. He had to act now.

He stumbled to the phone and dialed Devila's number. His hands shook so violently that it took several attempts before he was successful. It rang incessantly, and Albert banged the heavy black receiver against the table in frustration.

When it became evident that Devila wasn't home, Albert staggered toward the door, consumed with thoughts of a final solution.

He walked through the open portal into the dark, swirling air, intent on distancing himself as far from his home as possible.

He walked through the streets, into the arid hills behind the houses, and disappeared into the scrub brush. Trudging along like a zombie, he tried to squeeze as much energy from his aching body before *It* came back and found him. It didn't matter where he wound up, just as long as it was far away from his house and Thora.

Landis was ready to begin filming. The cameras were in position, the lights set, the sets arranged. His house had become a dream factory now. He sat in the living room, before the massive fireplace, and closed his eyes.

Tomorrow at the crack of dawn it would begin. From all the disparate elements Landis would form a cohesive piece. The idea he envisioned, the script he nurtured along with Neil, the actors he hired, the sets he improvised from his own furniture, the monster corpses that Buzzy fashioned, the morgue, the money for the film stock, it all waited to come together. And it would, under Landis Woodley's direction.

Now, after all the planning, the moment of truth was at hand.

He rubbed his eyes and yawned. He was alone in the great, silent house. But that silence deceived, for in the darkened quiet of those rooms a thousand fears scuttled. Landis Woodley was an insecure and lonely man.

He dozed until the telephone rang. It jarred him back from the sweet release of his fatigue.

"Hello?"

A husky female voice said, "Landis? This is Devila. I have the objects."

Landis shook off the layers of sluggishness that had draped his body while he slept. He looked at the clock. It was after two. He'd been sleeping for hours.

"Devila? It's a little late for this. I start shooting tomorrow at first light," he rasped.

"I'm sorry, Landis," she said. "I hate to bother you, but this is really, *really* important. I got those objects I told you about . . . I can't keep them long. We need to film them right away."

Landis sat forward and took a few deep breaths to bring the oxygen level in his blood back up to an alert status.

"But—"

"Listen to me. I know this is an inopportune time, and I apologize for that, but the situation presented itself to me today and I seized it. Now, I can't keep these . . . these objects, I can only have them for a short while. I could get into big trouble if I'm found out. Look, I know this is nuts, but we have to film this right now, *tonight!* Otherwise, we lose out."

Landis rolled his eyes. "Aw shit, Devila, I can't do it now. I got a million things to do. I'm tryin' to get some rest before—"

"Then forget it," she snapped.

"Hold on," he said, his throat scratched and dry. "Let me think about this."

The lights were set and the cameras were loaded. If he wanted to do it, there would never be a better time. If he just wasn't so damn tired.

Landis sighed, longing for a glass of water. He said, "You sound a little distraught. Are you all right?"

"No, I'm not all right, I've just been through something that scared the shit out of—" She paused, caught her breath, then evened her voice like a rope snapped taut, and continued— "Why am I telling you this? I called you first because I thought you might be interested. Common courtesy. I can always go somewhere else with it."

Landis heard the strain in her voice and knew instinctively that the woman was scared. He could smell fear like a wolf. "Okay, cool it. I got the message. Did you see the . . . the thing?"

Devila sucked air between her teeth. "I don't want to talk about it now," she said, biting off her words.

"It's got to be tonight?"

"Yes. Look, I can be there in fifteen minutes," she said breathlessly. Landis heard a truck drive by in the background, over the phone. It rumbled through the line with a blast of white noise, drowning out everything for a few seconds.

"Where the hell are you?" he asked.

"At a phone booth," she shouted over the roar of the truck. "I can't go home."

Landis was about to ask why not when he thought better of it. He could read the situation from the information he'd already gleaned. She'd stolen the objects, and now she had to use them right away, before she got caught. It didn't take a Rhodes scholar to figure that one out.

The more his mind cleared, the more he realized that he couldn't let this opportunity pass him by. If what she said was true, it could be a piece of film that might ultimately be worth more than the whole production of *Cadaver*. He wrestled with the decision.

Devila waited. Landis heard another truck rumble by.

"Okay," he said finally, "I have some cameras up here at the house. I guess I could do it . . . are you sure we can't do this in a day or two?"

"Absolutely not. It's now or never; otherwise, I go somewhere else with it," she said, her voice quivering. The road noises crept back as soon as she stopped talking. Her voice changed again, softening. "Landis?"

"Yeah?"

"I want you to do this. You're the only one who can do it justice."

Chet Bronski was asleep. He liked to get a good ten hours in before he had to work, especially with Landis Woodley. Landis usually planned twenty to thirty shots a day. Twenty to thirty! Most feature-length movie productions thought anything over three shots a day was incredible.

When the phone rang he tried to ignore it; when it persisted, he picked it up.

"Yeah?" he growled, his voice slurred and deep.

"Chet?"

"Who the fuck is this? I'm sleepin'!"

"It's Landis."

After a moment's hesitation, a cough, and a few deep breaths, Chet responded.

"What's the problem?"

"Something's come up, something important. Can you come over right away?"

Chet coughed some more. "What the hell for? I'm sleepin', I got a big day tomorrow. You know that, for Christ sake. Why are you bothering me?"

"I need you to film something. It's a private affair, just you and me and . . . a third party. Look, I know this is a pain in the ass, but I'll pay you."

"How much?" It was the question of the day.

"How about a hundred bucks?"

"Hmm, I don't know. Shit, I gotta get out of bed, drive across town, that's a lot of work . . ."

Landis said, "One-fifty."

"I don't want to get up. Call someone else."

"Two hundred."

Chet sighed. He'd do it now, but he didn't want to. Money was money. "I'll be there in forty minutes," he said.

He slammed the phone down, swung his legs over the side of the bed, and sat up. Reaching for his pack of cigarettes by the side of the bed, he fished one out and lit it. The strong smoke of the unfiltered Chesterfield King sent shock waves through his body from the lungs out.

The first drag made him dizzy, the second made him cough, and the third got him out of bed.

What the hell was going on? Landis never called in the middle of the night like this. It must be something really special for him to shell out two hundred smackers. For a tightwad like Woodley, that bordered on unbelievable. Must be some porn, Chet thought, something kinky or weird.

Chet knew the cameras were ready and the set was lit over at Landis's house. He knew that it would be a piece of cake for him to roll film. Figuring he could probably sleep the remaining few hours of the night over there, he packed his overnight bag.

Outside, the wind picked up. The smell of rain freshened the air. There was no traffic to speak of as Chet guided his Ford down Sunset Boulevard toward Beachwood Canyon.

14

Thora Beaumond panicked when she found the front door open and her father gone.

She called Dr. Segwick at home, her fingers clumsy and numb on the heavy rotary dialer. It took several tries before she successfully made the connection. He suggested she call the police.

She contacted the night desk sergeant on duty at the North Hollywood Police Station, who transferred her over to Lt. Garth Prease in the department of missing persons.

After listening to her story, Prease explained that an adult couldn't be declared legally missing until he'd been gone for forty-eight hours. Lieutenant Prease promised to keep an unofficial eye out for her father, should anyone report a man wandering around, but there was really nothing he could do for the time being. She pleaded, insisting that her father was ill and feverish and quite likely to be disoriented. Prease took down a detailed description.

Thora found her father's address book and called everyone she thought might be helpful, each conversation more rushed and desperate than the last. In return, she received a carload of advice. Everyone did agree on one thing; Thora should not, under any circumstances, go out looking for Albert alone.

She put the address book in her pocket. What was everybody so damned afraid of?

She drove to Devila's apartment.

She knocked on the door and, after a few minutes of silence, pounded on it.

"There's no one home, dearie," a rough female voice croaked behind her. The sound made her jump.

"You scared me!" Thora said, clutching her chest.

"Sorry, my voice does that sometimes," the old lady barked hoarsely. Her gin-soaked, cigarette-rough vocal cords put out a strange combination of sounds that seemed to be indigenous to sixty-year-old Hollywood matrons. It was a smoky, sensual sound that only time and tobacco could create. Her hair in curlers and her housecoat buttoned high, she looked like a dried apple doll that Thora had made in summer camp once many years ago.

"I'm looking for Miss Devila. Have you seen her?"

"She hasn't been home since yesterday," the voice answered. "I'm Myrna; I live across the hall." She lit a cigarette and blew smoke at the ceiling. "Are you a friend of Devila's?"

"Yes. Well, actually, my father is," Thora answered. "I'm looking for him."

Myrna squinted at Thora's face, saw the lines of consternation there, and smiled. "What's the problem, sweetie?"

Thora's forehead wrinkled, and her eyes cast down. The panic of the night's searching had now turned to resigned worry and sadness.

"It's nothing," she said.

"You've been crying. What's wrong, hon?"

Thora could feel the tears welling up again, her voice got that little hitch in it that meant she was going to cry any second. "I . . . I . . . my father is missing, and I thought—"

Myrna opened the door to her apartment wider and Thora could see the blue glow of a black-and-white TV screen showing an old movie and a room crowded with bric-a-brac and memorabilia. The smell of coffee drifted out.

"How about a cup of java?" Myrna asked.

Their eyes met. Thora could do little to disguise the pain she was going through, and Myrna couldn't help but feel concerned.

"I don't know," Thora mumbled.

"Oh, sure you do. Everybody likes a nice cup of hot coffee to cheer them up. You look like you've been out all night."

"I've got to find Miss Devila," Thora begged, her face distorted with the onset of tears.

Myrna handed Thora a tissue and led her into the tiny apartment. She sat her down gently at the kitchen table as though she was leading a child, and busied herself pouring a cup of coffee and buttering an English muffin. The food and drink seemed to revive her slightly.

"I'm sorry. I should go. I shouldn't bother you," Thora said with the halting speech of someone fighting to control their emotions.

"Nonsense. You just sip that coffee and tell Myrna what's troubling you."

Thora did as she was told. The coffee, a trifle too hot, burned her mouth and throat and brought the color of life back into her cheeks.

Thora, unpracticed at holding things in, began to explain. It felt good to tell it, as if the words themselves were bearing weight and once removed let her breathe again.

"My father was very sick, he . . . he had a fever, and he wasn't himself."

Myrna nodded. "Fevers can do that, hon. Go on."

"Anyway, I had to go to class, I go to college at UCLA, and I left him alone for just a few hours. Right when I was leaving, Miss Devila showed up, said she wanted to visit my dad, so I let her in. I thought it would be a good idea, you see. They dated one time."

Myrna poured more coffee. "I see," she said.

"So, anyway, I left her alone in the house, told her to go on up and stay with him, and when I came back, he was gone."

"Both of them?"

"Yeah, both. I thought that maybe they were together, you know, maybe he felt better and they decided to go out somewhere. But he's been gone all night!"

Myrna pointed to the muffin. "Eat some."

Thora put the dry biscuit in her mouth and began to chew. Myrna watched with sad, knowing eyes.

"Well," she said, "it sounds to me like they probably went out and had a good old time and he just forgot to call, that's all."

"I don't think so. He was very sick. It doesn't make sense."

There was a knock on the back door of Myrna's apartment. She had a small door that led from the kitchen to the parking court in the back. Myrna crossed the room and opened the door. Another old lady was standing there.

"Katherine! Do come in. We've got company."

Katherine entered the room looking very much like Myrna, without the curlers. Her housecoat was pastel blue and made of the same quilted material.

"Company! Well, isn't that—" She saw the tears on Thora's face and stopped. "What's the matter, child? Did old Myrna scare you?"

"I most certainly did not!" Myrna rasped. "She came here looking for you-know-who."

"Devila? That witch? Well, it doesn't surprise me one bit. She's made more than one person cry."

Myrna was trying to signal for Katherine to shut up, but the other old woman kept right on talking.

"What do you mean?" asked Thora.

"What I mean is, that hussy has been nothin' but trouble since she moved in here."

"I don't think she wants to hear that," Myrna protested.

"Please." Thora looked at Katherine. "Please tell me."

"You might as well sit down and pour yourself a cup." Myrna sighed. "By the way, this is Thora. She's looking for her father, who didn't come home last night, after seeing our lovely neighbor. Thora, this is Katherine Schlitz. Katherine lives upstairs."

"Oh," Katherine said. "I didn't mean to—"

"What were you going to tell me about Devila?" Thora demanded.

"Well, it's just that she isn't very honest, that's all."

Thora looked from Katherine to Myrna, searching for answers, her brow furrowed.

"Go ahead, tell her. You've already tipped over the apple cart," Myrna said with resignation.

"Well, I had an Oscar statuette," Katherine said proudly, "a real one. It was for best actress in the year 1931, won by Marie Dressler. She got it for a movie called *Min and Bill,* beat out Marlene Dietrich who was red-hot that year. Marlene was up for *Morocco* or some such trash."

Thora nodded, not really understanding what all this had to do with Devila and her father. "Yes?"

"Marie Dressler was a dear old lady who lived in this very building, up in 2B. She was already ill when she won the Oscar, and she passed away a few years later. They cleaned out her apartment and her daughter gave me the statuette because she said that Marie wanted me to have it. I was close to Marie, I guess you could say. Anyway, it was great honor to have the Oscar and I kept it on my mantle for years . . . until *she* stole it!" She pointed across the hall to Devila's apartment.

"She stole it?" Thora said.

Myrna smiled. "Well, we're not positive, hon."

"I am," Katherine said firmly. "I'm sure she took it! She took it while I was making brownies one day. She just came right in and took it!"

Myrna put her hand on Thora's knee and patted it affectionately. "I thought I saw it once when she left her door open. I can't be sure, of course, but I thought I saw it in her room."

"Who else would take it?"

Myrna shot Katherine a glance. So far the effect of all her furtive looks and "shut up" glances had been nil. Katherine obviously had a mind of her own and didn't care a whit for anything Myrna was trying to tell her through body language.

Katherine sipped her coffee noisily. "She'd been coveting the thing for months, you know. I could tell she really wanted it bad. It was a real Oscar, not some kind of fake knock-off. Julia is a huge movie fan; she collects memorabilia."

"Julia?" Thora asked.

"Julia Greenly is Devila's real name; it was on the lease. It seems that nothing about her is what it appears to be, does it?"

Thora nodded, interested in Katherine's monologue, yet still polite and timid. She had never considered Devila being anything but honest and sincere. After all, the woman was a star, wasn't she?

Myrna stepped into the conversation, eager to keep it balanced and unbiased.

"Julia wouldn't ever let us into her apartment. She was very secretive, very private. The time I thought I saw the statuette was when she left the door ajar for a minute. Of course, neither one of us has ever set foot in there to know for certain. The point is, and I don't want to worry you, but neither one of us likes that woman. She's dishonest."

Katherine interrupted. The two ladies seemed to edit each other constantly as they spoke, one hardly waiting for the other to breathe before she jumped in to make a point or disagree. "And then there's all the men!"

Myrna jerked her hand up and wagged a finger at Katherine.

"I don't think Thora wants to hear about that, remember, her father was dating—"

"Yes," Thora said sharply. "Yes, I *do* want to know."

Katherine cleared her throat and sipped again at the coffee cup. Thora noticed that it was decorated with a design that said "Elvis Presley is the King." She held her little finger straight out as she drank.

"I always thought she was a little tramp, what with that costume she wears on television and those dreadful movies she shows. She has a regular harem of boyfriends, mostly deadbeats with beards and dungarees. Usually she doesn't get home until after two in the morning, probably drunk. Men call on her at all hours. Sometimes she lets them stay all night."

Myrna smiled. "Well, you can see that she has no fans here, dearie. Between that and the missing statuette, we just don't trust her."

"The brazen hussy took it," Katherine snorted. "I should have called the police."

"Why didn't you?" Thora wanted to know.

"Oh, no! We never call the police," Katherine said.

"Why not?"

The two old ladies looked at each other, a flash of guilt passed between them. Myrna sighed. "Sometimes we make our own spirits."

Thora looked confused. "Spirits?"

"Spring tonic," Myrna said. "My father's recipe."

Albert Beaumond raced through the scrub brush on all fours, scrambling up and down the dark canyons. It didn't take him long to become completely lost. The lights of LA were gone now, just a ruddy glow over the horizon from where he came. Lizards skittered through the dried shrubbery, making frantic dashes across his path.

It seemed strange that just a few hundred yards from his home, from the orderly housing tract he lived in, was the wild.

Being a city built in a desert, the limits of LA were constantly being pushed farther out into the untamed brush that surrounded it. Mountain lions and other wild animals were finding rows of suburban ranch homes where just last year they'd hunted for food.

Out here over a few canyon walls, just a stone's throw from the freeway, was another world. The animals, crowded out by man's invasion, competed for food and territory in the shrinking unspoiled land.

Albert was aware of these things as he escaped deeper and deeper into the hillsides.

His brain writhed inside his skull, as afraid and panicked as those lizards. He kept moving, placing one foot in front of the other, trying not to think about the serpent.

He had no way of knowing when it would return, and the thought terrified him. At least, if it happened now, he would be far away from Thora.

Albert Beaumond believed in God, although he had never prayed to him. All his adult life, since he'd made the big rationalization that there was no good or evil, he'd wasted his time praying to the devil. Now, in his hour of need, he found his allegiance shifting. The blackness was closing in on him, staining his life beyond redemption.

It's been said that many an atheist prayed when their plane went down. He chuckled to himself softly, aware now of the truth of that statement.

What a fool I've been, he thought. *What a steaming pile of shit I've* been to be so naive. Greed and lust for power must have corrupted my heart easier and deeper than I knew.

I fucked my own self.

And now I pay. I only hope that Thora doesn't have to pay also. The sins of the father, will they also be those of the daughter?

Albert knew it was only a matter of time before the serpent returned, and only a short time beyond that before Thora became affected.

This he knew with terrible certainty.

He also knew the only way out for him.

He was desperate now, not afraid. The difference was that he knew, when the moment came for him to consummate the decision he'd made, that he would not hesitate. He had to do what he had to do without thinking, because thinking would only cause him to balk. That would be dangerous. In that moment of uncertainty, the serpent might return, take over his body, and force him back home to Thora. How much longer did he have?

I've got to save my daughter, he thought. Nothing else matters.

He kept that idea in the front of his mind, flashing like a neon sign, guiding him.

The night passed like a freight train. Time clicked off like the tapping of the rails. Eventually, a few hours before dawn, the wind began to pick up. It blew hard now, out of the west. It felt warm and ominous, bringing the scent of the ocean to the alien desert landscape, swirling through the canyons.

Dry bushes rattled in its wake. Albert knew that soon it would begin to rain. Rain was rare in LA and he couldn't remember the last time it had fallen. Tonight the smell of it hung in the wind and raced across the dry soil with the promise of a deluge. The animals of the desert, the lizards and rodents, had noticed it long ago.

Albert staggered up one hill and down the next, disoriented and aimless, with only one thought in mind. Get away, get as far away as possible.

He felt himself growing weak from the night-long journey, but he dared not rest. As long as there was an ounce of strength in his legs, a sigh of air in his lungs, he would push on.

Give me a sign, he asked the night. A sign.

Albert huffed badly as he topped yet another canyon wall. It seemed like the hundredth one he'd scaled tonight. His legs felt rubbery. He stood, looking down as his lungs fought for oxygen. Below him spread a wide valley, part scrub, part unattended orchard. The waves of endless canyons had ended, giving way to this panorama of flatland.

He squinted in the half-light and saw that a line of high-tension power lines bisected the valley neatly down the center. They marched like silent, unmoving alien robots, through the heart of the flatland and up into the next set of hills.

Through the center of the valley, at the lowest point, ran a dry creek bed. Its lower half was rimmed with concrete, forming a conduit for the infrequent runoff. *Flood control,* thought Albert. *It probably runs south into the Los Angeles River.*

The Los Angeles River seemed a grossly misleading bit of nomenclature. It was more like a big drainage ditch. The merest trickle of water ran through its cement course, not much more than a labyrinth of sewers and underground water pipe. The once-proud river had been, sadly, tamed by man. Its passage set, it now led a docile, schizophrenic life. Following its predestined route meekly, to flow like a piss stream of warm yellow water searching for the sea.

Until the rains came. Then it became a monster.

The power lines followed its meandering route through this particular valley, as yet unmarred by the urban sprawl.

Albert blinked, rubbed his eyes, and began shambling down the slope, toward the creek bed. The wind whipped up dust devils, and the abrasive sand assaulted his face. The sun made orange the eastern hillside.

The first raindrops began to fall.

15

Chet Bronski arrived at Landis Woodley's house at three-fifteen in the morning, demanding coffee and complaining that he'd been inconvenienced.

Landis met him at the door and ushered him into the huge living room, where he was surprised to find Devila in full costume and makeup, sitting demurely on the sofa.

"Thanks for comin', Chet," Landis said. "I really appreciate it. Have you met Devila?"

Devila stood, and they approached each other. She extended a waxen hand, and he shook it gently. "Of course, Devila, the horror show host. I never miss you, unless I'm working," Chet replied, smiling through his fatigue.

Devila didn't smile back, and Chet could see that she was very tense. His curiosity ran wild.

"So," he said. "What's the big deal to get me out of bed in the middle of the night? I must say, I'm intrigued." He looked at the two of them and caught the strange vibrations in the room. "Actually, I'm dying to know."

Landis stepped forward, his face emerging into the full light of the overhead chandelier. His expression seemed odd, as if Landis himself was unsure what would happen next.

"Chet, Devila has something quite astounding that she wants us to film," Landis explained. "It's something . . . supernatural."

"What is this, a joke?" He looked Landis in the eye and shook his head. "You want me to film a ghost?"

"Not exactly," Landis replied. "It's more like . . . like a demon."

Devila sliced into their conversation like a razor-sharp butcher knife. "The fact is, it *is* a demon, with the head of a snake."

Chet smiled. "What kinda dope are you guys on? You called me out of bed at this hour to film a demon with the head of a snake? You're out of your minds."

Devila shook her long black hair, swinging it out from her face. It was a haughty gesture, one she used all the time.

"Listen, I know this sounds nuts, but I can really conjure this thing. I've seen it with my own eyes. This will be the first time ever, in the history of filmmaking, that a real live demon has been photographed. It's the opportunity of a lifetime. You'll be famous as the man who shot the first bona fide supernatural phenomenon. If all goes well tonight, the footage that we get will change the world and make us all rich."

"And what if you're wrong?" Chet sneered.

"Then you can hate me," Devila answered softly, her conviction plain for all to see and hear.

Landis lit a cigar. "What do you care? You're gettin' paid, Chet."

"All right, it's your money. When do we start?"

Landis smiled. "Just as soon as José makes the coffee."

"José makes coffee?"

"The best in the West," Landis answered proudly. "Not bad for a gardener, huh?"

Just then, José entered the room with a steaming, aromatic pot of coffee and three mugs. Without being told, he poured and distributed the steaming cups of brew. He disappeared back into the kitchen.

"Pretty convenient having your gardener, who doubles as a

cook, live on the premises," Landis bragged. "He has a room above the garage and it only costs me a few bucks a month. The only problem is that he hardly speaks English."

"Shall we get started?" Chet asked, his eyes resting on Devila.

It was evident that she was growing more nervous by the minute. She bit her fingernails and wrinkled her brow. "Okay," she said. "I'll need a fairly big area."

"The basement projection room is already lit. We're using it first thing in the morning," said Landis. "Let's go down there."

They trooped down the stairs single file and made their way back to the projection room, which was all the way in the back of the building. The lights were already set up for the morning shoot. Chet made a few adjustments, and Devila unwrapped the tuning forks.

"Do you need anything special?" Landis asked.

"You know," Devila responded, "this is gonna sound weird, but I think I need someone to stand in for me."

"Stand in?"

"Yeah, to act as a . . . a host, sort of."

"You mean for the demon?" Chet asked.

"That's right. I think it might be necessary," she answered.

"You think? Don't you know?" Landis asked incredulously.

"I've only seen the ceremony once, and I'm pretty sure that it requires a host," she said.

Chet and Landis exchanged quick looks. Chet scratched his head and said, "You mean, you want somebody to play host to a demon while I film it?"

She nodded.

"You're crazy. I'm goin' home."

Landis grabbed Chet's arm, "Hey, give it a chance, man. I'm payin' cash, remember?"

"Where are you going to get a host?" Chet asked, suppressing a yawn. "You and me certainly ain't gonna do it, and Devila is—you know, the star, so—"

Landis looked back toward the steps.

"José!" he shouted, "José, could you come down here please?"

Devila's face was frozen in a mask of guilt. No one spoke as the slow, unsuspecting Mexican entered the room.

* * *

The buzzing sound was louder than the wind. It was alive, crackling with intensity, and came from the hundred-foot-high tension tower. Albert's eyes followed the Erector Set-style girders up until he saw a flash.

A power line had been blown loose and had wrapped itself around the crisscrossed metal beams about two-thirds of the way up. The live end dangled in the stiff winds, occasionally knocking against another cable. Each time they touched it emitted a shower of sparks and a loud zapping sound. The buzzing hummed like a swarm of angry bees, punctuated by the intermittent and explosive-sounding zap. Albert stood at the foot of the tower and stared heavenward.

The idea came to him with a clarity of thought he hadn't enjoyed for days. He made an instant decision.

A few raindrops fell in scattered flurries around him, lightly touching his face in a random pattern. The smell of the impending storm filled his nostrils with a musty bouquet, a smell that he knew and liked, but could never figure out where it came from. It was like the aroma of wet concrete, or maybe like moist dust, and it brought back pleasurable boyhood memories.

Memories.

They came flooding now, as if the door, unlocked by the scent of the storm, had now been kicked open forcefully.

Instinctively, Albert began to think about his life. It seemed to be passing in review behind his sunken eyes now, and he relived the pleasures and pains in a daze for several minutes. A spectator in his own world, he wondered about events, and his reactions to them, long past. What a cruel twist of fate for him to end up here; life could be so strange.

He had asked for a sign.

Now that sign loomed above him with unmistakable, irrefutable gravity. The strobe flashing of the hot cable hypnotized him, canceling out all other thoughts. With a Zen-like single-mindedness, he put his hand on the cold, rusted first rung of the ladder that ran up the base of the giant structure, and began to climb. He never took his eyes off the sharp brightness of the intermittent blue arc high above.

* * *

Landis insisted on writing a short script. "You can't shoot film without a script. It just isn't done," he said.

"Aw, who cares," Chet replied. "It's a waste of time. Let's just shoot the damn film and go home, okay?"

Landis made them both wait while he dashed up to his office and banged out the few pages he thought were necessary.

Fifteen minutes later, Devila had learned her lines and stood poised for her appearance.

Landis told José to sit in a high-backed wooden chair amid the brightest of the lights. He did what he was told, of course, uncomplaining and happy to be working.

Landis had allowed José to bring his wife up from Mexico, and even though they were both unregistered aliens, and therefore illegal, he found work for them. Maria did housework and laundry, José took care of the gardening and odd jobs. When it came to cooking, José would not let Maria near the kitchen. That should only be a man's sacred domain, he told her.

Landis had recently noticed that Maria was pregnant, and said nothing.

José sat patiently while Chet aimed the lights and fussed with the camera. At last, Devila was ready, and Landis called for quiet on the set.

"Devila, baby, I want to do this in one take, do you understand that? If you make a mistake, just keep going, we'll fix it in editing," Landis told her.

"Landis," she answered, "there's only gonna *be* one take, just make sure everything's running, 'cause what you're gonna see, you won't believe. We're about to make history."

Landis relit his cigar, checked his watch, and waved his hand in the air. José began to rise from the chair, but Landis pushed him back down in it. He looked up inquisitively at the filmmaker, then shrugged and sat back, content to be on camera or not, whatever Landis wanted. José didn't care. A smile crossed his lips when he realized that he would be on film, even though he hadn't the slightest idea why.

Devila took a fingertip of ashes from her cigarette and marked his forehead.

"Okay," Landis shouted. "Here we go! Camera! Sound!

Slate—Devila, take one—produced, written, and directed by Landis Woodley, filmed by Chet Bronski."

"Speed!" shouted Chet back at him.

"Annnnnnd, ACTION!"

Devila took a deep breath, tried to calm her shaky nerves, and looked into the lens. She was a professional, and she knew how to conduct herself in front of the camera, but the thought of seeing the snake demon again made her heart pound wildly.

Landis nodded and Devila began to speak. The mechanical whirring of the camera seemed loud at first, then, in a few seconds, faded from consciousness as if it didn't exist. *Funny how that is,* she thought. *There's no limit to what a body can get used to.*

Devila flashed a cruel, cinematic smile, her trademark, then let her face settle into an impassive mask, as cold and distant as the shores of Antarctica.

"Hello, I am Devila, queen of your nightmares. Tonight, I invite you on a great journey, a journey into the unknown."

Chet checked the film, made sure the Nagra tape recorder was running, too, then nodded to Landis who, in turn, nodded to Devila, who continued her monologue.

"What you are about to see is absolutely real. It is being filmed live, before our cameras, as it happens. There are no special effects or camera tricks. This is really happening. You will be shocked, horrified, maybe even sickened by it. It changes everything you have ever been taught about God and the church, about monsters, about what is real and what is illusion. But, make no mistake, what you are about to witness is evil, and it is submitted to you without judgment or opinion. That, my dear viewer, is up to you."

She paused, let that sink in, then continued. The camera panned out to reveal José sitting nervously in the background. Devila's ghoulish dress, tattered and revealing, played to the camera shamelessly. Her tiny waist seemed impossible. It was cinched up so tightly with a wide belt, which made it appear so small on screen, that you could put your hands around it. Her cleavage heaved and quivered, diverting attention from her face and her words. Chet got it all.

"Are you ready? Okay, let's begin. I am now going to conjure the supernatural entity. Remember, this is not a trick. The demon you are about to see materialize out of thin air is real. I want you to watch closely. This is the first time in the history of filmmaking that anything supernatural, anything beyond the reach of science and logic, has been captured on film."

She stepped back to a small table, on which rested the tuning forks.

Without explanation, for, in fact, she could not offer one, she hung the two, oddly sized tuning forks from a freestanding floor lamp. U-shaped, they appeared to Landis to be a set of polished silver bars, reflecting the lights sharply.

She struck the first fork, the larger of the two, the same one that she had watched Albert strike first. It hummed and vibrated, warming her ears strangely. The note seemed to sustain forever, suspended in the still air of the projection room.

From the moment the note was struck, Landis felt an uneasiness. Something in the low, mournful timbre of the note made his heartbeat accelerate. He felt a tightness in his chest and a tremble in his breath. He was watching, hoping that what Devila said was going to happen, actually *would* happen, but he was also uncharacteristically fearful. What was it that made the sound of the note so unsettling?

Devila struck the second tuning fork. The note it made was higher than the first, and wildly dissonant. Then, the peculiar oscillations began, slowly at first, but then faster, changing without any discernible pattern. It was the randomness of the dissonant notes, pushing and pulling against each other, that really put Landis's nerves on edge. He felt his teeth grind.

The notes had the same effect as a scratching fingernail, slowly wending its way across a dry chalkboard. It set the hair on the back of his neck straight up. Landis was not alone in his discomfort; all the people in the room: Devila, Chet, José and Landis, were affected. It was as if the air in the room had suddenly become unbreathable with anxiety.

The forks began to blur. They vibrated so vigorously and interacted to such an extent that they appeared to lose all visual definition.

Was all this going to film? Landis glanced at Chet.

The cameraman squinted through his viewfinder, sweat beading up on his brow. The alien atmosphere created by the dissonance was palpable; it prickled at their skin like thousands of tiny needles. None of them had ever felt anything even remotely like it. Fear lived in this atmosphere—it was the haunt of something evil.

For the first time, Landis wondered if he was making a big mistake. Danger had never been a factor, yet now he began to consider the possibility that what they were doing was terribly wrong.

Landis kept his eye on Devila, the expression on her face a mixture of dread and triumph. She knew that something impossible was about to happen. Time hung suspended. Indeed, all the rules of nature seemed to be suspended. Landis felt the pangs of panic begin to pierce the thin veneer of his control. Things were getting weird fast.

José squirmed in his chair, as uncomfortable and scared as a cornered ferret.

Landis kept checking to see that Chet was rolling film, although he knew that the strangeness that permeated the air in this room could never be captured on film. The oppressive, evil feeling of impending doom bore down on them like heavy smoke.

Then came the smell. A sewer stench assailed Landis's nostrils, then disappeared as he tried to locate it again, as if a door had opened and quickly closed. Landis tried to identify it, but couldn't.

The atmospheric pressure seemed to skyrocket, making it hard to breathe for a moment, worrying Landis further. What had he unleashed here in his own house?

Devila stared at the space in front of her. The air there began to change. It undulated like heat waves, distorting the images of things behind it.

They all saw it.

It was the first manifestation of the supernatural. Chet swung his camera in on the phenomenon, zooming in, trying to obtain a close-up of the rippling air in the center of the room.

"Behold!" Devila said in a choked, halting voice, striving for maximum dramatic impact.

"Behold the first sign," she said louder, gaining fresh confidence from her focus. Landis admired her professionalism, hanging in there in an increasingly hostile and malevolent environment.

This woman must be made of stone, he thought, *and she's a natural ham. What a combination.*

The air continued to pulsate, becoming more agitated with every passing second. The very molecules, it seemed, were excited, angry even, and couldn't control themselves. Like unstable heat waves, they shimmered within the influence of the ringing forks, tearing a hole in reality.

The sound of the vibration rang in their inner ears as if they'd been temporarily struck deaf. It was simply too much for the delicate human eardrum to cope with. Landis clamped his hands over his ears, but the sound carried right through the flesh and bone.

Coupled with the air distortion, it made all of them slightly dizzy and nauseous.

Then something began to materialize from the distortion. Chet dollied in for a better shot, realizing it was now "showtime," and he'd better not miss a single second of this.

A huge serpent's head appeared in the disturbance. Behind it, in a tangle, were its scaly coils, sleek and powerful with rippling, inhuman muscles. It writhed, tying and untying itself into iridescent, snake-flesh pretzels.

"Jesus," Chet muttered, but kept his camera focused and running.

The serpent's head wavered for a moment, its eyes flickering around the room, studying the occupants. José stood up, terrified, and screamed.

The snake's unlidded, wet, reptilian eyes immediately shot across the room to José and locked on him. José screamed again and backed up against the chair he'd been sitting in. He tumbled, falling backward onto the chair and collapsing in a tangle of arms and legs.

The snake's forked tongue flashed out, testing the atmosphere. It tasted their fear as a sweet, familiar odor carried by the moisture in the air. The odor came from their skin, from every pore, and they stank of it. The cablelike tongue lapped at the flooding mortal emotion, anxious to drink in all the delicious fear it could.

Then, with a whiplike movement faster than the eye could follow, it mounted itself, not on the hapless Mexican, but on the sinuous body of Devila.

The coils wrapped around her pale skin, pinning her arms at her side, then seemed to melt into her. The serpent became her. With a loud snap that sounded like the jaws of death clamping shut, it displaced her pate with its own.

Landis yelped, shocked beyond reason, yet fascinated by the most unimaginable sight he'd ever seen. The look of mind-numbing fear on Devila's face a split second before the demon encircled her, when she knew what was going to happen, was the darkest thing he'd ever seen. That look, even though it lasted only a fraction of a second, would be carried in his memory the rest of his life. It sent an electric current of horror through him that connected with the essence of his soul.

Landis, in a lifetime of trying to scare people, would draw continually on that moment and try to recreate the terror of that unexpected turn of events. But he would never even get close to the flash of hell in Devila's eyes as her face was replaced by the serpent's smooth, glistening countenance. Landis stood up and moved away. He could hear himself breathing like a wild animal, air coming in great ragged gulps, his heart hammering out of control.

"Holy shit!" he shouted. "Are you gettin' this?" he asked Chet.

"I don't believe it, but I'm gettin' it!" Chet shouted back, his voice cracking like a frightened schoolboy's.

The snake thing, attached now to Devila's slender body, turned, pivoting, and looked around the room. The camera followed its every move.

The tongue flickered. The eyes registered. The serpent took in the information from every sense.

Something excited it, made it keep rechecking the surroundings. The head swiveled and the beady black eyes swept the room again and again.

Something was different this time.

No fire.

There was no ring of fire!

These stupid humans had summoned it without the security

of the wall of flame that kept the demon contained. What could they be thinking?

No matter. The serpent was overjoyed to be, at last, after centuries of containment, free.

Devila's body jerked spasmodically, her skin crawled. Her silent scream filled the air.

16

Albert Beaumond looked up. The electric flash of the damaged power line appeared as a shower of heavenly sparks, raining down on him as divine inspiration. He climbed toward it, oblivious to the cold, unyielding surface of the metal girders. He clung to them like a spider to its silken web, working his way up the maintenance ladder, hand over hand, rung by rung.

The wind was intense now, and it threatened to blow him off the structure in wrathful gusts. But Albert would not be distracted; he stayed his course.

He could see that the dangling cable was wrapped around a diagonal girder some fifty feet above him, slapping against other bits of line with a loud zap. The pungent smell of burning insulation was detectable even in the wind. It mixed with the scent of the oncoming storm.

Albert feared heights, and he made a conscious effort not to look down. He was well over thirty feet high now, but the sparks seemed no closer. He realized that they were much higher than he'd anticipated.

It would be a Herculean effort on his part to make it that

high, but it was his only course of action. He stubbornly refused to entertain any other thoughts but those of further ascent. His arms ached, and he bit back the fear. The metal was cold and unfriendly in his grip, making each step up a battle.

The wind howled through the girders, whistling like a furious ghost. It moved the tower, making it sway dramatically. Albert could feel it bend, the metal groaning beneath the weight of the tempest.

Shit, he thought, *I'm never gonna make it. This thing is swinging like a cheap suspension bridge in a hurricane. It's gonna take every ounce of strength, every fiber of will I can muster. There won't be anything left when I finally get there. . . .*

Then, in another revelation, his mind jumped ahead. *So what? What difference does that make? It's time to overcome personal fears and physical limitations. Climbing up there is a spiritual quest, don't think of it any other way. To make it is to triumph, the soul over the body and mind, to fail is damnation.*

Landis Woodley heard a scream and was surprised to find it was his own voice. Chet hung on to the camera gamely, shooting every foot of film he could before something stopped him. The room was insane with apprehension. Devila, or rather the thing that used to be Devila, had begun to walk, to circle the room, arms outstretched, as if feeling for some invisible barrier.

Chet followed it with the camera, keeping a professionally focused and centered shot. Landis had dropped his clipboard and was backing away from the thing. José had never regained his feet from the backwards fall he had taken. He was scuttling back, crablike, until his back made contact with the wall, and he could escape no farther.

He whimpered like a frightened child, crossing himself and praying for deliverance.

The thing did not seem interested in any of them and made no threatening advances. Landis, his mind racing with the intoxication of fear, had time to consider the magnitude of the developed film.

He glanced at Chet. *Good man,* he thought. *He's rolling and he'll keep rolling until I tell him to stop. Good. That's the way to go. We'll ride this thing out and in the end have some of the most incredible celluloid footage ever exposed to light.*

He considered what he would ultimately do with it. He could always build a movie around it, that was no problem. Then, he began to see it as a documentary, *Devila's Mysteries from the Grave.* Whatever. The exposed film would be dynamite, and he knew it. Devila had been right.

He looked at her now, the snake head twisting grotesquely on the long neck, black tongue blinking in and out of her mouth, and wondered what would happen. Is this the kind of thing people recovered from?

Landis was fascinated.

He stayed away from the thing as it circumnavigated the room. At one point it passed precariously close to the camera tripod, and Chet nearly fell back, taking the camera with him. José gained enough confidence to jump to his feet and run screaming from the room. Landis kept moving, rotating away from the creature, staying a fixed distance from it as it prowled the room.

Albert's estimation that the climb up the high-tension structure would be a spiritual journey was not wrong. The flashbacks to his childhood that had begun to pull at his memory when he was on the ground continued. They grew stronger and more poignant as he gained altitude.

Memories dominated his already-reeling brain. He no longer had to concentrate on not thinking about the demon, the quest upward, or his own fate. He was overwhelmed by a flood of emotional recollections. Each one seemed to leave a different imprint on his heart; each one seemed important, indispensable. Each one seemed to aim him, focus him, give him pause for inspiration. He knew what he was doing was right and every passing chapter of his life, replayed now on the cinematic panorama of his soul, reinforced that understanding.

Albert was undergoing a massive spiritual catharsis. Canonized by each level he traversed, his inner voices were fairly shouting and singing the changes through.

It was as if every event in his life, every thought and theism, had been nothing but a preamble to this moment. He shook, sometimes with tears, sometimes with laughter, as he climbed.

Forgetting the height and the dangers above and below, Albert gained his wisdom one ladder rung at a time. He pushed on, higher, and eventually forgot who he was.

The sparking cable was almost parallel with him now, and ten feet out to his left. To reach it, he would have to shinny out across a narrow beam, a hundred feet above the ground. Albert did not consider the risk, and, without thinking, he stepped out onto the beam. He squatted and flexed his knees so he could reach down and grip the beam with his hands if he lost balance, and began to edge, crablike, away from the support girder.

The surface of the beam was wet and slick with an oily grit. It was six inches wide, hardly width enough to keep his balance under the best of conditions. He moved sideways, sliding one foot along at a time, inching his body laterally on the narrow beam. It was difficult and uncomfortable. He moved slowly out over the open space with the wind at his back.

Albert's feet slipped several times as he went, but after a moment of panic, he was able to retain his footing and continue.

The wind sang through the lattice of beams and girders, blowing his hair into his face, but he dared not wipe it away. To take one hand away from the task at hand would be foolhardy and dangerous. He fought against his natural inclinations and fears. He fought against them every inch of the way, with a tenacity he would have thought impossible a few short days ago.

The cable spit with a violence that almost knocked Albert off the beam. It crackled and sparked as the wind blew it wildly into the tangle of wires. The smell of burned insulation was stronger. The beam he walked on tingled slightly. Albert realized that some of the current that pulsed through the severed cable must be leaking onto the support beam beneath him. He shook it off and continued.

This is it, he thought. *The end is in sight. Just keep cool and all will be fine. Just a few more feet and I'll be there.*

Albert glanced down. The ground spun crazily below him as the terrible symptoms of vertigo played with his mind. He steadied himself on the beam, occasionally squatting lower and touching it with his hands. His palm pressed against the cold grit and he felt the tingle of electricity, like ants, invading his skin. The great power of the electricity in such close proximity seemed to throb through him. The electromagnetic field he was now within caused the hair on his head to stand up.

Don't look down, he told himself. *Just keep going.* His front heel slipped, and he fought to maintain control. For a moment he thought he was going to fall, and fright exploded in his chest with a flurry of heartbeats. He slipped and the beam came up and hit him squarely between the legs. Pain sent stars across his eyes. He gritted his teeth and endured it. He wrapped himself around the beam tightly, using both arms and legs. He was now curled around it like a giant tree sloth.

He realized he was crying. His breath came in gulps. He was losing it.

Carefully, he raised himself back up to a standing position. The muscles in his thighs began to spasm involuntarily, but he clenched his teeth and kept going.

The snake demon stopped. It looked at the ceiling and straightened its neck. The room became silent, as if a blanket of snow had been thrown over it. The whir of the camera was audible, and Landis was glad to hear it. That meant that he was still in business. Chet, shaken and pale, continued to stand by his post.

Then, without foreshadowing, the snake began to dematerialize. Devila's features returned. The coils fell away, and Landis got the distinct impression that the snake was being drawn by something; that something far off had diverted its attention and it was no longer interested in what was happening in this little room.

He got one last look at the face of the thing before Devila reemerged from under its diabolical embrace. It was a look that Landis would never forget. Half-woman, half-demon, it seemed neither. It made eye contact with him just before it faded, and the chill that coursed down Landis's back caused his whole body to shudder uncontrollably.

Then it was gone, and Devila was lying on the floor.

Albert Beaumond was ready to be purified. It had taken him his entire life to reach this point. The time was now upon him, and he looked up into the gathering raindrops with a mystical zeal that transfigured him. The power cable flashed, sparks danced into the wind, and the sound crackled.

He took a deep breath, centered himself, and took one last look at the world around him. Intuitively he knew that the serpent was coming. He knew that it was loose, no longer a prisoner of the circle of flame. There was no time left.

He did this for Thora as much as for himself. He could not bear another possession. His sanity hung by a thread, but in that second of complete and utter surrender, as he reached out, he was as sane and clearheaded as any man had ever been.

His fingers moved toward the flashing cable end. He smiled with contentment.

The wind blew it just out of his reach. It swung out over the concrete riverbed like a sparkler on a string. Albert felt a hissing behind him. The back of his neck crackled with tension. The serpent was back!

He was too late!

Albert cried out in desperation. He could feel the power sweeping into him, invading his brain. The raping of his soul had begun again and the terrible certainty that this time it was for good. The end had begun for Albert Beaumond just as a new era was unfolding. The irony made him weep spontaneously.

The wind blew the flashing end back toward him and Albert, driven as he had never been in his life, reached out and grasped it.

Cleanse me, he prayed.

Cleanse me and destroy this parasite!

The power, thousands of volts of pure, clean electricity, jumped through his body in the blink of an eye. Albert had no time to scream. The pain was nil.

It all happened so fast that he had no time to react physically in any way. Only his soul knew what had happened. He prayed to God, the same God he had denied all his life. Just like the atheist in a crashing plane, he prayed.

Albert no longer disbelieved. He had proven the existence of God by proving the existence of the devil.

Cleanse me.

Purify me.

His body, frozen by the massive amount of current running through it, clung to the live end of the power line. Flesh began to fry almost immediately. Smoke curled away from the palms of his hands, where the skin was in contact with the juice.

Albert convulsed. He jerked spasmodically, his body dancing to the tune of unimaginable electric power. He lost contact with the beam and began to fall. His hands tore away from the power line, leaving the skin of his palms behind, where it adhered to cook further in the unrelenting current. He was dead long before he hit the concrete drainage ditch.

The serpent fell with him.

Trapped in Albert's body as it died, the serpent cursed and writhed.

Cleanse me.

He lay in the cement creek bed facing upward, his mouth and eyes open. Rain began to fall on his face, the droplets growing in size and number.

17

Jonathon Luboff looked dead on camera. His skin was pasty white, and the dark circles under his eyes were impossible to hide. Even with liberal amounts of theatrical makeup, the old man looked worse than the mock-up cadavers Buzzy had created for the movie.

His eyes, however, were downright frightening. They held the camera like two burning orbs, hypnotic and unfathomable. You either stared into them and were sucked down, or you looked away. There was no middle ground.

Landis had managed to keep Luboff off drugs for the two days they were shooting in Landis's house. Not completely off drugs, of course, but just this side of dreamsville. Luboff never nodded out on the set, and that, to many who knew him, was an accomplishment.

Tad Kingston struggled. His lines were always kept short. In any given scene, he was never allowed more than a few sentences of dialogue. Even then, he often needed cue cards. Luboff helped him when he could, but Tad was thick as a brick.

In the end, Landis resorted to intimidation to keep both his stars in line. At the pace he worked, if you didn't know your lines, you wound up looking like a fool. Landis simply left mistakes in, unless they were monumental, and the actor had to endure watching himself immortalized on the big screen that way. It could be embarrassing.

If you looked bad in a Landis Woodley production, *nobody* would hire you. Ever. Just the fact that you worked with Woodley would have been the kiss of death to most, and that alone could keep you out of the mainstream for life. It happened more than once.

Many an actor, desperate for money, had accepted the Woodley "one-way ticket to Palookaville" (as Buzzy called it). For his two stars, Jonathon Luboff and Tad Kingston, it didn't matter. They were both going nowhere fast. One a dying shooting star, on its last crash through the atmosphere, destined to burn out long before it hit the ground, and the other a cheap skyrocket, hopelessly trying to compete with real celestial bodies.

"All right!" Landis barked through his bullhorn. "Shut up! Everybody, shut up! Now, here's what we're gonna do. First, we're gonna reshoot scene forty-seven. Kingston, learn your lines, you nutski! You fuck this up one more time and you're off the picture, got it? Okay, second, we get the pickup shots we need here, reaction shots from Jonathon, uhm . . . the monster sequence, front and back, then we tear down and get ready for scenes sixteen, seventeen, eighteen, nineteen, and, uhm . . . twenty four. While we're changing the lights over, the cast can grab a sandwich. Grips, lights, camera, script, and makeup don't get to eat yet. Any questions? Okay, let's go, we're running behind here. We've got to pick up the pace!"

There was grumbling, but nobody dared speak out. After all, this was Landis's movie; he was in charge. He was unorthodox and unpleasant, but every person there needed the work. Landis specialized in hiring people who, for one reason or another, didn't fit anywhere else. If he pushed them too hard, it was tough luck. How else could you make a feature-length movie in six days?

Assistant cameraman and key grip Bob Avelene, Chet's right-hand man, tapped Landis's shoulder. Landis looked up from his clipboard, the frown permanently fixed on his face. "Yeah?"

"Mr. Woodley," the young man said, obviously nervous, "Chet says he needs a sandwich. He said he's tired and hungry; he said you'd know what he meant."

"Yeah, yeah. I know," Landis answered impatiently. "Here, give him this." He placed a small packet of white pills in Bob's hand without a change of facial expression. "That's the cure for tired and hungry."

The kid looked at the pills, a little shocked, and nodded. "Yes, sir," he mumbled, and went shuffling back to where Chet was repositioning his camera.

Landis often handed out Benzedrine to his crew in an effort to make a deadline. The bennies filled two needs—you worked faster and longer, and you didn't eat. To Landis, that was money in the bank.

His mind kept returning to the incredible scene he and Chet had witnessed and filmed the night before. He mulled his options. The piece of film was spectacular, no question about that. He'd removed it from the camera and placed it in the locked storage cabinet in the projection room. It was in there among his master copies and important prints. As the day's shoot progressed he couldn't help but think about how he was going to handle it.

It would be a spectacular centerpiece for a movie, that much was a lock. But what kind? The documentary idea hung with him all day. *Devila's Mysteries from the Grave* had a nice ring to it. He could shoot a bunch of fake cinema vérité stuff, maybe a couple of cheap effects, a séance, a haunted house, a graveyard, the usual crap.

The thought occurred to him that he could use a lot of his own footage, stuff he had in the can. Cannibalizing his own work would save a ton of money, and who would care? The Great Romano could do his shtick. He could always trot out the old guillotine again. The money-making potential gave him a thrill every time he considered it.

Of course, with a scene like that, it would also make a hell of a horror movie. He could build a film around it, bang out a story, have Neil turn out a script in twelve hours. Devila had star potential. Maybe put her and Luboff together . . .

Landis decided to keep the same crew and sets he had for

Cadaver and just shoot an extra day or two on the Devila project. It was a natural. Two movies for the price of one! That was the Woodley way!

His script girl, the ubiquitous Becky Sears (who would work for next to nothing to be close to Tad Kingston), had been trying to raise Devila on the phone all day. Landis knew she was home because he'd driven her home himself at five in the morning.

The poor girl was a wreck. Whatever it was that took possession of her last night had taken a heavy toll. There wasn't enough functioning gray matter left in her brain to order a cheeseburger. Exhausted and traumatized as she was, he had to walk her to the door like a drunk. He carried her in, unlocked her door, and tucked her in bed. She kept mumbling about the tuning forks. Landis had wrapped them up and stashed them along with the film in his storage cabinet.

"It's all right, I've got 'em locked up. They're safe."

She started to rise from her bed, panic in her eyes, and Landis pushed her back down.

"Hey," he said, "I told you they were all right. You can have them back anytime you want, but I think they should stay locked away in a safe place for now."

She fell back onto the pillow and moaned.

Jesus, he thought, *what did she go through?* Something like that could drive a person stark raving mad.

All because of a couple of odd tuning forks.

The damn things were evil. Landis remembered the feeling when he touched them. The tingle of current and mild electric shocks made his skin crawl.

It made him wonder.

Radiation? The fuckin' atomic bomb is everywhere. There are tests in Nevada all the time. Jesus, could these things be radioactive?

He hated to handle them and treated them as if they were radioactive. He'd wished for asbestos gloves when he actually had to make contact with them, wrapping them quickly and shoving them in the back of the safe.

They gave him the creeps, but they were worth a fortune. God knows where she got them.

Landis lay in bed as the sun crept over the hills and wondered about the answer to that question. Where *did* she get them?

Rain had begun to fall in Southern California. It started innocently enough, a few showers, then the storm hit with full force. To the parched hillsides and canyons, the rain meant the end of a year-long drought that had dried out every living thing within two hundred miles. The bone-dry soil drank it up like a sponge. The runoff was minimal at first.

But, after two days of steady downpour, the ground reached the saturation point, and water began to fill the gullies and culverts. For the first time in over a year, the Los Angeles River flowed. It sluiced like an obedient serpent through the labyrinth of man-made spillways, staying well within the prearranged concrete shores.

The sewer system quickly attained its maximum flow and began to back up. A flash flood warning was issued for Los Angeles County and hundreds of tiny, normally dry creeks and streambeds overflowed their banks and began to cause problems. Every watercourse was at its highest stage.

Then came the mud slides. The TV news was full of images of homes skating down hills, of landscaping gone mad, of whole embankments avalanching down onto unsuspecting neighborhoods.

The storm dominated the headlines. The city was a mess.

Albert Beaumond's body began to move. Carried by the water, its odyssey began beneath the electric tower and carried it through miles of waterway, into the heart of LA.

"Goddamn it, Becky! Keep tryin'! If she doesn't answer, then go over there. Either way, I want to talk to Devila *today!"*

Landis Woodley's voice shook the room, his booming, authoritative baritone intimidated everyone within range. Becky Sears winced. She'd been trying the phone number that he'd given her for Devila all day. So far there had been no response.

Landis, although completely involved with his production, was concerned. He began to imagine all sorts of horrible things. At five in the afternoon, exactly twelve hours after he'd taken Devila home, he sent Becky Sears to find her.

The filming was behind schedule, as usual, and Landis was driving his crew like a team of Alaskan sled dogs. Part of Woodley's problem was that he compiled a production schedule that was completely unrealistic and called for superhuman efforts to maintain. He expected to get his full twenty or more shots a day, regardless of circumstances. That allowed for most every shot to be completed in one take, and that wasn't commensurate with his talent pool. Luboff seemed to flow with it well enough, but he was a veteran actor with hundreds of movies behind him. Just about everyone else had a problem. None of them had worked that hard for that long.

Except Landis Woodley.

It was the only way he could make money. *Cadaver* was shaping up to be his masterpiece. He already had a commitment for exhibition from a distributor with a chain of drive-ins across the South and that almost assured him of a winner.

Landis and his crew worked through the night, taking a short break for hamburgers at eleven-thirty. Landis, Buzzy, Jonathon, Neil, Tad, and Chet gathered in the kitchen for a much-needed break. Chet read the paper and sipped his coffee. Becky Sears had returned hours ago with the report that no one was home at Devila's apartment and that the two old ladies across the hall said that she had left late in the afternoon.

"Strange thing about it," said Becky, "was that the old ladies said that someone else had been around looking for her too, a young woman."

Landis raised an eyebrow. "A young woman? Probably a fan."

Becky shook her head, her dog-ears wagging. "I don't think so. They said she was looking for her father. Apparently, Devila had been out with the guy. What do you think?"

Landis shrugged. "How the hell should I know? All I can tell you is, I want her found."

Chet looked up from his newspaper and smiled.

"What are you smilin' about?" Landis sneered.

"I know where she is," Chet said coolly.

Landis leveled his gaze at Chet, but the canny cameraman deflected it like a slow housefly. Landis waited for Chet to speak, and, when he didn't, he walked over to where the cinematographer was sitting. Chet ignored him, reading his paper. Landis stood over him and glared.

Chet looked up in mock surprise. "Yeah?"

"You said you knew where Devila is," Landis growled.

"Yep."

"So, where is she?"

"It's Saturday night, ain't it?"

Landis and Buzzy looked at each other.

"Your brain cells are startin' to go, you know that, Landis? You better lay off the weed," Chet said with a smile. He liked yanking the boss man's chain.

"In case you don't remember, our girl has a horror movie to host every week about this time. Tonight it's *Mark of the Vampire*, one of my all-time favorites. You got a TV?"

Landis slapped his forehead. "Shit! How could I be so stupid! Let's go into the living room."

The huge wooden cabinet black-and-white Motorola took a full two minutes to warm up. Its tubes crackled and the speaker hummed. Everyone who had been in the kitchen was now gathered around the TV. Landis squatted, fine-tuning the sensitive set until he had a watchable picture. Then he stepped away and stared. The sound faded in with a sizzle of static a few seconds before the picture.

"—brings you the 1935 Tod Browning classic, *Mark of the Vampire*, with Bela Lugosi and Carol Borland. And now, your hostess of horror, the divine Devila!"

The screen went from gray to gray. Landis realized that he was watching a graveyard scene. The set was smoky, a graveyard, cheap cardboard gravestones. The camera panned in on a pale-looking Devila, leaning against a fake crypt. The crypt moved slightly, destroying what little sense of realism there was, as she put her weight on it.

Landis squinted. She didn't look good. Even with the indistinct picture on his TV, it was evident that Devila was not well. The circles around her eyes were not hidden by makeup, her face seemed somehow hollow, gaunt. Electric "snow" fell across the screen, the picture hiccuped, rolling upward, sending Landis scrambling for the horizontal hold dial.

That thing last night really took its toll on her, Landis thought. *She looks like hell. I'm gonna have to spruce her up a bit before we can shoot the rest of her scenes for the documentary.* Her dress seemed to hang off of her like a mannequin. She didn't move.

There had been a few moments of silence since the announcer had spoken. The camera came in for a medium close-up, framing her from the waist up. Her eyes stared off into space. Her face was expressionless.

"She looks like shit," Buzzy said behind him, but Landis was deep in thought.

The silence continued.

That's rare for TV, Landis thought. *Something's wrong here. These guys edit as tight as a gnat's asshole; they must be having cows in the control room. Maybe she forgot her cue.*

The camera stayed with Devila, staring at her with an unblinking eye. The uncomfortable silence stretched farther. Landis felt inexplicably nervous, a prickle of sweat crossed his brow.

Then, in slow motion, she brought her hand up. Landis wondered if this was planned. Still no words had passed her lips, and no change of expression flickered across her unnaturally vacuous face.

What the hell is she doing? She's gonna lose her job for this, he thought.

When her hand came into the frame, Landis saw the gun and gasped. He couldn't see what kind of gun it was, but it looked real.

She brought the gun to her head, and, in front of thousands of viewers, blew her brains out. The screen went blank, then was replaced by a test pattern.

18

The cloudburst conditions continued for several days. LA was the wettest it had been in fifteen years. The body of Albert Beaumond continued its sewer journey. It washed down the Los Angeles River, got hung up on some debris and stuck in a drainage pipe, and wound up wedged in the elbow of a culvert in North Hollywood. It stayed there with the muddy storm water cascading over it for twenty-four hours, becoming horribly bloated and waterlogged.

When the weather broke and the water level went back down, Albert was left high and dry beneath an underpass near the construction site for a new apartment building. There he stayed until two kids, playing nearby, discovered him. They later told police that they were alerted by the smell. They knew something dead was down there in the culvert, maybe a dog or a raccoon. Never in their wildest dreams did they ever expect to come across an honest-to-God human corpse.

The homicide squad made an appearance, inspected the scene, and made the announcement that this unidentified body had died of misadventure. His body, officially a "John Doe" case, was picked up by the coroner's wagon and packed off to the morgue.

The medical examiner made special mention of the advance state of putrefaction that had taken place because of the exposure to water. Most curious were the wounds: first-degree burns around the hands, especially the palms, where skin had been removed, a plethora of broken bones, including a massive skull fracture, multiple abrasions, and water damage. The medical examiner noted a lack of lividity, just a tinge around the buttocks, indicating that the person was dead prior to receiving the wounds, and was moved shortly after death, probably by the storm runoff. A quick, cursory examination by the medical examiner at the request of the police to determine if foul play might be involved, turned up nothing.

"John Doe" was taken to the morgue. Pending identification, he would be stored there until buried.

Thora Beaumond called Lt. Garth Prease at the North Hollywood Precinct missing persons department every day. When the forty-eight-hour waiting period was up, and her father had not returned, Prease went to work.

Albert Beaumond was declared officially missing, his description went out to all the appropriate agencies, and a search was instituted. Thora was not pleased that the police had waited to start looking for her father, and it only alienated her further from the authorities.

Dr. Segwick did what he could, which was very little except prescribe vitamins and sedatives. Thora had the support of family friends and a few distant relatives who had not yet disowned the part of the family sired by Albert. "A bad seed," he was called by most people who knew about his activities, "a misguided soul," by others. The members of his congregation, Satanic though they might be, were all sympathetic to Thora and offered their help, both financial and spiritual.

In short, she was not lacking for human attention and sustenance. Certain "mystical" friends of her father even conducted a series of séances and psychic readings, trying to contact the missing man, but they turned up nothing. After four days, it was hard for Thora not to assume the worst. She read it in the faces of those around her, and, try as she might, she could not tune it out.

They think he's dead, she thought. *They think my father's dead.*

Her mood deteriorated as the next few days went by, every day a little more. It was deflating like a slow leak in a balloon, but she would not, could not, give up thinking he was still alive. *He's out there somewhere*, she thought, *wandering around in the rain. Maybe he's got amnesia. He was so feverish when he disappeared, he could have wandered away, become disoriented, and lost himself. He probably needs me, he could be hurt, he could be sick, he could be—*

—dead?

No, she didn't want to think that.

The newspapers made a big deal out of Devila's televised suicide. It had affected people in various ways. In the classic LA tradition, one channel showed it several times with a telephone number across the bottom of the screen to call if watching it upset you. The number was for psychiatric counseling. They made a fortune over the weekend and kicked back a healthy share to the program director at the TV station. It was capitalism in its purest form. Even Landis Woodley had to admire their chutzpah.

For his part, Landis was confused. Had the serpent caused Devila's madness or had she been seriously depressed prior to the filming? Did she have other, secret, more debilitating personal problems that might have driven her to kill herself?

Or was she just plain crazy? And now that she was dead, what would he do with the film? And where did the cursed tuning forks belong?

As for Devila's mental condition, Landis was of the belief that the serpent, when it possessed her body, must have driven her mad. How could it not? The thought of ever having that happen again must have been so great in her that she chose to end her life rather than to take that chance. *God*, he thought, *it must have been horrible.*

He would sit on the film. Its value would not diminish with time, and it would be in bad taste, even for Landis, to release it so soon after her death. Devila already showed signs of becoming a cult figure, and in coming years, he reasoned, her suicide could take on mythical proportions. One thing was for sure—

people were going to talk about it for a long time. Besides, Landis was too wrapped up in *Cadaver* right then to think about anything else.

The tuning forks were another matter. Landis briefly entertained the notion of filming another possession, and wondered who he could get to act as a host. But after agonizing over it, Landis rejected the plan. He decided to return them to the rightful owner, whoever that might be, as soon as possible. They were obviously powerful and dangerous talismans, and having them in his house was unsettling. He didn't even want to touch them. They stayed locked in the safe, along with the film.

Devila's funeral was held in midafternoon on a smoggy, hot LA day. Landis was one of the pallbearers. It was a job he loathed but felt somehow obligated to do. Her parents came from somewhere in the Midwest. Landis could tell at a glance that they didn't understand what had happened, and that their daughter had always been a mystery to them.

From the name she had chosen for herself, to her job as horror hostess, none of it made the least bit of sense to them. Their plain, down-to-earth Christian sensibilities could not accept any of it. She was a lost soul, a failure. They would return to Iowa or Ohio or wherever it was that they came from, and try desperately to put it out of their minds. They would pretend they had never had a daughter.

Landis offered his condolences quietly at the cemetery, and her father had looked at him with thinly veiled contempt.

"Suicide is a mortal sin!" he hissed. The look in his eyes was as sharp and accusing as anything Landis had ever seen in his life. The mother cried quietly, sniffling into her tissue, saying nothing, and the father glared, then they went back home.

Landis couldn't get them out of his mind.

He wondered if they thought Los Angeles had been misnamed. It was not the City of Angels; far from it, it was the devil's city. It took their little girl and poisoned her beyond recognition. For that, the citizens of LA should all die and go to hell.

No problem there, Landis thought. *This town's already got one foot in the door.*

In the same newspaper that carried Devila's obituary, another article appeared at the bottom of page forty-one, "Albert Beaumond, Satanist, missing."

Thora was as shocked as everyone else about Devila. She was even more afraid that her father's disappearance was somehow linked to Devila's suicide. That was a frightening thought. She called Lieutenant Prease about it the same day, describing how Devila had been a visitor in their house the night before.

He told her to let the police be the ones who worried. Two days later he called to tell her there was no link.

Rubbish, Thora thought. *He was my father. I have more insight into his disappearance than all the stupid cops and psychics.*

Prease had the nerve to suggest that Thora go to church with him and pray. She told him she hated church; that was the end of that. He shook his head and said his own prayer, not for the safety of Albert Beaumond, but for the salvation of his bitter daughter. He told her so, and she cried.

It was a world gone mad.

Landis and Buzzy had made all the preparations to film in the morgue for two nights. They were as excited as two kids going to that new, million-dollar amusement park down in Anaheim—Disneyland.

They'd had several meetings with the coroner and even given him a speaking part in the film. He studied his script religiously. He played a coroner. It wouldn't be a stretch.

Everything was ready for them to begin shooting that night. They had, by arrangement, access to the three main rooms from the hours of 9:00 P.M. to 6:00 A.M.

Landis's plan was to get rid of the coroner as soon as possible, filming him first and sending him home. It was to be another Woodley production, on schedule or bust.

They loaded in their cameras and equipment shortly after the main staff went home for the day. The coroner, his assistant, and the night watchmen were thrilled to meet the great Jonathon Luboff, and he dispensed autographs in his usual aloof, spaced-out manner. •

Luboff was given the coroner's office as his dressing room and, after smiling graciously at everyone, proceeded to lock himself in and refuse to come out. It wasn't until Landis agreed to call his "doctor" so that Luboff might have his "medicine" after the filming was done that he cautiously opened the door a crack. Peering out, he could see that the coroner was still there, and refused to move until the man was finished and gone from the premises.

"But Jonathon, he's in the same scene with you. You're together in the shot. You'll have to come out!" Landis argued. He lured the old actor to the door with a decent cigar and a shot of whiskey.

"All right, but only one take," Luboff sneered.

Landis smiled. "No problem," he replied cheerfully. "I don't do second takes on location anyway."

Luboff thought Landis was a genius. Landis thought Luboff was a pain in the ass.

After midnight, and a few false starts, things quieted down, and the shooting began to run smoothly. Landis had, as usual, an ambitious schedule of production, and tonight, for some reason, it didn't seem all that impossible.

Chet was making every camera shot count, not wasting a single foot of film stock, and the actors were on a roll. Landis was happy, and Luboff was, so far, clean and sober.

Buzzy and his assistant, Beatnik Fred, were playing the parts of the monsters. They were demanding roles that required a lot of movement, and they were taking themselves very seriously. Buzzy was a stickler for realism.

The special effects were easy, although somewhat time-consuming. It was basically a heavy makeup job with a few latex open wounds. The white, death pallor war paint revealed the features of their faces. This in itself was not a problem. It was later, when Landis realized that he was using the same two zombies in every shot, that he voiced his concern. It was three in the morning, and everyone not essential to the production had gone home.

The crew, at this point, consisted of director Landis Woodley, cinematographer Chet Bronski, his assistant Bob Avelene, actors Jonathon Luboff and Tad Kingston, scriptwriter Neil Bugmier, gaffer Phil the gofer, and Buzzy and his assistant, Beatnik Fred.

The night watchman, a retired police officer named Charles Boone, stayed at his post by the front door. Buzzy had discovered that Charles was partial to wine, and had furnished him with a bottle of some decent California Chardonnay.

"Goes good with my peanut butter and jelly sandwich," Charles commented after the first swallow.

"I like to keep my people happy," Buzzy said, sharing a generous swig out of the bottle himself. "You just hang on to this, and I'll be back from time to time to wet my whistle, okay?"

Charles nodded vigorously. These film people were all right!

They were shooting in the main room, where the drawers with the corpses in them were located.

In the scene, a cadaver was rising off the slab and trying to strangle Tad Kingston. Luboff played the part of the doctor, and Kingston, his assistant. It was a fairly straightforward scene. Landis pulled Buzzy over to the side and confided.

"Buzz, we got too much of you and Fred already. This scene is important, it's the close-up."

Buzzy looked at the script and said, "Yeah, I see what you mean."

"Who else can you make up?"

Buzzy laughed. "There's nobody, man. Besides, even if there was, like, let's just say if I called one of the boys and woke him up and got him down here, it would take hours to get him ready. That white shit is hard to work with; it shows everything."

"I can't wait that long," Landis said automatically.

"I hear ya," Buzzy answered.

Landis pulled a pack of cigarettes out of his pocket and shook one out for Buzzy, then himself. They both lit up off of Landis's trusty World War II–vintage Zippo lighter. The smell of lighter fluid filled the air, pungent and manly, and Landis flicked the Zippo shut with a practiced motion. He exhaled slowly through his nose, tilting his head back, and looked at the ceiling. "Shit, Buzz. I guess we'll have to go with what we got. What do you think?" he asked.

"Gimme a second," Buzzy replied.

Charles Boone was snoring. He didn't know he snored. His wife complained about it from time to time, but he never gave it a second thought. A man never hears himself snore, no matter how loud it is, and Charles Boone was no exception.

Buzzy Haller could hear it from down the hall. It was a thunderous symphony of nasal honkings. He was on his way to check on the diminutive night watchman, but the wine had done its job and rendered the man dead to the world. Buzzy stuck his head around a corner to see what position he was in, and saw him hunched over his desk, the empty bottle of Chardonnay next to him. His head was cradled in his arms. Buzzy smiled.

He slipped back into the big room and pulled Landis into a corner.

"I've got an idea," he whispered. "It's a little nuts, but just go along with me on this, okay? All I want is for you to keep an open mind and hear me out."

Landis looked at him, a question mark on his brow. "What is it?"

"Well," Buzzy continued, "you know all the pressure we've been under lately, to compete with National? RKM has been down our backs to come up with something that will *really* scare the shit out of people, right?"

"Right. So?"

"Well, I know for a fact that they're using real pigs' blood in *Unearthly Terror*, and they used cows' organs for the big climax scene where they rip the monster's brain out."

Landis looked annoyed. "What are you driving at? Come on, I'm behind schedule. I don't have time to play twenty questions with you."

"Don't you see?"

"See what?"

Buzzy smiled, his teeth flashing sardonically in the fluorescent lights. He looked evil and mischievous.

"Here we are in the biggest repository of dead bodies in the state. The cameras are rolling, the lights are set up, there's no one around. The night watchman is sleeping off a bottle of vino that I gave him. Come on, man, don't you see it? We've got carte blanche! Nobody will ever know! It's the best special effect in the world, and it's right here under our noses!"

Landis cocked his head. "Are you saying what I think you're saying?"

"It's a guaranteed winner, Woody. A guaranteed total fuckin' winner. We use a real corpse or two. Nobody ever finds out. I tell everybody that I've got a new makeup technique. We get super realism! And it doesn't cost us a cent!"

Landis's jaw dropped. What Buzzy was saying was insane, but true.

"Nobody would ever know," he repeated.

Landis was still considering the last part, the part about its not costing a single cent. Buzzy was like that—he thought budget. He was a real production man. Budget first, everything else second. But this, this was crazy . . .

Totally out of the question . . .

Landis's mind began to turn. It *would* be just the thing to put this movie over the top. No denying that.

It's free.

No one would ever know.

Christ. Could he get away with it?

The more he thought about it, the more he knew it was the kind of radical, insane idea that would probably work. He thought about the close-up. It would scare the hell out of people. He thought about his crew. Would they keep their mouths shut? If something like this got out, his career would be over—wouldn't it?

Hell, if it did somehow leak out, that would be the kind of publicity that might actually have a reverse effect, he thought. A rumor like that could double the box office. Triple it! Landis would be a legend with horror fans. It would be the most outrageous stunt in the history of cinematography.

No one would ever know.

He looked at Buzzy.

Buzzy smiled back. "I watched him open the drawer when that dickhead coroner gave us the tour, remember?" he said, his impish smile broadening further. "I think I could get these suckers open with a screwdriver and a few minutes alone. The problem, the way I see it, would be those guys," he said, nodding toward the crew.

Landis looked over at them. They stood around smoking and talking. Not a care in the world. Landis's mental wheels were turning.

Could they be trusted? Would they understand? He found himself weighing each individual case. His eyes traveled the room, clicking off the players. Luboff and Chet? No problem. Bugmier the fruitcake? Probably. Kingston? Maybe. The flunkies? Yeah, not impossible.

No one would ever know.

Buzzy was in his face, hissing and swearing, doing the hard sell. He could tell that Landis was listening. He knew he was pushing all the right buttons. Buzzy Haller was no fool, but he *was* dangerously crazy. "I swear, we could make horror history, man. It's right here under our noses. *And it won't cost a goddamn cent.*"

Landis found himself nodding, agreeing.

No one would ever know.

19

Landis waved. The crew looked over at him, ready to get back to work. Cigarettes were crushed out; a few murmurs rose in the echo walled chamber. People were beginning to feel strange being in here, working in close proximity with all those dead bodies. It gave them the creeps. They had enjoyed their short break, talking nervously among themselves to chase the weirdness.

Landis gave them a big surprise.

"We're gonna take five, people!" he shouted. He fished in his pockets for a set of keys and threw them to Neil. "Here, I've got a cooler full of beer in my trunk. Let everybody have some. Save me and Buzz a couple, okay?"

The crew was already moving for the door. That's how anxious they were to get out of this place, Landis noted. Chet walked over to him and said, "What's up, boss? I've never known you to call a break in mid shoot. Something wrong?"

Landis shook his head. "Me and Buzzy have a technical problem we want to work out. It's no big deal, we just need a few minutes. Go have a beer with the rest of them."

"That's another thing, I've never known you to give away free beer either."

"Enjoy it while you can," Landis said, deep in thought. His eyes were far away. Chet didn't need to be told twice. He was gone in a flash.

As soon as they were alone, Buzzy went to work on the drawers holding the corpses. In truth, he didn't even need a screwdriver to get them open. All he had to do was unlatch them. Landis couldn't believe that they weren't locked.

"Who would steal a corpse?" Buzzy asked.

"I don't know. Somebody like us?" Landis deadpanned.

Buzzy didn't laugh. He was too busy pulling out the first drawer; it slid along a metal track, locking when fully extended. The cold and the smell hit them like a sledgehammer. Like a butcher shop, like raw meat. Behind that was a strong disinfectant aroma, bad enough to make a man gag. The combination was nauseating. Buzzy was too caught up in the moment to notice. He pulled back the sheet and gasped.

It was a woman's body, a bullet hole in her forehead. Her eyes were closed and severely sunken, as if her brains had been sucked out by the bullet. Buzzy pulled the sheet over her head and slid the drawer closed.

He opened the next drawer. It was an old man, too wrinkly and prunelike to be of use to them. His face was screwed up like a shrunken head. "He must have died of constipation," Buzzy cracked.

Landis was over his shoulder, fascinated by the ghoulish game. "Try this one," he said, pointing to the bottom drawer, marked number sixty-six.

"Okay, stand back."

The bottom drawer screeched when they slid it open, its echo snapping off the tile walls. The smell from this one was much worse. Landis held his nose. "Jesus, this one's ripe."

Buzzy pulled the sheet back. Landis reeled. It was the worst-looking body he had ever seen. "God knows what this guy died of," Buzzy whispered, "but he looks like he's been lying around for at least a week. Christ, look at the skin, man. It's greenish. This one's perfect. I couldn't have made one up any better. It's the right size and age, right condition, check out the bloating. I'm tellin' ya, this one will scare the shit out of *anybody.*"

There was a tag tied to his big toe which identified him as John Doe. In other words, name unknown.

Landis looked into Buzzy's face. There was a short silence, then, "What do we do?"

Buzzy eyed the corpse. "We lift him out, put him on the slab, cover him up, and . . . shit, I don't know. It's your ball game then. I already did my part; you're the director. Let's block out a shot."

"But how—"

Buzzy made a face. "I'll have to manipulate him from behind," he said softly. "Maybe I can rig up some wires or something. Here, give me a hand."

Landis hesitated. He looked down at the corpse and fought back a reflex to gag. He didn't want to touch the thing.

"Come on," Buzzy hissed. "Shit, man. I'm not doin' everything."

"Jesus," Landis said, "I don't know if I can go through with this."

"Sure you can," Buzzy answered. "Just don't think about it."

Landis had never touched a dead body before. He wondered if Buzzy had. Revulsion shuddered through him at the thought of it. That made two things he never wanted to touch in the past few days; first the tuning forks and now this. Of course, this was much worse.

At least the tuning forks were solid, hard. This guy looked as soft and rotted as an old mattress. Landis fought back the nausea. There was a very real chance that he might throw up.

Buzzy noticed Landis's reticence and frowned. He said, "Look, I know this is no day at the beach, but consider something, okay? You move this corpse with me, you touch this dead fuckin' decaying thing with your hands and move it over there on that slab, which is only ten feet away, and your life will change."

Landis stared into the dead man's face.

Buzzy continued, "Your life will change because you will have just made one of the greatest horror movies of all time, and you will have scared the shit out of millions of people all over the world."

Landis's head came up and he locked eyes with Buzzy. There was a question there. "The world?"

"Yeah, I said all over the world. Like Frankenstein or Dracula, this thing is gonna become a classic. It's not just for those shitty drive-ins with their pathetic double features that we seem to live on. No. This one's for all time, Woody.

"It's got that extra dimension that makes your skin crawl, and very few directors can do that. You've got to take a chance, roll the dice. You think these other directors would do it? Orson Welles? Tod Browning? You're damn right they would. They'd do *anything* to make a movie great."

Landis looked back down at the corpse.

"It's right here in front of you," Buzzy said. "Great men make great decisions. We're gonna do it, man, we're gonna make it happen. All you have to do is reach down and touch the dead flesh with me. That's not so bad, is it? Shit, that dickhead coroner does it every day. You think he can do something we can't do? It's easy. Are you ready?"

Landis was still. He said nothing.

Buzzy's voice dropped. "Touch it, Woody. Touch the dead flesh. Come on. It's for art. You want greatness, don't you? This guy's your star; treat him like one."

With that, Buzzy leaned over and put his arms around the dead man's back and lifted him out of the drawer.

"Get his legs," he mumbled. When Landis hesitated, Buzzy snapped, "Come on! The legs, damn it!"

Rigor mortis had set in with a vengeance and made the dead man most uncooperative. Buzzy almost changed his mind about it, based on the fact that he would have a devil of a time animating the stiff limbs. But, some movement was possible, and as long as he could get the arms and hands to move, he was in business. The stench, disturbed now by the movement, was putrid, and caused both men to hold their breath.

Landis got hold of the legs and hefted the dead man off the drawer. In the process, his hand fell off his chest and slid down by his side. It brushed Landis's arm and sent gooseflesh crawling completely over his back and down his sides like an army of fire ants. He recalled Buzzy's words, sung like a bad refrain, "Touch the dead flesh, Woody, touch the dead flesh."

Now that he had actually done it, and his warm, live skin made contact with the dead man's hand, he realized how disgusting it was. Landis would remember that touch, that first fraction of a second contact, for the rest of his life.

The flesh was cold. It chilled Landis to consider the temperature, like the inside of a refrigerator. It was also greasy, damp, almost oily. That must be from the putrefaction, he thought. The epidermis, being the first thing in contact with the air, probably begins to decay before the rest of the body. Landis shuddered at the thought.

The oiliness was the outer layer of skin, now dead, beginning to rot. It fell away to the touch like the skin of an overripe tomato.

They moved quickly, walking the dead man to the slab and laying him out. There was a stainless steel gurney nearby, but neither man had the idea to use it. They stepped away and breathed again. A curious deodorizing scent came off the body along with the smell of death. The coroner, evidently, had treated the dead man with an innocuous spray to minimize the overpowering aroma of a corpse in this condition. The flowery, totally inappropriate smell mixed with the stench of decay to form a new, bizarre combination that assailed their nostrils like a poison gas.

Both men gagged and backpedaled.

The slab itself was made of white enamel, grooved for the flow of liquids. Blood, Landis guessed. The dead man was laid out like a sleeping monster. Buzzy pulled a sheet over him and coughed.

"Jesus, that's bad!" he croaked. "I wonder where he keeps that spray?" It occurred to Landis that Buzzy knew about the spray, but he didn't think that odd. Buzzy knew all kinds of weird stuff.

As soon as the sheet had settled over the corpse's face, Buzzy was off looking for the spray. "It's gotta be around, within easy reach. It's the one absolutely necessary thing here," he said.

He found it in a cabinet nearby and read the label. " 'For forensic use only.' Hmm, must be the good stuff."

Without waiting, he pulled back the sheet and sprayed the corpse from head to toe, then returned the shroud to its original position. At that moment, Landis heard footsteps. The crew was returning.

Chet and Neil went right to the corpse and looked at Landis. "What's this all about?" Neil demanded.

Tonight, for the shoot, Neil had worn normal male clothes, and they gave him a modicum of respectability. At least people weren't laughing outright at him. His question was delivered firmly and deserved an answer.

Landis had been considering what he would tell them when they returned. It was time for him to explain.

"Buzzy had an idea, and I thought it was good."

He paused, measuring the disbelief on their faces. Then proceeded cautiously.

"We're gonna use one of the corpses in the movie."

They all stared. Neil's jaw dropped.

"One of the *real* corpses?"

Landis nodded.

"You can't do that! It's . . . it's . . . it's against the law."

"So is sodomy," Buzzy said from behind Landis. "It doesn't matter. Nobody will ever know."

Neil slapped his hand against the unoccupied gurney. "Nobody will ever know? Are you crazy? How are you gonna keep this a secret? Already, everyone in this room knows." He gestured around him.

Landis nodded. "Yeah, but I think that everybody here is trustworthy enough and loyal enough to keep a secret. Especially if they ever want to work for me again." He looked around the room at their faces.

"Now, Buzzy here thinks that by using this corpse in the movie, it will make it a hit, and I happen to agree. It might put this film, and everyone in it, in the horror hall of fame. It's a gamble, I know, and it's a radical idea, but, if we work together and pull it off, well . . . we'll be making cinematic history, and better yet, we'll all make money."

Chet stepped forward. "How will I make money?" he asked.

"Your career will take off if you do a hit movie, especially one with unbelievable special effects. I'll hire you again, for sure. If I make money, you make money."

Chet laughed. "That's horseshit. My career is what it is. If I was working at MGM, I wouldn't *be* here."

"Exactly. None of you people here are working," Landis said with conviction. "That's why I hired you. None of you can afford a scandal; all of you need the work desperately. Do this for me. Do this one thing for me, and I'll see to it that each and every one of you gets a bonus when the film comes out. That's fair, isn't it?"

Silence.

"How much of a bonus?" Chet asked.

Landis was ready for that. "I can't give you a figure right now, maybe a percentage of the profits over a certain amount, maybe points, I don't know. Whatever it is, I will make sure that you're all happy."

Neil snorted. "You're asking us to trust you."

"Yeah," Landis said, "I am."

There was a titter of laughter through the room. It echoed sadly off the tile walls and settled on them all like the sheet had settled on the face of the nameless corpse. The sound trailed off, and the room became quiet again.

"It's a sick fuckin' world when we have to trust the likes of you," Chet grumbled. Landis wondered how he had reconciled filming Devila the other night. That wasn't exactly normal either. He hadn't had a problem then, had he? Landis realized that he was being shaken down for more money, pure and simple. He respected that in a man. It was a God-given right. Chet was all right—he could be read perfectly.

"Nobody will ever know," Landis repeated.

"I'll know," Neil answered. The words hung in the air.

Landis turned to Neil. "Look, anybody who doesn't want to do this can leave now. We'll make it without him. I just thought that I could count on you guys," he said softly.

Jonathon came forward and approached the corpse. He peeked under the sheet and looked at Landis. "This is genius!" he said dramatically.

Buzzy smiled. "We have a winner!"

"Yes," Luboff continued, looking at the others. "It's genius, I say! This corpse is horrible, the worst thing I've ever seen. If you have it in the movie, it will scare everyone! Isn't that what a horror movie is supposed to do? Here we have a chance to do something brilliant, something truly grotesque, because of this man's vision." He pointed at Landis. "And you doubt him?"

Luboff pulled the sheet away suddenly, dramatically, like a matador, revealing the dead man in all his hideous glory.

"Look upon him! Look upon the face of death!" There were gasps. "He is magnificent! Let our young filmmaker create a masterpiece of horror, let him use the elements at his disposal, let him transcend this art form and make a statement that will live"—he paused and took a breath—"forever."

Luboff had spoken. The endorsement had come from such a strange quarter that it had taken them all off guard. If any one of them had the credibility to speak about art, it was Luboff. His speech was persuasive. It galvanized their feelings and directed their thinking away from the petty problems of impropriety and into the larger picture of art and substance.

Landis looked at their faces. He could see them all beginning to change their minds. Buzzy was lighting another cigarette and stealing a glance at Landis. Through the smoke he could see the faint outline of a smile.

"All right," Chet said. "I'll do it."

"Good," Luboff said, and stood by him. "Who else *is a man?*"

"I'm in," said Beatnik Fred. He had his own reasons to participate in history. He was a seeker of sensations, of experiences. This was, by far, the most bizarre, unorthodox thing he had ever heard of, and he wanted to be a part of it.

"Me too," chimed assistant cameraman Bob and Phil the gofer. They were following Fred's lead.

"Think about what you're doing," whined Neil. "It's sick!"

Jonathon raised his hand. "Galileo was a heretic, Van Gogh was mad. It's nothing new—we have to rise above such things."

"What about this poor man's family?" Neil pleaded.

"What family?" Buzzy pointed out, "He's a John Doe, a no-name. I'd say he was probably a drifter. Chances are he had no home. This could be his greatest triumph. Are you gonna deny this poor son of a bitch his big chance to star in a movie after he's dead? If you ask me, it's an honor."

Landis looked at Tad. "Tad, you're an important part of this. I want you to say yes. I've done a lot for you, made you a star, developed your career, I think you owe it to me to do this one favor. I've never asked you to do anything else, have I?"

Tad was about to say that he made him take Lana Wills to the Halloween party instead of his girlfriend, Becky Sears, but he held his tongue. It was not the time. Landis was right. He'd done so much for Tad. Tad basically owed him his career. Tad nodded and stepped forward, taking his place next to Beatnik Fred and Chet.

"I don't want to," Tad explained to Neil, "but I've got to, you understand."

Neil saw that everyone was against him. Hurt and anger welled up in his eyes, and he balled his fists. Landis thought he was going to cry. Instead, he stormed out of the room.

Landis went after him.

Tad started to follow, but Buzzy grabbed his arm. "Let 'em go," he said quietly.

Landis caught up with Neil near the sleeping night watchman. He put a hand on his shoulder and spun him around. "Neil, hey, slow down, man. Look, I can understand how you're feeling. Shit, I feel the same way. It's disgusting. But, think about it. Won't it make this movie unforgettable?"

Neil had a tear in his eye, just one, and it clung to his eyelash valiantly, trying not to fall. He looked into Landis's face and said, "It's wrong, Landis. It's so *wrong.*"

Landis put his other hand on Neil's other shoulder and held him in front of him. He shook those shoulders and spoke with as much sincerity as he could muster.

"I know it's wrong. But, shit, Neil. Listen. We don't have that many chances left. We either deliver a winner this time out or we can just about forget about making another movie. Think about it.

"You've got talent. I want you to be successful. But do you want your brilliant script to get buried here and never made?

"This world is full of compromises, and if you want to be a big-time writer, you need hits. Guys like you and me have used up all our favors, Neil. It's time to deliver. Nobody's knockin' down our doors with million-dollar offers, are they? Now, Buzzy has come up with an idea that definitely puts this movie over the top. Okay, it's sick, I'll admit that. But who are we to argue?"

"It's a *dead man*, for Christ sake!" Neil sniveled. "He can't defend himself."

"We all die, man." Landis's voice had taken on a soothing timbre. When it came to talking people into things they didn't want to do, he was slicker than a frozen pond.

"Put your feelings aside and come back in there with me. I need you, Neil. Honestly. You're my F. Scott Fitzgerald. Do it for me, okay?"

There was a full half minute of quiet. To Landis it seemed like an hour. Finally, Neil whispered, "All right, you win. I'll do it, but only for you."

Landis hugged Neil. "I knew you wouldn't let me down."

They walked past the sleeping watchman. His snoring was like the buzzing of a chain saw, very far away, carrying across a lake on a summer night. Landis leaned over, picked up the bottle of wine, and wiped off the top with his sleeve. He sighed and took a big swig. He handed the bottle to Neil, who raised it to his lips. "Thanks. I think we're gonna need it."

When they arrived back at the location, Buzzy was looking at his watch and pacing. "Come on! We're really late now! We've got a lot of catching up to do, and I've got to get this old boy back into the drawer before they start coming in for the morning shift. We don't have much time."

Landis wondered what time people started showing up for work here. He guided Neil back to his chair, picked up his script, and shouted, "Scene thirty-eight! Let's go!"

People snapped back into their jobs as if nothing had ever happened. Forty minutes had passed and not one shot had been completed, unheard-of for a Landis Woodley production. Chet lined up the next shot. Landis walked them through it, and when it came time to use the corpse, Tad Kingston objected.

"You mean, I have to touch it?" he whined.

"That's what the script calls for," Landis said.

"You never told me that. I'm not doing it!"

Landis looked at the script, then back at Tad. "Don't be a wimp, Kingston. Buzzy's gonna be right behind it, manipulating the arms, it reaches out and grabs you by the neck. We'll get it in one take."

"It *smells!*"

"Of course it smells, you knucklehead. It's dead."

"Can I talk to you for a minute?" Tad demanded like a petulant child.

"All right," Landis sighed. He stood up and pointed to the far side of the room, indicating that he would talk to Tad there. "Don't anyone move!" he shouted at the crew.

They walked together, and Landis was beginning to feel like a psychiatrist. He didn't like to talk this much. "What's the problem?"

"Well, I agreed to come back on the production with the rest of the crew, but I didn't realize I had to touch that thing. It scares me; I'll have bad dreams. Can't we work it out so that the close-up is Buzzy's hands instead of that . . . that thing?"

"You don't want to touch it?"

"No, sir. Please don't make me do it."

Landis looked at Tad, sizing up the situation. "Sure, Tad," he said with phony enthusiasm. "I'll get Beatnik Fred to do it."

Tad started to agree, but Landis cut him off. "No problem, and I'll get Fred to *star in the movie instead of you!*"

Tad blanched. "No, you don't understand—"

"Oh, I understand all right." Landis smirked. "You're just tryin' to fuck up my movie."

Tad shook his haircut. Landis noticed it was still perfect. He scratched his head and looked back at the crew, who were all straining to hear what was being said. Then, he reached into his pocket, pulled out a hundred-dollar bill, and stuffed it in Tad's shirt. "You can buy some bubble bath and soak for hours when you get home, just do the scene," he whispered.

Tad blinked. "But—"

"Do the fuckin' scene, Kingston!" Landis hissed. "And don't bother me anymore. This whole production is turning into a real pain in the ass!"

Landis turned and walked away from Tad Kingston. A fly buzzed around his head. Landis wondered how a fly could get all the way down here in the morgue. *Christ, it must be happy,* he thought.

20

Buzzy hunkered down behind the corpse and, using some wire that he'd attached to its wrists, manipulated it like a marionette.

The condition of rigor mortis made it hard, but by first bending the limbs and loosening them up a little, he was able to get limited movement.

The smell was a factor, but Buzzy was made of iron. He'd liberally applied the spray, but it couldn't work miracles, and a miracle was what was needed. All the crew members were appalled at the sight and smell of their guest star, and Buzzy was of a mind to minimize it as best he could. Stoically, he acted as if it happened every day.

Touching the dead body's skin and being in such close contact with it was horrible, not at all like touching the dead girl the coroner had shown him earlier, but as long as he kept moving and kept his mind on the finished production, he was all right. Focus was the key. *Focus your energy,* he told himself.

He was assisted by, of all people, Jonathon Luboff, who came to his aid when Beatnik Fred balked at having to handle the corpse. Luboff seemed to have a morbid fascination for the dead man that Buzzy found intriguing. It was almost as if he was checking the body out, wondering what it would be like when *he* was dead.

If anyone there on the set was close to the grave, it was he. Buzzy was grateful for the help, even though Luboff hands shook when he tried to tie off the wires.

"That's all right, Jonathon, I can take it from here," Buzzy said. "Thank you for your help."

Jonathon nodded. "What name will you give this man?"

Buzzy looked bemused. "He's marked as John Doe, so I think I'll call him Johnny. Johnny D. The 'D' stands for Doe, or Dead, depending on your mood. Johnny Dead. I like it. It has a nice ring to it. I can see it in the credits now. Corpse—Johnny D."

There was no smile from Luboff, not even a flicker. "You know, as an actor, Johnny Dead has dignity," he said, his accent thick and his eyes downcast.

"Why do you say that?"

"He has no ego, no vanity to get in his way. He's pure—his life is done and he's left this world. His petty problems and worries are behind him now. He is to be envied, I would think. Imagine to be as free as that."

Buzzy laughed. "No thanks. The day I start envying dead people is the day I stop drinkin'." He looked up, concerned at the seriousness of Luboff's words, determined to lighten the grave-heavy mood. "You dig?"

Jonathon's face was drawn and overcast, like a slate-gray LA sky. "I dig, young man, I most certainly dig," he said.

"Okay, let's get old Johnny D. in position."

The lights illuminated the dead man's face, sharply defining every decay, every failing of the human flesh. White as a fish belly, and just as soft, with subtle discoloration here and there, his skin seemed to come alive under the harsh scrutiny of the klieg lights. Their unforgiving carbon arcs showed nuances that only the camera wanted to see.

Chet peered through the viewfinder and whistled. "Christ, come here and look at this," he said to Landis. "Talk about scary. This guy's in his own league."

Landis hurried over and squinted into the eyepiece and nodded. "Yeah, it looks incredible. You like the light?"

Chet checked his light meter. "It's perfect. I got a little shine, but it works, keeps it wet. Powder would dry it up too much. Let's go before something happens."

Landis waved his hand and everyone came to attention. "We're ready to shoot. I want this in one take, okay?"

"You got it!" Buzzy said from behind the corpse. He sounded excited. Tad looked stricken, as if he might be sick at any moment. He was clearly terrified, and, of all the people on the set, appeared to be the most distraught. In a rare show of humanity, Luboff patted him on the back and whispered that it was time to go into character.

Neil Bugmier watched the situation with the detached interest of a funeralgoer. *This is madness,* he thought. *Am I the only one here who realizes the monstrous thing we're doing? This could ruin all our careers and haunt us forever. Have we become so desperate and so desensitized that violating the sanctity of the dead becomes just another Hollywood prank?*

He lit a cigarette and tried not to show his emotions.

Blame it all on Landis, he told himself, *blame it all on Buzzy. I am not even here.*

Landis Woodley shouted out commands. "Lights! Slate!"

Bob stepped into frame and barked, *"Cadaver,* scene thirty-nine, take one!" Crack! The slate box slammed down, and Landis leaned forward.

"Camera?"

"Speed!"

"Sound?"

"Rolling."

"Annnnd ACTION!"

Tad forced himself into the frame, moving stiffly. Luboff loomed behind him, the essence of pain. His face seemed to steal every scene he was in, whether he wanted to or not. It was just that everyone else looked so ordinary next to him. Tad Kingston bent over the corpse.

"Doctor, I—"

The corpse reached up and began to strangle Tad. Its dead hands pushed against his neck drunkenly, not actually closing around it, just pushing into it. The thumbs were pulled back, away from the fingers, so as to give the illusion of grasping. The touch of the cadaver was like fish.

It wasn't in the script.

It moved against him like an eel he had the traumatic misfortune to handle once when he was a child. The memory flashed in Tad's mind automatically, rushing in like an uninvited guest at a private party. His father had taken him fishing at the age of ten. In a tidal pool, trapped by the falling tide, a large, black eel swam desperately back and forth. Tad's father, in one of Tad's most vivid memories, went into the pool and clubbed the eel to death with a piece of driftwood. After the eel was dead, Tad's father made him pick it up and carry it back to the car. "What's the problem? It's already dead," he told him. Tad cried and cried to no avail. It felt like the most foul thing in the world, a seagoing worm.

That's what the touch of Johnny D. was like.

Tad's reaction was off the scale.

"Oh my God!" he screamed and stumbled back into Luboff, who deftly stepped aside, letting the young actor fall to the tile floor.

Landis thought Tad screamed like a woman. It was convincing, though.

The corpse had moved too soon; it wasn't going according to plan. Tad had been taken completely by surprise, and his fright was as real and deep as the realization of death. He wasn't acting. In fact, he'd forgotten all about the movie and everything else. To him there were only those hands on his neck, and the memory of the eel.

He nearly knocked the frail figure of Jonathon Luboff over, but the old man stood his ground miraculously. In front of a camera, he was a tower of strength. His spindly, discolored legs, scarred by years of injections, held like wire sculpture. Tad Kingston fell past him, brushing by as he crashed to the floor.

Kingston's face was ashen. "It moved . . ." he stammered. "That thing's alive."

From behind the corpse, Buzzy Haller was smiling. He'd jumped the gun a few seconds just to see what kind of reaction he would get from Kingston. It was worth it. Knowing that Landis would want only one take, and knowing that Tad would be scared shitless, he'd made the decision to go beyond what they had planned.

It was part of the magic. Not only would they get real death on film; they would get real fear, too. The horror in Tad's face was miles past his acting ability. It was true terror, and it transcended the movie. What Buzzy was doing was revolutionary, first with the corpse, and now with Tad. In a few short moments, he had taken this simple horror movie to the edge, then pushed it over.

Technique into passion, art into substance.

Real fear.

Landis let the camera roll; knowing Buzzy as he did, he suspected his partner's motives and sensed his gamble. It was a stunning bit of cinematography. Luboff watched it all and felt the heat of the moment like a heart attack. It was beautiful to him. To assure the whelp's performance like that was brilliant.

Buzzy pulled back the corpse's arms and let him swagger. Tad groveled at his feet shamefully, too lost in his own nightmare to worry about anyone else's.

The wires attached to Buzzy's wrists hurt. They cut into him and inhibited his circulation, but it was the only way to get realistic corpse movement. The wires cut into the Johnny's wrists too, but they were soft and cold, and in no time they were down to the bone. Without bleeding it was hard to tell how deep a cut was. Johnny's wrists were nearly severed by the end of the scene.

Buzzy didn't notice. Johnny D. never complained. His face was unchanged.

Tad Kingston was huddled on the floor sobbing for a good sixty seconds before Landis yelled, "Cut!"

People snapped out of their trance. Then, a funny thing happened. They applauded.

It wasn't for Johnny D. they applauded, or Tad, or Luboff. It was for the moment. It was for the magic. It was for the triumph. Landis and Buzzy had pulled off, within the shabby confines of their lurid little movie, a golden moment in cinematic history.

The sound of their hands clapping ricocheted off the brittle walls like gunshots.

It was a scene for the ages.

* * *

However, for all its gruesome intensity, the scene that most horror aficionados remember in *Cadaver* was not the Kingston/corpse interaction, but a scene that came a few minutes later. It resulted from another Buzzy Haller gamble.

Landis Woodley wanted a close-up of Johnny D. It was a pivotal shot, one that would establish Johnny's credentials and would be used several times. Johnny's face was so hideous that no special lighting was required to make it any more frightening. It sold itself. The only problem was the eyes. They were closed.

Landis wanted them open. A corpse with closed eyes didn't seem quite right. In the medium and long shots it wasn't a problem. They were sunken and distorted and pushed so far back into the skull that they seemed to disappear. In the close-up he wanted them open.

Buzzy told Landis that he thought he could get them to open by pulling back the skin along the top of the scalp.

"It'll look like he's opening them himself, man. It should be incredible," Buzzy crowed. They were both riding so high from the previous shots with Johnny D. that they felt they could do anything.

"I gotta warn ya," Landis told Chet as he prepared the camera angle. "I don't know what to expect under there. The damn things are probably rotten and runny as poached eggs. It could be pretty disgusting. Whatever you do, just keep rolling till I yell. Got it?"

"Got it," Chet acknowledged.

"Let's rock."

The camera whirred, the lens screwed in, bringing the viewer's eye close, close, closer to Johnny's haunted face. Everyone held his breath. At Landis's signal, Buzzy yanked back on the scalp and the eyes jerked open, first one, then the other. The right one had stuck for a split second, glued down by some dried putrescence. It popped open a heartbeat later.

Chet gasped. Through his camera lens he got the worst of it.

Worms. Hundreds of worms. Surprised by the light, they wriggled out of the sockets, squirming insanely. Somebody screamed. Chet kept the camera on it just as he was told, and its unblinking eye recorded it all faithfully. He stared, astonished at the grotesque mass of writhing hell, and tried to keep from vomiting. The supreme effort it took to keep his stomach down was second only to his dogged determination to keep the shot in focus.

Everyone else looked away.

It was as if the brains inside the dead man's head had come alive and were trying to crawl through the holes.

21

"Okay, that's a wrap!" shouted Landis Woodley at 4:30 A.M. "Let's pack it up, people! I want everybody back here tonight no later than five."

The LA County Morgue morning shift was coming in, eyeing Landis and his crowd as they broke down their equipment and loaded it back into their truck. Buzzy had been careful to put everything back exactly the way he'd found it, especially Johnny D.

No one noticed anything amiss. To the coroner, they were a model crew.

Landis was bleary-eyed when he came out of the dark building into the daylight. It had been a very long night. The light hurt his eyes, and he immediately donned his sunglasses. He was smoking his umpteenth cigarette as he walked through the parking lot.

An ambulance, bearing the day's first customer, pulled up. The paramedics took their time unloading a gurney with a sheet-covered figure on it. Landis watched the leisurely pace of the workers. *The time to rush is over now,* he thought. *This guy is no longer on the razor's edge, he's just another stiff checking into Hotel Hell. Looks like business as usual.*

Landis flicked his cigarette across the parking lot and yawned. Buzzy rolled down the window of his car and waved at Landis. Landis walked toward him, a thin smile on his lips.

"Hell of a night," he said.

Buzzy nodded. "We made horror-movie history, man. I think we really got something special in there last night."

"I can't believe we actually did it."

"Yeah, and it's all immortalized on film." Buzzy started his engine.

Landis looked at the sky. "Looks like the rain is over; it's gonna be fresh and clear for a change."

Buzzy put the car in gear. "Won't last. See ya later."

That night, to no one's surprise, Johnny D. made his triumphant encore. Buzzy and Chet joked about it, and Landis could tell that the horror of their actions was gone; it was almost normal now. Even Tad seemed less uptight, as long as he didn't have to touch a corpse.

All in all, things seemed more reasonable and less strained the second time around. The crew felt easier around Johnny D., and hardly flinched when he was hauled out of cold storage for his reprise.

They even used a few of Johnny's buddies. Buzzy was now an expert at corpse choreography, and seemed to have a real rapport with them. The other cadavers were just plain dead folk; nothing special, they were used as background mostly. None of them had the unchained charisma of Johnny D. Landis was beginning to feel that Johnny was the actual star of the movie.

Try as he might, Landis could never repeat the intensity of the Tad Kingston surprise-reaction shot, or the utter repulsion of the worm shot.

They wrapped up the last few scenes and went home ahead of schedule. A miracle. Landis was in heaven. His little production had worked out smoothly and showed every sign of being a success.

Landis took the exposed film stock to Fairfax Film Labs for immediate development. On the way he had to stop and see Sol

Kravitz to get the cash for the processing, because Fairfax wouldn't take a Landis Woodley check.

He couldn't wait to start editing because he knew he'd see it again on the film splicer—that stark terror and hungry weirdness that permeated the footage they'd shot at the morgue. He knew it would be there in black and white, waiting for him.

He'd created magic.

After sleeping all day, Buzzy Haller drove to Don's Liquors and picked up a bottle of Chardonnay, a pack of cigarettes, and a half pint of Seagram's. The sun was sinking low in the western sky, just beginning to touch the tops of the hills behind Sunset Strip. The palm trees were silhouetted vividly against a fleeting orange universe.

Buzzy sat in his car in the parking lot and cracked open the Seagram's. He brought it to his lips. It tasted wonderful going down, and he finished the swig in one long, smooth swallow. The burn in his throat felt good.

Lighting a cigarette from his new pack of Luckies, he sat back in the seat of his '48 Dodge Roadster and switched on the radio. The old gray car had a metal visor in the front that hung out over the windshield and cut the glare. He smoked while waiting for the radio to warm up. It came to life a minute later and throbbed with the deep voice only vacuum tubes can achieve, a kind of basso profundo that gently rattled the loose panels in his door.

Buzzy's car radio didn't have reverb, like some of the other models, but it kicked ass.

He scanned the dial, looking for some of that high-octane, new music that was sweeping the nation, that crazy rock and roll.

Buzzy was a jazz man, mostly. He was much too hip for the hillbilly cats who had recently invaded the airwaves. Yet, when he was alone, and no one could see him enjoying himself, he curiously tuned into the rock station. Some of the stuff, the hot rhythm and blues, was a jazz spin-off anyway. It was okay to dig people like Ray Charles and Fats Domino.

It was just that wild teenage stuff that was uncool. People like Elvis Presley, Jerry Lee Lewis, and Ricky Nelson were beneath him . . . unless he was alone. Then it was all right to tap his foot.

He zeroed in on disc jockey Art Laboe's show just in time to hear the second half of "Suzie Q" by Dale Hawkins. Leaning back in the roomy seat, he casually let the smoke drift out the open window and sang along. He liked the song; it was about a girl he thought he once knew.

Abruptly he thought of Roberta. *She was such a Goody Two-shoes. Cute, though. Nice butt, too. Too bad things turned out the way they did.* He almost felt a pang of guilt when he remembered the way she'd cried at the party.

God, I'm scum, he thought. *That's why I don't get any chicks anymore, because I'm pond scum. What girl wants pond scum?*

He visualized Roberta's smile.

That's what I like about her, he thought, *her smile, and the fact that she's a nice girl. That's what Woody digs too—the nice girl scene. Who wouldn't? Chicks like that are hard to find.*

I got dibs on her anyway 'cause I found her first. Not too many nice girls in this town anymore. My mom would have liked her. Maybe if I apologized . . .

Thinking of his mother caused Buzzy to squirm in his seat. It was impossible to think of Mother and not recall the same scene every time. He wondered why he couldn't remember anything else, just that one grotesque moment. He tried to shove it out of his mind but it persisted. He was only five years old.

Mother in her bathrobe, dead on the bathroom floor, the water running in the tub. Turn off the water and kneel down beside her. Alone for two days. Afraid to close her eyes.

Buzzy shivered and rolled his head.

Fuck this. He took another hard swallow of Seagram's and turned up the music. Thinking about Mother hurt, and he hated to hurt.

"Suzie Q" ended and Laboe introduced the next song. "It's a little ditty from New York City. Paul Anka singing about that crazy chick, 'Diana.' " The song started.

Buzzy turned the music down again, and his mind returned to Roberta. *She couldn't take a joke. That's all. If I explain it to her, she'll understand.*

Suddenly calling Roberta seemed like the most important thing in the world. He got out of his car, walked across the street to a pay phone, fished out a dime, and dialed her number. He let it ring three times before hanging up. Then he leaned against the cool glass of the phone booth door and closed his eyes.

"You got a match, Daddy-O?"

Buzzy looked up. "Huh?"

"You gotta match?" a young voice asked.

Buzzy looked at the guy in the blue jeans, T-shirt, and black leather motorcycle jacket, and nodded. They all wanted to be Brando now, he thought, the rebel, the wild one. Buzzy was cool; he knew the score with all the hipsters. He handed a match over to the kid and watched while he lit a cigarette.

Life is passing me by, Buzzy thought. *This punk is living more than me. I'm falling behind. First the chicks, then the whole scene. What's next?*

Buzzy felt every one of his twenty-five years weighing down on him like boulders.

He watched the kid walk away and remembered how he felt when he was like that, a young rebel. He would have felt exactly like that kid, that he had just bummed a match *from a square.*

Is that what I am now? A square? No, I'm still a rebel, damn it. I'm still the wildest cat in town.

He eventually drove to Scrivener's drive-in, near Hollywood High School, and had a hamburger. Watching the high school chicks tease their boyfriends made him feel even older.

He drove on, knocking back another long swallow of the Seagram's at the next light. He drove in the direction of the morgue.

Pulling into the parking lot there, he waited a while longer, had himself several more drinks, and listened to some more rock and roll. At eight o'clock he went in.

"Say man, how're ya doin'?"

It was Charles, the night watchman, at his usual post.

"Oh, I'm doin' all right. 'Course there ain't no excitement since you boys left."

Buzzy smiled. "I'll bet."

"That was the most action we ever had down here," Charles said. "Not that I minded it, you understand. It's just that it gets pretty quiet around here at night."

"Do you ever get spooked?"

"Spooked?"

"Yeah, with all those stiffs back there, and you the only living soul in the building?"

Charles smiled through his bad teeth. "Sometimes it does get a might creepy, especially after I been watchin' one of them horror movies y'all make." He chuckled. "Seriously, though, once in a while I think I hear something, and I go back there and have a look."

Buzzy offered a cigarette. The old man coughed and took one. He continued speaking after lighting up.

"Yeah, I go down there and have myself a nice long look. Sometimes I swear I hear voices. Of course, that's impossible. When I get down there I halfway expect to see all the dead bodies sitting around having a party, and when I walk in the room they all stop talkin' and look at me. They don't look too happy to see me. In fact, they probably hate me. They all think, well, he's still alive, and we're dead, so fuck him. It ain't fair."

Buzzy looked past him, down the hall into the shadows of the dead room. "Yeah, I'll bet you hear all kinds of shit in a place like this, night after night."

"I gotta go back there to check." Charles nodded in the direction of the abattoir. " 'Course, there's nothin' there, there never is. Then I come back out here and have a smoke and forget about it. Still, sometimes . . . voices. Ya know what I mean? Fuckin' voices. Whispering. Kinda gives ya the creeps."

"I can imagine," Buzzy said honestly. "Hey, I almost forgot, I brought you something, a little gift, from the guys on the crew." He pulled the bottle of wine out of the brown paper bag he carried and smiled.

Charles stood up and shook his hand, admiring the bottle and smiling back at him like he'd just found a ten-dollar bill.

"Well, I'll be damned. That's awful nice of you, Buzzy. Damn. You know, in all my years down here, nobody ever gave me a gift until you came along."

Buzzy nodded. "Yeah, it's a rotten world. You deserve a little reward, Charlie. You're doin' a hell of a job guardin' the stiffs. What do you say we have a taste right now? I got a corkscrew and some paper cups."

Charles smiled. "Don't mind if I do."

They shared a few glasses and some small talk. Twenty minutes later, Buzzy stood and said, "Well, I gotta go. Take care of yourself Charlie, okay? Keep the bottle."

Charlie held up the wine. "I sure will."

Buzzy left the building and found his way back to the car and the rock and roll.

"I'm still the wildest cat in town," he said to himself.

Lieutenant Garth Prease walked up the front path to the Beaumond house marveling at what a nice, normal place it appeared to be. He'd expected some sort of Satanic temple, not the white picket fence and well-tended lawn that greeted him.

The path to the door was made of flagstones, set into the earth and measured carefully so that each stone was approximately where your foot would land as you walked at a normal pace.

Garth smiled. This was not what he'd expected at all. It was evening, just after ten o'clock, and the house was illuminated from within. Squares of warm yellow light shone like color slides projected on glass.

Thora's face appeared at the window, pale and drawn, the black circles under her eyes visible even through the gauze curtains. His heart sank. The girl was already fragile enough. He didn't want to upset her further, but it was part of his job. He chose to do it in person, rather than over the phone.

He cursed the medical examiner for being so tardy with the forms, but it was typical. When the unclaimed-body notification came in from the morgue, it was already quitting time. It had taken several phone calls to set the wheels in motion. The coroner didn't like being disturbed at home during dinner, but Garth didn't like having to work after five. If the damn note had been filed when the body first arrived and not a day and a half later, maybe they all could have done their jobs during normal business hours. Bureaucracy was like cancer.

After arranging to meet the coroner and view the body, he called Thora and told her he wanted to come over and talk. The John Doe matched the description of Albert Beaumond.

Some things are best not discussed over the phone. Garth, a good Christian, appreciated that, and, if nothing else, he was sensitive. He'd done this before, and it was never easy, but it had to be done face-to-face.

Thora opened the door before he rang the bell. The door

opened a crack, her face loomed from the shadows like an apparition, ghostly and tortured. It struck him as incredibly sad.

"Hello, Miss Beaumond," he said.

"Lieutenant Prease," she replied. "Have you found my father?"

He answered her question with a question. "May I come in?"

The door swung in a little farther and he slipped through. It was subdued inside, the lights tastefully kept at a low wattage. What had looked so bright and cheerful from the outside appeared now to be of minimal candlepower and somewhat depressing. He stood in the hall with his hands at his sides.

"Have you found my father?" she asked again automatically.

Garth looked away and began his prepared speech. "I'm sorry, I don't want to upset you, Miss Beaumond, but I may have some bad news. There was a body found yesterday. It hasn't been identified, but it matches the description you gave me. I think maybe you should come with me and have a look."

"Oh my God," Thora said in a rushed breath, a sob already erupting through the thin layer of control. Her eyes quickly filled with fluid. Garth wanted to comfort her but didn't.

"Look," he said, "it could be nothing. I just want to make sure . . ."

"Of course," Thora, dazed, said in a barely audible whisper. "I'll get my things."

Garth watched her climb the stairs, and for the first time noticed how much of a woman Thora Beaumond was becoming. She was young, but her youth was tempered with a quiet maturity that comes with tragedy. He found himself wondering about her life. How much had she suffered already? With her father a devout Satanist and the family home a pagan temple, how had the child's adolescent years been distorted?

Garth looked around the hall and peered into the living room. No signs of devil worship were visible.

Thora came back down the stairs, drying her eyes with a balled tissue.

"I can drive you, if you like," he offered.

Thora's eyes lifted to meet his. The dewy sadness that he'd seen there before had now been replaced by an agitated, steady weeping.

Garth wanted to look away. The fear on her face hurt to watch. He could tell she was silently praying that the body was not that of her father. And so was he. There was something about this girl.

He dreaded the moment.

"Okay," she said in a fragile, frightened voice.

"My car's outside."

22

When Buzzy Haller returned to the morgue at ten o'clock in the evening he was not surprised to find Charles, the night watchman, asleep at his post, the empty bottle of Chardonnay next to him.

Buzzy was drunk himself, but with him it was an entirely different animal. Buzzy drank, not to forget, but to remember. He didn't want to pass out, he wanted to conquer the world. He laughed at old lushes like Charles, who only wanted to use the booze for sleeping medicine. *What a waste,* he thought. *There are things to do, places to go, applecarts to upset.*

He opened the front door, walked past the desk, and strolled down the hall to the abattoir.

Drawer sixty-six had not been opened or disturbed in any way since the night before. Buzzy slid it opened and said hello to Johnny D.

"Hey, man, how's it goin'?"

Buzzy laughed. *How could it be goin'? The man is dead. To him, every day is basically the same.*

He'd actually missed the ripe old guy since their last dance.

"You know, Johnny, I been thinkin' about you, my man."

Johnny didn't move. His closed eyelids stared at the ceiling, and his sagging face remained the same.

Buzzy gave old Johnny the once-over and was shocked by the deterioration that had occurred in just one night. The man was going fast, like hamburger going bad. Whatever Johnny D. was going to do, Buzzy thought, whatever his destiny, it better happen fast or forever hold his peace.

"I been thinkin'. It's a shame to know that a major talent like you is down here with no work, no agent, and no publicity, while all those other stiffs are out there making millions! It ain't right. Well, I'm here to save you, my man. I'm here to save you from this fuckin' place, where they don't understand and appreciate you. From now on, you're a star."

Bluish lips stayed shut. Were the eyes full of worms still? Buzzy almost checked, then decided to do it later, when he could be more thorough. Besides, what was he going to do about the maggots?

Buzzy considered it for a moment.

Well, let's see, he thought. *I could always spray some ant and roach killer in his eyes, that would probably do some damage, but then the rest of them, the ones not killed by direct contact with the spray, would just crawl back into the skull where I couldn't get 'em. They would multiply back there and there wouldn't be a thing I could do about it. No, the worm thing is problematic, but it's one of Johnny's many charms. There's not a damn thing I can do.*

"The strong silent type, aren't you?" Buzzy murmured. He hoisted Johnny out of the drawer and onto a nearby gurney. Not bothering to cover the corpse, or obscure it in any way, Buzzy began to wheel the gurney toward the door, then he caught a whiff of decay and stopped long enough to pick up a can of deodorant spray, which he stuffed in his pocket.

"Deodorant for corpses, what will they think of next?"

Buzzy rolled the gurney up the hall, past Charles, and out the front door. With wheels squeaking, he taxied the gurney right up to his car. Without even bothering to look around, Buzzy casually unlocked his trunk and put Johnny inside.

He left the gurney in the lot and drove away.

As he accelerated, he felt Johnny's body thump against the

rear wall of the trunk. Buzzy lit a cigarette and turned up the radio. "In The Still of the Night" by the Five Satins was playing. The pimply teenage harmonies made Buzzy smile. To some people, this was a serious piece of music, the definitive Doo-wop song. To Buzzy, it was a joke. Everything was a joke. Life was a joke.

As Buzzy drove away, he was passed by a black sedan traveling in the other direction. The car pulled into the parking lot of the morgue, into the spot vacated by Buzzy's car. The gurney stood alone in the lot, ominous and enigmatic.

"What's that thing doing out here?" Garth Prease asked aloud.

"What is it?" Thora asked. Then she knew, she knew in a twinkling. Garth didn't answer.

They got out and made their way to the door. The sound of Charles's snoring echoed up the hall like machinery. The distinctive nasal snort that identified his particular snore rattled and hummed, bouncing off the walls in happy, irresponsible chaos.

"Guard!" Garth shouted. The snoring changed meter, modulated upward, then dropped back into the predictable pattern. "Hey! Wake up!" Garth shouted again.

"Huh?" Charles's head came up, his face lined by the folds on his sleeve. He squinted at them. "What? Who are you?"

Garth had his badge out and in Charles's face in less time than it took Charles to realize that his ass was grass. "Lieutenant Garth Prease, LAPD. The coroner is on his way down here right now. We came to look at a body."

Charles was up like a slow shot. "Yes, sir! Right this way, sir!" He motioned for them to walk farther down the hall, in the direction of the main room. Charles realized, with a sinking feeling, that the empty bottle of wine was sitting on his desk, a branding iron. He was busted, plain and simple.

He decided to take it like a man, and deny everything.

"That your wine, fellah?"

"No, sir!"

"Were you asleep?"

"No, sir!"

"What were you doing when we came in?"

"Resting my eyes, sir," Charles said quickly, as if speed of response would get him back any of the points that he had lost.

Prease was already in his face. Charles knew the gig was up.

Just then, Dr. Milburn, the assistant coroner, walked in. Charles picked up the bottle and placed it on the floor next to his chair. Milburn saw it anyway.

When they discovered that the body in drawer number sixty-six was missing, along with the gurney, Charles was relieved of duty.

Buzzy Haller got drunk with his new best friend that night. They spent a jolly time knocking back shots of tequila and smoking reefers. Sometime around midnight, Buzzy got the bright idea that he wanted to shoot some publicity photos of his new superstar, Johnny D.

Being a decent photographer with professional equipment, he took several rolls of 35 mm film in color and black and white. Johnny was a real sport as far as Buzzy was concerned. He posed him this way and that, even reproduced the famous "eyeball full of worms" shot.

Garth Prease took Thora Beaumond home. He stayed in touch with her and whenever a possible clue manifested itself, he was quick to draw it to her attention. Nothing, however, seemed to bring Albert Beaumond back into the picture, and soon, even Thora would begin to doubt that he was still alive.

23

When the processed film came back from the lab, Landis dived into the editing, working furiously around the clock. He spent the next several days hunched over his old Movieola Editing Machine, hand-splicing his masterpiece, until a rough cut of *Cadaver* was ready.

That Friday night he'd arranged for a wrap party at his house. It was a tradition and a good-luck charm. He intended to show the film at the party.

Roberta Bachman didn't usually answer the door in her curlers; but, then again, the doorbell didn't usually ring after eleven o'clock at night. She swung the door open, expecting an emergency, maybe a cop standing there saying, "Your dog's been hit by a car, miss." Except she didn't have a dog. Or, "Do you know this person? They've just been arrested for armed robbery." And one of her friends would be standing there looking guilty.

Her jaw dropped when she saw Landis Woodley.

"You!" she gasped, and began to close the door. Landis reached out and held it open.

"I'm sorry to disturb you," he started to say.

She cut him off. "You've got a lot of nerve coming around here. After what you did at that party—oh, you make me sick!"

"Hold on a second!"

"Let go of my door!"

"I just want to talk to you."

"Send me a letter."

She pushed on the door with renewed vigor. "Aren't you going to invite me in?" he asked with a smile.

"No!" she snapped. "Now, go away."

"I just wanted to say I'm sorry about what happened."

Roberta shook her head. "I don't believe you. Look, we've been all through this already. I don't especially want to see you, hear from you, know you, or listen to your apologies."

Landis kept smiling, even though his hand, wedged in the door, was beginning to hurt. He decided it was time to play his trump card. "I've got pickles," he said, holding up a white deli bag with his other hand.

She kept pushing. "So?"

"Not just any old pickles."

Landis had heard from Buzzy that Roberta loved homemade deli pickles. Everyone knew that the best pickles in LA were from Canter's Delicatessen on Fairfax Avenue.

"From Canter's," he said.

Roberta's face changed; the scowl went out of it. She relaxed her pressure on the door. "Canter's?"

"They're for you."

Roberta snorted. "Oh, you are so slick. You think you can bribe your way in here with those? How did you know I liked pickles?"

"Research. I've been workin' on this for a while."

"I still hate you."

"That's understandable."

"You're still mule puke."

"Okay."

"But let me see the pickles."

She let Landis inch the door open until he could hand her the pickles. He stepped inside with the exchange.

"I can't believe I let you in here," Roberta said. "I must be out of my mind." She sighed. "You can only stay a minute, understand?"

"Sure, a minute's fine."

"Say what you gotta say and leave."

"I'm sorry you got scared. Those stunts were part of the party. Buzzy took a lot of time planning them. They were for publicity."

"We've been all through this."

"You know, I'm in production on a new movie right now. It's called *Cadaver.*"

Roberta made a sour face. "Your movies are sick."

"People watch 'em anyway, just like they slow down to look at a car wreck on the side of the road."

"What's your point?"

"My point is—scaring people is my job. I'm sorry you got in the way. I never meant to hurt you."

Roberta looked at Landis suspiciously. Her soft, honest eyes bored into his cheesy smile. He melted a little.

"You're pathetic, you know that?" she said. "You can stay for one cup of coffee. Just one. Then you leave."

Neil Bugmier strung crepe paper across the room, looping it over the top of the ten-foot movie screen in the projection room in Landis Woodley's basement. He was wearing a simple turquoise housedress and had his shoes off. It was difficult to stand on a chair and hang decorations in high heels.

The acrid smoke from Landis Woodley's cigarette drifted in his face, spicing the air and making him want to light up a Chesterfield himself.

Landis was hunched over his film-editing machine, checking the footage from *Cadaver.* From the grunting sounds he made as he squinted through the eyepiece, Neil deduced that Landis was pleased with what he saw. Landis jealously guarded that eyepiece, and refused to let anybody see even one frame of film until he deemed it ready. Landis was funny like that.

He'd promised that he'd have a rough cut of the film ready for viewing tonight at the cast party. It would be the centerpiece of the celebration.

Everyone from Luboff to Kingston would have an opinion,

Landis knew, and he would ignore them all. Landis didn't need anyone to tell him when something was good or bad. He knew from experience.

At any rate, the rough cut he would show tonight would be stunning, if he did say so himself.

"It's fuckin' beautiful," he told Neil. "The corpse is scary, Luboff is completely believable, and the sets look great. I gotta tell ya, this is the best one yet."

"My script?"

"It smells like a rose."

Was that a compliment or a put-down? Neil screwed up his face behind his makeup and climbed down off the ladder. He surveyed his work and was pleased enough to put the ladder away.

"You didn't have to do all that, Neil. Nobody cares," Landis remarked.

"I care," Neil said. It was becoming his standard answer. "It makes it more festive."

"Well, this old place always did need a woman's touch," Landis said, baiting the trap.

"Thank you," Neil replied, taking it. "I hear you dropped in on Roberta Bachman."

"Who told you that?"

Neil fished a cigarette out of his pocketbook and lit it from a book of matches from Frederick's of Hollywood.

"I know Roberta. We worked together over at National."

Landis looked up from his eyepiece. "I didn't know that," he said slowly.

"There's a lot you don't know, Landis Woodley," Neil exhaled loudly. "You're in your own little world working on these pictures. I'm not some shut-in who only comes out to work for you. I got a life, you know."

"Are you spying on me?"

"Why on earth would I do that?"

Landis grunted. "Well, to answer your question, yeah, I did see her. I brought her some pickles from Canter's a few days ago."

"You know, she was very upset after your party. Apparently, Buzzy and you really made a great impression. God knows, you two guys can alienate anybody. But why go after Roberta? She's a sweet innocent thing."

Landis clicked off the light in the film splicer to avoid heat damage to the celluloid. He rubbed his eyes. Editing was tiresome work, but he insisted on doing it all himself. No one else could touch his film. If he could, he would also do the processing, but that was impossible.

He sighed. "That's the whole point, Neil. You see, everyone around here, everyone I work with, all the people we know . . . are all freaks. She's the one person I know who is totally normal, who I can talk to and get a real opinion once in a while. I think she's just about the sweetest, nicest, most honest person I know. And that's no jive. I like her a lot."

Neil sat next to Landis. His bizarre combination of colognes and perfumes assailed Landis's nose. It mingled with the cigar and cigarette smoke to form a dense toxic jungle of aromas. They both coughed.

"Let's go out on the porch," Landis said.

"Okay. I could go for some coffee."

"Fuck coffee. I want a beer."

"Done."

Three minutes later they were looking out at the brownish LA sky and relaxing in a pair of cheap lawn chairs.

"Roberta is vulnerable. I wouldn't want you to hurt her," Neil said.

"I won't hurt her, for God's sake. I like her. Hell, maybe she's the woman I'll marry someday."

Neil snapped his head around. "Am I hearing this straight? Did you say the word 'marry'?"

Landis smiled sheepishly. "Well, not—no. I mean, not for a long time. And she doesn't really feel the same way about me."

"I thought she hated you," Neil said.

"She kinda does. I've only been to see her twice, and I don't think she enjoyed my company all that much. I think she was just being nice. She heard me out, though, and it helped to have a person like that to talk to," Landis concluded.

"What did you—oh no, you didn't tell her about—"

Neil didn't finish his question. Landis's face remained granite.

"Landis! You didn't! That shit could ruin you! It could ruin us all!"

Landis looked out at the smog and said nothing.

"Jesus Christ! I don't believe it! You told this girl you hardly know, about . . . about *that?*" He hooked his thumb back toward the house, indicating the movie Landis was editing.

"I didn't say that!" Landis replied defensively.

"Well, what did you say?"

Landis leaned back in his chair and said nothing.

Neil grabbed his arm. "Don't hurt Roberta and don't tell her things that she'll never understand. Damning things, ruinous things. She's just a child, for Christ sake."

"I didn't say that I told her anything," Landis answered.

"Well, did you?"

The sliding door opened and Buzzy Haller stepped through. "Where's the beer?" he asked.

Neil kept his eyes locked on Landis, waiting for an answer. He asked again.

"Did you?"

"Fuck off, Neil," Landis replied without venom. "You're not my mother. I don't have to tell you shit. You work for me, remember?"

The party was sedate compared to the Halloween bash. There were substantially fewer people in the house, only the cast and crew. Buzzy Haller didn't get stinking drunk until after ten o'clock, a record by most people's recollections. Landis ran the film at midnight.

They all gathered in the projection room and he got up to address the crowd before switching off the lights.

"I would just like to thank everyone here for doing their part in making this movie possible. I thought we did a pretty damn good job."

There was polite applause.

Landis continued. "I did a very rough edit today, just so we could have something to look at tonight. The real edit will take a week or two, so just keep that in mind. I think you're going to like what you see. The acting is excellent. Jonathon, as usual, you were brilliant."

Luboff, the consummate ham, stood and took a bow. "Thank you, my friends," he said, his pupils as constricted as pinpoints.

Landis smiled. "And a fine job was also done by our costar, Tad." Addressing Tad directly, he said, "You were very convincing. Although I don't know how much of it was acting and how much was real fear. Either way, you did your best work yet."

"Thank you, Mr. Woodley," Tad said from his seat.

"And Chet, you were magnificent. The camera work was, how can I say it, beyond anything we've ever done before. The morgue stuff is absolutely the scariest stuff I've ever seen, and the lighting was atmospheric and spooky as hell. In short, a masterful job."

Chet waved his hand and chugged a beer. He was a man of few words and fewer emotions. "Thanks," he muttered.

"Okay, that's it. Before we roll film I just want to say one more thing. This film is scary. Not just a little scary, a lot scary. It's a good film with decent production values. The overall feeling is very disturbing; I think you'll be pleased. We have created a masterpiece of horror, folks, and I am very proud. Let's roll film!"

The lights clicked off and Buzzy started the projector. The film credits had yet to be included, so the action jumped right into the first scene. Everyone watched with rapacious intensity.

Buzzy periodically swigged from a silver flask. Others politely sipped beer or wine at their seats. No one dared to move while the movie was showing.

The grainy, black-and-white texture of the film gave it a dark, atmospheric dimension.

Luboff's manic eyes filled the screen. In the first shot he was digging up a grave. It was night, in a graveyard, and he labored over the freshly dug earth. The camera started with his eyes, then panned back and away to encompass the scene as he looked around frantically. Then, assured that he was alone, he went back to digging.

Chet had made brilliant use of the zoom lens and subject framing. Luboff's eyes struck the right chord of insanity and terror from the very first second of film. It was the kind of beginning—an extreme close-up of the eyes—that would jar the audience right into the mood of the thing.

There was scattered applause for the opening scene. Landis

and Chet smiled. As the movie wore on, Landis watched the reactions of the people around him. They gasped at all the right
moments, and, at the climax of the morgue scene, they
screamed. All of them. Even the hardened veterans like Luboff
and Beatnik Fred. It was the terrible shot of Johnny D.'s eyes. It
was the maggots.

Landis waited until the lights came up and congratulated his
cast and crew. They were all impressed. This time he had really
done it. He had really done what he set out to do, scare the hell
out of everybody. God, it felt good.

Landis had himself a few drinks and enjoyed the moment.

Buzzy, in the meantime, had gotten more inebriated with
every passing hour.

Why did Buzzy get like this? Landis wondered about his
friend. It seemed like he had to get thoroughly smashed every
time there was a party. Was it the social aspect? Did he feel uncomfortable around people? That might have been the excuse
for Halloween, but not here. These were people he worked with
every day.

Buzzy was out of control, and Landis thought that maybe it
was time for his good buddy to dry out.

The movie had been shown, the guests were happy, the drinks
were flowing, it was getting late. Then Buzzy Haller staggered to
his feet.

"Can I have yer attenshun?" he shouted drunkenly.

Heads turned. Landis thought, *Oh shit, here he goes. He's chewed
through the leash again.*

"Attenshun! Please!"

Someone, almost as drunk as Buzzy, kept talking.

"Hey!" Buzzy shouted in an ugly explosion. "Shut the fuck
up!"

The room went quiet. All eyes went to Buzzy's face, which was
now twisted in an evil, maniacal smile. His red-rimmed eyes
sparkled like demonic sapphires. Warning lights were going off
in Landis's head. He instinctively moved closer to Buzzy, in case
he had to restrain him physically. He signaled to Neil to do the
same. Together they inched nearer the drunken monster maker.

"You people . . . you people are fulla shit! You wanna know
why? Huh? Ya wanna know? I tell ya!"

Buzzy stumbled backward a half step. Landis moved another few feet closer. Buzzy's eyes locked on him and glared. "Get back, Woody! I'll be good, I promise! I jush wanna say one thing, okay?"

Landis held up a hand. "You're drunk, Buzz. Come on, let's just cool out now."

"Fuck you! I'll show you cool. You wanna see cool?"

Neil moved in next to Landis.

"Oh, look at this," Buzzy slurred, pointing to Neil. "It's Rebecca of Sunnybrook Farm. He's gonna help Woody restrain the drunken party guest. Well, stay the fuck back! I swear it, I'll deck the next guy who tries to make a move on me!"

Everyone held their ground, watching and waiting.

"Now, where was I? Oh yeah, you people are fulla shit! You know why? 'Cause the real star of this movie was not even invited!"

Landis shook his head. "What are you talkin' about, Buzz?"

"Oh, as if you didn't know!" Buzzy roared back at the top of his lungs. "There's one star and one star only that makes this pukin' picture worth a half a shit! He's the guy who saved all your asses, the one who's gonna fill the theaters and scare the teenagers, *and you pompous assholes didn't even invite him!*"

Buzzy took another stumbling step back, nearly tripping over his own feet. Landis couldn't figure out his actions or where he was going with all this. Buzzy was just smashed, too drunk to make any sense, he thought.

"Ladies and gentlemen, meet the real star of this picture! Don't look in your programs, you won't find him there! He's that hot new prospect that's got all the ladies talkin'."

Buzzy took another halting step backward. His hand went out and met the wall. Supporting his weight, he moved along the wall until his hand found the closet door.

The closet! Landis thought. *That's what he's been moving toward this whole time.*

Buzzy twisted the handle of the closet door, grinning like a mad dog all the while. The door opened a crack and Landis could see a hint of something white leaning against it from the other side.

"Here he is, the man of the hour! He's hot, he's sexy, and he's dead! Folks, meet Johnny D.!"

Buzzy jerked the closet door open and the white, bloated, dead body of Johnny D. fell out. It hit the floor with an ungodly slap, facedown. The sound it made as it impacted with the hard-wood was unimaginable. A solid, wet thud, like two hundred pounds of beef hitting a butcher's counter, reverberated through the house. The sound of cartilage breaking as the face crunched into the floor was as clear and unmistakable as a fart.

People screamed. Becky Sears fainted into Tad Kingston's arms. Beatnik Fred hunched over and began to vomit onto the floor.

The body settled. Then, the sound of a massive bubble of es-caping gas hissed from somewhere deep in its throat and a stench from beyond hell filled the room.

Landis reeled, his eyes watering, toward the hall. There was a crush of hysteria and people fighting to make the stairs and fresh air.

Most ran out onto the porch. The unbelievable sound of a group of people vomiting over the railing filled the night.

Tears filled Landis's eyes.

Buzzy Haller was completely insane.

24

"You're the sickest piece of shit in the world, you know that?"

Buzzy just smiled. Landis slapped him across the face, his hand stinging as it hit bone. Buzzy turned with the blow, still numb from the liquor.

"Don't smile at me!" Landis screamed.

Buzzy put his hand to his face and felt for damage. The red mark was spreading, but the skin was unbroken. He blinked and resumed sipping his coffee as if nothing had happened.

Landis continued to rage. "How *could* you? Jesus, you must have broken fifty laws to get him here. How did you do it?"

"It was easy," Buzzy replied.

"Do the cops know?"

Buzzy shook his head.

"You are one sick muthafucker. What am I gonna do with you? I think you need psychiatric help. The morgue was one thing, but bringing him here . . . what the hell were you thinking?"

Buzzy smiled a crooked, goofy smile. He really was beginning to resemble a lunatic, Landis thought. Watching him now, hours later, while he coolly fended off questions, he actually seemed to be pleased with himself.

"I just thought that you couldn't very well have a cast party without the real star of the picture. It's not fair," Buzzy mumbled.

Landis exploded again. "Cut the shit! *The man's dead!* You've lost your mind, Buzz, you really have! Bringing him here last night was dangerous. Now there are witnesses."

Buzzy laughed. "They're the same witnesses you already swore to secrecy. What are they gonna say?"

Landis paced. He ran a hand through his rapidly thinning hair. "You're gonna have to get rid of him. That's all there is to it. The sooner the better."

Buzzy looked up, the steam from the coffee swirling around his face. "What do you mean?"

"Just get rid of him," Landis snapped back.

"You mean take him back?"

Landis stopped pacing. "No! No, don't take him back. That would only make things worse. You might get caught. You're gonna have to get rid of him the same way that people always get rid of bodies. Dump him somewhere."

Buzzy snorted. "Where?"

"I don't care where! Just get rid of him!"

Buzzy raised an eyebrow. Landis always wondered about that move. Buzzy could raise just one eyebrow at a time, arch it, and hold the position for sixty seconds. It was a gift. Landis could only raise both eyebrows at the same time. To be able to control them separately like that was a gift from God. Buzzy was touched.

He watched Buzzy's eyebrow until the man spoke. "Sure, I'll get rid of him. No problem."

Later that morning, Landis went to meet with the distributors. His film was on the table, and it was now time to see what kind of action he could get. This was the side of the business Landis hated, the ass-kissing and the politics. He had never excelled at impressing people from a business standpoint. In fact, Landis repulsed people. That was part of his problem. Landis braced himself against the bullshit and drove into Burbank with his window down and his mind open.

He had told Buzzy to sober up and get rid of the body before he returned. Landis was shaken; Buzzy had actually succeeded in scaring him. The man was out of control. When Buzzy lost it, it meant that Landis, whose life was continually on the edge, might lose too. Buzzy was more than a friend—he was an integral part of Landis's cinematic operations.

He was the monster maker. You can't have a monster movie without a monster. Now, it seemed to Landis, Buzzy had become a monster himself. Dangerous and unpredictable, he threatened to bring down the whole house of cards on Landis's head.

He had to do something.

First, Buzzy had to dry out. It was time for a trip to the hospital. Landis had taken Luboff in so many times they knew him by name. What must they think? That he was a friend to all the winos and junkies of the world?

Landis thought. *Who cares? If I cared what people thought about me all the time, I'd be out of business. The main thing was to get Buzzy help.*

Nineteen fifty-seven came to a close. The papers were full of Sputnik and the Dodgers were coming to town. Rock and roll had taken over the radio, and juvenile delinquents had taken over the high schools.

All over America, teenagers flocked to the drive-ins and became enamored with monsters. Aliens, vampires, creatures from lagoons, dinosaurs, giant bugs, mummies, mad scientists, and their hideous creations dominated the outdoor screens. The exploitation movie business boomed. Sales of cosmetics, blue jeans, motorcycles, guitars, leather jackets, and chewing gum skyrocketed.

Cadaver became a hit at the drive-ins, but, because Landis had oversold all the available shares in advance, most of the profits were gobbled up by the investors. Although he would never get the respect and recognition he longed for from his Hollywood colleagues, he did make a splash with the kids and became, for a short while, the king of the B-movies.

Then America changed, leaving Landis Woodley behind.

NOW

25

STUDIO CITY, CALIFORNIA 1996

Roberta Bachman's office was elegant. She favored leather couches and modern desks. The art pieces that hung on her walls were all original lithos, signed and numbered by known artists. She bought the prints at an art gallery on Ventura Boulevard in Van Nuys, where she knew the owner. Roberta was chic, but not dumb; she never paid retail. She had learned over the years in the Hollywood community that it was not how much money you actually had, it was how much money people *thought* you had.

In other words, the image game.

Roberta played that game well. She enjoyed it. It was tailor-made for a woman who made good money yet wanted to be perceived as a woman who made great money. Attractive and slim for a woman of her years, Roberta kept her hair shade of Lucille Ball red as a sort of trademark. Thus was she known and instantly recognizable around town. She had a self-contained prettiness that endured, and a confidence that overcame.

Savvy and tough, she knew Hollywood like a mapmaker. She'd held every kind of job in the movie business, and she knew all kinds of people, the good and the bad. Roberta owned her own home and business, had never married, and loved her life. She was the prototypical LA career woman—a buyer of designer clothes, a diner at exclusive restaurants, a driver of exotic cars.

Clint Stockbern was the exact opposite. His beat-up Volkswagen bug looked like what it was—barely adequate transportation for a man who barely made a living.

He carried the scars of a terrible case of adolescent acne but he was an otherwise handsome youth. His wardrobe consisted solely of T-shirts and jeans.

He sat in Roberta's office, careful to keep his sneakers off her furniture.

"You didn't tell me you knew him."

"That's right," Roberta answered.

"But why?"

"This is your story, Clint. If you knew I knew him, you'd have wasted a lot of time bugging me for details. Hell, I could just as soon write the story myself."

Clint looked out the window at the afternoon traffic in downtown Thousand Oaks and cleared his throat.

"He invited me back to look at some film," Clint said proudly.

"What kind of film?"

"Rare stuff, outtakes, stuff the censors made him clip, I don't know. He was vague about it. All I can tell you is I want to see it. It's a collector's dream."

Roberta nodded. "Okay, but be careful."

"Why? He's just an old man."

Roberta drummed a pencil on her desk absently. "What would you say if I told you that Landis Woodley was, at one time, madly in love with me?"

Clint smiled automatically. "I'd say, 'Jesus Christ.' "

"And what would you say if I told you that we actually went out together a couple of times?"

"I'd say, 'holy shit.' "

"And what would you say if I told you he confided all his deepest, darkest secrets to me?"

"I'd say, 'why the fuck have I been all over town digging up rumors when you've got the facts?' "

It was Roberta's turn to smile. "A story is a story. You still have to do your homework."

"You're the boss."

Roberta sniffed. She was the boss, and as long as she was running the show, she'd put whatever writer on whatever story she wanted. It just so happened that Clint was a natural for this one. He was familiar with the subject matter, he was sharp and resourceful, and, she thought, a talented young writer.

"Why do you think I sent you out on this?" she asked.

"I don't know. Because I like his movies?"

"Crap," Roberta snorted. "His films are garbage. How you can watch 'em, I'll never know. You're a sick puppy, kid."

Clint shifted in his seat.

"From what you've gathered so far, tell me what you think," Roberta said.

Clint hunched forward, his face aglow. The sparkle of excitement in his eyes was intense. "I think there's a curse."

Roberta smiled. She looked over his head, letting her eyes drift across a Peggy Hopper Hawaiian print. She gathered her breath and asked, "Okay, why do you think that?"

"Because, several of the people who worked on *Cadaver* have all met untimely deaths. Most recently, a year ago, Buzzy Haller committed suicide. In 1989, Chet Bronski was murdered in his apartment, strangled. It's still in the 'unsolved crimes' file at the LAPD. Before that, in 1971, Neil Bugmier disappeared off the face of the earth, again, no clues."

Roberta nodded. "And you think it's a conspiracy?"

"Conspiracies are for wimps. I think there's a curse, a big, fat, juicy curse, and that's the story I'm gonna write."

Roberta smiled anew. "I knew you'd think that."

"You did?"

"Of course. That's why I put you on it."

Clint's jaw dropped. "What?"

"First of all," she continued, "just getting in to see Landis Woodley is a challenge. I know that. He's turned into quite the recluse, not to mention he's just about the most unpleasant man in the known universe. *I certainly wasn't going over there.* And it's too good a story to go to waste.

"With your enthusiasm for his films and your encyclopedic knowledge of the man, the myth, the miracle, I figured you would find a way in. Then, once you got in, you'd be able to hold his attention, even if it was just some kind of sicko hero worship."

Clint nodded. "Yeah, you were right about that."

"He likes hero worship. He never got his due in the glory years," Roberta explained. "I figured you were just the man for the job. A good curse story is dynamite, and you're a good writer, Clint. Good writers are worth their weight."

Clint ran his fingers through his hair, raking it back loosely. "The thing is—the story about real corpses in *Cadaver* is true. He actually confessed to it on tape. Now, that in itself is a hell of scoop and would sell a ton of magazines, but then I started thinkin'. I thought, hey, most of these people are dead."

"Good, good, go on," she said.

"Well, think about it. They use real corpses, later on people start dying. It's like—they're pissed off, you know? The dead are pissed off and they want revenge."

Roberta nodded. "So?"

"So, they're back from the grave and they want their residuals!"

Roberta thought Clint's idea of a joke was weak. She let it crash and burn on her desk without flinching.

"What about the others?" she asked.

"What others?"

"Didn't you check the rest of the cast and crew of *Cadaver*, to see who was left alive?"

Clint shook his head.

"Fred Sanchez, AKA Beatnik Fred, was Buzzy Haller's right-hand man on the film. He was one of Buzzy's pot-smokin' buddies from San Francisco. He disappeared a year after Chet. They found his shoe out in the driveway."

"Wow! Just one shoe?"

Roberta nodded. "There was blood on it."

"Jeez."

"Jonathon Luboff, overdose of heroin, October 31, 1958."

Clint cocked his head. "I knew that."

Roberta took a sip of some mineral water that had been sitting on her desk all afternoon. It was as warm and flat as the air in San Fernando Valley that day.

"Yes, I would have thought you'd know that, Clint. Everybody knew that Luboff was a junkie, and it was only a matter of time before he died, but, he *was* the star of the movie. Who's to say it wasn't an accidental overdose?"

Clint nodded. "I lost track of Tad Kingston," he said with a tinge of resignation in his reedy voice. "I tried everything, tracked him every way I knew how, but he's a blank page. Now, if he—"

"Canada," she said.

Clint stopped talking.

Roberta continued, "He moved to Canada in 1966, made a few more terrible films and retired. He married Becky Sears. You wouldn't know her, she was a script girl who worked for Woodley."

"Great. I'll look him up right now."

"Dead," Roberta said flatly. "Dead. Dead. Dead."

Clint's eyes widened. "Jesus Christ! Dead? Are you sure?"

"Yes, I'm sure. Same deal, as far as I know. Strangled. He'd come back to Hollywood to bury his mother. They found him in his hotel room."

Clint slid back into the chair. He started to put his frayed sneakers up on the chair across from him, but stopped in midswing. Roberta's knowing eyes bored into him, and he lowered his feet back to the carpet. "Don't even think about it," they seemed to say, and Clint didn't.

"Did you see *Cadaver* when you were young?" she asked.

"Sure. Of course. It scared the shit out of me."

Roberta nodded. "You're not alone. Aside from *Night of the Living Dead*, it's most people's favorite horror movie of that era, certainly the most frightening. Did it give you nightmares?"

"Boy, did it ever. I was one of those kids who had all the plastic models of monsters all over his room, and I also had my army men. At night, I was so scared that the dead bodies from the movie were gonna attack me that I set up my army men all around the room, facing the windows and doors. I had tanks, bazooka guys, everything, plus the model monsters to protect me. The only problem was that I thought that maybe during the night, the model monsters would come alive and turn bad and attack the army guys, then come for *me*. I was one screwed-up kid, let me tell ya. A couple of times I woke up to find that some of them had moved or gotten knocked over during the night. *That* made me wonder."

"You're still wondering, aren't you, Clint?"

He nodded his head thoughtfully. "Yeah, I guess I am."

"Well, there's something sinister about that movie, something downright evil. I was convinced of that way back in '57. If I was to tell you that there was a curse on that movie, even if you didn't know about the corpses, you'd believe it, right?"

"I think I would," Clint replied.

"Well, so would a lot of our readers. I think this story is huge. As far as the curse goes, I've suspected it for years. When Buzzy Haller died, I knew. I just knew. Landis Woodley is a very bitter man. I guess you found that out. Buzzy Haller was his best friend, his only friend. Buzzy was the last one to die. They all shared a secret. A terrible secret."

Clint blinked. "Are you saying that Landis Woodley is behind it?"

Roberta didn't answer right away. She let Clint ponder the situation before speaking.

"Landis is a very unhappy man. His career is over, he has nothing left except that crumbling house, and he's the only one who knows what's happening. I'm sure he's kept track over the years. I'm not saying he killed them . . . I'm not sure what I'm saying. All I can tell you is, I think he knows the truth, and I think he's hiding something."

The office was still. It was a weekday afternoon. The staff only came in three days a week to do the layout and sell the advertising. The rest of the time they worked at home. Roberta preferred it that way. She liked it quiet. It allowed her to think. In this age of computers, fax machines, and fiber-optic telephone communication, her people could work at home all they wanted. That left her with a quiet office most of the time, until a deadline loomed.

Clint broke the silence.

"Shit. You knew all that?"

Roberta nodded.

"But you still let me go out and dig like a gopher?"

She smiled, tapped her pencil on her desk again, and pointed it at Clint. "You're my best writer. I think this story will be the biggest thing the magazine's ever done, I want a first-rate job, an honest job."

"But, if you knew all along . . ."

"I detest Landis Woodley," Roberta said sharply. "I think he's scum, and I could never be objective about this story, even though I've been sitting on it for years. I've been waiting for someone like you to come along and pick up the pieces. Me write the story? No, Clint, this one's yours. I want it done right."

"I wonder if we'll ever find out the truth," Clint wondered aloud. "It's been a long time."

"Yeah. Either way, we'll know soon."

"Why?" Clint asked.

Roberta's expression turned hard. It was a practiced move. Her face clouded over like a stormy sky. "Didn't you learn *anything?*"

"Well, I—"

"All the murders, deaths, whatever you want to call them, occurred in October–November. Look at the calendar. It's the end of November now."

"So?"

"So, Landis is the last one left."

Clint closed his eyes. "Oh, I see. If it is a curse, and he's the last one, maybe it'll come for him, but if he's behind it, maybe nothing will happen. Sounds like the plot of one of his movies."

"And now, Landis Woodley is the last one. Are you sure you want to go back now?"

Clint smiled and nodded. "Are you kiddin'? I love this kind of stuff. It's cool, it's scary, and that's my bag." He glanced at his watch. "I gotta get workin'. I'll let you know, okay?"

She threw a folder that had been on her desk into his lap.

"Newspaper photocopies. Nineteen-fifty-seven. Read 'em."

He stood up and smiled.

"Be careful," she reminded him.

He went back to the desk that she let him use in the office and began to scan the photocopies of newspapers for October–November 1957.

He found the first mention of Landis Woodley for November 1, 1957. It was an account of his Halloween party in the gossip column. There had been some noise complaints, parking problems, a few angry neighbors, that kind of thing. It must have been quite a bash, he thought. There was a published guest list. He scanned it, jotting down the names.

Reading on, he came across a curious article. A few days after the party, Devila, the horror show hostess, blew her brains out on TV. He remembered the name. She had been a guest of Woodley's. Coincidence? Clint was beginning to suspect that there were no coincidences. He dug farther.

Twenty minutes later he came across an account of the disappearance of Albert Beaumond, the celebrated Satanist. Thora Beaumond was quoted as saying her father was still alive somewhere, probably suffering from amnesia.

He went back to the guest list.

Albert Beaumond was Devila's date at the party! More coincidences?

Clint decided to find Thora Beaumond and talk to her.

Former Lieutenant, now retired Captain Garth Prease, found Clint first. As soon as Prease got word that someone was sniffing around looking for the former Thora Beaumond, now Mrs. Thora Beaumond-Prease, he left his home and came down to confront the stranger. He was surprised to find a man as young as Clint.

"Sir, I need some information about Albert Beaumond."

"That's ancient history," Garth said brusquely. "I don't see—"

"I'm a journalist. I'm working on a story about Landis Woodley."

"Woodley? That old rummy film guy?"

"Yes, sir. You see, Albert Beaumond was Devila's date for the Halloween party he gave in 1957. As you may recall, she committed suicide a few days later, at about the same time Albert disappeared."

Garth scratched his chin and looked around. "Let's go in my office," he said softly.

As soon as the door closed he turned and said, "It's taken me years to bury this Albert Beaumond thing, and I don't want you dredging it up and upsetting my wife."

"Your wife? You married Beaumond's daughter?"

Garth nodded. "Yes, I . . . she needed help, we grew close, I married her a year later. I don't see what any of this has to do with Landis Woodley."

"I'm looking for a possible connection between Woodley's party, Devila's suicide, and Beaumond's disappearance."

Garth went behind the desk and sat down, motioning for Clint to do the same. "That was a long time ago. Devila was a freak, Albert Beaumond was a Satanist. They were like two peas in a pod. Thora was lucky to get out when she did."

Clint made a note of that and continued. "I read about Mr. Beaumond in the newspapers. He was quite a controversial person."

"He was a devil worshiper, for God's sake!"

Clint pulled out his pad and began to write.

"You never found him?"

"No."

"Not even a clue?"

Garth eyed Clint suspiciously. His upper face narrowed, producing a squint that locked his eyes in shadow. "Who did you say you were with?"

"Bachman Publications," Clint replied, using the name of *Monster Magazine*'s parent company because it sounded a hell of a lot better.

"Hmm. Okay. Well, there was one thing."

"Yes?"

Garth cleared his throat, pausing.

"They found a body a few days later. It fit Beaumond's description to a tee, even the clothes. I got a note from the medical examiner and it seemed like a match. That night I went out to Thora's house and called the assistant coroner to meet us down at the morgue so she could identify him.

"When we got there, the body was gone. It must have happened earlier that night. The night watchman got drunk, fell asleep, and somebody made off with the body. Can you believe that? What kind of ghoul would do such a thing?"

"They stole the body?"

"Somebody did. It just didn't get up and walk out of there on its own."

"Sick," Clint said succinctly. Then, he had a thought. The connection came together so fast in his mind that he scarcely had time to consider the ramifications before he spoke again. Landis Woodley had been filming in that same morgue the night before!

"Were you aware that Landis Woodley was shooting a movie in the morgue that week?" he asked.

"No," Garth replied.

"Well, there's a connection between Devila and Albert Beaumond, that would be Woodley's party, and between Landis Woodley and the morgue."

Garth shook his head. "This case is closed, Mr. ahh—"

"Stockbern."

"Yeah, Stockbern, let's just leave it at that. This thing happened forty years ago. I have no further comment."

He stood up and shook Clint's hand.

"Are you a Christian, Mr. Stockbern?" Prease asked as they stepped toward the door.

"Well, yeah, I guess so."

Prease lowered his voice. "Albert Beaumond worshiped the devil. He consorted with other deviants. That doesn't surprise me. He could have met his end in any one of a number of ways. When you deal with the unclean, you're liable to get your hands dirty."

Prease opened the door. "Let it be, Mr. Stockbern."

26

The gardener's house was nothing more than a one-room hovel above the garage. Emil, José's feebleminded son, lived there alone.

After his father had died, he learned to fend for himself and did pretty well, all things considered.

Mr. Woodley was always there to help him, but during the last seven years he had come to rely less and less on the old man.

He didn't like the big house and avoided going in there unless it was completely necessary. But now it was. He was hungry. Yesterday he'd opened his last can of Spam, and he was even out of the dog food he'd eaten on more than one occasion. He knew people weren't supposed to eat that stuff, but it wasn't that bad, just a little gelatinous. Mr. Woodley had made a mistake once, when he was drunk, and bought a whole case of the stuff thinking it was budget-priced beef stew.

The market man knew Landis Woodley didn't have a dog, but he didn't say anything. Landis shuffled around the store, absently loading his basket, and paid cash, usually in the form of ⬚⬚n nickels and dimes.

Whenever Emil went alone, the market man was always nice to him, but still counted the money carefully.

Emil hadn't been to the store in two weeks. All the food was gone, and Mr. Woodley hadn't called him. He waited until after when dinner should have been and went over to the big house.

The kitchen door was unlocked, so he went in.

Mr. Woodley was asleep sitting up at the kitchen table, his head cradled in his arms, making grunting sounds.

Emil was tempted to wake him. His stomach was grumbling, but he was afraid. The old man was mean when he first woke up. Emil slid across the room toward the cabinets. Maybe some tuna fish . . .

Landis stirred. Emil froze.

"Mr. Woodley?" His voice trembled whenever he addressed his master. "Mr. Woodley, I'm hungry. Can I have some food?"

There was no response. Emil took a tentative step closer.

"My tummy hurts, Mr. Woodley."

Woodley's head stayed down, his breathing slow and labored. The old man drooled onto the Formica tabletop. Emil traced the slender thread from his lip to the counter. An empty bottle of whiskey sat near, as still as fossilized amber in the slanting rays of the afternoon sun. Emil knew what that meant.

He took a can of Vienna sausages and left.

The kitchen door clicked shut.

Landis snorted and lifted his head. Had someone been there?

Then he smelled it; something was burning.

"Shit," he muttered. "S'fire."

He squinted around the room. His head was clearing as the frail adrenaline pump inside him pushed a measure of consciousness through his smoky brain. He sat up straighter and sniffed the air. It was coming, he thought, from the living room. He looked in that direction.

Something sailed through.

A tiny flying saucer flew into the room through the open doorway and landed on the kitchen floor in front of him. It was on fire. He was too stunned to move.

"What the hell—"

The burning saucer began to curl up at the edges. The smoke had a familiar smell.

It's paper, he thought. *The goddamn thing's paper. Wait a second, just hold everything.* A flood of fear rushed into his heart as the recognition hit him.

It was two paper plates glued together, soaked in gasoline and set on fire.

That was Buzzy Haller's ending for *Attack of the Haunted Saucer.* Who would pull a trick like this on him? His heart began galloping in his chest. No. It couldn't be. Buzzy was dead, twelve months in the ground.

Landis watched the saucer burn and realized that it was scorching his linoleum floor. Suddenly he jumped up out of his chair and began to stamp out the fire. The burning plates sent large flakes of gray ash toward the kitchen ceiling. Landis ground his foot into the smoldering ruins of the plates and wanted to scream, but something was wrong.

His arms felt heavy.

"Who the fuck's in there?" he shouted angrily. "This ain't funny!"

He tasted an acidic dot of fear on the tip of his tongue and felt a tightness grip his chest. *I'm hallucinating,* he thought. *I'm losing my marbles. This can't be happening.*

Landis lurched forward. Somebody was going to pay for this bullshit. Who? The kid reporter? Emil? Who the hell else was around?

"Okay, joke's over. Come on out!" he growled.

He put one foot in front of the other, making his way toward the living room. His heart was galloping in his chest, and it was beginning to hurt when he breathed.

A few gasps and a few more steps and he was in the doorway, on the threshold of the living room. He steadied himself and extended both arms against the wooden molding.

The room was in deep shadow. Motes of dust hung suspended in the air, moving in their own currents. Landis fought to regain his breath. He gulped air like a tired swimmer and willed his heart to slow down.

What happened next nearly killed him.

In his weakened condition he was vulnerable, and that angered him. It angered him because he couldn't bull his way into the room and tear it apart until he found the perpetrator of this cruel hoax and kick his ass.

His chest hurt.

From the shadow directly in front of him, another paper plate flew out, tossed with uncanny accuracy. He saw it streaking toward him like a white blur and he held his breath. The shock his system went through at that moment took Landis Woodley to the brink of death. His heart was on the verge of bursting. The saucer hit him squarely in the chest and bounced off. "Huh!" he gasped.

Landis yelped. There was no disguising the terror now. It was burning in him just as the plate was burning on the floor at his feet.

"Oh Jesus," he cried. "Oh, sweet Jesus!"

He took his hands off the doorjamb and gripped his chest. The lack of support propelled him sideways until he was leaning against the hinges, barely able to maintain his footing and balance.

I'm having a heart attack, he thought. *I'm hallucinating while my brain is starving for oxygen. I gotta calm down, try not to panic.*

The two paper plates were burning nicely, sending a thin plume of smoke into the dusty air. Landis closed his eyes and opened them again.

Somebody was trying to kill him. Somebody was trying to scare him to death so he'd have a heart attack and drop dead on the living room floor. As that thought presented itself, he grasped at it like a lifeline to sanity. Of course, it was the only answer.

The idea pissed him off and he decided right then and there not to die, but live to spit in whoever's eye.

"It won't work," he gasped. "You can't kill me. I'm too mean to die."

The room was silent.

"All right! The party's over! Come on out here and let me see you, you sadistic son of a bitch!"

The room seemed to grow even more quiet. Unnaturally quiet, as if he'd stepped outside on a snow-blanketed night. Landis felt the hair rise on the back of his neck. Something was terribly wrong here.

Then he felt a presence step into the room. It was the cold, unyielding presence of death.

Clint listened to the tape of the Landis Woodley interview. The sky over LA was going from blue to violet. One good thing about smog, thought Clint. It made for some spectacular sunsets. He could tell that tonight's would be no exception.

"Drawer sixty-six," the voice on the tape said. "Get your kicks on Route 66."

All he had to do was find out what body was in drawer number sixty-six on November 5, 1957, the night of the shoot, and November 6, 1957, the night of the theft. Easy, right?

Clint called the morgue but found, to his dismay, that they destroyed their records every ten years. *Great,* thought Clint. *That makes all kinds of sense. Keep records, throw them away. Logical.*

He listened to the tape all the way through and then, at the end, he heard the sound that had scared him so badly when he was at the house.

It was the moan.

Hearing it now, on tape, made his hair stand on end. Jesus, what was that thing?

He immediately thought of Landis Woodley's famous hoaxes. Could this be one of them? Like the bats, the owls, and the rest of that creepy shit? It was hard to say. There was something alien about that moan, something genuinely tortured. It came across on the tape like a cold spot in a haunted house. The amazing thing was that Clint had forgotten all about it until now, as if his brain had erased the memory.

Jesus, he thought, *what was that thing?*

He rewound and played it several times. Something inside told Clint that the moan was not a fake; it was real. Something was under the house, and it sounded piteous.

His mind searched for all the logical answers first, of course. Maybe it was a raccoon, caught in a trap. A cat, maybe a dog, and it was howling for its life. He'd heard cats fight outside his window, heard the eerie mating cries in the night. They rose in a crescendo of pain and desire that was most definitely subhuman. This sound was nothing like that.

There was a tortured hysteria to it, as if whatever it was were trying to communicate some terrible, unknowable pain. The range was almost human, he decided, yet utterly deranged. It almost seemed like it was trying to form words.

No, that's nuts, Clint reasoned. *It was probably one of the old man's animals. A bat or an owl or a fuckin' iguana. How should I know? Best to forget all about it. I have bigger fish to fry. There's a mystery to unwind. No time for the creepy crawlies now.*

Clint concentrated on his notes, the jumble of facts and the patterns that emerged. The people who died were either strangled or committed suicide. That was an odd combination. What was troubling these people? Was the memory of the *Cadaver* shoot that horrible? It didn't seem likely to Clint.

He looked up at the ceiling, as he often did when searching for answers. Sometimes they were written up there like graffiti. The thought occurred to him that maybe those people feared the curse so much that they'd rather kill themselves before it got them.

Landis Woodley stood in the doorway, too mad to think and too pained to move. His chest had constricted into a fist, holding his breath to short, desperate gasps. The paper flying saucer lay on the living room floor at his feet, smoldering enigmatically. Landis looked down at it, wondering what the hell was going on.

Out there, in the room, beyond the saucer, something moved. His head snapped up and caught the subtle shifting among the shadows. He squinted into the gloom and fought to control his heart.

"Who's there?"

Something stepped closer, white against the gray backdrop.

"Who do you think it is? Johnny D.?" a hoarse voice whispered.

Landis's jaw dropped. Johnny D.? Who knew about Johnny D. that was still alive? Nobody, that's who.

"Johnny D.?" Landis gasped.

It stepped closer. Landis was reeling, trying to keep his legs from buckling. They supported his body begrudgingly. He placed more weight on the doorjamb.

"You remember old Johnny D., don't you, Woody?"

A patina of slick perspiration appeared on his face. He tried not to consider the only explanation he could think of, but, the fact was, *he knew that voice.*

From behind the ragged vocal cords it grouped words in familiar patterns. Despite the unusual raspiness which sounded the vowels and syllables in coughs and gasps, he knew it.

He prayed he was wrong.

It stepped closer, emerging now from the shadows. A terrible humidity permeated the air, accompanied by a stench, a gutter-like rottenness. Landis breathed it in with all the rest of the dust and dread he could manage to suck into his worried lungs.

"Don't be such a stranger, I won't bite. Come over here so I can see you," the voice hissed. Landis clutched his chest. "Oh, what is it? Are you having a heart attack? Jesus, Woody, that's no way to go."

It took another step, fully visible now, and the shock that shuddered through Landis Woodley's frame would have killed a lesser man.

"Buzzy?" Landis croaked.

"You rang?" Buzzy had always been a big Maynard G. Krebs fan.

"It can't be you," Landis said. "You're dead! I went to your funeral."

Buzzy stepped closer. Landis could now see that his flesh was as pale as a fish's belly, discolored here and there with spots of purple decay. His lips were drawn back into an imitation smile, but the flesh surrounding them had deteriorated to the point where a true smile was impossible.

"Quite right," Buzzy said with a snakelike hiss. Landis supposed that the tissue in his throat and mouth that supported speech had undergone a similar decomposition. The man sounded as if he had advanced cancer of the throat. Landis trembled as though he had stumbled into a walk-in freezer. "But you know, there's dead, and then there's *dead.*"

It hobbled forward, drawing close enough for Landis to see that he was dressed in costume as one of the zombies in *Cadaver.*

"Hey," Buzzy's voice sizzled, "too bad you don't have a camera rollin'. You could get some killer footage. Better than the stuff we put out, huh?"

Landis swallowed. He didn't know what to say. He was trying

to decide if this thing that stood before him was real or not. Could too much alcohol or a strained and swollen heart have possibly produced a hallucination like this? Was it a delusion? Do you talk back to delusions when they ask you questions?

"What do you want?" Landis managed to ask through clenched teeth, deciding to play along with the dream.

"Tonight's the night."

"I beg your pardon?"

"Tonight, Woody. Tonight is D-Day."

Landis rubbed his eyes. "I need a drink," he said.

"Yeah, me too. Whatcha got?"

"You're dead! The dead can't drink!"

Buzzy laughed. It was the same laugh he had in life, only more phlegmy. Landis's heart began to calm down, and the chest pains began to subside. He could take deeper breaths now.

Buzzy noticed the change and took another step toward him. The heart attack was passing.

"Sure we can, Woody. Haven't you ever heard of dead drunk? You just can't taste it, that's all," he said. "Taste buds are shot."

Buzzy stepped closer, leaning in to look at Landis. "You look like shit, you know that?"

"You ain't no matinee idol yourself."

"I came here to warn you," Buzzy said, suddenly serious. "Old Johnny D.'s gonna be payin' you a visit, man. I know because he dropped by my pad last year about this time."

Landis shook his head. "Johnny D.?"

"Yeah, he ain't right. He's pissed, Woody, and he's already killed everybody else on the movie."

Landis shambled toward a chair and sat down hard. He exhaled sharply as his butt hit the cushion, relieved to be off his feet. Color was returning to his face. "Why?" he asked, swallowing hard. His mouth was as dry as a strip of sandpaper.

"Don't play dumb with me, man. You can't bullshit a bullshitter, you know that."

Landis felt in his pocket for a cigar, a foolish thing to do right after chest pains. He came up empty. He looked at Buzzy as if he were the manifestation of all his guilt.

"It was your idea, Buzz."

"Yeah, but it was your movie, and you made the money. He

made you famous with that close-up, remember? Legions of horror fans cut their teeth on that scene."

Landis pointed at Buzzy. "I don't believe you're real. I think you're just a dream." *Guilt. This is a guilt thing,* he thought.

"Don't change the subject, Daddy-O. He's been savin' you for last. You're the only one left. It's your turn."

Landis wagged his finger at Buzzy. "You were the one who manipulated him, you were the one who stole him and brought him to the party, you sick fuck! Now you tell me that *I'm* gonna die for something *you* did?"

Buzzy chuckled. "Listen, we were friends. I just thought I'd do a little Jacob Marley impression and warn you about Johnny D. It ain't pleasant, Woody, it really ain't. When he gets you he makes you pay. I personally preferred to blow my brains out, like Devila."

Landis threw a glance up into Buzzy's rotten face. A flicker of recognition passed over his face. Devila—he hadn't thought of her in years.

Buzzy continued talking, his putrid breath blowing across the room as he spoke. Landis smelled it and turned away.

"It's your choice," Buzzy hissed. "You can do it yourself and avoid the unpleasantness of having that fucker's bony fingers down your throat."

"Jesus," Landis muttered.

"Either way you cut the cake, tonight you're dead meat. Judging by the condition of your heart, you might not even make it that far, which would be a blessing, believe me. He's moaning, Woody, and he don't stop moanin' 'til he gets what he wants."

Landis thought about the dreadful moans he'd been hearing for the past several days. He blinked at Buzzy and rubbed his eyes.

"You're still tryin' to figure out if I'm real, aren't you?" Buzzy said. "You might be dreamin', you never know. You might be hallucinating. You might even be dead yourself, and on your way to hell. Those chest pains can be a bitch, Woody. You should have that checked out. But consider this. Real or not, it doesn't matter. The warning is true."

Buzzy shifted. His worm-eaten clothes were hanging off of him like dead skin. He cocked his head and attempted another smile. Landis could see the brown gums receding from his root-baring teeth.

The thing spoke again.

"Hey, look, I'm wasting my time here. Two things, okay? One—there's no escape from this thing. Johnny D.'s not human, Woody. He's like a demon or something. He's got a fuckin' snake head. Can you believe that? The thing has no soul. It can't exist in either world.

"When I stole him from the morgue, he was already cursed. He can't die. No matter how decayed his body becomes, and believe me, it's just about beef jerky now, he still rises up from the grave. I made a big mistake when I chose him for the scene, didn't I?"

Landis nodded slowly. He was numb and afraid.

Buzzy continued, "Two—and I know you're gonna shit when you hear this one." Buzzy paused. "He's buried in your basement."

Landis looked back, a rage crossed his brow like a flaming arrow. "What?"

"Remember when you told me to get rid of him after the cast party? Well, I figured the quickest way was to bury him under the house, down in the crawl space."

"You what?" Landis stood up, forgetting all about his heart attack. "You asshole! I wish I could kill you some more," he shouted, stepping toward Buzzy menacingly. His hands were fisted and he had blood in his eye.

"You're an amazing person, Woody. A dead man comes to warn you that you're gonna die, and you try to kill him even more than he already is. You're a real piece of work!"

"You buried him under my house? Jesus Christ, after all the things I did for you! How could you? That's it! You're outa here!" he shouted in a rage. "But first I'm gonna kick your ass!"

Landis lumbered toward Buzzy, his hands out and ready to grab. The thing that was Buzzy Haller whispered, "Fuck you. Go to hell," and faded into thin air. Landis walked right through him.

When he realized that Buzzy was gone he bellowed at the top of his lungs, *"Asshole!"*

27

Clint Stockbern put fresh batteries in his cassette tape recorder, threw a few spare tapes on the seat, and cranked the Volkswagen engine. It started reluctantly, protesting in a constricted, metallic, German voice. A little Hitler, it was trained against its will to haul his pimply American ass around town. Friction warmed the metal and the motor relaxed into a predictable pattern.

The "Shit Happens" bumper sticker had been partially peeled off by the weather and now it simply read, "—it Happens." That was all one could read as the billow of blue smoke farted out the tailpipe and he pulled out into traffic.

He was going back. This time he had his camera, an inexpensive autoflash that he sometimes used to immortalize his friends. He wanted some pictures of Woodley.

The excitement was hard to control. For him, it was the culmination of all his work. He was nervous and more than a little afraid.

The prospect of going back into the creepy old basement and watching those grainy black-and-white films of real corpses, while something moaned and groaned under his feet, made him sweat. But it was more than that. It was the scare factor.

The old man scared him. The house scared him. The movies scared him. The moaning scared him. Hell, the whole situation scared him, and that was part of the thrill. He had the same feeling that he got when he was going to see a really great horror movie that he knew was going to blow him away. Anticipation. It always drove him nuts.

The goose bumps he felt when he visualized sitting down in the projection room were delicious. He had been waiting all day for this and now it was time. The research he'd done primed him, sharpened his curiosity to a razor's edge.

This time he found the house without any trouble and parked on the tree-lined street without incident.

The sun had gone down and the few stars visible above LA twinkled fiercely through the thermal induction layer. He descended the steps casually, confident that this time he'd not be turned away.

He rang the doorbell six times, knocked twice, and was about to step back when the viewing grate opened and the haunted eyes of Landis Woodley peered through.

"You again," he said. Not a question, not a statement, not anything, just his number being called.

"Yes, Mr. Woodley."

The door swung inward, the hinges as dry as sawdust. They sang a long melancholy note that ended in a grunt. Clint stepped through the portal and back into the nightmare. His senses tingled wonderfully.

The smell of bats. The scent of cigar.

Landis looked different. The man was as pale and drawn as a ghost. He looked ill. The circles beneath his eyes were darker and even more sunken than before and his walk was less steady.

"Are you okay?"

Without answering, Landis led the way through the house to the basement stairs, and put his hand on the doorknob. Since his chest-constricting panic attack that afternoon, Landis had not left the kitchen except to check the floor to see if the burning paper plates had been a dream. Twice he checked and twice he saw the ashes. Then the pattern repeated; some whiskey, a cigar, another catnap, back again. The color had yet to return to his face, and his hands still shook.

The basement door opened and allowed the musty, foul-smelling air to billow into the hall. Clint's nostrils flared as the aroma of decay assailed him. The basement smelled bad; worse, he thought, than before. A light switch clicked, and an inadequate bulb illuminated somewhere below.

Landis went first, Clint following behind, watching the stooped back and dry skin of the old man's elbows as he descended. The passageway was narrow. Huge dust balls hugged the base of each step. Clint looked down, studying the angle. He didn't want to stumble here.

They passed through the owls' room, the smell of their fecal matter pungent, and Clint realized that that was a primary source of the odor he smelled when the door was open. But there was something else, something worse.

The second door opened, a light switch was thrown, and the projection room came to life before him. It stood like a torture chamber. In the back of Clint's mind he realized that this was the room *with the fear in it*.

"I got some stuff out," Landis said. "Unbelievable stuff. You'll see. Take a seat in the front row there, and I'll get the show started."

Clint settled into the hard wooden theater seat and waited. He put his tape recorder in his lap and turned it on, wanting to get any descriptive dialogue the old man might utter. A minute later, the lights went down and the screen glowed smoky silver.

The flicker of film started and a numbers sequence counted down to the first outtake. Clint recognized the *Cadaver* set. There was the great Luboff, hunched over a table, Tad Kingston behind him. The corpse on the table was real, Clint knew. It was the same dead body that appeared in most of the morgue scenes, the one from the famous close-up. The first scene showed Buzzy behind the corpse, obviously manipulating it. The second scene was Luboff and Buzzy playing around with the corpse. Luboff appeared to be—and Clint had to look twice to confirm his suspicion—*dancing with it*.

What kind of sicko was this guy? Clint thought. Behind him, backlit by the projector, Landis read his mind and made a comment to that effect. "Old Jonathon had a strange sense of humor."

Clint saw the window of opportunity open and launched his first question like a scud missile, hoping it would acquire a decent target. "Whose corpse was that? Did you ever check?"

Landis moved closer to the projector, his face lit from below now as the powerful bulb inside the big machine glowed savagely. It did frightening things to his face. He looked like a still from one of his own movies. Clint was enthralled.

"Whose corpse?" The light, shining up through Landis's eyebrows, made weird patterns in his forehead. "Why do you ask?"

Suddenly they were both on guard.

Landis, naturally suspicious, narrowed his eyes and stared at Clint. "Huh?" he demanded.

Clint moved defensively. "I don't know, it just occurred to me, that's all. It's a hell of a thing to be a movie star after you're dead. I thought maybe you kept track of the name." He tried to sound as cheerful and upbeat as he could.

"It was unmarked. A John Doe. Buzzy called him Johnny D."

Clint nodded. He watched the black-and-white images on the screen go through their act. There were close-ups of the corpse, a few too gory for the censor, several shots where Buzzy was plainly visible, a couple of morgue shots in which the camera panned the room. These were establishing shots for the entire sequence. The camera swung around the room. Clint saw the white tile walls, the steel gurneys, the drawers. His breath caught. The drawers! The camera panned slowly past them and he could see that drawer number sixty-six was open! The camera lingered on it for a second more, then continued around the room.

The creepy atmosphere of the morgue was undeniable. Clint could understand the reluctance of the crew to work down there. The place looked positively chilling.

As he watched the outtakes and censored material, Clint was struck by the overall darkness of the film. It was almost too real. Luboff's eyes, the dead bodies, the bizarre lighting by Chet Bronski. Clint shuddered.

This was horror *film noir,* a genre occupied by only a handful of films. Films that made you sick with dread, films that scared you a little too much, that went a little beyond the norm. Like a real snuff film, *Cadaver* lived up to its reputation. Clint could not take his eyes away.

A strange fascination held him; the fascination with all things horrible. It was his only addiction.

"This stuff is incredible," Clint said, more to break the mood than anything else. "I'm surprised that most people didn't suspect the real corpses, it's so damn . . ."

"—Real. Yeah, I know whatcha mean, but I had to be as careful as possible. Believe it or not, at the time, people just thought it was great special effects. That's a tribute to Buzzy, I guess."

Clint watched each scene carefully, studying the movements of the corpse, trying to get a good look at its face. Ironically, the only really good look at it was in the world famous close-up with the worms. Clint saw that twice, from two different angles. The first time they shot it, the worms grossed everyone out so badly that the camera moved. In the background was someone saying, "Oh shit! I can't believe it." Clint wondered if it was Landis.

The second time, a worm wriggled out a little too far and touched Buzzy's thumb as he prepared to open the eyes. Buzzy gasped and let go of the head as if he'd touched a lit match. It fell forward and clunked against the tile with a sound too graphic to be described.

Clint watched, his eyes like saucers. Then, the screen went black—the horror show was over. The film continued to roll when the tail end passed through the machine and started flapping wildly. Landis switched it off.

Clint turned to face Woodley. "Great stuff, unbelievable, I loved it. It really gives you a feel for what it must have been like to be there."

"You can't imagine what it was like," Landis replied. "You just can't imagine . . ."

The lights came up. Landis pulled the take-up reel without rewinding and placed a new reel on the spool.

"Okay, now this next part is different," Landis explained. "This is some footage I shot for a movie that never got made."

Clint twisted in his seat. He watched the old man fooling around with the projector. Two dinosaurs, Clint thought, one preening the other. Landis treated the machine with a respect that he seldom, if ever, showed human beings.

"It is, with a doubt, the greatest few minutes of film I ever shot. Maybe even the most remarkable piece of film *ever.*" He paused, watching for Clint's reaction, then sighed. "It's a shame I couldn't do anything with it way back when, but maybe now, with our enlightened society—" His words trailed off and he coughed deeply. "Ah, who the fuck am I kiddin'?"

Clint looked perplexed. "What were you gonna say?" he asked.

"Nothing," Landis muttered. "Judge for yourself."

When it was film he was dealing with, Landis's ancient, gnarled fingers were suddenly as nimble as a surgeon's. Clint watched the old man thread the wide 35 mm celluloid through the maze of toothed spools and running gears. It seemed like a needlessly complicated process, full of endless loops and twists. Old-time film equipment was like that.

Then, it was ready. Landis dimmed the lights and said, "What you are about to see, no human being besides myself and the cameraman has ever seen before. I think you'll recognize the principals, if you're half the horror fan you say you are. I gotta warn ya, this is very strong stuff. It was never released, for one reason or another, as you'll see. One more thing—it's all real."

"What do you mean by that?" Clint asked immediately.

"You'll see," Landis replied cryptically.

Clint shifted back in his seat, anxious to see what was so incredible in the old man's eyes. Another countdown filled the screen, the film blinked, then stabilized.

A pale woman with black hair and dark lipstick appeared on the screen. She looked familiar.

She spoke. Clint listened closely. "Hello, I am Devila, queen of your nightmares. Tonight, I invite you on a great journey, a journey into the unknown."

Devila! The connection Clint had been looking for was in front of him. He looked back at the old man, saw he was absorbed with the image on the screen, then turned his attention back to Devila. She went through a short monologue saying that everything they were about to see was real. She appeared to be very nervous. Clint wondered why.

"I am now going to conjure up the spiritual entity. Remember, this is not a trick."

Clint was transfixed. She took two huge tuning forks, hung them on a floor lamp, and struck them.

The sound they made was distorted on the film, but it seemed to be an intense vibration, too much for the microphones, and they canceled out. Clint was suddenly fearful. The feeling of dread coming off the screen was overwhelming. The sound on film went to white noise, yet even then, it seemed powerfully evil.

"Watch this part closely," Landis rasped.

What happened next made him sit up straight and study what his eyes told him they saw. The woman transformed into a snake, or rather, her head became a serpent's head.

If it was a special effect, Clint couldn't see it. It appeared to be real. Clint realized that the only way to fake something like that was to use the clay-dynamation process like Ray Harry-hausen.

A clay model could be photographed one frame at a time, but even then, by its movements you could tell what it was. This was definitely not that. Clint watched, studying the screen for a clue, but could find nothing that would give the effect away. The serpent's head fit on her seamlessly; its coils seemed to meld into her flesh.

In his heart, Clint knew that it couldn't be real. Such things don't exist. It was impossible, but it *looked* real. *It must be the old man, screwing with my head again,* thought Clint.

His eyes were riveted to the horror occurring onscreen.

The snake thing moved around the room and flicked its tongue, the camera wobbled but kept rolling. Some guy in the background screamed. Clint studied the film. Then, abruptly, it ended. The screen went white as if an eye had opened into the sun.

Clint turned to face Landis. "What was that thing?"

"I don't know, but it scared the shit out of me."

"You never did anything with this film?"

Landis switched the lights back on, but the atmosphere stayed dark and ominous. The only difference was now you could see.

"What could I do?" Landis asked. "Devila blew her brains out on TV a few days later; we were all watching. I only had the couple minutes of film you just looked at . . . I was stuck. But, as you can see, it's powerful stuff. That was completely real; it actually happened."

Clint hesitated, gathering his strength, then made the decision to let the cat out of the bag.

"Devila was just one of the people involved with *Cadaver* to die, right?"

"Devila wasn't in *Cadaver*," Landis answered quickly, "and I know what you're driving at. You're going to tell me that each and every person who worked on that movie is dead, and that most of them died mysteriously, either by suicide or murder. You're going to tell me that there's a curse, aren't you?"

"Yeah," Clint said, "I was. I've been doing some research."

Landis snorted. "I'll bet you have."

"There are those who might believe that the corpse you used in the movie has come back to, how should I say it, even the score?"

Landis laughed. "Like who? That's horseshit."

"And you're the last one left."

"Pure crapola."

"Aren't you scared?"

Landis laughed another one of his humorless laughs. The skin of his face had sagged noticeably since he'd arrived, and Clint wondered if he wasn't going to start gasping for breath any second. The laugh turned into a sharp, dry cough.

"Me, scared? Shit, boy, I invented scared. What do you think?"

Clint stood up, his notebook and pen in hand. He gestured at Landis, waving a hand over the room. "I think all this is part of something else, something bigger," he said.

Landis sneered. "You're crazy."

"Hear me out," Clint continued. "Yes, I do think there's a curse, but that's not what I wanted to say." He took a deep breath. "I think I know whose body that was in drawer sixty-six. It was Albert Beaumond."

Landis shook his head. "The Satanist?"

"Yeah, he came to your party with Devila, he was involved with devil worship, and he disappeared at the same time. He was never found. The cop in charge of the case said that they did find a body that matched the description, but before it could be identified, somebody stole it from the morgue!"

"Buzzy!"

"The body was in drawer sixty-six."

Landis stared off into the distance of the blank movie screen as if he were looking out into a polar landscape. "Johnny D.," he muttered.

"Johnny D.? Albert Beaumond."

"Jesus."

Clint leveled his gaze at the old man and began to weave a web of impossible logic. "Suppose that Albert Beaumond stumbled onto something truly supernatural, like those tuning forks. Suppose Devila got them from him after *he* used them and went crazy, then *she* used them herself in the film, and *she* went crazy. Albert probably went out and killed himself, but his body wasn't found until later. Those forks are the connection. Then you come along and make *Cadaver* and trot out Albert's body for one last fling."

"Buzzy ripped it off and brought it here," the old man said.

"Here? He brought the body here?"

Landis sighed. "The asshole . . ."

Clint continued. "That was the corpse of Albert Beaumond, a man who worshipped the devil, a man who had become host to a demon."

"That explains a lot of things," Landis said, still staring at the snowfield.

"But that's not the curse, is it?" Clint asked bravely.

"What do you mean?" Landis hissed.

"Well, that story about the demonic possession might account for Devila, but someone else, someone alive killed those other people, unless you're willing to believe that something truly supernatural was responsible. Personally, I don't. I think somebody did them in and made it look that way. Why? I don't know."

"Revenge," Landis whispered.

"Maybe. The secret of *Cadaver* and the missing corpse was protected. The people who were part of it are all dead."

Landis pulled his face back from the empty screen and narrowed his eyes. "What are you saying?"

"Who knew?" Clint asked.

"Buzzy Haller."

Clint nodded. "And you."

Landis didn't seem surprised. His face showed no emotion whatsoever. Clint, unschooled in the fine art of subterfuge, wore his heart, soul, and guts on his sleeve.

"Me," Landis said flatly. There was no inflection to give away what he was thinking.

"You had the most to gain," Clint softly said. "You knew the score."

"Landis Woodley is not a murderer," the old man spit. "Say what you want about him, but he doesn't kill people. Your theory is good, but you left out one little thing."

The old man stared off into the arctic snowscape of the screen again and sighed. Clint could see the fatigue on his back, grinding him down. He stood hunched over, frail and sickly.

"The curse," he said, "is real. And the body of Albert Beaumond is right underneath us."

As if on cue, something pounded the floor at his feet, causing the floorboards to rise. Clint nearly jumped out of his skin. Then the moaning started. He felt a flush of fear race through his system.

The old man could see that Clint was completely unnerved.

"What is it?" he cried. "What in God's name is it?"

Landis moved away, his eyes on the floor. "I just told you, it's the body of Albert Beaumond."

"But that's impossible!" Clint shouted.

"Accept it, kid. I know it's hard to believe, but accept it."

There was another moan, louder than the last, and a scraping noise that seemed to move along the underside of the floor across the center of the room. Clint was not ready for that. It was as if he'd gotten on an amusement park ride and realized too late that it was the suicide big dipper.

"It's buried in the dirt of the crawl space," the old man droned. "It's been right under my feet all these years, and I never knew it."

Clint flinched. This was something he was not prepared to deal with. "But, it's dead!" he yelled.

"Undead," Landis replied, the hopelessness in his voice rising above the dreadful sounds of pain coming up from below. "With the demon trapped inside."

"That's impossible! It's a hoax!"

"The body is undead." Landis looked away, disbelieving his own words as he said them. "Undead," he muttered, "and tonight . . . tonight it's coming for me. I'm the last one, kid."

The moans were getting louder and more agitated. Clint looked at the floor as if it were on fire. His dread swam unchallenged through his bloodstream, and the wild taste of terror was on his lips. "You're insane," he whined.

"Suit yourself." Landis laughed, coughed. There was another escalation of moaning, sending shivers down Clint's back as if he'd been doused by a bucket of ice water.

What the fuck is it?" Clint screamed, his voice trembling now, brittle and unsteady as he began to back away.

"I told you, but you don't believe me," Landis said.

The pounding shook the floor.

"Let's get outa here!" Clint shouted.

Landis shrugged. "No place to run, no place to hide."

Clint grabbed Landis's arm and shook the old man's frail body. "Out! Now!" he shouted.

Landis looked into his eyes. The atmosphere in the room was becoming unbearable; the terrible moaning and pounding shook the air itself.

"Yeah, okay. Upstairs."

Clint grabbed his cassette recorder and camera and stumbled toward the door. The old man stumbled behind him. Together they reached the steps, the owls screeched and flew from their perches. Clint slammed the door behind him when he realized that the old man wasn't going to.

"Hurry up, for God's sake!" Clint choked.

Behind them the sound of the floor buckling upward cracked the night. The trapdoor, set in the floor he'd been standing on a few moments ago, creaked and split, pulling the rug up. It hovered for a second, opened a few inches, screeching like a banshee, then crashed open with enough force to shake the house.

"Oh, shit," Clint brayed. He pushed the old man aside to mount the stairs. Landis bounced off the wall like a skeleton. The kid flew past him with the swiftness of youth.

"Come on!" he shouted at Landis.

The old man arrived at the top of the stairs what seemed like hours later, puffing and gripping his chest, laboring across the threshold.

Clint slammed that door and fumbled with the lock.

He then turned and noticed the old man. His face was as white as parchment; a sheen of sweat had broken out and he seemed to be fighting for every breath.

"You don't look so good," Clint said.

Clint had never seen a person have a heart attack before, but he knew that's what it was. The color of the face, the shortness of breath, and the dangling left arm gave it away. The old man leaned against the wall, looking like death itself.

"You got some medicine or something?" Clint asked.

Landis shook his head. He couldn't talk anymore.

Before Clint could begin to worry about Landis Woodley's health, the sounds from below drew closer. The first door banged open. The moaning continued.

"This ain't real, is it?" Clint asked, his heart galloping.

In spite of his pain, Landis smiled.

Something began to climb the stairs. Heavy footsteps thudded closer.

Clint looked like he was going to cry. Landis's smile was frozen on his face as he watched the kid. The terrible burning in his chest was overwhelming. He was in real danger of falling down, but he held on like the tenacious survivor that he was.

The kid knew that he should run, and, for some perverse reason didn't. But the old man wasn't going anywhere. His heart was too weak.

The thing trudged slowly up the wooden stairs, as if the weight of the world were on its shoulders. The kid realized that he was staying.

He rationalized it by saying that the thing, the bad thing, was slow. Even if it splintered through that door and made a lunge at them, Clint was young and quick and would be able to escape.

Besides, he wanted to see it. He had to get a picture. He had to. He fumbled with the camera, popping the autoflash up and sliding back the lens cover. *Whatever it is,* he told himself, *I'm going to get at least one good shot of it.*

All those years of horror movies had culminated in this, face-to-face with real terror. He shuddered, as much thrilled as afraid.

The fear, like a drug, was numbing, intoxicating. It filled his blood as if injected there by a mainline fix.

Let me see it. I want to see it before I run.

The door shook. The thing on the other side had reached the top of the stairs and was leaning into it. The old wood creaked, then cracked. A thin fissure appeared in the thick molding, splitting the length of the oft-painted wood. Funny that Clint could see so much in so short a time, but he noticed the colors it had been before, at least three different layers of paint.

He was rooted, poised to escape but not wanting to, just yet. Like a child covering his eyes when the monster came on the screen, he was aware of the intensity of his fear. It was a rich, heavy opium that paralyzed and stupefied. Was that how a cornered animal felt? Unable to find his legs, he stood by the old man and waited for death to make an entrance.

Let me see it. I just want to see what it looks like.

What would the monster do? Was it only after Landis Woodley, or did it want to destroy everything in its path? Clint realized, in a moment of lucidity, that he was measuring his chances. Apparently, his subconscious thought they were pretty good, because he had yet to move.

Why am I like this, Clint wondered. *Why can't I just turn my back on this shit and beat feet? Any normal person would be out of here. What is it inside me that makes me want to stay?*

He thought about the army men he placed around his room at night; he thought about the plastic monster models and how they were so hard to control. Were they really his friends or enemies? He built them, but would they turn on him after the lights went out, as Frankenstein's monster had done? The army guys had a dual role. Not only did they guard against the creatures from without; they guarded against the far more dangerous creatures from within.

Clint watched the door buckle. The hinges, screwed deep in the rotten wood, groaned as they were pulled out of shape. The bad thing moaned again, this time louder than Clint had ever heard.

The sound was terrifying. It pushed all the panic buttons in Clint, sending overdoses of adrenaline into his heart. He brought the camera to his eye and positioned his finger over the shutter release.

He was like a runner in the starting box, every muscle taut. Ready to explode. Ready to take flight. Yet, he waited.

Let me see it. I just want to see what it looks like.

Landis was waiting, too, but for a vastly different reason. He knew that he should run, but his body would not, could not, respond. So, he waited for his fate.

Then he remembered Buzzy's warning. *Somebody had to die.*

Landis looked at the kid, the poor ridiculous kid. He considered his options and made a swift decision.

Could I live with myself? he asked his tarry heart.

Yep. No problem.

Landis was not surprised by his answer. Maybe the fact that he was five or six heartbeats away from a massive cardiac arrest influenced his thinking.

The door splintered open, not with a great thump and smash, but more like gradual pressure. It sounded like ice cracking.

It caved outward toward Landis.

The kid was trembling, camera at the ready. The flash went off as he clicked a picture. Landis grabbed his arm at the bicep. As the thing came through the door, he used the last ounce of strength he had to shove the kid into the oncoming monster. They collided and both went tumbling back down the stairs. The moaning reached a crescendo, then stopped abruptly.

Two seconds later, Clint screamed loud enough to wake the dead.

In the gardener's house, Emil looked up from his can of Viennas. The scream was coming from the house. The old man, he thought, always with the horror movies.

This one sounded almost real.

EPILOGUE

Roberta Bachman's phone rang, but she was too depressed to answer it. Life had taken one of its mean plot twists and left her feeling very guilty. She had sent Clint out on an assignment she knew could have been dangerous, and he had not yet returned.

It had been two days now, and she was beside herself with worry. She took full responsibility for whatever had happened to him. She realized that the only way for her to know for sure was to go over there.

She dreaded it.

Forty years ago she had fled that place in tears and vowed never to return. Now, to find her missing reporter, she knew she had to.

The prerecorded message came on and she listened to a tiny metallic imitation of her own voice. "Hello, you have reached Roberta Bachman's office. I'm away from my desk right now, so please leave a message."

Beep.

A gruff voice, deep and resonant but with none of the charm, spoke.

"Roberta," it said.

She inched closer to the idle phone, chilled by the sound of the voice, debating whether to pick up the receiver or not.

"Roberta," it repeated. "I know you're there. Pick up the goddamn phone."

Roberta froze.

"The kid you sent is gone. We both can live another year . . ."

Suddenly she snatched the hand set off the cradle. "What do you mean, he's gone?" she shouted into the mouthpiece.

"Ahh, I knew you were there. Are you avoiding me?"

"What do you mean, he's gone?" she repeated.

"Gone . . . that's all. Just, gone."

She let the words fall. Her eyes watered and she felt the tremble of anger.

The voice on the other end of the line sensed it and picked up the silence. "Gone," it continued. "Just like Buzzy and all the others."

"What did you do to him? If any harm comes to Clint, I'll—"

"I didn't do a thing to him. But, like I said, he's gone."

"Gone?"

"Somebody had to go, somebody who *knew.*"

"Goddamn you!" she screamed. "You are the lowest form of life on this planet, you know that?"

"Yep," the voice said smugly. "People keep saying that. I guess it must be true. Listen, I just wanted to thank you for sending that little shit over here. He was just what the doctor ordered."

Roberta's face went crimson. "What are you saying? That I knew something would happen? Clint wasn't involved; he was outside the loop. You're sick!"

Landis chuckled, his laugh low and sinister. "You're cute when you're mad."

"Where is he, Landis?"

"The curse . . . it got him." Landis was breathing heavy now, like an obscene caller. "I don't know how it's possible, but he figured everything out. That thing . . . it knows. It knows when somebody is too close to the truth. It protects itself. It takes a life and goes away for a while."

"I'm going to the police," she snapped.

"Go," he replied.

"I'm gonna see you fry," she blurted.

"Do it," he whispered. "Just don't forget me . . . because I won't forget you."

She slammed the phone down hard. Her hands were shaking. She crossed the carpeted floor of her office and found the framed litho hanging prominently on the wall. She gripped her fingers around the right edge and pulled.

The picture swung away from the patterned wallboard. Behind it was a sizable wall safe with a combination lock. Skillfully she spun the dial, feeding in the numbers, feeling the tumblers click. In a moment it was open. She reached inside and removed a wrapped package. She placed the package on her desk and undid the rope that bound it. The plastic bubble wrap gave way to some cotton toweling.

Then she pulled the cloth away.

There were the tuning forks. They gleamed dully in the recessed halogen light. She stared at them hypnotically, the sense of wonder and awe that visited her every time she looked at them returned. It was followed, inevitably, by fear and nausea.

Her trembling hands went for the telephone book and began to thumb the pages.

Why have I waited so long? Why did I procrastinate? God, I only hope it's not too late.

She'd been smart years ago when he came to her uncharacteristically repentant and afraid. She'd been smart to use his infatuation with her to make him relinquish the tuning forks. She'd been smart to keep them where they couldn't cause any more trouble—out of people's hands, out of *Landis's* hands. But, she'd been stupid to wait this long to deal with them.

She scanned the pages for "M" until she found what she was looking for. Not sure of what she wanted to say, she dialed the number. A man answered on the second ring.

"King's Precision Metal Casting. Stephen speaking, how can I help you?"

"Can you melt something down for me?" she asked.

"We have a foundry, ma'am. What kind of die cast would you need?"

"I don't care, I just want it melted down into any shape you want."

The man at the other end of the phone line hesitated. He was unsure of what this woman wanted. "Uhm, let me get this straight. You have a piece of metal that you want me to melt down and you don't care what shape it becomes?"

"Yes, that's it basically. Can you do it?"

The man smiled. This lady was nuts. "Well, that's highly irregular, we usually melt something down and cast it into another shape."

"I want this thing melted down to nothing. I want it destroyed," Roberta said.

"Wait a sec."

There was a pause. Her eyes strayed to the tuning forks. They seemed to pulse, but Roberta was sure that was an optical illusion. She covered them and waited for a reply.

The voice returned. "Sure, we can do it. Bring it on down."

As he was about to hang up, Roberta heard another man ask what that was all about.

"Hell if I know," he answered truthfully. "Some crazy lady."